TOXIC SHADOWS

Tim Curran

I

Already the city was quiet.

Already the smell of death twisted inexorably in the chill air.

Tom Haynes could smell it, feel it. It was in him now, too, a black infection spreading cell by cell.

In his blood.

His bones.

His brain.

It felt cold. There was no other way to describe it—a frigid numbness that was sliding through him with pernicious fingers. This morning it had been different. There had been pain, convulsions, and that awful burning in his belly at the very spot where the dog had sunk its fangs. But thankfully, that was all gone.

Now there was only the saliva that ran down his chin.

The stomach cramps.

His fingers hooked into claws.

And in his head, that odd sense of unreality which told him all was not as he thought it to be. That he could not trust what he saw, what his brain was thinking.

Drooling and delusional, he shambled through the streets.

Trees were down, power lines dangling. Half the city was without power, telephones still out. The storm had been a biggie—eighty-mile-an-hour winds, lashing rains, lightning that split trees—yet it was little more than a minor inconvenience compared to the truly dark thing that had the town in its savage grip. But the storm had done its job, all right, severing the town from civilization long enough for it to go bad.

Haynes looked at the sky but the sun was so bright it seemed to burn his eyes. It made his face feel tight and hot. Nearly sundown. He could trust his instincts on that.

The shadows were long and the air had a nip to it. Night wasn't far off.

1

And when the sun went down, he knew, they would be in the streets.

Men, women, and children.

He stumbled along the sidewalks and fell against a parked El Dorado. It was a nice older one with jutting fins in the back. The upholstery was shit. The fender walls were more Bondo than steel, but still not too bad. In another life he had worked at an auto body shop. He could still vaguely picture that life in his mind. It was all gray and convoluted, peopled by shadows and a routine that was alien and somehow exotic now. But it was there.

How long ago had that been?

He told himself months or years, but as he concentrated, collapsed on the hood of the El Dorado, he knew it had only been two days ago.

Two days.

That meant it was only last night he was bitten.

He wanted to be startled by this, shocked even. The tenuous strands of humanity in him demanded it, but he did not have the strength. For a split second there was a surge of panic, but then it, too, was lost in the chill gray fog.

An agonizing wave of muscular spasms swept through him. He writhed and contorted and finally slid off the car into the street. His lips were bearded with bloody foam, his eyes glazed and yellowish.

Am I the last one?

Are there no others left?

Is that even possible?

Yes, he knew it was.

In two days, the town had been swept into the dustbin. It probably started a few days before that, he supposed, being that's when he first heard about it. That rain—dark, bloody, bizarre. By the time anyone realized how bad it had gotten, it was too late to do anything about it. Flu bug. That's what everyone said.

Ha, ha. Flu bug, all right.

Then when the storm passed, Cut River was a graveyard.

Haynes made a choking, gargling sound in his throat that was supposed to be a laugh. But it was laughter like a scream is a whisper.

His body grew very cold as his core temperature plummeted.

Weakness moved through him in sluggish waves.

His eyes focused one last time and he saw the Last Call Tavern. Northland A & P. The Drill Sergeant Army/Navy store. Cut River Cinema, formerly just the Rialto. It was good to see those things. He remembered them from when he was a kid. And memories, sentimental memories, were good to go to sleep on. They made him feel like maybe he was still a man, still a human being.

As he slipped into a coma, he prayed he would hurt no one. Prayed that someone, somewhere would shoot him down like the animal he would soon be.

These were Tom Haynes' last rational thoughts.

2

Lou Frawley rounded the bluff just outside Cut River and saw the little town lying in the hollow below, pretty as a postcard and about as exciting as ten feet of fence. He piloted his Grand Am down the winding stretch of blacktop that fed into town. He slowed, passed over a bridge spanning a rushing, restless river. It must have been the Cut. The moon had just come up and its ghostly reflection rode the waters, rippling, shimmering, but never disappearing entirely.

He slid a cigarette in his mouth and sped over the bridge.

On the other side, in the yawning fields, he caught a momentary glimpse of...*what?* He wasn't quite sure. Almost looked like scarecrows strung up on crossbars, dozens of them. And then he was past it.

Some crazy rural custom, he thought without much interest.

He exhaled a stream of smoke, stretched his back.

He drove up a main thoroughfare which was probably called Main or Elm or something equally as bucolic and quaint. When you pushed plumbing supplies in several hundred small Midwestern towns on a yearly basis, you got to know all their secrets. He had once kept count. On his yearly travels through

Michigan, Wisconsin, Illinois, Indiana, Minnesota etc. he jotted down in a travel book how many streets were named Main and how many named Elm. Elm beat out Main six to one.

The main drag.

About what he expected.

Stores were squeezed together on either side—sporting goods, drug stores, video stores, clothes shops, party stores. All the essentials. He saw the spires of churches climbing in the distance, old homes, a sprawling park along the riverbank, and, separated by a stand of gnarled, leafless trees, a cemetery hugging a series of shadowy hills. He saw old hotels, coffee shops, sheet metal Quonset huts that housed garages, auto body joints. There was a huge building in the distance, lots of pillars and stone work, a big clock set in its face.

A lot of the town was dark. There were trees down all over the place and telephone poles, too. Maybe not as bad as out on the highway, but bad enough.

Lou was looking for the local Ace hardware, Shinneman's Hardware.

He'd tried to call them from Green Bay that morning, but the operator told him that service hadn't been restored yet to Cut River and probably wouldn't be for a few days. Even the cell towers were down. Entire place was cut off.

Oh, well. Come bright and early tomorrow morning, he'd be hawking PVC pipe and flushing kits to some bored local zombie.

Right now, however, he'd have been glad to see anyone.

Because, thing was, he hadn't seen a soul since arriving.

Not a car, a truck, nothing.

He thought: *These places, Jesus, they sure roll up the sidewalks at seven sharp.*

It wasn't a bad-looking little town, he decided. Much better than some. One thing he liked right off the bat was all the saloons. Every block seemed to have a few, PABST and BUDWEISER signs competing for attention. He pulled to a stop across from a place called the Town Tap. Just to be different they had a neon OLD STYLE sign glowing in the window. There were a few pick-up trucks and a couple cars crowded in front. Looked like the place to be.

Lou got out, tossed his cigarette.

The air was chill and damp, screaming late September at him. Waterlogged leaves were plastered in the gutters. His stomach wasn't feeling too good about then; he'd had a couple burritos at a Taco Bell on the highway a few hours before in Wisconsin and now they were beginning their obligatory march to the sea. He decided he'd feel more at home in Cut River after a good, healthy shit.

The door, an old weathered oak affair, gave a groan when he pulled it open.

He was expecting muted laughter, Hank Williams Jr. on the juke, the Monday Night Football game on the tube, the overpowering, reassuring stink of stale beer and cigarette smoke.

But what he got was absolutely nothing.

The place was empty.

He stood there in the doorway, feeling oddly like a stranger at the borderland of some ghost town.

He stepped in.

A bar ran along one side, booths along the other, a scattering of tables in-between. The light was on behind the bar—he could see all those bottles of liquor lined up like soldiers, like hookers offering him a hard, fast time—but everything else was dark.

He licked his lips, went to the bar.

He could smell a faint trace memory of old booze, old smoke, but vague, a ghost of what was, was no longer.

"Hello?" he said, his voice echoing emptily like a whisper in a tomb.

Nothing. Nobody.

He turned, made his way out of there quickly, gooseflesh prickling his arms and the nape of his neck. He wasn't an imaginative sort, but damn if there wasn't something eerie about the silent vacancy. The breeze was slight, chill, peppered by tiny drops of rain. It felt good, cementing him back in reality.

Don't make sense, he thought. *Door wide open...but the joint's closed. Everybody head for the hills when the storm hit?*

He saw the lights on in a café a few doors down.

He walked over there, noticing with an almost palpable sense of alarm how incredibly *quiet* the town was. No cars passing, close or in the distance. No far-off barks of dogs, shouts of children.

Nothing.

Just a heavy, almost brooding desolation...a sense of creeping expectancy, like something was about to happen any minute.

A surprise party, is what he was thinking.

The town, its residents, were holding their breath, waiting, just waiting to jump out, to throw open doors and start screaming.

The image of that made his flesh crawl.

He shook it off, lit another cigarette, moved up the sidewalk consciously making as much noise as he possibly could. At least, he wanted to, but in reality he moved very soundlessly, afraid, maybe, that someone *would* hear.

Oh, for chrissake! he told his runaway imagination. *Quit being so fucking ridiculous here. It's a small town. Excitement here on a Monday night consists of doing the wash, trimming your toe nails, and getting a piece off the old lady while the kids are plugged into the tube.*

He started when he saw a shadowy form slip behind a parked truck.

He kept staring, blinking his eyes, not sure if he'd seen anything at all.

His hand on the door to the Chestnut Street Café (there was one for his notebook, a Midwestern anomaly for his memoirs—a Chestnut Street), he could see the graveyard in the distance, a covetous expanse of heavy trees and marble.

The Chestnut Street Café was just a little counter joint. Places like this, Lou knew, always had the best burgers, the best breakfasts. Nobody knew this better than he did...or the expanding sack of his belly. The café was all lit up...but empty.

His heart started pounding then slowed when he saw a man in the corner, back to him, just standing by a huge coffee urn.

"Hello, there," Lou said, flicking his ash into a tray on the green Formica counter.

There was a blackboard above the malt machine and deep fryers. In fluorescent chalk the specials were scrawled: FRESH PERCH FRY $3.99, HAM AND SCALLOP BLUE PLATE

$4.99, HOT BEEF $4.50. Yeah, it all sounded good. Beat the living shit out of Taco Hell.

The guy still hadn't turned around.

Lou was about to sit down on one of the red vinyl stools, but he didn't. He stood there, cigarette smoldering in the corner of his drawn lips, a numb, empty feeling spreading out in his belly.

"Excuse me..." he said, lacking the breath to finish whatever might have come next.

The guy turned around.

He wore a red plaid hunting shirt. It was open to the waist. His bare chest and face were the color of graveyard marble. One eye was missing from its socket, a crusty trail of blood smeared down his cheek. The other eye was wide, unblinking, and yellow as a cat's pupil.

Then the guy made his move.

All Lou knew was that there was some crazy, one-eyed shit coming at him with a meat cleaver. He looked frantically around for a weapon, saw a broom leaning up against a booth. It was either make a stand with the broom handle or he was going to get sliced up like a Christmas ham.

He went for the broom, knowing that a run for the door would have been suicidal at that point.

The guy kept coming, his face tight and bloodless. He was making a low gurgling sound in his throat. A tangle of foamy drool hung from his lips, swayed back and forth as he shambled forward.

Lou got his hand around the broom handle just as a small pale hand grabbed him by the ankle from under the booth. He yanked his foot and the hand pulled back.

He saw a girl hiding under there, no more than seven or eight, stark naked, her eyes yellow and faintly luminous.

She made a low growling sound and dove out at him, scampering on all fours like a mad dog, snapping at his legs. He kicked her in the head and she yelped, rolling away.

At that precise moment, the one-eyed man lunged, swinging the cleaver wildly. It slashed within two, three inches of Lou's face. It came again and he stepped under it. The blade slit open the booth, stuffing spilling out like the guts from a road killed hound.

The girl scampered forward again and Lou cracked her on top of the head with the broom handle. There was a hollow pop and she went still.

The one-eyed man threw his cleaver and it spun end over end, just missing the crown of Lou's skull and shattering a tower of water glasses behind the counter.

"Listen, man," Lou found himself saying. "I don't know what the fuck this is about here. But you need help. You and the kid. I didn't want to hurt her, but—"

The one-eyed man, hands hooked into claws, made a sharp barking noise and threw himself at Lou. Lou got around him, cracked him on the side of the face with the broom handle. His head snapped back and came around again.

Lou hit him two, three more times.

He did not got down.

Lou slammed the tip into his belly and the one-eyed man doubled over, crying out. Lou turned and bolted out the door.

His keys were in his hand and he couldn't remember digging them out of his coat. His shoes made slapping sounds on the wet pavement. The Grand Am was open. He fell in behind the wheel, trembling fingers fumbling the keys, trying to get them in the ignition. Click. There. They slid in.

As he made to turn the car over, he suddenly realized he wasn't alone.

Oh, God, the backseat, the backseat...

In the grainy darkness, he heard a high, muted giggling and felt cold fingers at the nape of his neck, hot and feverish breath that stunk of sick wards at his ear. Sweat running down his forehead, he ducked forward, brought his elbow back and felt it connect with a solid thud.

He threw open the door and launched himself into the street, an obscene growling rising up from the back seat. He saw huge yellow eyes, glistening teeth—both set in the narrow, hungry face of a young woman.

He found his feet and dashed up the street.

He made it maybe a block before his wind started to give out.

He slipped behind a van and went to his hands and knees, his lungs aching, gasping for breath, more out of sheer panic than exertion. Cautiously, he peered around the bumper.

The street was empty and wet. Bits of streetlight reflected from puddles.

But he was definitely alone.

Why hadn't they come after him? What in the name of Christ was this all about? What had happened to these people? This town?

The reels of his brain were spinning crazily, but found no answers. A guy with one eye. A naked kid. A woman. All demented, savage. Not human anymore. Animals, monsters. All they wanted to do was kill.

And those eyes, Lou thought in terror, *Jesus Christ, those eyes, not right, not right at all.*

Down the street, he could see his Grand Am.

It looked harmless, door wide open.

He didn't see anyone around it. But it was hard to know, the town washed in clutching shadows.

He crouched there, unable to move. Afraid to do anything and afraid not to. His throat was full of cotton, his tongue stuck to the roof of his mouth. He needed a plan. Something. He kept trying to tell himself that those three...*people* were isolated cases, but if that was true, how come he hadn't seen anyone else? Not a soul. Nothing.

Think! Goddammit, think!

All right, all right. Maybe the town had *gone bad,* maybe some weird pathogen or something had ravaged it. Okay. He would proceed with the assumption that they were all crazy. So, what he needed was a weapon, some way to defend himself.

And then a phone.

He would call the cops...

Oh, Jesus the fucking lines are down. This place is cut off. Even cells are useless here.

All right. No panicking. All he had to do was use his head.

He thought he'd been to Cut River maybe four, five years before. But that had been in broad daylight. Not at night and not with mental cases roaming the streets. Still, a town this size had to have some cops. What did the sign say back on the road? CUT RIVER, Pop. 2400. Yeah, there had to be a police force here, sheriff's department, something. Somebody had to get his ass out of here. If all else failed, he'd steal a car or a truck.

But, dammit, he was getting out.

Steeling himself, he rose from his hiding place, wondering if any of those predatory, lupine eyes were even now tracking him, stalking him, waiting to get him somewhere where he could be easily brought down.

But he wouldn't let himself think that.

He moved off in the waiting, sullen darkness.

He got up on the sidewalk, tried to press himself into the brick facade of shop fronts. He sought shadows, but none that were large enough to conceal any surprises. He decided the thing to do was to make for the end of the road, the end of Chestnut. That big, gothic-looking building at the end, squatting darkly on the hill. It had to be the town hall, probably the police station and fire hall as well. Maybe the courthouse, too. If there was any law in this town it would be there.

The shadows were everywhere, clawing and conspiring.

Lou had a nasty feeling this was his last night on earth.

3

The night was dark and wet.

Lisa Tabano climbed from her car, greeted the chill air with a shiver. She opened her purse, made sure her stash was still there and breathed a sigh of relief.

Yeah, okay. It was cool. Everything was in order.

Her heart rate slowed, her hands stopped trembling—or as much as they ever did these days—and something unknotted in her belly. And all this over the remote *possibility* that she was out. It was getting bad, she knew, but she wasn't going to think about that. She needed a hot bath, a long sleep. Then tomorrow—

Then tomorrow, a voice told her, *you'll get up and start right away. Because, girl, you don't have a choice any more. It's not just social now, it's chemical. You need it.*

She went to the trunk, tried to get the key in the lock and scratched the shit out of the paint job when a wild, almost convulsive shudder passed through her. She got the trunk open, staring blankly at her suitcases, travel bags, and her guitar case.

The idea of lugging all that into a house she might not be welcome in anymore was fatiguing. It made her slump over.

God, she was tired.

I'll compromise, she decided, *I'll take the guitar.*

Like her head, she didn't go anywhere without it.

She had other guitars—twelve other guitars as a matter of fact, everything from customized Strats to Flying-Vs—but it was this one she would not part from. An ultra-rare '59 Gibson Les Paul Flametop. Mint condition. A beauty, a collector's dream, worth mega-thousands.

It did not get out of her sight.

She left just about everything else at her apartment in LA— her custom leathers, her other guitars—but never the Flametop. She wouldn't even let the roadies touch it. Sometimes, she even brought it in the can with her, slept with it nearby. Obsessed? Yes, she was and would happily admit it.

Taking the guitar in its hardshell case by the handle, she moved up the walk to the porch.

Surely they'd heard her pull up.

Surely they'd seen the lights.

She knew damn well they didn't sleep that soundly; when she was sixteen coming home from some drunken binge, they'd always heard her.

But not now?

At the door, she hesitated, figuring this was probably a real colossal mistake. But what was she to do? She'd tried to call, but that goddamn storm knocked everything out. She'd lived in Cut River most of her life (before you went big-time, she reminded herself) and if that experience taught her nothing else it was this: Cut River would be one of the last places to get their juice and phones back. It had no true factories anymore, no mills, no real industry to speak of. Places like that weren't a priority.

The storm had really trashed the countryside.

They were saying on the radio that even a few twisters had touched down.

It didn't look too bad.

When Lisa came into town, she drove by her old haunts—the school, Chestnut Street, the football field—and found nothing damaged very badly. Somehow, this was what she needed: to find her hometown unchanged. After the frenetic pace of the past three years, she needed that sense of sameness, of roots.

She was about to knock—*knock* for chrissake at her own door, except it wasn't her door anymore and she knew it—but decided, on a whim, to try the doorknob.

It was unlocked.

She opened it, went in.

God, it smelled like home. Mom's incense, dad's cigars...but overpowering these was a strange, almost forbidden odor. Metallic, savage.

Smelling it, Lisa instantly tensed.

She stood there, just inside the door, feeling somehow naked and vulnerable, at risk. She tried the lights. They came on. She set her keys on the hallway table, but couldn't bring herself to set down the guitar, her purse.

The house looked the same.

Dad's chair, his pile of newspapers and magazines alongside it, his ashtray, TV Guide, remote controls. And over there, mom's chair, a stack of paperback romances on the end table, a few cooking magazines, a bag of cashews.

Very normal, very ordinary.

Memories flooded her head. Above the fireplace mantel was what really caught her eye. There was a framed reproduction of the band's first CD cover. It showed a blighted, saffron-colored field of stunted grasses and gnarled bushes. In the background were the crumbling ruins of a medieval castle. In the foreground, a svelte raven-haired woman, arms outstretched. She was flaking away into tatters, flames climbing up her black dress.

ELECTRIC WITCH, it said in red Gothic print, and at the bottom, BURNING TIMES.

It brought a lump into Lisa's throat.

Her father had raged at the idea of her being a musician, a guitarist in what he called an "acid-rock" band (though progressive Goth metal would have been more accurate). When Lisa had left home, journeyed to Chicago and formed up the band months later, he'd refused to speak to her. Even when Electric Witch landed a recording contract, a top ten single and video, he still looked on her in shame. It was only in the past few months that he began talking to her again on the phone, offering her a sort of begrudging respect.

But this...the CD album cover on the wall.

That was something.

It proved that he *was* proud of her.

Dad was old-fashioned; he ruled the roost like something from the 1950's. Mom, though staunchly independent in her own way, was very submissive when it came to him. The dutiful little wifey of lore.

But one thing was for sure: if dad hadn't wanted the album cover on the wall, it would not be there. The fact that it was displayed so prominently spoke volumes.

Proud of me, Lisa thought, close to tears, *he* is *proud of me.*

For reasons she didn't completely understand this was very important.

As much as she denied or dismissed parental acceptance, she very much needed it. But the smile on her face suddenly began to dissipate. She wondered what dad would think of her habit, what it would do to him if they found her OD'd backstage or in some shitty motel room.

Not now, she told herself.

There were always rehab centers, methadone clinics. They worked...if you could stand the agony of going cold off junk. It took real balls to kick it, to willingly throw yourself into the arms of a nightmare.

"Mom?" she called out. *"Dad?"*

It was so silent she could hear herself breathing, hear the wind rattling the eaves outside. She swallowed down hard, chewed her lower lip. Maybe they were sleeping. But for some reason she didn't think so...she only knew that she was definitely not alone.

Footsteps.

She heard them coming up the hall, slow and stalking.

Not the way her mother or father walked at all.

Not unless they were trying to sneak up on her.

She turned quickly, the hairs at the back of her neck rising up, something thick and heavy stirring in her belly.

From the darkness of the hallway she could make out a vague shape moving stealthily in her direction, see eyes shining in the gloom like strobes. As it got closer she could see it was a woman. Lisa could hear her breathing, raspy and hollow like wind through bellows.

"Who..." Lisa started to say right before her throat seized up.

No, not her mother.

A stranger.

Some strange woman dressed in a business suit of all things, barefoot, her hands held out before her, the fingers trembling and slicked red with blood.

Lisa, a wave of raw fear washing through her, set down her guitar case, dropped her purse. She backed up slowly as the woman advanced, her face twisted up in an insane grimace that was more like the death rictus of a corpse than an actual smile.

Lisa kept backing up.

She reached down and took a poker from the brass sheath of fireplace tools.

"Listen," she said, her voice barely above a whisper, "I don't know who you are or what you want, but you can't be here."

The woman's lips pulled away from her teeth. Foamy drool slid from the corners of her flaking lips. *"What I want,"* she hissed in awful congested voice like a backed-up drainpipe, *"is you, is you, is youuuuu..."*

Long before Lisa even had a chance to be locked-up with horror, before her nerve endings had a chance to seize-up with raw fear, the woman came at her. She didn't move like a human being, but with a perverse see-sawing motion.

A predator sneaking up on its prey.

Lisa stood her ground and swung the poker.

It caught the crazy woman in the head, snapped her skull around and took her body with it. She landed bonelessly in Lisa's mother's chair. She struck the arm and tipped over with it. But her face came up immediately, eyes still burning, her forehead gashed open just below the hairline, blood running over her pale face in rivulets.

The fact that she could be knocked down, could be made to bleed, heartened Lisa.

She advanced on her and as she came up again, growling, Lisa brought the poker down.

But the woman was ready.

As the hook of the poker sunk into her shoulder—if she felt any pain there was no indication of it—she took hold of Lisa's wrists, flung her sideways with a near-psychotic strength.

Lisa hit the hardwood floor and conked her head.

But she still had the poker.

As the madwoman came on again, Lisa rose to meet her, jabbing the pointed end of the poker into her belly. The woman howled with a bestial roar, stumbled back. The poker was stuck in her belly. She gripped it and pulled it out, about three inches of tempered steel that was glistening red and dripping. She flung it away.

But by then Lisa was on her feet.

She dove past the crazy woman to the fireplace, grabbed a two-foot birch log and when the woman rushed her yet again, she brought it down on her head with everything she had, screaming as she did so.

The woman shuddered, her eyes rolled shut, and she collapsed like she was made of Popsicle sticks. She lay on the floor, bleeding, but not dead. Unconscious and twitching, vile foam dribbling from her askew mouth. A pencil-thin line of it oozed from her left nostril.

Lisa stood there with the log in her hand.

Her body felt heavy, slack, and useless. She had a sudden need to vomit, to cry, to start shouting. But she did nothing but stand there. After a time, she dragged herself into the kitchen.

She didn't find her parents there, either.

But she did find a lot of blood.

4

"What would really speed things along here," Nancy Eklind said to her husband, "would be for you to just admit I'm right."

Ben had a nasty urge to wrap his hands around her throat. Not that he was going to, mind you, he just had a nasty urge to. So he compromised: he said nothing. He kept his hands on the steering wheel and studied the dark road ahead, the minivan's headlights splashing across it. Safer that way.

"What?" Nancy said.

He kept staring forward. "You say something?"

"I believe I said *what*," she told him. "I said *what* in reference to my comment about you admitting I was right."

He nodded, wouldn't go there.

He looked in the rearview.

He could see Nancy's brother Sam sitting in the back, looking everywhere but at what was going on in the front seat. Poor guy. Sixty days courtesy of the county and his first night out he gets a belly full of this. Dinner and a little gambling at the Chippewa casino, they'd told him. A few drinks. Help you relax.

Ben decided he looked anything but relaxed.

She's your sister, buddy, he thought acidly, *at least I'm only related to her by marriage.*

Nancy snorted. "You know, Ben, maybe you're not involved in this conversation. Maybe I'm having it all by myself. Would you like me to bring you up to speed on what we're discussing?"

"No, Nancy."

"All right, then. Feel free to jump in anytime."

He mumbled something.

"Sorry? Couldn't quite make that out. Jump in a little louder."

He wanted to jump with both feet in her fucking face. "I said, no." *He scratched his beard.*

"See?" Nancy turned and looked at her brother cowering in the backseat. "See what it's like, Sam? It's like this all the time.

He can't discuss anything. Doesn't matter what it is, if it's the least bit sensitive, just forget about it."

Ben sighed, slowed the van, made a left onto a country road. "Let's change the subject, okay? I think you've beaten this to death for one night."

"Oh really?" Nancy folded her arms across her sizeable bosom, cocked her head, considered it. "No, I don't think we're done here. Nope, don't think so."

"Hasn't it gone far enough? Change the record already."

"You know what, Ben? If you would just discuss things with me, spit out what's on your mind, we wouldn't have these problems. But, no, talking with you is like pulling teeth."

Ben sighed again, thinking that for the past five years since he'd slid that noose...er, that *ring* on his finger, he'd been doing a lot of sighing. "We'll discuss this later, okay? We're making Sam uncomfortable."

Nancy turned around again. "Are we making you uncomfortable, Sam?"

He kept staring out the window. "Listen, I just wanna go home. I'm tired. I want to hit the sack. A real bed, not a county mat. Jesus."

Nancy snorted at him, too. "All I'm saying to you, Ben, is that for a man your age, you're not very responsible. Being eighteen is great, *when you're eighteen*. But you're thirty-five, dear, time to put away the fantasies and what-ifs, live life like a great big man."

"I think you're being really impatient," he told her, trying to sound calm, in control, very rational, so Sam would think *she* was the crazy, belligerent one and not him. "Every business loses money the first year or so. Ask anyone."

She kept nodding her head. "Well that's fine. Problem being it's my money you're losing. These past five years, Ben, it's been one crazy scheme after another. First the trapping business. Lots of money in beaver and raccoon fur, you said. So I put up the money like an idiot. That fell apart. I should've known better—people don't wear real fur anymore. Then the extermination business. Okay, that sounded reasonable. So I put up the money for your licensing, your equipment. What happened? Big fat nothing. All that stuff is out in the garage collecting dust. Then the house painting scheme. Never mind that there were more painters in town than hairs on a dog's ass. That fell through." She slapped her knee, laughed without humor. "And now, ah yes, your latest business, striping parking lots. Parking lots have to have those yellow lines, honey, and somebody's gotta put 'em down. There went my entire tax refund, right down the old drain. And why? Because all those jobs are contracted out, but you didn't look into that. Oh well."

Ben was gripping the steering wheel for dear life now, wondering what was keeping him from punching her head right through the windshield. She was right, in essence. All his *schemes,* as she'd called them, had fallen through. But not for lack of trying. She was pissed off because their income tax refunds, savings etc. were always dumped into his business ventures.

But, goddammit, at least he tried.

Tapping her hands on her knees, Nancy said, "Listen, baby, all I'm saying is you tried and you failed. Okay. Turn the page. The mill is hiring. You have an uncle there, he'll get you in. Good pay, good benefits. What's so bad about that?"

"The minute I walk through those doors, I'll be there all my life."

"So fucking what, Ben? I've been at the credit union for ten years and I always will be. I've accepted that. Each week I bring home a paycheck. And that's the bottom line. Christ, if not for me, then for the kids."

That was low. Nancy, a widower, had four kids from her first marriage and Ben loved them like his own. Using them against him...that was bullshit.

"Yeah, well, I'll think about it," he said, beaten now.

"Damn right you will."

White-lipped, teeth gnashing, Ben kept driving, luxuriating in the sudden silence. He could hear the engine humming along, feel the tires bumping along the road. God, what kind of life was it when you took great pleasure in such things?

But the quiet lasted no more than five minutes. "Just where the hell are we?" Nancy demanded to know.

"Short cut."

She rolled her eyes. "Not another short cut."

"We're just going to slip through Cut River, it'll take twenty minutes off the drive."

Nancy studied the black farmland, heavy woods encroaching from all sides. "Oh, I'll just bet."

"He's right," Sam said from the back. "It's the shortest way."

Nancy said nothing to that.

"Cut River's up around the bend," Ben said.

Nancy giggled deep in her throat. "Sure. Probably be Milwaukee or Altoona, PA knowing you and your short cuts."

As they rounded the bend in the darkness, thumping over railroad tracks in the process, Ben saw the lights of Cut River. But for one moment, one glaring awful moment, he took his eyes off the road. "You know what, Nancy? I've had it right up to here with you and your goddamn mouth. Just keeping running it and see where it gets you. You want me to apply at the mill? Fine, I will. If that's what it takes to shut you up, God knows I'll be there with bells on my freaking toes. But right now, how's about shutting the hell up and letting me drive?"

In the backseat, Sam made a strange stuttering sound. "Hey, hey, hey, you guys—"

"If you could drive worth a damn I'd gladly shut up, Ben. But you have a nasty little habit of getting us lost," she said, ignoring her brother. "And further more...*Jesus Christ, Ben, look out, look out*—"

Ben brought his eyes back onto the road long enough to see, not five feet in front of the van, a man standing in the road.

Just standing there.

Shirtless despite the weather, his arms were spread out and, just as Ben saw him, he could've sworn this guy was smiling. Ben let out a cry and spun the wheel, hitting the brakes, but it was just too damn late.

He heard the sickening, fleshy thump as the minivan slammed into the guy, tossing him sideways. And then, the wheel spinning crazily in Ben's hands, the minivan careened off to the left, leaped the culvert and slammed into a tree stump.

And there it died.

Everyone was belted in. Ben always made sure of that.

When he found his voice, was able to drag it up his throat, he said: "Everyone okay?"

"Yeah," Sam said, his voice shallow. "I think...yeah...Jesus, Ben we hit him."

Nancy hadn't said a word.

She just sat there holding her face in her hands as if it would fall off without support. Ben kept calling her name, but she ignored him. Finally she looked up, saw the damage to the van in the glow of the headlights, and looked to her husband. "You ran him down," she said. "You ran him down...you goddamn moron...oh my God." She slumped down in her seat, went the color of cheese, and looked like she was going to pass clean out. Ben put a concerned hand on her arm; she batted it away like a pesky fly. "Oh, Ben, oh dear God in Heaven..."

He sat there, staring, thinking, incapable of unbuckling his belt. "This didn't just happen," he said. "This couldn't have just happened."

All that got him was an evil look from his wife.

Sam popped his belt, slid the side door open. The night came in, cool and damp. "Van's trashed. We'll need a wrecker. The...that...the other thing...shit, we better go look..."

Ben nodded, licking his lips with a heavy tongue. All he could smell was the wet foliage. It had a dark, earthy smell of loam and soil and decay.

"You pegged your first one," Nancy told him, showing no mercy. "Had to happen, right? Way you drive." She popped her belt and opened her door, stepped out.

Ben smiled grimly. He didn't even have the energy to tell her to go fuck herself.

He saw her climb out, step into the grass, lean for a time against the van. He could see she was shaking. Every bit of her was shuddering, trembling. After a time she moved on, jumped the culvert and joined her brother out in the road.

The darkness out there was heavy, absolute.

Ben flicked the emergency flashers on.

He got out himself. The headlights illuminated the woods, the flashers turning the road into some crazy, dancing shadow show of yellow strobing lights. He felt dizzy, disoriented until he realized that he'd been timing his breaths with the rapid flashes of the emergency lights.

He took a deep breath and walked around the front of the van.

It was mashed-in but good. The radiator ruptured, the stink of coolant raw in the air. He could hear other things hissing and dripping in there. The stump they'd hit was all that was left of a huge elm bigger around than a tractor tire. Like some modern version of a druid sacrificial tree, he bet it had claimed a lot of Detroit steel, a lot of flesh and blood. Probably why it was cut down. Good idea, except the fools that did it left about three feet of stump jutting up.

They'd have to walk into town.

He was looking into the woods, thinking how dark and thick they were, impenetrable, like maybe you could wander into them and never find your way out again, just listening to the breeze filtering through the boughs with a sound like someone sighing.

Losing himself in there didn't seem bad all of a sudden, especially since he had manslaughter on his mind.

Vehicular manslaughter.

But he'd only had two beers at the casino. That was good. Guy just jumped out, was all. It wasn't his fault. Maybe he hadn't been watching the road like he should have been what with the old wenchbag pissing at him, but that guy…shit, he'd jumped out at them.

Ben knew he'd skate the charges.

That made him feel better, at least a little.

"Where is he?" he said to his wife and brother-in-law, both of whom were wandering the road in circles like somebody had dropped a contact.

Sam shrugged. "I don't know. I don't see him. No blood, no nothing." His pleasant face was drawn with worry. "Couldn't have walked off."

"Maybe…maybe I didn't really hit him," Ben suggested.

"Oh, no," Nancy said, "you hit him, bright boy. You ran him down like a dog. Yup, Ben, that was a good idea of yours, this short cut. Good thinking."

Ben, recovered somewhat now, was about to kick her ass into the culvert, but Sam came between them. "Now's not the time, Nancy," he said. "It was an accident and we all know that, so please quit with the recriminations here. I'm not in the mood for it."

Nancy looked like she'd been slapped. "Well, excuse me all to hell."

They looked up and down the road, seeing nothing, hearing nothing. If he was out there, then he was surely dead. But it was so damn dark. The only lights were coming from Cut River, less than a mile below in the little valley. But out here...Jesus, nothing but the glow of the headlights, the surreal staccato of the emergency flashers.

"A car should be along pretty soon," Nancy said. "A truck or something."

That got Ben to thinking that he hadn't actually seen a car in some time now.

The old highway swept by Cut River to within maybe three, four miles, the new one farther away yet. So there wouldn't be a lot of traffic out here and especially not on a Monday night. Yet...there should've been *something*.

A logging truck.

A semi.

Kids out joyriding.

Something.

He tried to remember the last time he'd seen a car and knew it had been before the short cut.

What did that mean exactly?

"Over here," Sam said. "He's over here."

Ben joined him, Nancy dragging at his heels.

The guy had been thrown into the ditch. His head was in the culvert, half under water. He was sprawled in an unnatural position, legs splayed out, arms folded under him.

"We better get him out of there," Ben said.

As Sam and he got down there, Nancy said, "You're not supposed to touch an injured man, you idiots. You know that. Never move an injured man." She shook her head. *"Hello."*

They ignored her.

She was right, of course, but leaving him in the cold water wasn't going to do him any good either. His flesh was clammy, frigid even, as they lifted him up to the shoulder and set him there. Now with the intermittent illumination from the flashers, they could see that the crown of his skull was split open, blood caked in his hair. The water had cleaned the wound thoroughly. Bloodless, they could see his brain in there like some fleshy sponge. His entire left side from armpit to asshole was one huge, livid bruise.

"Oh my God," Nancy said, turning away.

She began walking in tight little circles, laughing and crying, shaking and gasping. She was hysterical, out of her head now with terror, shock. This was bad for her. But compared to the man with his head split open like a ruptured tire, she was doing all right.

Ben pushed past her, went back to the van.

He popped the hatch, dug a blanket out. It was kept in there for roadside emergencies. This little scenario seemed to fit the bill. He brought the blanket back, spread it over the man.

Nancy was on her hands and knees, vomiting out her dinner into the grass.

"Dead," Sam said, a statement.

Ben nodded. "We're gonna have to walk into Cut River, get some help."

"Nobody on the road tonight."

"Yeah. Monday night, you know—"

Nancy, finished now, screamed.

"What?"

"He moved," she said, her voice cracking with panic. "I...I saw him...the blanket moved. He's alive in there."

"He's not alive," Sam told her.

Ben went to her, put an arm around her shoulders. "He's dead, honey. You don't live with a head wound like that. Trust me. When you feel up to it we're gonna walk into town, get some help."

Nancy kept shaking her head. She wiped bile from her chin and said, "I'm not freaking out here, Ben. *I saw it.*"

"Jesus Christ, Nancy," Sam finally said, sick of this night, sick of his sister, sick of all the bullshit and just wanting it to end. "He's dead. He's fucking *dead*, all right?" He stooped over, clutched the blanket, pulled it back. "See? He's dead. He can't move."

And he did look pretty dead with that nasty gash in his head, the bruising. His face looked pale, discolored…or was that just the flashers bathing him in yellow light? Didn't matter. Sam started to pull the blanket back over him…and hesitated. There was something about him, something that had changed. He wasn't sure what.

Then the guy's eyes snapped open.

They were shining, the eyes of a stag transfixed by headlights.

Nancy made a choking, screaming sound.

"Easy," Sam said. "Just take it easy. We'll get you some help."

But the guy didn't care.

Run down, head sheared open, he still sat up, one cold hand grabbing Sam by the hair, pulling him forward. Before Sam could do much more than protest, the guy's mouth was at his throat, teeth digging in through skin, finding the carotid and severing it.

Sam let go with a scream—high, despairing, and hopeless.

There was suddenly blood everywhere, pooling, fountaining, and spraying. Nancy was screaming and maybe Ben was, too. Sam, however, wasn't doing anything now but bleeding to death.

Ben moved quickly, coming up fast and giving the guy's head a punt to get him off Sam. He rolled to the side, making gurgling sounds, his face black with fresh blood. Incredible. Impossible. It just couldn't be, none of it could be.

Sam was curled up on the pavement, his body wracked with awful spasms. Ben went to him, pulled him up, but his brother-in-law was either dead or close to it. He was limp in his arms.

The guy was on his feet now, going for Nancy.

"BEN!" she cried. "JESUS H. CHRIST, BEN! GET HIM OFF ME!"

She was backing away as the crazy bastard came on, grinning and gnashing his teeth, his hands clutching wildly at the air before him. Nancy kicked at him, ducked by him, kept screaming and shouting for Ben to come to her aid.

Ben let Sam slide from his arms, his brain full of alarm bells.

His wife was being attacked, but he was suddenly powerless. Tapped. That man...Jesus...dead, but walking...no, maybe not dead, but surely not alive in the traditional sense. His gait was jerky, more of a shambling than anything else. Like seeing a scarecrow pull itself from its bracket, limbs spindly, face lifeless, straw and rags imbued with ghastly life.

That's what this was like.

Not a man, but an effigy almost. Jaws snapping open, inhuman gibbers and glottals coming from his throat as slimy, bloody foam bubbled from his lips.

Ben got to his feet, got his hands on the guy's shoulders, pulled him back.

The guy spat something cold and gelatinous into his face, took hold of Ben by the arm and flung him away. Ben tumbled across the pavement. Nancy helped him up and they began running towards Cut River.

The dead/living man did not follow.

He watched their retreat and turned to Sam's body. Still making those horrible sounds, he dragged Sam off into the woods and the night went deathly silent again.

5

Some streets were lit, Lou Frawley saw, while others were completely dark.

Parts of Cut River still had no power. He kept away from these areas. He wanted some shadows, enough to conceal himself in, but not enough to drown him in a sea of clutching white hands.

The farther he went down Chestnut Street, the more he realized how total all this was, how the entire town must have been infected with...with whatever the hell this was.

And it was oh-so-perfect, wasn't it?

The storm.

The power outage.

Then this.

Almost like it was planned or something.

He saw people from time to time, alone or in groups, but he did not approach them; he didn't like the way they moved, the aura of menace coming off them.

Wait.

He paused there on the sidewalk. Yes, he could hear them. They were coming.

He dashed into the black mouth of an alley. So dark in there. Maybe they were drawing him in. But he didn't have a choice—he could see the crazy ones coming now, five or six of them, their eyes shining with evil influence.

He ducked into the alley, crouched behind a dumpster.

He sat there, trembling, his heart doing a drum solo, his face wet with mist.

Closer.

He practically sank his teeth through his lower lip as they passed the alley...paused, then moved on.

God, he'd wanted to scream.

Looked to be four men, two women. They were in a various states of dress and undress. One of the men was naked. One of the women shrouded in a ratty mink coat. Another of the men carried an axe. Still another had a butcher knife. A fetid odor blew off them.

What chilled Lou the most was not the insanity on an individual level like he'd experienced back in the diner or in the back of his car, but this mass...*dementia,* this organized savagery where these groups of...*psychos,* for lack of a better word, formed themselves into gangs and patrolled the streets. The ones that had just passed, for instance. They were grouped with almost military efficiency—two in front, two in the middle, two in the back, equally spaced.

Like a fucking platoon, he thought with a shudder.

And what did that mean? What did that say about all this?

When they stopped at the entrance to the alley, they stopped en masse, as a bunch. Without a word, they all just stopped there. They did not look around. They kept their heads pointed directly ahead, and then, without reason, they moved off *at the same time.* Like maybe they were plugged into the same brain, some mass consciousness.

It was scary.

No words, no nothing, just wet slithering sounds.

Lou wondered if they were looking for him.

The idea made his flesh go cold, made his brain race with wild thoughts.

Sure, he thought, *they're out hunting. They're seeking the normal ones, the human ones. Like a cancer they're searching out the healthy, uninfected cells so they can kill or contaminate them, bring them into the fold, make them like themselves, one huge body of pestilence.*

Normal human beings were the abnormal ones now...the ones to be persecuted, exterminated, and maybe infected in this pernicious witch hunt.

But how did they know?

How did they know which ones were infected and which weren't?

Lou figured it wasn't by sight or smell, but something more basic, more primal. Maybe a biochemical thing. A chemical signature they gave off. Same way one spider knew another spider and didn't end up mating with a housefly.

Yeah, okay. All and fine.

Pure speculation and plenty of it.

But it didn't get him out of this cemetery, now did it?

Crouched behind the dumpster, he lit a cigarette, very badly needing it. He'd wanted to smoke before this, but he hadn't dared. Now...well, he just had to before he faced the streets again.

When he'd first made his run he found his fogged, reeling brain thinking all kinds of crazy things. Like the fact that maybe this epidemic, this plague was not biological, but supernatural in origin. It was nuts, but what *if?* Vampires. Zombies. Something like that. These psychos definitely would fit the bill...but the idea of that was nonsense, of course. The guy in the diner had bled, he'd felt pain. Neither of which had stopped him, but it proved he was living flesh and blood. And in this nightmare, God knew, the knowledge of that was something.

And Lou knew, also, that they could die.

A block back he'd found one of them on the sidewalk, a middle-aged woman in a bathrobe curled up like a dead snake. He knew she was one of them because there was foam all over her lips. Her skin was a mottled gray, but he figured that had little to do with her death. Her head was nearly cleaved from her neck, as if she'd been worked on with a crosscut saw.

But it proved they could die.

Maybe he didn't know what this disease was. But he knew that much.

He butted his cigarette.

He wasn't going to get anywhere like this.

Steeling himself, he got to his feet, his back and legs protesting with a series of tiny popping sounds. It had been years, too many years, since he'd gotten any real exercise other than walking. And the smoking, drinking, and fatty foods had not helped. Yet, his body was responding just fine when you considered he was on the bad side of forty.

He made to leave the alley.

And that's when he realized he wasn't alone.

6

After all these years, the war finally came home.

It finally rose up from the violent collective blackness that is America's love of combat, of war, of death, and bit Uncle Sam right in his fat, lazy ass. God knew, it had been a long time coming.

Johnny Davis positioned himself high above the town.

He sat in the belfry above St. Thomas Catholic Church.

It seemed like a good place from which to watch the town go to shit. Safe, defensible. He was invisible in his roost. He didn't think the rabids would find him up here. Most had emerged from the fog as little more than animals, savage evil beasts who knew only knew two things: fucking and killing. But the others? Yes, some of them—quite a few, in fact—were capable of organization, of tactics, of subterfuge.

These were the dangerous ones.

The ones that could and possibly would lead the others.

But if they came for him up here, if it's a fight they wanted, then it would be a fight he'd give them. Maybe they'd get him in the end, but he wouldn't make it easy for them.

Johnny was wearing Vietnam-issue tiger stripe camouflage (pants and shirt), waterproof nylon jungle boots, and a black bandanna. It was the way he'd dressed in the war. And when this happened—like he knew it would eventually—he suited up and got ready.

Funny thing was, everyone in Cut River thought he was out of his head, some stoned-out, brain dead, shell-shocked Vietnam vet who lived in a tarpaper shack outside town at the edge of the marshes. Maybe they were right, he often thought. But the real funny thing, the ironic thing, was that he was the only one who knew what was happening here.

Wasn't that poetic justice?

After the war, he returned home in '73, worked a variety of jobs—factories, mills, auto garages, even yard work and construction—but found, like a lot of vets, that he couldn't hold them. The war was too fresh, the atrocities too close for him to simply shift gears from a world of bloody survival and attrition to one of small-town monotony, hypocritical morals and value judgments. There'd been bar fights, petty crime, then the real thing when he'd hooked up with a local motorcycle gang, now defunct. It had all led to jail, the V.A. hospital, and the psycho ward at the state hospital. Nowhere good.

In the end, Johnny was only glad that he had no family to witness the self-destructive wreck he indeed became.

Lot of vets had seen bad things, had experienced mind-numbing horrors that their Main Street, USA upbringings had definitely not prepared them for, but he had seen things far worse.

The war had been history for roughly thirty years now.

He had seen his fiftieth birthday come and go.

And what had he learned in all that time?

Not a thing, not really. Nothing he didn't know at twenty in the Delta. Sure, he'd mellowed after they let him out of the hospital, he'd gotten a grip on reality again via intensive therapy with other vets. He'd even managed to hold jobs. But what never changed in all that time was that the war still left a bad taste in his mouth.

And, more so, the government that waged it, its citizens who allowed it.

He sat there, cheek packed with chew, thinking, wondering why he hadn't just gotten the hell out when he'd seen this coming, because he had. Maybe it was that all these years he'd been looking for some action, looking for a good fight, a reason to do some serious damage and now he had found it.

The belfry had been screened-in to keep out birds and bats, but Johnny had cut the screens out with his K-bar. So, up there in the tower he had himself a four-sided gun port. With his Winchester and its telescopic nightsight, he could pick the rabids off a block away. Not that they'd stay down unless you got them just right, but he could still drop them.

He studied the town.

He had a .357 Smith in a holster at his belt, along with a Browning 9mm semi-auto and .38 in his shoulder sack. Plenty of ammo for all three. Then there was the K-bar, a machete, and a sawed-off twelve-gauge pump with a pistol grip.

Loaded for bear?

Damn right he was.

Bears were nothing compared to what he was facing.

What would have been nice would have been some grenades, some Claymores for perimeter defense. Maybe a sixty or an over-and-under CAR-15. Yeah, sure, and while he was at it maybe an RPG and a Stoner machine gun like he'd carried in the war.

He watched the streets and hated what was happening, while knowing something like this was inevitable. He hated the innocents getting caught up in it, especially the children. They always suffered. He didn't like the government (never voted, thought they were all corrupt, self-serving facists owned by rich special-interest groups) and hated authority in any form. He knew he was a dinosaur with his revolutionary, anti-establishment attitudes that stunk of sixties' radicalism.

But he didn't care.

He was getting old and he was going to die this time, probably. And the thought of that didn't scare him, it energized him. He decided he was just going to watch this get out of hand, wait for those in power to send in the troops to clean this up, to stop it (if they could), and when they came, he was going to start killing them. Until then he would—

Jesus H. Christ, what was that?

He saw it, but didn't believe it.

Down there, walking up the sidewalk was a woman. She looked confused, dazed, lost. At least, that's what her stumbling gait told him. Crazy thing was that she carried what looked like a guitar case.

Was that possible?

"Going to a jam session with those animals, dear?"

He took up his Winchester, sighted her with the night scope. He watched her in the field of green, brought the crosshairs to bear right between her shoulder blades. It was the best way to grease someone. A slug in the spine would explode the vertebrae like shrapnel.

Killshot.

He kept watching her, wondering what her deal was.

She didn't move like one of them.

He didn't like the idea of shooting, of announcing his presence to the rabids. But this woman, she had to be fucked-up to be wandering around like that. Had to be. Besides, it was only a matter of time before they got her and he needed a target to sight his rifle in with.

He'd save her from them.

Winchester balanced on the lip of the belfry, eye pressed to the sight's eyehole, he breathed in and out slowly, bringing himself down, willing a total calm to descend over him. Killing in war was a business and had to be handled in a business-like matter.

Nothing personal, bitch.

He applied pressure to the trigger.

7

The voice was clotted, full of dirt: *"You got a smoke for me, mister?"*

Lou Frawley almost fell right over, knowing he was not only in imminent danger but that he had been since he'd hid out in the alley. The voice belonged to a woman...no, not a woman, a young girl. A teenager, he guessed.

He made his way out of the alley into the streetlights.

He saw no one around. Heard nothing.

He stood there, his throat tight, his heart pounding, wondering if maybe he'd imagined it all. He waited a moment, two, three. Nothing.

What if that girl was still *human?*

What if she needed help?

Then he smelled something.

An odd odor. Sharp, pungent. A chemical smell. That and a vague stink of decay, like what you might smell at the bottom of a pile of wet leaves. Not revolting, really, simply earthy, unsettling.

He cleared his throat. "Come out where I can see you."

First, he heard a slithering sound.

It turned his guts to jelly, made him take a few steps back. Nothing sane made a sound like that. It was low and wet-sounding. He expected to see a nest of snakes come slinking out of the darkness, all knotted-up together like when they hibernated, a great tangle of reptilian motion.

He heard a wet dragging sound, heard it getting closer.

It was time to run, but he couldn't.

Like the aftermath of a head-on collision, he just had to look.

She came out of the alley on her belly, eyes lit yellow like Christmas bulbs. She was grinning, a wild and deranged smile, all teeth and gums, a froth of foam coming from her nose, her mouth. She slithered along on her belly in a hideous, side-to-side serpentine motion. Her hands were out before her, clawing at the pavement as she came on, the fingertips scraped to bloody nubs.

And Lou, who'd grown up in the mean streets of Milwaukee and had witnessed the aftermath of a gangland execution before his twelfth birthday, fell back, but did not go down.

His head grew dizzy, his lungs seized up and ached from the lack of air.

Then it came, from down deep, somewhere distant and primal, a ragged manic scream that made his bones rattle.

It snapped him out of it.

Like a snake, an emotionless voice told him, *she moves like a python, a crawling, legless thing.*

And the crazy part was, she moved very quickly.

When she was within a few feet—about the time he screamed—her head and torso rose up like a cobra preparing to strike. He could see that her abdomen had been rubbed raw, her breasts worn to bleeding sacs that hung like skinless polyps.

He also saw why she moved like a snake-woman.

She had no feet.

There was nothing beneath her ankles, just crusted, ragged stumps.

Her bleeding hands reached out for him. *"Can you help me, mister? Can you? I'm sick, mister...help me..."* she asked, her voice black and soulless. Her tongue came out, seemingly five or six inches of it, white and swollen, tasting the air and looking for life to steal. *"Please, mister, I'm so cold...help me..."*

But he couldn't help her.

He couldn't even help himself.

For one crazy moment while his mind teetered on the edge of some yawning black pit, he almost went to her, pulled her into his arms. He could almost feel the chill of her damp flesh against his own, smell her acrid chemical stink, feel her teeth sinking into his throat.

He ran.

His brain a hive of turbulent thoughts, he kept going, not caring if he ran into a pack of the psychos as long as they would make it quick. That girl...she was inhuman, a thing from the slime of evolution, an obscenity. All he could see was her grotesque form in his brain, inching forward like a slug.

He had a pretty good idea he was going crazy. But there was nothing to stop it now. He just went with the flow, a twig caught in a stream heading out to the dire, churning sea of eternity.

Then he tripped over something and went sprawling face-first into the street.

He split his lip, tasted the blood, and felt the pain. His eyes welled with tears at the hopelessness of it all.

He couldn't accept this shit.

He couldn't accept that some lunatic prick of a god had tossed his ass into this...this *bedlam*. So he lay there, waiting for the end. He had run blind from the snake-woman, didn't even know where the hell he was anymore. At least before he'd been eyeing up cars, looking for one with a set of keys in it. Now...now he was just lost.

He pulled himself up, saw what he'd tripped over.

Another body.

This one was crushed, splattered.

A man, or what was left of him. It looked like he had taken a swan dive off the roof of the building behind him—three stories up—rather than become like the others.

Or maybe he'd been thrown off.

Lou went to him, not shocked by his slaughtered remains. A corpse was a corpse. Much better than those things that pretended to be people. He had something in one undamaged hand. Lou reached down to see. The dead man's stiffened fingers were locked death-hard around it. Lou snapped them free.

A gun.

Sweet Jesus, it was a gun.

A revolver. A little .38 police special.

Lou broke it open. Not a shot had been fired. Looking around like maybe someone might take it from him, tell him it wasn't allowed in the game, he clutched it tightly in his hands.

He saw the big building in the distance, the place he thought was maybe city hall or the municipal building, an island in the storm. Armed, he would go there now.

They haven't beaten me yet.

This part of town, though partially lit up, showed the abuse of the storm. Trees were split open and tumbled across sidewalks. Cars wrecked. Plate glass windows shattered, storefronts ravaged, doors kicked in. And there were more bodies, of course. Four of five of them sprawled on the walks, another (headless) lying in the street.

It made him wonder how much was the storm and how much was the psychos out venting themselves.

It was about then that he heard the sound.

First he thought it was running feet in the distance. But as he listened, he understood all too well. Clomp, clomp, clomp. The sound of paws on concrete. The rattle of collar chains.

Dogs.

They came around the corner just ahead, three mongrels trotting side by side. Two bigger ones—shepherd and setter mixes—and a smaller beagle mix. They came forward, tongues flopping from side to side, moving with an ordered, businesslike efficiency that belied a set destination.

Then they stopped dead.

They saw Lou, raised their hackles, began growling.

Lou brought up the gun, made ready.

His heart skipped a beat when he saw the fierce yellow of their eyes, the foam dropping in clots from their tongues. The small dog launched itself first.

Lou put a bullet in its head.

The slug punched through its left eye and scrambled its brains. It flopped over, squealing. The other two approached it, more interested in their fallen comrade now than Lou. They sniffed its twitching corpse. Then, without hesitation, they began to devour it.

But were they devouring it?

They seemed to be ripping it open, yanking out lengths of viscera, chewing them, tearing them and vomiting them back out again. Their only purpose here seemed to be mutilation.

Quietly, very quietly, Lou backed away, one silent step at a time.

Then he slipped around a corner and ran like hell.

8

Lisa Tabano left her mother's house in something of a daze.

Had she been able to think clearly, to process and sort the details of her little fugue, she would have known she was in shock. But that blood, all that goddamn blood, splattered, pooled. Like a slaughterhouse.

That crazy woman there...had she murdered her parents?

Maybe killed them in the kitchen, dragged them outside? Maybe that's what she'd been doing when Lisa arrived. Feeding on them, maybe, mutilating their bodies at the very least. Just finishing up when Lisa arrived, taking out the scraps.

Yes, Lisa saw it all in vivid, shocking Technicolor and, seeing it, her traumatized mind simply closed-up shop, pulled in on itself. The reality of it was simply too much, so it was filed away in some dark shadowy closet where the worst nightmares were stored.

Then Lisa, bewildered and confused, her dazed brain running on auto, wandered off in an outraged stupor. Guitar case in hand she toured the city. She made it quite a few blocks before she was seen.

Two young punks, is what she thought.

Then she really saw them as they stepped into the glow of the streetlight. They wore leather motorcycle jackets that were crusted with filth, no shirts beneath. Their flesh was the color of tombstones, their ribs jutting like ladders of bone as they breathed. Their eyes were huge, empty, devoid of anything remotely human. Wide, staring pools of electric neon yellow rimmed in red.

Maybe this is what brought her out of it.

Like a slap in the face with a wet towel or a boot to the crotch.

She blinked, blinked again, felt a scream clawing its way to her lips. It brought her back to the real world, to reality, the reality of survival in her hometown which was now a barbarous netherworld. It showed her that Lisa Tabano was about to become a victim. And there she was, head full of dreams and dust, guitar case in one hand, purse thrown over her shoulder (*gotta protect the stuff inside, God yes*).

Then she did scream.

The two punks grinned, snarled really, lips pulling away from teeth, tangles of terrible translucent foam running from their mouths. Their chests were crusted with it.

"Oh, Christ," she managed, knowing she was mostly fucked here.

The two punks separated, moved to either side of her, coming in slow and stealthy, breath rattling from their lungs with the sibilance of wind through pipes.

Lisa tried to go back, tried to duck forward, tried all the easy moves but they kept pace with her all too effortlessly.

The punk to her left got within three, four feet when there was a thunderous, distant crack and his head literally *exploded*, shattering like a crystal vase in an eruption of blood and bone. His head neatly split open, his face actually dangling by threads of meat, he took two, three drunken steps forward and went down in a heap. He should have been motionless, divorced of life, but his body trembled, his fingers clawing madly at the wet sidewalk with shrill scraping sounds.

Lisa let out some kind of cry, went down on her ass, confused as ever now.

The second punk studied his fallen comrade with amusement, turned back to her.

He bent his knees, made to leap like a cat on a sparrow. His hands clutched to either side, he actually moved maybe a foot before his face caved-in. One minute he was coming at her, whispering hungry death, and the next there was another loud report...and his face *imploded*, actually blew out the back of his head.

She saw it spray in the air, white crown-shaped things tinkling over the walk.

She realized they were teeth.

He slumped over, went face-down. Did not move.

She pulled herself to her feet, jogging away. Bile kicked up into her mouth, her stomach trying to push its way into her throat. She stumbled off, not even looking where she was going until she slammed into a wrought-iron fence. Then she cried and coughed, her head echoing with dark noise like a scream in an empty room.

She looked up and saw the church.

Yes, St. Thomas'. She knew it very well, having made communion there. She took catechism in the school out back. It loomed up before her gigantic and black and gothic. She pushed her way through the gate, fell on the stone steps.

I'll be safe in there.

They can't get me in there.

They can't come in here, not their kind.

In her brain was everything she ever was or wanted to be. Her life, her goals, her aspirations. She thought of the next CD Electric Witch was working on. The songs were better than the first. Her playing was so much better, so much more professional, not rough and raw. She could hear her own voice telling her that, *yes, yes, girl, you're gonna be a rock star, you're gonna be big, band's gonna be big*...and then all that faded away into grayness as she saw how easily this town had stripped it all away from her.

She opened her eyes, looked up.

There was a man standing above her.

He was not a big man, but hard-looking, powerful, wizened.

"I guess you think you're going to live, eh?" he said.

And then he descended on her.

9

The town was dead.

Cut River was a graveyard.

Ben Eklind and his wife Nancy cut through darkened yards, up shadowy streets, across lonesome boulevards. The chill night wind was at their backs, dead leaves skittered up walks, and everywhere, everything was sullen, empty, abandoned. The houses were dusty tombs, the buildings mausoleums. There was no one, nothing, just that awful creeping, electric stillness that buzzed in the air.

They'd run into town, breathless and bewildered, needing only to be free from the scene of the accident. From the dead guy who was anything but dead, maybe not truly alive in the human sense of the word, but definitely not dead. Caught in some twilight limbo in-between perhaps.

So they ran...into this.

"Sam..." Nancy kept saying under her breath. "Sam. *Sam*. He's—"

"Yes," Ben told her, holding her tight against him. "He is, darling. But we can't think about that right now. We've gotta think about us."

And that made sense to her.

They knocked at the door of the first house they found.

Nothing. No one answered.

Same at the one after that and the one after that. All the houses were dark, uninhabited. Phones were dead. Cars were in driveways. Yards were neat. Hedges trimmed. Everything looked normal...yet, there was something wrong here. They both knew it. It wasn't just that psycho on the road, either. That was minor compared to this. Nobody anywhere. Not that you could see, anyway. But, down deep, down where the aboriginal being lived, Ben knew they were still here.

Somewhere.

Hiding.

Playing some wicked game of cat-and-mouse.

More than once, he'd been sure there was someone in the dark, someone just watching them.

"Maybe the world ended," Nancy said, "and somebody forgot to tell us."

Ben shook his head. "No, this is localized."

"And how do you know that?"

"I just...I don't know, just a feeling."

"Oh really?" she said, as they moved up a nameless street. "I hope it's not the same sort of feeling that told you to take the shortcut or we're seriously screwed here, I think."

He ignored that.

Something was wrong...but what?

He'd been through it all in his mind, the usual things. Nuclear war. Plague. Foreign attack, terrorists, alien invasion. Some natural catastrophe. Everything he'd sucked in from a lifetime of watching old movies on the late show. But none of it fit. None of it seemed to wash in his way of thinking.

Something had happened.

Something pretty bad.

He kept thinking chemical spill. Maybe some tanker truck had overturned, spilling a load of some toxic substance. The town had been evacuated. And maybe...*yeah,* maybe that guy on the road had been contaminated or something. He liked that scenario, it covered all the bases. He liked it until he stopped to consider that they, Nancy and he, might get tainted by the stuff, too.

But he kept thinking about it.

It was something rational to hold onto.

"Look," Nancy said as they crossed an avenue. "Over there."

Ben saw it. In the middle of the block, a small ranch house with its lights on. They'd been in Cut River for some time now and this was the first sign of life they'd come across.

Up ahead, he could see, there were more lit up houses.

Even streetlights shining like beacons in the murk. He sighed with relief. It meant they were still on planet Earth, anyway. Crazy as it sounded, he was starting to think they'd stepped off into some alternate universe.

The first three houses were dark, festooned with creeping shadows, wound up in webs of blackness. Scary, sure. It was all scary. But why was it that this ranch house, lights glowing in its windows, seemed more...*threatening?* There were other houses lit-up on the next block and street lamps, too, but this one, all alone in the tenebrous sea, really got under Ben's skin.

He could feel a formless dread rolling in his belly.

It didn't bother Nancy, though.

When they reached the house, he hung back. It wasn't a conscious decision. Something atavistic, maybe, wouldn't let him get any closer.

Nancy, however, went up the walk, totally at ease.

Ben looked around—a bird feeder, thick cedar bushes, a fence in need of paint, a newer pick-up in the drive, a few newspapers on the porch, rolled-up and unread—there was nothing wrong with it.

Yet, he *knew* there was.

Something.

"A cup of coffee," Nancy was saying. "That's what I need. Or maybe a drink. You don't know us, but here we come."

"Maybe we should just make for the main drag like we said," Ben said.

She looked at him over her shoulder, annoyed. "Why?"

"I don't know," he said, realizing he couldn't put it into words. "Why not?"

"*Why not?* Because this town is giving me the fucking creeps, Ben, that's why not. We're going here. Maybe their phone works."

He followed her up onto the porch. "I doubt it. Lines are down."

"Well, maybe they've got a computer. Maybe they're on-line."

"Not if the phone lines are down."

She shook her head. "A lot of people use cable now, bright boy, or haven't you heard?"

"It's probably down, too."

"Oh, quit being such a moron. I don't need it, Ben. You hear me? My brother's dead and I don't need your bullshit right now."

Yeah, Sam *was* dead. But Ben knew they weren't that close, never had been. Right now, he knew, she was worried about her own ass despite what she said. It was funny how her insults didn't bother him now. Any other time he would have been thinking about putting her down on her big butt, but right now her caustic tongue was almost *reassuring*.

She was knocking at the door.

She kept at it, on and off, for maybe three, four minutes. Then she opened the screen door, the inside door. Ben's protests went unheard. She walked right in. He had no choice but to follow.

First thing that struck him was the smell.

It wasn't the usual household bouquet of lingering food odors, tobacco, pets, room deodorizers. This was heavy, pungent. A strange, heady chemical brew almost like ammonia.

He caught a good whiff of it and then it was gone.

He had to wonder if it was ever there.

"Hello?" Nancy called out.

Her voice echoed and died.

Ben felt the flesh on his arms begin to crawl; he didn't like this in the least.

"Hello?" Nancy called out again. *"Is anyone here?"*

The heavy echo of her voice told them the place was empty.

Funny, Ben was thinking, but the very quality of an echo can tell you so much. It can tell you that a house is empty. It can tell you that something is wrong, that something nasty is about to happen.

They walked from room to room to room. Bedrooms were empty. Living room ditto. The TV was on, but there was nothing but static on the screen. Nancy picked up the remote, clicked a few channels. She found the Weather Channel.

"See?" she said. "Cable's working." She tossed the remote on the couch. "Where the hell is everyone?"

There was a blanket on the floor at the foot of a rocking chair. Next to it was a side table, an ashtray sitting on it. A cigarette had burned down to ash long ago. A pack of Marlboros and a lighter were next to it.

Nancy shrugged, put one in her mouth, lit it. "It's cold in here, Ben. It's so cold in here," she said in a low voice.

Ben was going to remind her that she'd quit smoking six months before, but he didn't; he had an urge to light up, too, and hadn't smoked in eight years. Right now, he needed something.

In the kitchen, the back door was open to the night, frigid air funneling in. Ben closed it, the texture of the darkness outside somehow unsettling. There was a ham sandwich on a plate, a pile of chips at its side. A bottle of Coke, opened, sat on the table, untouched.

It was eerie.

Like the fucking Mary Celeste, he thought.

Except this place wasn't out in the middle of some gray, empty ocean. It was just an average house in an average town in the upper Midwest in the very average state of Michigan. Yet, he had a pretty good idea now—if he hadn't before—that something extremely un-average had swallowed this place whole and spat something back in its place, something sinister, something malevolent.

"Lets go," he said, barely able now to contain the horror he felt.

But Nancy, stalwart and self-deluding, maintained her sense of normality. She tried the phone, shook her head. Then she started leafing through bills by the phone. "Gerald and Shiela Bricker," she said. "I wonder where they've gotten to?"

"I'm leaving," Ben announced.

"Oh no you're not," Nancy informed him. "There's a truck outside. Help me find the keys. Then we'll drive out of this mess."

"We can't steal their truck."

Nancy raised an eyebrow, looked him dead in the eye. "Oh yeah? And why the hell can't we?"

But he couldn't seem to come up with an objection. He'd never stolen anything in his life. It wasn't in his make-up to do so, but right now grand theft auto sounded perfectly fine. He started rooting through drawers, but quietly, as if someone might hear.

And maybe that's what he was afraid of.

He found a cell phone on the floor. Looked like somebody had purposely smashed it. He picked it up, but it was useless.

Nancy searched around in the living room, checked the hall closet. The Bricker's bills in hand, she went to the back bedrooms. The last one was not a bedroom at all, but a computer room. She sat down at the desk. The screen was black, but she clicked the mouse and it came up. Somebody had been chatting.

"Ben, come here," she called, afraid now, too.

He came in, his usual windburned, hearty complexion wan and sickly.

"Look," his wife said. "Shiela8. That must be Shiela Bricker."

Shiela had been at the keyboard trying desperately to reach the outside world apparently. She'd last logged-on some two hours before.

6:28 P.M. Shiela8: help me

6:31 P.M. Shiela8: help me

6:39 P.M. Shiela8: help me please is there anyone

6:42 P.M. Shiela8: is anyone out there

6:55 P.M. Shiela8: alone am alone am alone help me out there

7:02 P.M. Shiela8: last one am i the last one am i the last i

7:07 P.M. Shiela8: nobody nobody help me help me godhelpus

7:11 P.M. Shiela8: youareout areyou out help meeeecan you

7:14 P.M. Shiela8: happeningnowhelpmememe helpmeee

7:15 P.M. Shiela8: help usssss

Ben cleared his throat. "What the fuck happened here?"

"Look," Nancy said then. "Somebody answered her."

8:35 P.M. XXX: where are you

8:37 P.M. XXX: tell me and i'll come for you yes

8:40 P.M. XXX: i'll help you tell me

"I wonder who the hell that was?"

Nancy shook her head. "You never get out and chat, Ben. You don't know what it's like."

"Sure I do," he said, crossing his arms. "Chat rooms are full of dipshits with too much time on their hands."

"Sometimes." She shrugged. "Maybe this XXX person was trying to help."

"Probably thought it was all a joke."

"Let's find out."

"No." He put his hand on her shoulder. "Let's find those keys and get out of here."

"Ben. This might be our only contact with the outside world."

He looked angry. "I said no. Let's find the keys, get in that truck and get the hell outta Dodge."

"And if we can't find them? Then what? We go house to house looking for a car to steal?" She fixed him with those dark eyes of hers, that don't-be-so-fucking-stupid stare. "Let me try this, get a message out there. Then we'll go."

He didn't like it, but he submitted. "All right. Whatever."

Nancy typed a message.

9:31 P.M. Shiela8: Hey, is anyone out there? This isn't a joke. I need help.

The minutes ticked by. Ben stood there, feeling superior but not enjoying it at all. They were wasting time. For some reason, he felt time was very precious. They had to get out of this mess now. They couldn't afford to wait.

9:34 P.M. Shiela8: Please we need help. We're in Cut River Michigan. Something's happened here. We're trapped. We need assistance immediately.

9:35 P.M. XXX: cut river yes where are you

9:35 P.M. XXX: where are you

"Don't answer that," Ben suddenly said. "There's something wrong about this."

"Oh, quit it for godsake," Nancy said and typed.

9:36 P.M. Shiela8: We're at 809 Kerrigan Street. The Bricker's residence

9:37 P.M. XXX: yes i'm coming yessss

9:37 P.M. XXX: coming through the rye yessss

Nancy kept staring at the screen, slowly shaking her head. "It's a big joke to them."

Ben grabbed her by the arm, pulled her roughly to her feet. "It's more than a joke, you dumbass," he snapped at her. "Whoever XXX is, they're in this town. Don't you see? They're here and now they know where *we* are."

Nancy began to argue, but Ben didn't give her the chance to do more than cuss. He dragged her straight through the house and out the front door. He pulled her down the porch, nearly tossing her into the yard. She fought with him, made to slap him, kick him. It did her no good. He clamped a hand over her mouth and put a wristlock on her he'd learned in high school wrestling. It wasn't until they were hidden behind a row of cedars that he let her loose.

"You stupid sonofabitch!" she railed, but not too loudly. "Who the fuck you think you are? You don't lay a hand on me, you don't—"

He clamped his hand over her mouth again. "Shut your hole," he said sternly, his voice hard, trembling with authority. "Someone's coming."

Nancy listened, turning her head this way and that. She heard nothing but the wind in the trees overhead. But then...yes, something. In the distance.

Click, click, click.

She narrowed her eyes.

What the hell was that?

It was getting louder, from the direction they'd come from, from the blacked-out section of Cut River...one of them, anyway. She licked her lips, suddenly aware of the cool mist on her skin, the thunder of her heart. She drew in quick, shallow breaths, trying to do this quietly. Quiet mattered now. Mattered more than anything.

Click, click, click.

Very close now.

Nancy was gripping Ben's arm with everything she had. He was doing the same. Any other time it would have hurt, now it was just a solid, firm pressure that she needed more than anything. She could smell the damp air, cold and gray, smell the thick green odor of the cedars they hid behind. These were physical things. They grounded her.

Click, click, click.

A woman came up the sidewalk, her stride casual, yet...odd.

Just a woman, Nancy knew, that was all...but that shape coming from the darkness...it filled her with a nameless dread, made her flesh crawl in waves...a woman, yes, but not really. More like something ebon and malignant pretending to be a woman.

She kept coming, tall, thin, hair swinging at her shoulders.

She paused at the walk and they both got a good look at her. She was wearing high heels, a purse on her arm. She carried a high, noisome stink of violated crypts about her.

And she was stark naked.

They could hear her breathing. It was a horrible wet sound like water sucked through a hose. Her white, grinning face said all there was to say about the black depths of human madness, of incarnate evil. Her eyes were yellow, gleaming.

Nancy was shaking, willing herself not to scream.

The woman carried a big knife in one hand.

She walked right up onto the porch, went through the open door.

"Helloooo," she said, "anybody home?"

Dear God, Nancy thought, *that voice.*

Raw, rasping, and bestial. The snarl of a mad dog contained more humanity. She kept calling out in the house. Sometimes her voice was remotely human, other times more of a barking, growling noise, an enraged wolf attempting speech.

About the time Ben and Nancy were thinking of making a run for it, she reappeared at the door, electric yellow eyes glistening like wet chrome. She scanned the yard, drool foaming from her lips and dropping in clots to her taut, jutting breasts.

"Hide and seek?" she hissed into the night air. "Is that our game...yesss...come out come out wherever you are. I can smell you out there..."

Nancy wasn't sure what was holding her together by that point.

Maybe it was Ben. Maybe she was just locked-down hard with superstitious, unreasoning fear. She watched the woman step out into the yard. She started in their direction and then abruptly turned, making towards the truck parked in the driveway. She pressed her face up to the windows, leaving a sticky smear when she pulled away. Then she went to the garage, threw open the door and disappeared inside.

"Now," Ben said under his breath. "Quietly."

Still holding onto each other, they rose and darted out from behind the cedar bushes. They scampered across the neighboring lawns, staying on the grass to avoid any noise. Three houses down the block, they paused behind another parked pick-up. In the distance, the Bricker's house looked peaceful. They waited maybe five minutes, but didn't see the woman again.

It took some time for Nancy to find her voice. For too long she was concerned only with staying alive, living long enough to draw another breath. "Oh my God, Ben, oh Jesus..." her voice trailed off into sobs. "What are we...what can we do?"

"We have to get out of here. This whole town is bad."

Nancy nodded silently.

They moved off again through dappled shadows.

There were other lit-up houses ahead and they made for them. They didn't really expect to find people now, but maybe keys to vehicles, weapons to protect themselves with. *Something*. Anything that could give them an edge of security in this nightmare.

Whether it was safe or not, they kept away from the road and sidewalks, sticking close to the houses, the shrubs, the bushes. Ben knew very well that at any moment white hands might reach out for them, drag them into the forever night, but there was no choice.

They came around the corner of a neat two-story cracker box, saw something dangling from the porch overhang. They both saw it, there was no way not to. No breath left in his lungs to scream, Ben teetered there on rubbery legs, wondered what could possibly top this.

"My God," Nancy whimpered. "My God..."

The body of a boy was swinging from a rope.

A frayed noose encircled his throat, cutting into the flesh. He couldn't have been more than ten or eleven, if that. He dangled in the breeze, turning back and forth slowly, his hands knotted into fists.

This was the epitaph of Cut River, the ghastly monument reared in its passing. A young boy hung by the neck.

It couldn't get worse than this.

That was, until his bloodless face hitched into a sneer, lips hooked into a smile, a chattering death grin.

His body began to dance.

Just a shudder at first, then a more fluid motion, arms and legs flopping limply in some macabre imitation of human locomotion. He was like some gruesome puppet, some marionette dangling by the neck, his limbs flowing as if he were walking on air.

Ben stood there, mesmerized by this latest statement of sheer lunacy.

His brain was filled with a thundering black sound like the flap of huge wings, like birds taking flight in his skull. It was maddening. And all he could think of was that old music video by Herbie Hancock, the one with all the motorized mannequins and automatons mimicking human beings—walking, kicking, turning, gyrating. And that's what this boy was, some cold, whirring machine mocking a little boy, jaws snapping open and shut, head bobbing, limbs thrashing, a garbled dry croaking erupting from his throat.

Nancy began to shake all over.

She started sobbing, then tittering, then both it seemed.

Ben wanted nothing more than to go quietly mad, but now wasn't the time.

With tremendous effort, he got his legs moving. He spun his wife around by the shoulders and her face, bathed in the yellow moonlight, was crazed, pulled into some tight crying/laughing mask. It frightened him. Probably worse than anything he'd seen thus far.

She came alive under his grip, fighting him, hitting out, trying to scratch his face. He slapped her and she slumped into his arms. He half-carried, half-dragged her away, wondering how long it could possibly be until that rope around the kid's neck snapped and he came looking to bite at something other than empty air.

"Gonna be okay," Ben heard himself whisper to Nancy as she collapsed completely and he scooped her up, carrying her away and across the avenue onto the block with the lights on.

He found a row of high bushes and set her gently down behind them.

He sat beside her, stroking her hair.

She was awake then, sobbing. "It can't be happening, Ben, can it?" she asked. "I know it can't, I know I'm crazy. I gotta be. That boy, he's dead, but he's still moving and that woman...oh Jesus, Ben, I'm losing my mind..."

He pulled her tight against him, kissed the top of her head. "You're not crazy, girl. This town is crazy, but not you."

After a time she quieted down and he was afraid for her.

Afraid because she was a tough, ballsy woman who didn't take shit from anyone or anything and now she was weak and beaten, whimpering like a little girl.

This is what scared him.

She was always a rock and now she was wearing down, flaking away before him.

"Sam and all this...I can't think straight. I don't know."

"Sshh. It's gonna be okay. I'll get you outta here."

Then they both heard something coming up the sidewalk.

At first it was muffled and indistinct, but then it became obvious: the slapping of bare feet. Many of them.

Ben and Nancy hugged one another, drawing strength.

The parade of bare feet came and went, their owners making a series of wet, almost reptilian hissings as they passed. Ben had this almost suicidal, crazy urge to peer over the hedges and see what manner of people made such sounds.

But he didn't.

He just held Nancy and was held, waiting.

Ten minutes later, they were still clutching one another. Waiting for what came next and not having to wait long. It came from across the street, from a bank of dark homes. Ben could feel his breath catch in his throat and hold there. It was merely a sound, but it conjured an almost physical horror in him.

I can't take anymore of this, oh God in Heaven, I can't.

Across the street, he could hear a shrill, eerie giggling.

The giggling of a little girl, demented and loathsome.

10

"All I want to do is live," Lisa Tabano told the bald, mustached man who carried her into the church. "I don't even want to know about this...I just want to live."

Johnny Davis nodded in the darkness. "Seems a simple enough thing, doesn't it?"

"I used to think so," she said, her voice weary.

"I'll try to get you out, but I can't promise anything."

"Thank you. Then we can get the police, the army, I don't know. The authorities. Someone in charge. Maybe...maybe my mom and dad...maybe they're alive somewhere."

"Maybe they got out," Johnny said.

She ignored that. "We'll get out, get the cops, whatever. Let them sort it out."

Johnny laughed low in his throat. "Oh, you are naïve, aren't you? You don't get it, do you? You don't even know what this is all about."

Lisa looked at him. "Do *you?*"

All that got was laughter.

She saw him shaking his head, massaging his jaw (something he seemed to do whenever confronted by something he didn't like). "No point in getting into any of this," he said. They were just inside the main door of the church where Johnny had taken her after finding her on the steps out front. He opened it a crack, peered out. "If you want to get out, we might as well start on that."

"I was kind of thinking that maybe you were coming with me," Lisa said. "Or am I mistaken on this?"

"Sadly mistaken, dear." He pulled a pack of RedMan chewing tobacco from inside his survival vest and stuffed his cheek. "I'm staying right here."

"For godsake, why?"

"You wouldn't understand. It would take just too long to explain it and we don't have the time."

An enigma?

Oh yes, and then some.

Here was a guy who obviously was some sort of survivalist—dressed out in fatigues and survival vest, armed to the teeth. A guy who had positioned himself in the church belfry and, thankfully, picked off those psychos who were about to make hamburger out of her. Hard as a concrete piling, he was built thick and heavy and was definitely no stranger to the business of killing. Not some weekend warrior here. No gun freak wannabe who dreamed of action and jerked off over back issues of *Soldier of Fortune,* but would piss his pants at the first taste of the real thing.

No, Johnny Davis was the genuine article.

But there was an undercurrent to him Lisa just couldn't put a finger on, some secret agenda. A mystery.

But right now, despite everything that had thus far happened, neither Johnny Davis or any of the rest of it was a priority for her. She was beginning to feel nauseous and sweaty like maybe she had a good flu bug going.

But it had nothing to do with that.

"We should leave before things get...worse," he said.

"I have to go to the bathroom."

He sighed, shook his head. "Goddamn women and their bladders."

She ignored him and he led her through the church to the rectory in the back. He motioned towards the bathroom and left her alone. She closed the door and clicked on the light. She set her guitar case and purse down. When she was sure he was out of earshot, she relieved herself (though that wasn't the real reason for this visit).

When she was finished, she splashed some water in her face and looked at herself in the mirror. Good God. She was wasted, drawn, her dark eyes and hair standing out in marked contrast to the pale, sweaty skin of her face. Twenty-three years old and already she had discolored rings under her eyes, worry lines at the corners of her lips. Like Keith Richard's junkie sister.

God, she felt horrible.

She opened her purse, took out a baggie of brown powder. She didn't have a spoon, so she scooped up a tad and shoved into her nose, sniffing it up. She repeated this and sat down on the toilet, shivering, her eyes watering, her guts flipping and flopping.

When's the last time you ate? she asked herself. *The last time you actually put some food in your body?*

But she couldn't remember.

A day? Two? Three?

Got so after awhile all you needed was the junk, you didn't need anything else.

She was pencil-thin, nearly emaciated, sporting a classic hard-living rock and roll look: haggard, gaunt, a big head of hair and a skeleton for a body. All those years as a teenager she'd gone on one crazy, punishing diet after another trying her damnedest to look like her heroes—Johnny Thunders, Joe Perry, Nikki Sixx—and now, at last, a rock star in her own right with a hit album, she'd discovered their secret: heroin. You didn't need diets or fasting or any of that nonsense, all you needed was H. Food of the gods, yes oh yes oh yes.

Already she could feel it canceling out the bad stuff.

Her personal cloud found her, wrapped her up tight. She'd peak in fifteen minutes or so, but the climb was oh-so delicious. Nose full of junk, she could laugh at the psychos outside.

Euphoric and revitalized, born again, she gathered up her stuff and left the bathroom, had a foolish urge to skip and whistle.

This was more like it.

She had nearly six grams left. Plenty to last.

God, if mom and dad are dead, if—

Don't think about it. That's for later, she told herself, *when you're safe.*

"Took you fucking long enough, rock star," Johnny said when she returned.

It was dark and Lisa was glad for it. She didn't want her savior, Johnny Davis Rambo, seeing the change coming over her. She had a pretty good vibe on the guy now and it told her he was not stupid, that he'd been around.

"You gonna lug that guitar case with?"

She looked at him like he was mad. "Of course. It's very rare, man, worth a bundle. It's everything to me."

He was peering out the door again. "No, you're wrong there, girly. A guitar ain't nothing but a guitar, just wood and strings and steel and what have you. Your life is all that counts."

"I'm not going to argue with you."

He shrugged. "Whatever. Seen cherries like you in the war. Always fretting over good luck charms and religious objects and prized possessions. Didn't do 'em no good. You got one life, that's all you get and all you need. Rest is bullshit. Materialism."

"Oh, you got me pegged, eh? Material girl."

"You said it not me."

"You don't know shit." She fished a pack of cigarettes out of her coat pocket, fired one up. "You don't know anything about me."

"No, you're right. I don't know, don't wanna know."

This guy. Jesus. He was ruining a perfectly good buzz with his attitude. "What about you? That must be quite a story. Look at you...what is that getup about?" she asked him, giving him a sneer she usually reserved for the cameras. "Camouflage for chrissake? Didn't notice any jungle around here, Rambo. Time to leave Da Nang behind, Chuck Fucking Norris."

He closed the door. "You wanna get out of here, rock star? That what you want? Then you'd best zip up that pisshole you call a mouth." He turned back to the door, muttered under his breath: "Fucking broads. Cooking and sucking dick are their high points, rest is crap. Can't trust 'em. Can't trust anything that bleeds for a week every month but don't have the good sense to lay down and die."

"*Excuse me?*" Lisa said, her blood boiling like hot molasses. "What did you say?"

"You heard me."

"You arrogant, macho shitbag." She shook her head. "Yeah, just my luck. I get stuck in this fucking mess and who do I get for company? Sexist goddamn loser. What happened, Rambo? What gave you such a high opinion of women? You get dumped too many times? Small penis? Or don't you even like girls?"

He smiled thinly. "How bad you want to find out?"

"About as bad as I want my tits stapled to the sidewalk."

"Good place for you, long as your ass is up in the air."

Lisa was wondering how he'd look with a guitar case shoved up his back door sideways. "Okay, macho man. Save it. Show me the way out. You can do that can't you?"

"I can do all sorts of things, woman."

Though there seemed to be no sexual undercurrent implied, she said, "Spare me, Sarge. You couldn't get laid in a fucking leper colony."

He pulled off his watch cap, stroked his bald head, put it back on. "You'd be surprised."

"No, I'd be disappointed." Her buzz had peaked now. It would hang around for a time, but already this guy had ruined a good thing. She wasn't going to let him get away with it.

Johnny took two quick, very quick, steps toward her. She saw his hand come up and was powerless to stop him. She saw her life flash before her eyes like a low-budget movie. His hand stopped inches from her left temple.

His eyes, locked with her own, belonged in the head of wild boar, not a man. Finally, he let out a breath, grinned at her, started giggling. "I like a woman with balls that puts me in my place. You're okay, rock star. You married?"

"Only to myself."

"Wanna be? You think you could go for a mutt like me?"

"Doubt it."

She suddenly felt connected to this guy, antithesis to everything she loved about the male species.

He nodded, shouldered his rifle and pulled a shotgun from its sheath at his back. It was a sleek, nasty-looking piece of hardware with a pistol grip. "Let's go, rock star."

Lisa stuck her tongue out behind his back, but followed.

Back out onto the streets. The damp. The cold. The grainy darkness.

Yeah, Rambo here was a real piece of work. It wasn't so much that he'd insulted her or women in general (she'd been gone over by the best), it was just that she had to wonder what sort of combination of circumstances produced a guy like him. He was rough, sure, about as polished as a rusty nail and liked to give the impression he was an A-number one badass lifetaker. And maybe he was, but she had a pretty good idea he was more than that. Something else entirely. There was warmth under that roughhewn exterior.

Like a coal in a firepot, warm at its center, but covered in ash and dirt.

That was Johnny Davis.

"Follow the leader, rock star."

Meaning: don't lag behind.

But she had no intention of doing that. In a situation like this, even a complete asshole like Johnny Davis came in pretty damn handy.

He motioned for her to stop.

He did everything with hand signals like he was humping it up the Ho Chi Minh Trail again. Up ahead, he was studying what lay before them.

He was real careful, real professional.

Good man to have on point, she figured.

Especially when the war came home.

II

Lou Frawley's world was one of madness and damp and perpetual dark.

It was a compacted microcosm of horror and survival where the worse things not only could happen but did with shocking regularity. His world was Cut River and the madhouse it had become. Pretty little snow-globe town. Shake it up and the snow fell on the quaint little village. Except the quaint little village was haunted by monsters that lived in the skins of men, women, and children.

Quite a change, really.

His was a salesman's life—town after town, one bad meal piled on another, ulcers, failed relationships, promotions that never materialized, shitty hotel rooms, drunken nights, ass-kissing sales managers, one night stands with painted-up bimbos and the only drama in it being what sort of social disease you might bring home like a sick puppy to care for and feed until it did you in, and the road went on forever.

That was pretty much what it was before Cut River.

All that dark revelation and this in only a few short hours.

Maybe it wasn't much of a life when you stuck it under the scope like a new microbe, but it was his and he tended it well. Watered it, fed it, and kept it growing.

Now there was only survival.

Stay alive long enough to maybe get out of this godforsaken town or, at the very least, to die knowing the answer to the grim puzzle.

I should've stayed in Green Bay, he thought. He almost did. Instead, he drove a couple hundred miles north into this.

Sound thinking, all right.

After his little rendezvous with the Snake Woman (as he now called her), he kept moving, keeping in the shadows, keeping his eyes on the big brick building perched on the hill. It had to serve some official function. He knew that much. But what if it didn't? What if it was some old condemned rathole waiting for the kiss of the wrecking ball? What then?

That's what he kept thinking.

He was half a block away from it now and could've been there a long time ago if he hadn't had to hide all the time. No matter, there it was.

He was in the doorway alcove of a little craft shop, pressed up stiffly to the plate glass display window, enclosed in bands of darkness.

Safe?

Yes, about as safe as any other place in this town. And that, of course, wasn't saying much.

He hadn't seen any more psychos since the Snake Woman, but that didn't mean they weren't out there. He could hear them from time to time—wild shriekings and cries. Sometimes the sounds of shattering glass. Oh yes, they were out there and very active. No doubt about that. But not just them; he could also hear dogs barking and whining...at least he hoped it was dogs. And earlier he could've sworn he heard gunfire, but it was too distant to be sure.

He liked to think that it was just that: gunfire.

Sounds of humanity, bugle call of his brothers and sisters in the resistance.

The resistance. That made him smile.

Knowing it was probably a mistake but not giving a ripe shit since he had the gun now, Lou lit up a cigarette. He lit it quickly, then cupped the cherry, waiting to see if it drew any attention.

As badly as he wanted out of this nightmare, he also wanted answers. He needed to know what had happened here. He knew that during the past week or so the area had been nailed by storms and that within the last couple days they'd been severe, bad enough to wipe out telephone poles and their attending lines without mercy.

But what else had happened?

What took possession of this town when the light failed? Was it a plague or a contagion and, if so, what kind? Was it in the soil? The air? The water? And better yet, was he already contaminated?

Jesus, it was all such madness.

He kept watching the big building up ahead.

Very gothic with the moon washing it down in a ghostly ambiance. It sat on a low, sloping hill, surrounded by denuded elms and craggy oaks. Three rambling stories of stone and brick, domed belfries, widow's walks, drooping eaves, gabled roof dormers, all capped by a jutting expanse of sheer-pitched roofs and rusting weather vanes. It had lots of scrollwork, a marble-cut frieze wrapping around it like a scarf, too many oblong and oval windows that glared out, dead eyes in a stone face. There was a huge clock set in the facade of a rectangular tower, telling him it was nearly half past nine.

Quite a place. About as inviting as mausoleum at midnight.

He thought maybe he saw some lights on in there...but couldn't be sure with moonlight the color of cornsilk turning the windows to somber reflecting pools. He dragged from his cigarette, knowing that now, this moment, more than ever before in his life, was not the time for impulsive action. Whatever he did had to be plotted out carefully.

He looked around.

Nothing but the town everywhere he looked—buildings and homes and church spires and leaning chimneys painted the color of coal dust, all frosted by the moon. Black, patchy clouds above and cold, mean streets below.

Or maybe not.

To the right of the big building was an open expanse like a park and beyond that what looked to be a cemetery. Same one he saw earlier, but from a different perspective now. A mutiny of stones and marble vaults...and beyond, nothing but dark woods, empty meadows.

So there it was.

He could either take his chance with the building or he could just do the smart thing and slip out of town. Through the boneyard and into the fields beyond. Easier than promises in the dark. Maybe *they* were out there, too, but probably very few, he figured, the best hunting being here in Cut River.

Grinding his cigarette beneath his heel, he moved out.

Across the street, past the monolithic building, into the park. He didn't like it there too much, either: too many dark hiding places, dank little holes where the monsters could spring out at him like trapdoor spiders from their webby lairs. He hid behind a war monument, listened, watched, kept the .38 in his hand. Okay.

Go!

Through a perimeter of stout pines and across a winding dirt drive.

So far, so good.

The cemetery was right before him now. Low stone wall, irregular and mounded, encircling it. He hopped over it, nearly flipping himself into the dirt. Just inside the wall, he crouched down, panned the night, looked for anything that reeked of danger.

Nothing.

The cemetery was laid out over hilly, grassy turf crowded with manicured shrubs and ancient oaks. The tombstones seemed to glow under the eye of the moon. Silent, jutting sepulchers trimmed in dead ivy were cut from charnel shadow. This was worse than he thought, more places to hide than he could've imagined—everywhere gravestones, markers, biers, marble shafts, leaning funerary crosses. A maze of stone and foliage and knife-edged shadow.

Lou darted forward, his legs pumped with concrete from all the unaccustomed exertion.

Headstone to headstone to headstone.

Silence, waiting and pregnant with sinister possibility.

He was thinking that he was perfectly safe. Chances were he was wasting his time with these cat-and-mouse evasion tactics. Too many old movies coming home to roost in the rotting rafters of his panicked brain. Yeah, it was cool, it was—

Up ahead, movement.

He stayed put, the gun trembling in his sweaty grip.

Shadows were everywhere out there, throngs and multitudes created by the moon, the trees, and the stones.

But then he saw, yes, *they* were here, too.

Dim forms threading slowly through the monuments in his direction. His heart skipped a beat, skipped another, kicked with a sharp pain in his chest.

Why here?

Were they waiting for him? Were they part of some group consciousness, knowing and thinking and acting as a single entity, but composed of hundreds of parts? Ridiculous. Again, too many late night movies vomiting drivel into his head. No, not that, but something, something...

He could hear muted thuddings now, muffled clangings.

Terror then, flooding through him like icy creek water, horror. The revelation was grisly. They weren't out here looking for the living, they were out here after the dead. Rooting through graves and burial vaults and crypts like grave robbers, hungry ghouls.

But maybe they did know he was here.

Some of them were getting closer, moving in his direction with less than casual interest. He could see their eyes now, flat and yellow like the eyes of rabid dogs.

They were spreading out now, six or seven of them. He could hear the wet sounds of their breathing, the chattering of teeth.

Lou's heart was literally in his throat, flabby and fibrillating uneasily, choking off his air and squirting sour bile onto his tongue. He sprang from his crouch and ran with everything he had out of the cemetery and into the little park and away until he was in the cyclopean shadow of the building.

Behind him, it was quiet.

They hadn't followed. He fell to his knees in the wet grass.

After a time, his panic lessened. He saw a sign.

CUT RIVER MUNICIPAL COMPLEX
City Hall Offices
Hall of Records
Public Safety Department

Bingo!

And, yes, he saw, studying the recessed windows, that there *were* lights on in there. Not all of them, but some. He licked his lips, calming himself. He could see a parking lot now in the back with a couple police cruisers and a few city trucks. If there was still law here, why weren't they doing something?

No time for that, no time for reasoning and analysis. That was the province of civilized men and civilization had now become something of an abstract concept here in the Devil's backyard.

Wiping a sheen of icy sweat from his brow, Lou got to his feet.

Move!

He was running again, galloping through the courtyard of the municipal building like a fox with a pack of slavering hounds at his tail. Through the wet grass, over glistening pavement, ducking into shadows, becoming shadows. And above, always, that huge and full moon, that hunter's moon, brushed by dark clouds like scars across a blind eyeball.

Lou's breath was misting sludge in his aching lungs, his brain raging with storm clouds.

He jogged up the steps to the entrance.

Huge double doors. He turned the knob, pushed, his heart going off like a cluster bomb, and then he was inside. Dark corridors, stairs climbing off to the left, a bank of elevators. A few panels of overhead lights were on, enough to see and navigate by. There were doors studding the hall, windows set in them. CITY TREASURER. CITY MANAGER. COUNTY CLERK. UTILITIES DEPT. There was a directory on the wall. Lou studied it, seeing that what he wanted was on this floor.

So far, so good.

He would've liked every light in the place to be burning, but at least it was warm. He hadn't realized how cold he'd been until the warmth touched his hands, his face.

God, he was numb.

A corridor wound off to his left, very dim, and that was the way he needed to go. He started off, the shadows alive with secret threat.

The police offices were all lit up.

But empty.

There was a bullpen securing a few desks and filing cabinets, stiff plastic chairs for visitors, safety posters on the wall, wanted bulletins tacked to a corkboard. All illuminated by buzzing fluorescent lights overhead.

Lou entered carefully, moved into the bullpen, holding the swinging gate so it wouldn't make any noise.

And his heart fell.

It looked like a tornado had howled through the place.

The floor was heaped with papers and folders as if someone had cleared the desktops with a broom. Computers were smashed under desks, keyboards jammed into their screens. Drawers were empty, their contents strewn about. Wastepaper cans kicked aside, a coffee maker and its attendant pot smashed in the corner. A letter opener was imbedded nearly two inches into the wall.

Yeah, the crazies had been here, too.

They'd made a thorough job of it by the looks of things. Probably the worse thing was the smell—like old piss. As if the crazies, monsters—whatever in fuck's name they were—had urinated all over everything to mark their territory.

Lou went to the first phone he found, picked it up.

Dead.

Even the cops didn't have working phones. There was a radio, but the microphone was missing, wires ripped out of the back.

Don't you see? a voice said to him. *Don't you see what's going on here? You're completely cut off from the real world. It's what they want. You're normal and they can't have that. This is a mousetrap, and you're the mouse, my friend. No way out. The storm took care of the phones, they did the rest. And moment by moment, the noose is tightening.*

Lou slumped against a desk, a crude mockery of a smile etched into his face like somebody had slashed it there with a knife. Okay. All right. Yes, indeedy. This is what it was like to go insane, eh? Worse than he thought. Maybe it would be easier if he just surrendered.

No.

He plugged a cigarette into his mouth, lit it, drew hard off it. The nicotine woke up his brain, parted the mists of bullshit. Like a worn-out TV set that needed to be slapped on the side, it started working again. The picture rolled a bit at first, sure, but it was receiving and processing again.

There was a door off the bullpen, another entrance leading into darkness.

He chose the door, a restroom.

He walked right in there, gun raised. He was feeling like Dirty Harry or the guy in *High Plains Drifter*, a man with a gun and a past and a serious need to kill some people...or, in Lou's case, things that looked like people but were people like a rubber glove is a human hand.

Typical bathroom. A few urinals with rust stains against one wall, sinks against the other. Above them a mirror. It was spattered with water stains, flaking in the corners. But none of that caught Lou's attention. He only saw what was scrawled across it:

GOD HELP US ALL

By this time, it took quite a bit to unnerve him. Two days ago, had he walked into an empty, vandalized police station and saw something like this he would've pissed in his shoes. Now, as ominous and menacing as it indeed was, he only studied the message, wondering vaguely what that crusty, dark stuff was.

Blood?

Lipstick?

He turned away, his brain still asking the same shopworn question: What exactly happened here?

He paused before the sink, dragging slowly off his cigarette. A long gray ash dropped away. He let the butt fall with it into the basin. Setting his gun aside, he turned on the faucet. That still worked. His cigarette butt sizzled out, ashes sucked down the drain. He splashed water on his face, wetted his lips. Oh Lord, it felt so good, so—

Jesus H. Christ, you fucking idiot!

He pulled away like it was acid...or he'd been splashing water from a urinal in his face. Only this was much worse. The water. Something happened here. Something had gotten these people and had gotten them bad. Too fast, he figured to be strictly from body contact, had to be airborne, maybe, or in the water. His imagination shifted into high gear. He could almost feel whatever it was coming through his pores, oozing into him like cold syrup, settling into his cells.

Fuck it.

He went to the sink and started gulping water.

Yeah, better. Goddamn right it was better! Ha, ha!

And then he happened to look in the mirror, saw the blunt tips of black shiny shoes under one of the stall doors. He was not alone.

He reached for the gun.

12

Ben and Nancy Eklind were on the move again.

"We're going to walk right out of this town," he told his wife. "No stops, no bullshit, no nothing. No stolen cars. We walk out, get our asses somewhere safe."

It was a plan.

Ben decided then and there, after they were a safe distance away from the hanged boy and the child laughing in darkness, that they weren't going to bother with anymore of the houses, lit up or not. All of them were potential traps. Better on the streets where you could run, maneuver.

They simply had to get out.

That was all that mattered; leave this clusterfuck to the authorities. But to get out they had to purge their minds of all the horror, wipe the blackboards clean, so to speak, so they could concentrate.

As they approached Chestnut, he pulled Nancy behind a tree.

"Are you okay?" he said.

"Yes."

"You're sure?"

"I'm just fine, Ben. What could possibly be wrong?"

Good. Sarcasm. Meant she was indeed okay or as okay as she was going to get this night. They crossed Chestnut at a jog, holding hands. They saw no one or nothing and that was perfectly fine. Soon enough the houses ran out and then there were warehouses, a few decrepit factories behind locked fences, a public works garage, a junkyard, and beyond, more dark buildings and a train yard.

"We make that train yard," Ben said, "and we're free."

Nancy had nothing to say to that. She simply nodded.

Ben studied the streets.

God, so many shadows, so many traps waiting to be sprung.

He remembered reading *To Kill a Mockingbird* in high school. There was a line in it about nothing being as dangerous as a deserted, waiting street. It had stuck in his mind all these years, buried with the attendant trash of daily living, only to emerge now. As if maybe it had been waiting for this, waiting to be applied to this spook show.

Hand in hand, they started walking faster, practically jogging.

He could feel the night air on his exposed hands and face like the breath of something long dead.

Not far now: the weedy fields of the train yards were just ahead. He studied them in the deadly moonlight. A gravel road wound along the edge of Cut River. Beyond it were the silent hulks of the trains themselves, huge and segmented worms clinging to the rails, waiting to be woken.

He could feel Nancy's hand gripping his own tighter and tighter, feel the breath aching in his lungs. Yes, this was it. So simple and easy, of course, he hadn't thought of it until survival instinct had pointed the way: *the fields, the woods, you dumb shit, make for the open spaces.*

They stepped onto the gravel road and seized up like their hearts had stopped.

On the other side of the road there was a ditch, another deep culvert separating them from the train yards and freedom. And out of it loped three or four bulky, panting bodies. *Dogs.* Mangy things covered with greasy pelts, tongues lolling from their mouths, teeth bared.

They saw Ben and Nancy, froze.

And then in unison, they started to growl, baleful yellow eyes fixed on the intruders.

"Oh no..." Nancy managed.

The dogs watched them.

They came no closer but stood their ground, growling, teeth exposed like white spikes.

Two or three others came out of the ditch, joined their comrades.

The fact that he and Nancy had even made it this far, Ben knew, was a blessing. Her hand in his own was hot, greasy, and crushing. They were close enough to one of the abandoned factories to make a run for it, to climb over the fence. He doubted that dogs, even *these* dogs, could climb an eight-foot storm fence.

As they slipped away, the dogs started growling simultaneously.

It was a low evil sound that rose up to a cacophonous whine.

The dogs launched themselves forward at the same time.

Nancy let out a scream and Ben thought he might have, too.

They turned and ran, both instinctively going for the fence. They would make it, maybe, mere seconds before those teeth ripped into their ankles like knives into soft, fat bellies.

They heard a rumbling, saw lights wash over them.

A Jeep Cherokee came whipping down the street, bearing down on the dogs, scattering them to the four winds like hornets in a cyclone. The Jeep cruised right up to the curb, the passenger side window slid down.

"What's happening, people?" a woman said to them. "You walking the dogs or are they walking you?"

Ben and Nancy stood there, staring at this woman, this vehicle. Too good to be true. A taste of civilization.

"Yeah," Ben told her, wanting to start crying with relief. "Jesus Christ, are we glad to see you."

"Climb in," she said.

The driver's side door opened and a mountain of a man got out. The Jeep seemed to actually rise up a few inches when it was free of his weight. He had wispy, shoulder-length hair and a full ZZ Top beard. He was built like a linebacker, carried a gut on him like a feed sack, but given his size, it seemed to belong.

He nodded to all present. "What the hell's going on around here?" He went to the back door, opened it with a key. "Lock's fucked," he said. "Gotta have a key to open it. Hop in."

Ben and Nancy did, melting into the soft leather seat, the warmth, the safety.

The big guy slammed their door, walked around the Jeep, scanning the darkness, looking and looking.

"He better get in," Ben said, "those dogs..."

"Don't you worry about Joe, hon. Dogs mess with him they gonna be sorry."

Ben almost believed it.

He was like a recruiting poster for the Hell's Angels.

He moved quickly for a large man, carrying a certain deadly intensity about him. He stood out in front of the Jeep, daring the dogs to come on. Slowly, they did. They came from all directions, making that awful growling sound again as they joined forces. Joe came around the side and hopped in, slamming his door. The Jeep rocked from his girth.

He hooked an arm the size of a carpet roll over the seat, turned to face his guests. "What in Christ's name is going on here?" he asked. "Goddamn town's like a graveyard. What gives?"

Ben broke up into laughter, despite himself. Wasn't that the $10,000 question? He kept laughing until he started coughing and gagging. Nancy laughed, too, patting him on the back.

"I say something funny?" Joe asked.

"We've been through a lot," she told him and, having found her voice, couldn't stop talking.

She told them about the hit-and-run on the road outside Cut River. About the dead guy who wasn't dead at all. About Sam getting killed (that wasn't easy), about them running. All the craziness they'd seen. All she left out was the bit about the hanging boy because it was just too...insane. Now, in the warmth of the Jeep, she was certain she'd hallucinated that.

"Jesus Christ on a stick," Joe said. "Nice place. All that and mad dogs, too."

Nancy nodded. "Not just them, but the people. Rabid. They're all rabid or something."

"You don't say?"

Nancy's hackles rose. "I'm telling you the truth."

He held his hand up, palm out. "Easy, lady. I believe you. Something's majorly fucked here. Even I can see that."

He told them that when they'd pulled into town about fifteen minutes before, the road coming in was nearly blocked with cars. Smashed cars.

Ben felt the skin at the back of his neck crawling. "Blocked off?"

"Almost," the woman said. "We just squeezed through, man. It was unreal. Remember, babe? Remember what I said? Heavy weather ahead for sure."

He nodded. "Yeah, we should have just turned around. Place didn't feel right, if that makes any sense. After we got past those smashed cars, shit, there were others in the streets—windows broken, bumpers torn off. And bodies. A mess. Looked like a goddamn riot passed through."

"Maybe one did," Nancy suggested grimly.

He shrugged. "By the way, I'm Joe," he told them. "This is Ruby Sue."

"Nancy Eklind."

"Ben Eklind."

"Married, eh? That takes some serious balls," Ruby Sue said.

She was thirtysomething, Ben figured. Short, thin, her face dominated by huge sleepy eyes. She was friendly, very warm, though maybe a little dizzy like she was hitting the pipe a little too often.

"That guy you hit...he just went crazy, eh?" Joe asked them.

Ben sighed. "Never seen anything like it. I hit him hard. He popped out of nowhere. I turned my eyes from the road for a second or two...and, well, there he was. *Bam.* We found him in the ditch. We were sure he was dead...head split right open, ribs crushed in on the side, and then he jumped up and started throwing us around. Christ."

"Like he was possessed," Nancy added.

"Hit and run. Wow." Ruby Sue stared at the ceiling, overwhelmed by the concept. "Know what? There was this guy...what was his name, Joe? Oh, *Crazy.* Remember Crazy? We had this bash, you know? Everybody drunk and naked, booze, chemicals...oh, man. Crazy, though, he snorts half of Peru, been drinking thirty-six hours straight. Tripping, speeding, totally fried, man, wanders off, starts dancing out in the highway. BAM! Big Peterbuilt. Hamburger Helper, you know?"

Joe looked at Nancy. "Your brother," he said, saying it very gently, compassionately, "Sam was it? You sure—"

Nancy chewed her lower lip like a strip of jerky. "Yes. That psycho ripped his throat open...blood everywhere..." She fell silent.

"I'm only asking because if he's not, well, shit, we wouldn't want to leave him out there."

"Yeah, Joe would help him if he could," Ruby Sue admitted to Nancy. "He was a medic in the army once. Like that one time, eh, Joe? Those two Banditos at Sturgis? Going at each other with knives? Bad news. Bleeding all over the place. Joe stitched 'em up, took care of 'em. Hey, babe?"

The bearded giant ignored her, folded his massive forearms over his chest. "Barefoot, no shirt, you say? This time of year? Again I ask, what the hell is that all about?"

"That's what we were wondering," Sam said.

"Dude must've been baked," Ruby Sue decided. "Some of that shit, man, look out. You just never know. Sometimes you get stuff that's been treated or sprayed with shit. Been there, done that. You get some herb treated with dust or something, cancel future appointments." She laughed. "Happened to me. I thought everyone was after me. Major paranoia, for sure. I thought my roommate had a spider for a head and snakes for hands. God, I was dusted for twenty-four hours."

Again, Joe didn't pay any attention.

Probably kept his sanity that way, Ben figured.

"We have to get out of here," he told them. "That's the bottom line."

"Agreed," Joe said.

There was a sudden thudding and the Jeep started rocking. It came again and again. Thud, thud, thud. The dogs were back, throwing themselves at the Jeep. They dove at the windows, enraged and filled with maniacal bloodlust, jaws snapping, eyes bulging, snouts spraying tangles of saliva and foam into the air.

"Jesus Christ!" Joe cried. "They're attacking my fucking Jeep!"

An immense black lab clawed its way up onto the hood, throwing itself at the windshield, teeth biting, tongue licking, paws clawing. Its eyes were huge, bulging, on fire with that profane yellow shine, raging with blind hatred. Its jaws closed around a windshield wiper, ripped it free, and snapped it in half like a chicken wing. It kept smashing its snout into the glass with a savage ferocity until the windshield was painted with foam and slime and blood.

"Wow," Ruby Sue said. "Un-fucking-*believable*."

Joe threw the Jeep in reverse, swinging around in a perfect arc, tires squealing. The lab tumbled through the air, disappeared. The Jeep popped the curb and Joe already had the transmission in drive. They swung back onto the street, knocking dogs aside like bowling pins. The Jeep gave a sickening lurch as it rolled over more than one of them. And they were away and gone, tooling down the road.

Ruby Sue said, "They're rabid, man. I seen a show once."

"It's worse than that," Nancy said, pressed up close to Ben now.

Joe was shaking his head as they wheeled around a corner, sliding into the street. "I've seen rabid. I've seen it more than once," he told them. "And that ain't rabid. It's like rabid to the tenth power."

Joe had the Jeep wailing up Chestnut, doing an easy seventy miles an hour.

The dogs had sent home the message that Ben and Nancy had been unable to: that there was something seriously wrong here and it was like nothing you could possibly imagine.

Now they know, Ben thought and was satisfied with that.

But he knew that the message wouldn't truly hit home until they saw the people of this town...or what they had become. The dogs were bad, yes, God knew they were, but the people...savages, monsters, inhuman things.

"Let's just get out of here," Joe said. "We'll sort the rest out later."

Joe brought them straight up Chestnut until they crossed Magnetic Street, and entered one of the blacked-out sections of Cut River. Houses were dark. Cars parked. Bodies sprawled in the streets. Lifeless, empty. A cemetery. At least that's how it looked, but Ben knew better. He knew what sort of things populated the darkness, their pale faces and grinning mouths and hooked fingers.

Yes, he knew all about those things.

Joe kept putting her to the metal, squealing around corners, firing through intersections, handling the Jeep with a near-suicidal mastery like he was piloting a fighter-bomber through enemy airspace. And, in some respects, that was true. Only thing lacking here was the heavy firepower.

"Up ahead," Ruby Sue said. "That's where those cars were, I think."

Joe nodded. "Yeah."

Ben sat silently waiting for something, anything. He didn't know what, but he knew it was coming. Knew it wouldn't be this easy.

Nancy was feeling it, too, he knew.

Her breathing was deep and labored, her body tight and rigid like it was held together with wire.

The headlights of the Jeep cut through the night like scalpels, peeling back the blighted darkness and revealing the festering underbelly of Cut River: cars with smashed windshields, flattened tires; garbage cans overturned, litter strewn on the sidewalks; tree limbs down from the storm; a pick-up truck driven right through a garage door. The homes squatting dismally in the gloom didn't look right either—windows were shattered, furniture spilled out onto lawns. There were other things in the yards, too, shapes nestled in the leave-strewn grass.

Ben thought he saw bodies, but it was hard to be sure.

But he did know he saw what he thought were effigies, scarecrows dangling from second-story windows and porch overhangs.

At least, he hoped they were effigies.

"Check that out," Ruby Sue said. "Did you see it?" Nobody answered, so she elaborated. "Looked like...I don't know, man...like symbols and shit painted on that house. This place has gone totally fucking pagan."

Pagan.

It made all the sense in the world to Ben.

Whatever had gotten this town, whatever pestilence had infected its citizens, it almost seemed to have freed something primal, something atavistic dwelling within them. Like the veneer of civilization had been peeled free, baring the dark, feral underbelly of the human race and the calculated barbarity that went with it. These people, like our ruthless, bloodthirsty ancestors fifty, a hundred millennia before, were predatory monsters, killers who reveled in the art of butchery, of slaughter.

"I thought it was the storm," Joe said to them or maybe to himself. "But it isn't; not all of it."

He had his window open just a crack. No more, no less. The air smelled of smoke like maybe there was a fire nearby. It stunk of other things, too: ripe, raw things. Nameless odors that stirred some shadowy race memory in the occupants of the Jeep. Some distant, dark memory of barbaric times when civilization was an unrealized dream.

Yes, Ben thought, these people have reverted somehow. And wouldn't it be easy, when you came right down to it, to tear off your clothes and join them? Celebrate death and sex and blood?

"What's that smell?" Ruby Sue inquired. "That burning? What is that?"

Good question because the wind was carrying a stink far worse than charred wood now.

The Jeep slowed down and everyone saw why.

The street was entirely blocked-off now.

Cars were wedged three deep across the road and right up onto lawns, blocking any possible avenue of escape. There were a few battered, mutilated bodies lying on the pavement before them.

And Ben was thinking: *Yes, exactly! They've marked the perimeters of their territory and everything within is their domain. And the bodies? Sacrifices, blood offerings to whatever it is they think rules the night. A primitive version of breaking a bottle of champagne against a ship. Because it wasn't always champagne, not in the dire, forbidding days before history. Good luck, good hunting, fertility...*

Maybe he was overwrought (he was) and maybe he was giving them too much goddamn credit, but he didn't think so. This was not as simple as he'd originally thought. This was not just a bunch of crazies acting impulsively, satisfying their basal desires. Oh no, not at all. The blockade proved that; this was organized. Maybe at some aboriginal, tribal level, but organized it was.

Joe clicked on his hi-beams.

"Look," he said, "by God, look—"

And they were all looking and all seeing, knowing there was no need for explanation here. At the back of the blockade, at the rear row of vehicles, bodies had been lashed to tree limbs and posts jammed into the ground, set afire. They were blackened and smoldering now, curled and withered by flame. The fires had gone out, but the thick nauseating stench of cremated flesh hung in the air like a poisonous envelope.

No man's land, Ben thought wildly. *Clearly marked. Do not pass go. Do not exit. This is the end of the world, their world.*

"Turn 'em off," Nancy whimpered, "for God's sake turn those lights off!"

Joe did, speechless, afraid as he'd ever been in a life where his sheer size made terror an impossibility.

He threw the Jeep in reverse, spun it around and headed back the way they came.

"There's other roads out," he said in a whisper of a voice. "Other ways."

He said nothing more and neither did anyone else.

But it was building in Nancy.

Ben could feel her shuddering next to him, not with horror, but with rage. It was only a matter of time.

"Are you—" she sucked in a dry breath "—trying to tell me that fifteen minutes ago when you came through here, you saw none of that?"

Ruby Sue turned in her seat, looked at her, then looked at Joe. "Oh, for chrissake, tell them the truth, babe. What does it matter now?"

He nodded. "We've been here for a couple hours."

Silence.

Nancy licked her lips. "And you lied about it because..."

"Because," Joe said, "the reason we were here in the first place wasn't exactly what you'd call legal. Okay? We came to see someone. They weren't home. So we waited around. They didn't show, so we took a ride. Then we found you guys."

"It doesn't matter," Ben said.

"Hell it doesn't," Nancy snapped. "What else are you two lying about?"

Joe sighed. "Listen, lady. Way I see it we're the only game in town, so why don't you sit tight and I'll try to get us out. How's about that?"

She grumbled under her breath.

Ben didn't like where any of this was going.

He managed to calm her down, but he knew it wouldn't last. The silence in the Jeep was thick like honey, dripping with innuendo. They couldn't afford to piss Joe off. They needed his ride. Like he pointed it out, it was the only game in town.

Through the streets again.

Joe drove slower this time, no theatrics, no NASCAR bullshit. He navigated the roads, taking his time. Maybe he knew now what was at stake here. That if he wiped the Jeep out, the story ended right here.

Nancy was suspicious of the both of them and, dammit, so was Ben now.

What bothered him at first is why they didn't offer their last names when everyone introduced themselves. It was a small thing, yes, but the smallest of bones could choke a man. And why lie about how long they were in town? They said they were in Cut River for a reason that *wasn't exactly what you'd call legal.*

Okay.

Fine.

But how bad could it be?

From the looks of Ruby Sue, Ben was figuring drugs. But from the look of Joe—and it took a while to look at Joe, he was so goddamn big—it could've been just about anything.

Ben massaged his temples.

He couldn't think anymore. He was drained, emptying fast.

Next to him, Nancy was grinding her teeth. It wasn't a good sign. It could've been anxiety or fear or she could've been pissed off, simmering like a pot of chili on the back burner.

As they drove, he swept his eyes over what he could see of Cut River.

They were driving through a part of town that had electricity: streetlights were working, shop fronts were lit, squares of light in apartment windows. It all looked so positively normal, so completely average it was frightening.

But six, seven blocks back, in the darkness...Christ, how could things change so quickly?

What bothered him the most was that he knew the psychos were around.

Maybe he didn't see them, but he definitely felt them. The way a man could feel something hunting him in the black jungle or cold steel about to be pressed to his throat.

Yes, they were out there. Many of them.

The bad part was how they didn't show themselves.

But then, neither does a tiger until it's time to sink its fangs into your throat.

Ben licked his lips, his eyes wide and staring now. He had a pretty good idea he knew where Joe was taking them, out to where the country road merged with the town. The very way

Nancy and Sam and he had planned coming in. More turns, more little shortcuts, then finally a main road, maybe part of Chestnut (Ben had only been in Cut River once or twice, so he couldn't be sure).

The electricity had failed here now, lights were patchy, few and far between.

It was going to be bad and he knew it.

He didn't think they'd be able to get out this way either. Just a feeling, but it persisted like a nasty itch. When Nancy and he had come into town earlier they had taken a footbridge up river that led into a little park. They hadn't gone over the main bridge. Maybe that was a good thing.

As they sped down the final stretch of road and Cut River fell behind them, dread thick as tar settled into Ben's belly.

The moon lit up the countryside pretty good.

He could see the bridge up ahead, other things, but he couldn't be exactly sure what. Joe must've seen them, too, because he started slowing down, clicking his brights on.

"Whoa," Ruby Sue said expectantly, "don't look good, people."

And it didn't.

Ben and Nancy were sitting forward in their seats now, mutually shaking.

The bridge was blocked with more cars.

No real surprise. There were clearings to either side of it, meandering open meadows.

Ben could see shapes out there, indistinct but there, all right.

As Joe backed up and swung the Jeep around, the headlights turned the clearing on the left to day. Ben kept looking, so did Nancy. He felt a serious necessity to scream, but he couldn't. His lungs were empty. He sat on the edge of his seat, that cold, gnawing feeling in his guts.

Nancy kept shaking her head. "My God," she whispered, defeated now. "My God."

The meadow was full of scarecrows mounted up tight and secure on crossbars, except, of course, they weren't scarecrows at all. They were people, maybe too hideous to even be called that. Corpses, really. Some recent, others decayed and withered into gray husks. And not just a few, but fifteen or twenty within the range of the headlights and many more hunched in the darkness beyond. Some were little more than skeletons dressed in the moldering cerements of the grave. They were not crucified as such, but lashed with wire, with ropes.

Joe idled there maybe two, three minutes, enough for the morbid impact of it to take root in their minds, to find soil and grow to ghastly fruition. When he pulled away, the fleshless skulls and cadaver faces faded, but were still livid and hurtful in their minds.

Nancy started sobbing.

Ruby Sue kept shaking her head as if it was beyond belief.

It was.

"Those people," she said bleakly, "those people...oh, man, they must've dug 'em up or something. You think they dug 'em up?"

"Shut up," Ben told her.

There was no argument on that and no time for one.

The townspeople were making their appearance.

They walked straight up the road en masse towards the Jeep. Mostly men and women, a few children. There had to be thirty or more, marching in unison, although it was more of an inhuman shambling. They were organized and fixed of purpose. A wall of humanity, a throng of white faces and glaring unblinking eyes.

"I'm going through them," Joe announced coldly. "I'm fucking plowing through them sonsabitches."

Ben felt Nancy slump against him as the Jeep picked up speed.

He felt his flesh crawl in undulating waves as reality spun wickedly out of control, as his mind narrowed and squealed with white noise.

When the Jeep started hitting them, his brain fell into darkness.

-DARKNESS ON THE EDGE OF TOWN-

13

Described by waxen moonlight, Cut River was a cemetery.

The buildings were leaning headstones and the homes were shadow-crawling crypts and the cars and trucks were caskets and burial vaults, lids sprung open, their cadaverous armies spilled into the night.

Lisa Tabano, her buzz bottoming like a freighter scratching its belly on a shoal, stumbled along behind Johnny Davis, he of the guns and the war that never completely ended. Disillusioned, distrustful, paranoid, but ultimately a good man, she decided. It was just that Uncle Sam had pissed on him so many times, he couldn't keep his head above the stink.

She was starting to feel the need again.

Not bad yet, but it was coming.

In an hour or so it would be there, all right, nibbling at her insides. And the really bad part was that day by sufferable day, the highs were of shorter duration. She was only snorting heroin right now, but really, how long would it be until she was shooting?

Johnny walked point ahead of her, pausing now and again, crouching down low, then signaling her to continue.

It made her think that he'd probably been waiting for some action since the war ended.

And now he had it.

They crept past a row of blank storefronts and Johnny stopped. "In here," he said to her.

It was a sporting goods store.

The plate glass door was shattered.

Inside, battery-powered emergency lights lit up the exit in the rear, casting ghoulish, lurching shadows everywhere. Displays were trashed, tipped over. Glass cases were obliterated. Shelves were emptied. It looked like looters had danced a merry destructive dance here.

But that wasn't the case and she knew it.

"What the hell do we want here?" Lisa asked, setting her guitar case down and stepping over heaps of camouflage hunting clothes that smelled like urine.

Johnny had a Tekna flashlight out, scanning the debris. "They really went through this place, eh? I was in here just before sundown, picking up a few things. They must've come since."

Lisa slid a cigarette in her mouth, lit it up. "Mind?" she said.

"You might draw them in, rock star."

"But I've got you, my own little Rambo. What me worry?"

He chortled deep in his throat as he dug madly through outdoor clothing—hunter's orange, Carhartt work clothes, waterproof tarps. He pulled a dark rubber poncho from the jumble, held it up, examined it carefully. He threw it at Lisa. "Catch."

She pulled it off her face. "Are we going on a mission or getting out of here?"

"We're evading, baby. E and E. Escape and evasion. It's the name of the game." He leaped over piles of winter boots, hiking shoes, slid a canoe out of the way. "Here, these'll look sweet on you." He tossed a pair of rubber boots at her. "They're all the rage, baby. I hear Hendrix wore 'em at Monterey."

She laughed, pulling the boots over her Nikes. "Christ, you are old."

"You know it."

"Should I ask why I have to wear boots or is that some mission secret?"

He grinned at her, all teeth and eyes, his face darkened with black camo paint. "I'd tell ya, sweet thing, but then I'd have to fuck ya."

"Yeah, I've always wanted to do it with Al Jolson. Nice makeup. It's so you."

Johnny found the freeze-dried backpacker's food and stuffed some in his pack. He pulled out a pistol, broke it open, snapped it closed and handed it to Lisa. "Know how to use it?"

She held it like it had been dipped in feces. "I don't like guns." She looked from it to him. "I don't approve of them."

He made a face, said, "Listen, I don't approve of condoms either. No fun. But if I'm gonna slap skins with a hooker, I wear one. Assures my survival. And if you're gonna stay alive in this shithole, you'll need a gun. Maybe not, but maybe so." He waited for an argument, was surprised, maybe, at how tolerant, how patient he was with her. It had been a long time since he'd been that way with anyone, let alone a female. "It's a thirty-eight. Revolver, doesn't jam. Six-shots. Safety is off. Bad guys comin' down on ya, aim it and pull the trigger."

Sighing, she accepted his logic and slid the little .38 into her coat pocket, hoping like hell she wouldn't have to use it on anyone. She wasn't a pacifist really, but violence was negative and solved nothing...that was, under normal circumstances. But here, in this hellzone where civilization had ground to a halt, all that mattered was who survived, not what sort of principals or moral integrity they possessed.

Somebody (or some thing) came looking for trouble, goddamn if she wasn't going to give them some (to paraphrase the old Johnny Winters' tune).

"Put that poncho on," he said, more of an order than anything else.

She did, not liking the idea too much, but once it was over her head it made her feel warm and protected. She put the .38 in the front pocket.

She walked around.

The phone had been ripped off the wall, the cash register and computer smashed on the floor. She saw the remains of a cell phone.

Whatever these things were, they had a definite hard-on for technology.

Savages, she thought. *They worship darkness, hate anything modern.*

Johnny was still searching through the mess. He finally held up what looked like a short boat hook and nodded, satisfied.

"We going fishing for big ones?"

"You'll see. Let's go."

Lisa was glad the windows were broken so she didn't have to catch a reflection of herself, how utterly foolish she must've looked in that huge poncho and squeaking boots. She picked up her guitar case and purse and led the way back out onto the sidewalk.

And heard it before she saw it.

Low, guttural growling, the sound of claws scratching concrete.

She froze up tight as cherries in a deep freeze, motionless, helpless, staring at the huge, mangled German Shepherd a few feet away. Its left ear was missing, its coat filthy and stained with blood and bits of clinging leaves, sticks. There were great patches of skin ripped free from its battered skull, one of its eyes a gored hole. Its snout was bloody pulling away from lethal white teeth. Ropes of vile foamy saliva dangled from its mouth. The good ear was flattened against the skull as it made to leap.

Johnny shoved her out of the way as the dog leapt.

It made it maybe three feet before it took a load of buckshot straight on that vaporized its head into bloody mucilage. Its body tumbled out into the road, legs still pistoning.

Johnny took Lisa by the arm. "C'mon, lady, time to march."

She realized then that she was lost in a dream for nearly a block, Johnny leading her like the good shepherd with a lost lamb. Then she came out of it, thinking that she needed a fix.

But now wasn't the time.

She'd been lucky so far, way too lucky. First with the woman at her parent's house, then with the two punks that Johnny had clipped for her, and now with the dog.

How long could it possibly hold? How long?

Johnny stopped on a quiet street. "Way I see it," he explained to her, "they're not going to let us just walk out of here. My guess is that by now they've got this town closed-up tight. Which means, essentially, we're prey."

"Prey?"

He nodded. "We're the enemy here, baby. Don't you get it? We're the weird ones, they're normal. Normal because they're the majority. They've got two choices with us: make us like them or kill us."

Lisa thought about it. "And how are they gonna make us like them? What're they gonna do? Bite our throats?"

"Don't be too surprised."

He slung his shotgun over his shoulder and walked a few feet away to a manhole cover. He took his boat hook and inserted the tip into the drain hole. With everything he had, he pulled and the lid came up. He dragged it onto the pavement.

"After you," he said.

Lisa had been watching him with a mixture of amusement and confusion, now she said, "You've got to be out of your mind."

"Maybe. But down you go." He handed her the flashlight. "You want out, don't you? This might be the only way."

"How about we find a cell phone instead?"

Johnny laughed. "Cell phone? They've destroyed every piece of technology they could lay their mitts on. You think they overlooked cell phones?"

"They couldn't get 'em all, Johnny."

He shook his head. "Don't have to. There's only one provider here. Its base station and transmitting antennas are located at the edge of town. In one of the blacked-out areas. No power, baby. I tried my neighbor's this afternoon...nothing. Just a dead piece of plastic..."

Man proposes and God disposes, Lisa thought helplessly.

She shined the light down the throat of the sewer.

It was dank and misty below. A built-in ladder led down to the water beneath. She looked back at Johnny. He was smiling, enjoying the hell out of this. Now she knew what he had in mind with the poncho and boots.

She handed him the light. "Keep it on me," she said.

Setting her guitar case on the street, she lowered herself down.

The rungs were greasy, slicked with mildew. Halfway down, Johnny fed the guitar case to her. It fit, all right. And if it hadn't, Lisa wasn't going either. It seemed like a long climb down, holding the guitar case and maneuvering with only one hand. The shaft opened at the bottom into a large central drain. Plenty large enough to walk through without hitting your head.

But the stink, oh God.

Stagnant water, organic rot. Like a brackish swamp.

She dipped one boot into the water, found the bottom, and then went all the way in. It was deep, nearly two feet. And cold. The boots kept her feet dry, but she could feel the chill wetness sucking out her heat.

Johnny dropped the light to her and swung down into the shaft. He pulled the lid closed after them, then moved down the ladder like it was something he'd done many times.

He smiled. "Not so bad, eh?"

"Says who?"

He took the light from her, played it around.

The passage was maybe seven feet in height, little more in width. A brick tunnel, more or less. She was surprised to see graffiti on the walls.

"This is the main drain line," Johnny explained to her. "It runs beneath the entire length of Chestnut Street. Most of the rainwater sewers in this town are only big enough to crawl through on your hands and knees. Some are a lot smaller. This one feeds to a culvert that empties into the river. That's where we're going."

Lisa lit a cigarette. "Only you would think of something like this."

"I been down here lots of times."

"I believe it."

He seemed surprised. "You grew up here and you never been down in the sewers?"

She shook her head. "Guess I missed out on that. I feel so incomplete."

He laughed, leading the way through the darkness, splashing just ahead of her. "We used to come down here, get stoned and drunk when we were teenagers. Usually there's only a trickle of water down here, half a foot, if that. But we've had a lot of rain lately, what with the storms and all, so it's pretty deep."

Lisa caught up to him, stayed at his side. "So we're going to crawl through a pipe into the river?"

"Got a better idea?"

"Yes. The streets above."

He shook his head. "No, not a good idea. There's lots of them up there. Rabids everywhere."

"Rabids?"

"It's what I call 'em. They're crazy, foaming at the mouth. *Rabids.*" He paused, scanned the light along the walls. "See that?"

There was a crude, ancient pot leaf carved into the discolored face of a brick.

"Nice," she said.

"Yeah, me and my buddy Tommy did that. Tommy Haynes. I was sixteen. Before the war."

They splashed along, shoulders touching. "Was it bad?" Lisa said.

"What?"

"The war? Vietnam."

He rubbed his jaw, sighed. "Yeah."

Lisa didn't push it.

"Christ, I hate it down here," she admitted.

Johnny smiled. "Reminds me of somewhere else, another set of tunnels."

"The war?"

"Yes."

Everything echoed in the sewer.

The sound of their boots slopping through the water was like thunder. Water was dripping and running, the sound of it amplified. The entire situation was surreal. It was the sort of place that would have driven a claustrophobe crazy—the stone walls pressing in, the sluicing water, the cloying darkness, and the ripe stench of rot and buried things. And above it all, the seepage from above, dripping and dripping.

Like a cave in an old movie.

They passed another ladder leading to a manhole above.

Lisa looked to Johnny hopefully, but he plodded onward into the subterranean maze.

The dampness was everywhere.

It came from the gently flowing river of rainwater, it came from the air, it bled from the damp stone walls. Lisa hugged herself, trying to keep warm, trying to hear anything but the dripping, the hollow splashing sounds, the noise of rainwater running from outlet pipes.

After awhile, it got on your nerves.

And when you had the need, the habit, things were only magnified as you came down. She tried to keep it out of her head, tried to think about her mom and dad and what the chances were that they had escaped (but that blood, all that goddamn blood, sticky, stinking). It only made things worse, though, so she examined her current situation minutely...unpleasant as it was.

She thought: *I came home to see my family after being gone for five years. I came home with a hit record under my belt, a lot of money from a successful yet grueling tour which nearly killed me (nearly killed all of us), and a heroin habit. I came home, not expecting much, but finding that my dad had accepted who and what I was, was maybe even proud of me. That would have been enough. I could have been happy. Maybe it was what I needed all the time, just that. Not the music or the life or the money or the drugs, just acceptance, understanding. Yes, I could have been happy. Except, I wandered into this goddamn nightmare and what the hell is this all about, what—*

Johnny concentrated his light on something bobbing in the water. "A dead one," he said.

"What is it?"

"Just a rat," he told her. "Lots of 'em down here. Always has been. The heavy rains probably drove most of 'em to higher ground, the rest maybe drowned."

"Rats. Christ."

Johnny shrugged. "Not so bad. They won't bother you. Trust me, rock star, infinitely preferable to what walks above."

So they kept going and Lisa kept trying to forget about the gnawing in her belly while making concessions about rats being preferable to the rabids, as Johnny called them, haunting the streets above.

It was not easy.

She felt ready to crawl out of her skin.

There was something indefinably eerie about all this.

"Hey, Rambo?" she said, needing badly to hear a voice, even her own. "Before you said that I was naïve. That I didn't know what this was all about. What did you mean by that? Do you know?"

He looked at her, looked away. "I know some things."

"And?"

"Take too long."

Great. Mystery man clutching secrets to his bosom. "It had to happen quick, right? I mean, the whole fucking town? If it took weeks, the authorities would have been involved. They would've stopped it or quarantined this place or something. Right?"

"Maybe. Maybe not." He touched her arm, paused. "It depends what they're up to. Who can say?"

She sighed. "You speak in riddles, white man. I'm just saying whatever this is it went fast. You were here...how fast did it happen?"

"I live outside town. In the woods. I wasn't here."

"You were close enough."

"You wanna know how it happened? I'll tell you that much. There was a storm. Not the bad one. Just a rainstorm a few days before. I was out of town, didn't see it. Old guy who lived out by me said it was strange...a black rain. Ink-black."

Lisa stared at him. "Black rain?"

"Yes." Johnny shrugged. "That's what he said. Lasted only for a couple minutes, he said, that blackness. Other than that, it was just a normal rain. Next day, people were getting sick. Flu symptoms. Closed the school, lots of businesses. Nobody thought it was odd, what with all the flu raging around the country. Then we got that bad storm, shut the town down. When it was over..."

"It was like this?"

"Yes."

"You think there was something in the rain?" she asked.

"Could be," he said, his tone lifeless. "Could very well be. Like I said, I never go into town much. But I can imagine how it went—everyone calling into work and what not, laying around in their beds, dizzy and weak, puking maybe, not liking the sunlight at all. Sleeping a lot. Maybe when they finally woke up, they weren't the same anymore. They'd changed. And what happened then? They started seeking out the ones who hadn't been infected so they could spread it, whatever got to them. A race purge, you know? Eliminate the normal ones, the different ones. Bring 'em into the fold or kill 'em."

"This is creeping me out," Lisa admitted. "Like they're...they're..."

"Vampires? Is that what you were thinking?"

"I guess."

"Why not?" Johnny said, finding the comparison acceptable.

He wouldn't say anything after that, but he really didn't have to. Oh, Lisa knew he knew more than he was saying. But she honestly didn't *want* to know more. Enough was enough.

Whatever happened was evil.

And maybe that was silly and superstitious, but it was the only word that seemed to apply: evil.

Of course, being down here in the sewers wasn't helping a goddamn thing.

She didn't feel any safer down here.

It was like wandering through the musty confines of a tomb. In her head, despite her attempts to steel herself, there was that voice telling her there was danger here. No, maybe it wasn't exactly a voice as such, but, God, it was clear, it's meaning crystal. She couldn't do a thing to dissuade it.

Maybe it was instinct.

Logic and reasoning were impotent in its shadow.

It made her heart thud dully like a hammer into a bag of sand, made the breath positively wheeze from her lungs as if her throat had constricted down to a pinhole, her air sacs thick with dust. Her skin was cold, damp, and shivering and it didn't have shit to do with this sodden, inundated pesthole. It came from within, bled through every swollen pore, every dilated blood vessel. It filled her guts with warm, rolling jelly, snapped her eyes wide and unblinking. The hairs along the back of her neck were straight and taut as wires.

She'd never known such complete and total terror before.

Maybe it had something to do with the monkey on her back, but she honestly didn't think so. Her adrenaline was high, electric, surging in every cell and for once, the need seemed to be nonexistent.

Is that what it took to go clean?

Either days of agony in some dark room or mindless fear?

"Stop," Johnny said to her.

"Why? What is it?"

There was an edge to his voice and she didn't like it at all.

Her heart practically kicked out of her chest like a boot through wet cardboard.

Johnny cocked his head to the side, narrowed his eyes.

He kept playing the light ahead, but the beam made it only fifteen, twenty feet at best before being swallowed by the stygian murk. Fingers of mist curled from the gently sluicing water.

Lisa wiped a sheen of dampness from her face, became very aware of the beat of her heart, her breathing.

She kept watching.

A cigarette butt floated by.

A few leaves.

Water dripped and dripped.

"I thought I heard something," he whispered. He turned around, flashing the beam behind them. "Maybe I was wrong."

Yeah, and maybe I'm ready to piss my pants out of sheer imagination, she thought fearfully, *but I seriously doubt it.*

They moved on wordlessly, communicating their dread silently. It rode on their backs like some black amorphous shadow, one with weight, with awful texture. It slid frozen fingers around their throats, whispered horrid truths in their ears.

And ahead...that tunnel, the burrow of some huge and obscene worm twisting into utter blackness.

"Stop," Johnny said, this time a frantic whisper.

He had clutched Lisa's arm, holding it tight and sure, not letting go.

And there it was.

A brief moment after their splashing footfalls ended, so did others.

Johnny swung around, bringing up the shotgun and the flashlight. Yes, behind them. He stood motionless and Lisa stood at his side, formed concrete, the guitar case oddly weightless for a change.

A minute.

Two.

Three.

Splash, splash, splash.

No more cat and mouse, the hunt was on.

Prey had to be brought down with claws and teeth. And it wasn't only the sounds of approaching feet—many of them, in fact—but worse things now, echoing through the black throat of the sewers. Muted screams, cries, chattering, shrill childlike laughter. And scraping sounds like sticks were being dragged along the bricks...or sharp, bony fingers.

"Get ahead of me," Johnny told her, afraid, but very much in control. "There's a manhole up ahead. Run for it!"

Lisa needed no further urging: she ran.

Running, running, running.

No easy matter in two feet of thick, turgid water.

Running with Johnny at her back, the flashlight casting wild, creeping shadows in every direction, knife-edged black phantoms washing over them.

And the echoes—thundering, reverberating. Their own and those of the things that gave chase.

Lisa's legs were filled with sand as they pumped along, aching, tired, but refusing to give in until the hunters brought them down. Splashing, water spraying in her face, soaking her guitar case which she knew was waterproof but could've cared less if it wasn't. Vintage, expensive guitar? Fuck it, there were others. She planned on beating off her attackers with it if it came to that.

And they were gaining.

She was sure of it.

Maybe she could not hear it with all that echoing noise, but she could feel it just fine. She almost went on her ass half a dozen times, but through luck or pluck she stayed upright and then before her, thank God, there it was.

The ladder.

"Gimme your guitar," Johnny said, pulling it from her hands and replacing it with the short-barreled shotgun and the flashlight.

Lisa did not argue.

He went up the rungs like a monkey, pulling the guitar case with him. At the top she heard him grunting and exerting, heard a metallic groan, iron scratched over cement. Then light...feeble, but light...spilling in from above.

He pulled himself up and out.

"NOW!" he shouted to her. "COME UP NOW!"

But she didn't move as fast as she wanted to, almost as if some grim curiosity had to see what could make such sounds.

But then she smelled them, offensive, ripe like wet dogs.

Something kicked into her throat, maybe her heart, maybe a clot of raw terror.

But it got her moving.

She clawed her way up the rungs and she could hear the rabids shrieking and snarling, feel the cold air they brought with them, smell their breath like raw, spoiled meat.

And then Johnny somehow had hold of her and hoisted her out effortlessly.

He held her to him, maybe a moment too long, but it felt good, right, necessary. Then they were on their feet and Johnny was pushing the lid back on the manhole and he almost had it, but it was too late.

A tangle of clawing, clutching hands erupted around the edges of the lid, a mutiny of dead white fingers. The lid went clattering into the street. So many hands, four or five anyway, but small, delicate.

The hands of children.

Somehow, this was worse.

Yes, Lisa thought madly, *the kids still hang around down there, Johnny. It's still their place, even now.*

Then they were running again, the feel of the damp night, the chill breeze so beautiful, so refreshing after the cloistered, suffocating underworld. The moon brooded above, huge, round, the color of fresh bone. A lonely, omnipotent killing eye, it described the city in a wan glow.

A harvest moon, a hunter's moon.

The very thing to hunt and die by, as it was in the ancient world.

Although Lisa was exhausted, her legs rubbery and knotted with pain, she kept going, trying to stay up with Johnny who, despite the fact he was nearly twice her age, was in much better condition. So it wasn't that surprising that she didn't see the curb that spilled her to the sidewalk, made her nose kiss the cement, brought blood.

And maybe they smelled it.

The rabids.

Because it brought them, a swarm of them.

They came crawling and leaping out of the shadows like hyenas for fresh meat. They moved with a perverse, slinking motion as if they were more snake than human, boneless and fluid. They crept from behind the hulks of cars, from the mouths of alleys, through broken windows, and, yes, from manholes.

Jesus, so many.

Hissing and slavering, they came. An inhuman throng grinning with cruel mouths slashed in red against clownwhite faces, sinister yellow eyes, huge and unblinking, fingers hooked, matted fright wigs for hair. Naked, clothed, dressed in rags and what might have been the bloodied skins of domestic animals and human beings.

And the sounds.

Chatterings and chitterings and throaty growls. Shrill pipings and congested whisperings as they advanced.

A teenage girl came hopping out on all fours, screaming, teeth snapping.

Johnny cut in her in half with the shotgun, racked it, and killed two others.

In the span of less than thirty seconds there were five bodies on the pavement, limbs still twitching, mouths still chomping, teeth still grinding.

Johnny and Lisa made their break as the rabids set on their fallen comrades.

Lisa, her brain a hive of rushing noise, looked back once and saw them.

Dozens now, tearing and feasting and fighting.

But what really wrecked her was the sight of a little girl, no more than five or six, clad in stained yellow Dr. Denton's, ripping free a decapitated head from a strand of bloody meat. Tearing it free and clutching it to her bosom like a soccer ball and scuttling off into the shadows with it.

That's what made Lisa start screaming.

14

Lou Frawley watched the shoes under the stall door.

They did not move, did not do anything. Like a knife in the shadows, they waited for him, waited for his soft neck to get in range.

There was something caught in his throat.

It was cold and slippery. When he swallowed it back down, it landed thick in his belly like a shivering clump of coagulated grease. It could not be digested, could not be voided. It hung there, spreading out tentacles of nausea and making him want to vomit very badly.

Terror. Yes, terror so absolute it physically manifested itself.

How long, he had to wonder, could a person live on a raw diet of such continuous horror? How long before it brought on a coronary or a stroke?

He clutched the .38 tightly in his fist and approached the stall door.

The bathroom lights buzzed overhead as if the fluorescent tubes were full of wasps. A trickle of sweat ran down his spine. Every time he thought he could know no more fear, no more trembling apprehension, this town threw something new at him. Its menu of dread lunacy was inexhaustible.

He paused a few feet away from the stall door.

Far enough back that whoever was in there wouldn't be able to kick it open and get the jump on him. He stood there, wondering what he should do—get the hell out or look this in the face and kill it if it indeed needed killing.

He stepped around the side of the door so he was out of range.

His palms damp with perspiration, he reached out for the catch on the door.

If it was locked from the inside, he decided right then and there, he wasn't bothering with it. No way in hell he was going under or over the walls.

Too damn dangerous.

This was bad enough.

He could smell the owner of those shoes just fine. It smelled like he'd just shit his pants. But there was another odor there, too, a sharp, lingering stink that made Lou's flesh go tight. Eyes bulging, teeth locked together, he took hold of the latch and gave it a little pull.

Unlocked, the door swung noiselessly out.

A man was sitting on the toilet, his eyes glazed like those of a dead fish on a toxic beach, staring sightlessly. He wore a dark blue cop's uniform, badge in place. There was a shotgun clutched in his hands, the barrel jabbed under his throat. Behind his head there was a great smear of dark, sticky material.

Lou reached out to touch him, his brain screaming, *did he do it? Did he do it? Did he—*

He touched the man's arm.

It was stiff and unyielding.

Dead, yes, certainly.

Lou sighed, letting some of the terror run out of him as if somebody had pulled a drain plug somewhere in his soul. It subsided.

He jabbed a finger at the cop's shoulder.

The shotgun and the hands that held it slid down a few inches and his face fell right off. Not just his face, but the entire front of his head slid free like ice from a roof and landed in his lap with a wet, bloody thud, a few pounds of raw hamburger.

Lou wheeled around, teeth clenched, dry heaves convulsing his belly.

Blew his head off, sure. Nothing to be afraid of.

This cop had balls. When whatever took this town settled into him as well, he'd taken his own life. That took courage, foresight. For even death was better than becoming an animal like those prowling the streets.

Lou could almost picture him coming in here, perhaps even calmly, the infection clawing at his brain. Sitting on the toilet and doing what he knew must be done.

Yes, this guy—his name badge said FRANK CONVERS— was strong.

The weak ones were outside.

Lou closed the stall door, giving Convers the only respect and privacy possible in this convoluted, primeval world that eons ago had been called Cut River. He mumbled some half-remember prayer from his childhood and left the restroom.

Out in the station, he studied the other entrance off the bullpen.

No door, just an arch. But it was dark in there, horrible, forbidding. Like the entrance to the cave of some voracious beast. Such darkness...as if someone had hung a blanket on the other side of the doorway. It bled into the bullpen, tendrils of it, a creeping midnight fungus.

Fuck it.

Lou waltzed right over there, reached inside along the wall. He found a switch right away, turned it on.

It was sort of a duty room, he guessed.

There were more desks, a podium, lockers against the wall. Nothing threatening, only his fevered imagination this time creating monsters out of whole cloth.

But if he didn't have the right, then who?

There were places for *them* to hide, of course: under tables, behind cabinets. There were always places. But his sense of perception was getting preternaturally sharp by that point. A tool of instinct reborn in a world of computers and biotechnology gone to ruin.

No, this place was safe.

He made a quick inspection, hoping for something, anything, that might give him a clue to this horror show and how it had happened. But there was nothing. Duty roster on the podium. Scraps of paper here and there with crabbed phone numbers or license plate numbers, addresses, descriptions of vehicles.

No, no answers here. Only more questions.

Beyond the row of lockers, set in a little ell, there was a heavy steel door with a wedge of safety glass in it two-thirds of the way up. There was a red sign to the right of it that said:

WARNING
AUTHORIZED PERSONS ONLY
CONTAINMENT AREA

Containment area?

Lou went up to it and looked through the glass. It was brightly lit within. There were what appeared to be three or four small holding cells. Probably kept the bad guys here until they were delivered to the county lock-up.

He was about to turn away when he saw a shadow shift in there, in the far cell.

Was he really seeing it?

He pressed his face up to the cool glass. Yes. Someone was in there, hunched in the corner. He kept watching them. They made no aggressive or questionable movements.

What was there to worry about, really?

They were in a cell for chrissake.

Only in movies did maniacs or monsters burst through iron bars.

Lou opened the door and there was a loud buzzing sound from an alarm.

He knew if he went in and let the door close behind him, there would be no getting out; as a safety precaution, he saw, you needed a second party to let you out from the other side.

Good he noticed that.

He let it close and found a chair, dragged it over there. He opened the door, that damn buzzing rattling him again. He put the chair in front of the door. But it was heavy and made to close automatically. It dragged the chair with it, but could not close all the way.

He climbed over the chair and into the containment area.

Cells against one wall, a small desk opposite with a keypad on it. Sure, the buttons opened the cells. If he didn't touch those he was safe.

He walked to the far cell.

Some guy was hunched up in the corner. He wasn't moving.

Lou found his voice. "Hey," he said. "You in there."

The head snapped around.

Some young guy, unshaven, face slack, eyes darting from his skull. "You...you're not one of them?" he asked like he couldn't believe it.

"No, I'm normal. You?"

The guy was on his feet and up to the bars so fast Lou stepped back. "Jesus Christ...oh shit...get me out of here before she comes back. *Hurry.*" He pressed his face to the bars, looking nervously towards the door. "If she comes back, she'll kill us both. I've been pretending I was dead every time she came in here. Come on, man! Don't just fucking stand there!"

Lou went over to the desk, to the keypad. He pressed one button after the other. There was a buzzing and the cell doors each made a metallic clicking sound and opened an inch or two.

The guy came running out, grasped Lou happily by the shoulders.

"I'm Steve," he said.

"Lou."

"Okay. You got a gun. Good. Might need it." He kept casting a wary eye towards the door as if he was expecting the Devil to waltz in any moment. He couldn't have been more than twenty-two, twenty-three years old, but his eyes were ancient. "Drunk driving. They threw me in for drunk driving. And then that shit happened...oh for Christ's sake, did the world end? What happened?"

"I don't know. I got here a few hours ago," Lou told him, the idea that it had only been a few hours sucking the wind from him, "and, well, everything's gone crazy here. But, no, the world hasn't ended. Just Cut River. It's gone."

Steve looked like he needed to cry badly. His eyes were wet, his lips trembling. "We have to get out of here, man. We gotta be gone when she comes back."

"She?"

Steve looked exasperated. "She's...well, shit, there's no time for that," he said, pulling Lou to the door. "I'll explain later if we make it out."

Out the door they went into the duty room.

Steve was holding Lou's arm like a frightened child. He started blabbering about how terrible she was, how she'd slaughtered the prisoners that weren't infected. How she'd released the ones that were. How he'd played dead every time she came around, mimicking the coma the infected ones went into at the end, right before they woke up—

"How about we just be quiet?" Lou suggested, the guy's frantic, droning voice getting under his skin.

"Yeah, yeah, sure," Steve said. "You're right, you're right."

Lou figured this woman was probably another psycho and he knew how to deal with them, thank you very much...at least he hoped so. Then he started wondering if guns would stop them. But he put that from his mind. They were flesh and blood (he hoped), they were alive. Sick, contaminated, insane, but still living. Yes, they would die. If you asked them the right way, they would die just fine. He had the .38, but something a little heavier would have been nice.

"Do you know where they keep the guns?" he asked Steve.

"No. I mean, there's gotta be a weapon's locker around here somewhere, but it's not something they tell us convicts about," he said, half-joking, half-serious.

"Don't suppose then, you'd know where the keys to those cruisers outside are?"

Steve nodded happily. "Sure. They're right in the cruisers."

"They leave the keys in 'em?"

"Small-town, man. Nobody steals too many cars here and especially not a patrol car for chrissake. What would be the point? Kind of obvious aren't they?"

Lou shrugged.

Well there, at last, was something he could use. If the keys were in them and the radios were working, then he could contact the state police or drive out of town and probably both. It was a plan.

As they eased out into the bullpen, Steve said, "Unless, you know, one of them got to the cars. It's possible. They're not stupid, you know. Not at all."

They made it out of the police station and started down the long, shadowy corridor. Steve was still stuck to Lou like a wart on a witch's ass. Lou kept trying to give him the hint by trying to gently push him away, but it did no good.

As they moved quietly down the hallway, Lou was struck by the emptiness, that awful pressing, confining sense of claustrophobia that he was a mouse in a maze, every movement being studied, the walls trembling, ready to crush him at any moment.

They made it to the entryway and the front door was standing open, blackness and damp blowing in. And that stopped Lou dead because he was certain he'd closed it behind him. He could've sworn he had...hadn't he? It was all such a muddle in his brain it was really hard to say.

His grip was wet on the .38. He thought the gun might slip from his hand like a greasy banana.

"Okay," he said to Steve in a whisper, "we're going to go straight out those doors and then we're making for the parking lot and one of those cruisers. You lag behind, you fuck up in any way, I leave your ass. You understand me?"

Steve nodded sullenly. "Yes. I know. I know we..."

But his voice faded away as a sound came drifting down the stairs off to their right, a cold inhuman cackling like marbles rattling in a metal can. No more human than that and maybe even less.

"Stay with me...stay here with me."

Lou wheeled madly about, bringing the gun up.

The stairwell was a well of grainy shadows.

Steve let out a strangled gasp and *she* came.

One minute there was darkness brooding before them and the next...the next she came out of it, seeping like oil. And maybe had Lou been smart he would have opened up on her, but he didn't. Whereas the Snake Woman had appalled him, filled him with a sense of crawling horror, this one inspired lust.

She poured out of the darkness, smooth and easy as cream, wearing a gun belt and nothing else, a nightstick in her hand. She was tall with a cap of short spiky black hair, her skin white as marble. Her legs were long and shapely, her breasts jutting like traffic cones. She moved with such a pure animal grace, with such a fluid sweep of muscle, she was on them in seconds, her eyes yellow drowning pools.

Lou took a step backward or maybe forward, because, Jesus, crazy as it was, he wanted her badly. Wanted those taut arms and legs wrapped around him, wanted those full lips on his own. She was a woman from a fantasy, from a skin magazine. And, God help him, he couldn't keep his eyes off the sliver of pubic hair between her legs.

And then two things happened.

Steve screamed.

And the woman touched Lou...and her hand, cold as refrigerated beef, took his wrist and he saw that she was not beautiful or desirable at all. Streaks of something sticky had dried in slashes across her belly and down her legs like the dark flow of menstrual blood. Her hair was wild and greasy, her teeth gnashing, chattering, begging to be put to use.

And those eyes, those horrible eyes, rimmed in silver, two yellow miasmic holes that looked down into a snakepit.

And she was growling.

Her head darted forward like a viper's, anxious to bite into his throat.

Steve was yelling something at him, but Lou couldn't seem to make it out.

"SHOOT HER!" he cried. "SHOOT HER YOU DUMB GODDAMN IDIOT!"

And Lou understood as pale white arms encircled him like the frigid tentacles of some deep-sea squid. She was a monster and he had to kill her. Simple as that.

He pulled the trigger and the chamber explosion rocked him back into reality, but the barrel of the gun was *behind* the woman and the bullet drilled harmlessly into the paneling.

And then she slapped the .38 from his fist.

Her hand, palm flattened, struck him in the chest and he went down on his ass.Steve made a run for the door and she caught him by the collar and spun him around in a perfect circle, his head slamming into the wall with a hollow thud. His knees went to putty and he collapsed.

Lou was screaming now as he crawled madly on all fours for the gun and actually felt his fingertips brush it as she took hold of one of his ankles and flipped him over effortlessly.

And then she was on him.

He could feel her marble skin sucking the warmth from him as she pinned him down, rode him like a lover, legs to either side, pelvis grinding against him crudely. He clawed and punched at her and she trapped his arms. Her face came in closer, closer, a ribbon of foamy slime hanging from her lips and running down one of his cheeks, cold as Freon. Then her lips brushed over his and her tongue licked his face like a lollipop, leaving a burning trail in its wake and all he could think of was the germs, that pestiferous infection eating into him like acid and that revolting stink like rotting fish.

It was over and he knew it.

She was too strong. He couldn't fight her.

Her teeth flashed and she made to bite him in the throat...and then there was a clap of thunder and she fell off him.

Steve was on his knees a few feet away with the gun in his hand.

The woman came back up, a bloody hole in her shoulder.

Steve fired again and the bullet pulverized her cheek, leaving a raw bleeding cavity draped by a flap of smoking skin.

He never got another one off.

She launched herself at him and struck him like a freight train exiting a tunnel. They went down in a heap and her teeth sank into his throat and Steve's screams turned to a watery gurgling and then there was blood everywhere as his jugular painted them both red.

And then Lou had the gun.

She snapped her head in his direction, red ruined face electric with triumph. Her mouth was hanging open, lips drawn away from bloodstained teeth.

Lou put a bullet in her head.

She flopped over, limbs twitching.

He put another slug in her head and she was still.

Making a shrill moaning sound, he ran for the door and was outside into the night, the air so fresh, so welcome, so cleansing.

He nearly fell down the steps and if he had, if he had—

They would have gotten him.

He would have fallen right into their midst.

They were everywhere now. Like locusts swarming a field, they were thronged at the foot of the steps, leering and howling, driven into a rage at the smell of blood coming from inside.

He fired at them until the .38 clicked on an empty chamber.

He threw it and turned, running back inside.

He could hear them coming, hear them screeching and hissing. He went back to where Steve and the woman lay in a spreading ocean of blood. He flipped her over, popped the catch on her gun belt and slid her 9mm semi-auto out of its holster. He worked the slide and put a round in the chamber.

And they were on him.

Two, then three of them.

Snarling and snapping, their hooked fingers tore at him like claws.

He rolled away and brought the 9mm to bear. He gave them each a round that did little more than distract them, buying him time, and then he was sprinting down the corridor and into the police station. He found the door marked EXIT he'd seen before and threw himself out into the night, missing the steps entirely and coming down hard on the sidewalk.

Dazed, he pulled himself up, the gun still—miraculously—in his hand. He'd split his lip on the concrete and his mouth was wet, metallic-tasting.

Not much time now.

But the parking lot was before him, he could see the cars.

Going to make it, a voice in his head was saying. *You're going to make it, by God.*

He started running towards the cruisers, his body aching, his lungs raw, but it was just a little further, a little further.

Behind him, the EXIT door flew open and they began pouring out, dozens and dozens of them, the citizens of Cut River.

Men, women, and children.

A pack of dogs, shrieking and yelping, an insane sea of white faces and clutching hands. Lou fired a few more rounds in their direction and then he was in the parking lot.

He threw himself behind the wheel of the nearest cruiser, noting the riot gun in its holder, and his fingers sought madly for dangling keys and found them.

Bless you, Steve, God bless you.

He threw the locks on the doors and started the cruiser up, his body thrumming with a mixture of joy and terror. He could hear traffic on the radio and knew that the world still existed. Really, truly existed out there somewhere.

He squealed in reverse and saw the lot was full of them.

Like human insects they hopped and careened and spread out. They rushed at the cruiser and he drove straight through them, casting them aside as he roared out into the street, the last straggler sliding from the hood.

And then he was in the streets.

Safe. Free.

15

"We ain't getting out," Joe said with sobering finality. "None of us are. Not by road, anyway."

He tooled slowly up the streets, driving nowhere in particular. Just driving and driving and driving. There didn't seem to be anywhere to go. Not until something occurred to them, some escape route.

Nancy and Ben had both been quiet since Joe plowed through that army of psychos. But inside Nancy's mind, it was not quiet at all. She didn't know much about these people, about Joe and Ruby Sue, but what she did know, she did not like.

They had an agenda.

It was illegal and they freely admitted as much. They'd lied about when they arrived in town and for some reason this really ate at Nancy. And what for God's sake were their last names? Maybe that was a small thing, but it mattered.

Just Joe and Ruby Sue.

She supposed bikers were like that. Christian names. Nicknames. Nothing more. But she was not part of that world and did not want to be part of that world. What it came down to was that she did not trust these people. And the more she didn't trust them, the more she didn't like them.

"This is so weird," Ruby Sue was saying. "Totally wild. I saw this movie once, you know, where this city was, like, taken over by vampires. This guy—he was the last human being left— he lived in this house and hung garlic and crosses and shit on the door. At night they'd come banging on the doors, the vampires would, and he'd sit there and get drunk."

"I don't think they're vampires," Ben said.

"Yeah, I know. But wouldn't it be wild if they were?"

Ben and Nancy looked at each other, shook their heads.

Joe kept on driving. "What we need to do people, I think, is find some place to hole up in. What do you think?"

Ben nodded. "Sounds good. It's obvious they won't let us leave."

"Right. So we hole up somewhere for the night, see what day brings. This town can't just fall off the edge of the planet without somebody noticing. My guess is by morning, people are starting to ask questions. Maybe then the cops or the army or somebody will come in and clean this place out."

Ruby Sue said, "Right. And, hey, maybe they only come at night. Maybe they'll hide in the daytime."

"Oh, would you get off the vampire-thing already?" Nancy said, sterner than she'd meant to.

"It's just an idea."

Yeah, right, Nancy thought, *like you've ever really had one of those.*

Any other time, she would have been all over someone like Ruby Sue.

Nancy had a real low tolerance for airheads and dizzy blonde bitches of any variety. Usually by now she would have been tearing into Miss Ruby Sue, jumping on every vacuous remark, every twirl of her hair, but tonight she just didn't have the strength.

She kept thinking about Sam.

Wondering if it was even remotely possible he was still alive. She decided it probably wasn't...but she still clung to the possibility. They weren't that close, really, for a brother and sister. Seldom saw each other, seldom had time to take interest in each others' lives...but Sam was still her brother. She still felt his loss, kept seeing them playing together as children, saw the good times and the golden moments. She had everything she could do not to start crying.

But that would be for later.

For now, there was this mess...and Ruby Sue.

Joe pulled the Jeep to a stop on Chestnut right before a grocery store, Northland A & P.

"It looks quiet here," he said. "This is as good a place as any."

"A grocery store?" Nancy said with amazement.

"Yeah, why not?"

"No, it's a good idea," Ben said, warming to it. "Food. Drinks. Everything we need. What could be better?"

"An armory, a police station."

Ruby Sue laughed. "You guys ever see that movie where this gang attacks the police station? That was wild. There was this one part where—"

"Let's go," Joe said.

He popped all their door locks and they got out. He went around back of the Jeep and opened the hatch. He took out a black duffel bag and went to the door of the A & P.

"It's locked," Nancy said.

Ruby Sue laughed. "So what?"

Joe took a small leather bag out of his duffel. Using a penlight, he sprayed some lubricant into the lock and began manipulating the tumblers with a little L-wrench. Within five minutes, the lock clicked open. "After you," he said, holding the door open.

"What if this trips some sort of alarm..." Nancy began to say and then realized how stupid that sounded. "Ignore me. Just ignore me."

They'd all been looking at her, but now they went in.

Joe locked the door behind them.

"I was thinking the same thing," Ruby Sue said. "What if we trip some silent alarm, you know? But then I thought, so what? Send in the fucking marines, man. Good to go."

Nancy squeezed her eyes shut tightly, was truly frightened because she was starting to think like Ruby Sue. And that *was* a very scary thing. She decided she'd probably rather become like one of those zombies out there than a total airhead. It would be less painful to everyone concerned.

The display cases at the front of the store were lit up and there were occasional fluorescent ceiling panels illuminated throughout. It was dim in spots, but not dark. And the food—snacks, drinks, the deli, bakery. Nancy hadn't realized how hungry she was until this moment. Now her stomach was growling.

She followed Ruby Sue to the donut case and started chewing on a long john, while Ruby Sue found a Bavarian.

Ben and Joe were eating slabs of ham from the deli case, slugging back beers.

It was a fine, peaceful moment.

Nancy sat there on the counter, eating and thinking this was the most relaxed she'd been since they stumbled into this hellhole. It was funny, she'd only lived an hour or so away from Cut River most of her life, but she'd never once visited before this day. It was all very ironic, she supposed.

Fucked-up, ugly, sadly ironic.

She wondered how the kids were doing. Just fine, no doubt. Watching TV. Playing games. Maybe raising hell. Never for a moment guessing that their Uncle Sam had been murdered or the nightmare their mother and stepfather were wading through.

Better it's us, she decided. *I couldn't handle this if they were here.*

Joe and Ben were eating silently. They hadn't really warmed to each other beyond small talk. Nancy was wondering exactly what sort of man Joe was. He went through the door like a professional. What did that say exactly? She decided they were damn lucky to have him with them, a guy who knew shit like that. He would probably know other stuff, too.

"We're going exploring," Ben announced.

Which left Nancy with Ruby Sue.

Whereupon, Ruby Sue began to ply her with questions about where she was from, how long her and Ben had been married, if they had children, what they did for a living. It went on and on. By the time Ruby Sue took a breath, Nancy's head was spinning madly.

"There's an apartment upstairs," Ben said when he returned maybe five minutes later. "Nobody home. Only way in is up a stairway in the back. Joe says it will be a good place to hide out later on. If...if they try to come after us, we can go up there. They'd have to come up the stairwell to get us, so we could hold 'em off."

"With what?" Nancy wanted to know. "Loafs of rye bread? Cans of Mini Ravioli?"

"Guns," Ruby Sue piped up. "We'll stop 'em with guns."

Nancy looked at her. "And where, pray tell, will we get those?"

Ruby Sue grinned. "You gotta be prepared, girl. It's what the Boy Scouts say." She opened her coat and pulled out a shiny black automatic about the size of a paperback book. "Course, they don't pack this kind of firepower."

"Jesus," Ben said, running a hand through his beard, "is it real?"

Nancy shook her head. "No, it's a fucking squirt gun, Ben."

"Yes, it's real," Ruby Sue said.

It seemed a reasonable question to her.

She hefted it in the air, taking up a firing stance and mouthing *Bang! Bang!* soundlessly. She went up to Ben, rubbed against him, pressed the gun into his hand like she was offering her tit—which, Nancy decided, probably would be next—and wrapped his fingers around it. "Take it, Ben. It's yours. You know how to work it?"

"Yeah, I guess."

She showed him the safety catch. How to work the slide to jack a round into the chamber. "See? Easy. Easy as pie, honey."

Nancy sat there, thinking: *I can't believe her. Right in front of me yet.*

Nancy was looking her up and down now.

Yeah, she was a slutty little airhead, all right. And that would have been fine except that she had a nice body on her, too. Face wasn't the best, but cute in a girl-next-door sort of way. Nancy's skin felt hot. She hadn't had curves like that since she was nineteen.

"Is this legal? Full auto?" Ben asked.

"Fuck no!" Ruby Sue said, still maintaining body contact with him via hip and arm. "But I won't tell if you don't."

Ben smiled. "You should keep it. In case there's trouble."

"Don't want anything happening to me?" Ruby Sue seethed. "That's cool. Don't worry, Joe has others."

"Others?" Nancy said incredulously.

"What do you think's in his bag, Nanc? Cookies? We came here to do something. We came prepared," she said and said no more on the subject. "You keep this one, Ben. I want you to have it."

"Thanks," he said.

"Just point it and shoot. *Bam!* Dick through a donut."

"You're definitely handy," he said and Nancy did not like his tone at all.

"Oh, you'd be surprised how handy I can be." Ruby Sue's words dripped with sex.

Nancy hopped off the counter. "Excuse me," she said. "But I'm right here and I happen to be his wife."

"Lighten up," Ruby Sue said. "I won't break him."

Nancy stared, eyes gone liquid green.

"Way I'm thinking," Ruby Sue said, oblivious to it all, "is that these people here are, like, infected with something. But they're still human...or almost. What we gotta do is shoot 'em in the heads. You know, like zombies? Blow their brains out. Bet that stops 'em."

"Shut up!" Nancy cried.

"What—"

"Listen," she said in a haunted voice. "*Listen.*"

They did.

They had company.

A group of people had assembled out on the sidewalk. They stood stock-still as if waiting for some sign, some command to begin the inevitable. And then apparently, they received it. They pressed in, a tight knot of white faces and leering eyes.

They pushed up against the glass.

Ruby Sue said, "Oh shit."

Ben started walking towards the front of the store, the automatic in his fist.

Nancy called to him to come back, but he didn't. Maybe the gun had given him courage, had turned his balls to drop-forged steel. But maybe he just wanted to see, *needed* to see what the hell this was all about. Get a good look at these savages, prove to himself that, *yes*, it was okay to kill them because they weren't men and women (and children) anymore, just berserkers wearing the skins of the same.

They started beating on the plate glass windows.

A tall man, his chest infibulated with numerous gashes and lesions, pressed his hands flat against the glass door. He seemed to be weighing the possibility of gaining entrance. He tried the door, rattled it violently in its frame, then decided to do things the hard way. He let out a maniacal, blood-curdling scream like someone being roasted over a bed of coals.

It went right up Nancy's spine like fingernails.

Grinning and foaming at the mouth, he began slamming his face into the glass. Not his fists. Not his feet. His *face*. He pounded it savagely against the glass, leaving a sticky smear of blood and slime with each impact. With each passing second, he put more and more force behind it until the glass began to bulge with each collision and the pounding reverberation of it rang out like the dirge of a funeral bell.

Then a series of tiny cracks fanned-out, met, and the glass shattered, exploded inward in a rain of jagged spikes.

The tall man stumbled in, his face a bloody ruin, his eyes bright and yellow like a stalking wolf's. Bathed in blood, he seemed no worse for wear.

A dozen others followed him in.

One, a teenage girl wearing a stained pair of cranberry sweatpants and nothing more, stooped down and scooped up a blade of glass. She held it in her hands, seemed fascinated by it. Then she drew it in a straight line between her breasts down to her navel, slitting open the flesh. Then repeating the process with a transverse cut across her sternum, fashioning a crude, bleeding crucifix.

The blood ran.

She dipped her fingers into it and licked them clean.

Ben stood there, rooted to the spot like an old elm, just watching.

Nancy screamed to him and it seemed to break his trance.

He brought the automatic up and started shooting. He put four slugs into the tall man before it slowed him down. He shot an elderly woman in the head and she fell back, fountaining blood. Next came a set of twin boys, no more than ten or eleven. Only remotely human by this point, they scrambled forward on all fours.

Ben put more bullets in them.

He kept shooting until he used up his ammunition, then he turned and ran, shouting to Nancy to get upstairs, get upstairs.

Nancy turned and saw that Ruby Sue was gone.

No, not gone.

At the deli.

A cadaverous man in a Carhartt jacket had her by the hair and was dragging her back. She stomped on the instep of his work booted-foot, pivoted and kneed him in the groin. He released her, more out of surprise than anything else.

In that brief respite, she snatched up a plastic knife from a tray of them and sank it into his left eye. Then she ducked away and Nancy saw no more of her. Just her retreating form and a naked man with an eagle tattooed on his chest who brandished a severed arm, his penis obscenely erect like a missile.

None of the savages had taken notice of Nancy yet.

Five or six of them were in hot pursuit of Ben.

In the center of a cereal aisle, they boxed him in and lunged forward for the kill. Ben climbed right up the shelves, an avalanche of Cheerios and Frosted Flakes in his wake. He made it to the top of the shelves and stayed there.

A few followed him.

The smarter ones ran to catch him in the next aisle.

But he didn't jump down, he ran straight down the flat top of the shelves kicking displays and signs out of his way, ducking the ceiling. At the end he dove off, straight at the man in the Carhart jacket, the guy who carried the plastic knife in his gored eye without concern. Ben slammed him flat and rolled off him, making for the rear of the store.

The savages were all loping in that direction now, howling and screeching and making horrible congested sounds.

Nancy flipped herself over the bakery counter, knowing there was no way she could join her husband or the others. She heard gunfire and peered over the lip of the counter and heard Ben shouting her name madly, saw him disappear in a clutching profusion of white hands. Then more gunfire.

She was thinking about those zombies from *Night of the Living Dead*...but they were nothing like these animals. Cinematic deadheads, crafty as rusty coat hangers, all the cunning of petrified rabbit shit, but these...these things, they were smart...and fast. Whatever contagion had consumed the population of Cut River, it had only amplified their cunning.

She pressed herself under the counter, her body rigid and jumping with terror.

A weapon. She needed a weapon. Something.

She looked around. Deep fryers. Cake pans. Pie tins. Bins of flour, sugar. A rolling pin. Her hand snaked out and grabbed it. Better than nothing. She could still hear them, gibbering and hissing, so very inhuman.

There was more gunfire. Moanings. Wet sounds. Thuds. Then...silence. She waited under the counter, her heart too large for her chest, banging like drum.

Were they all dead?

Everyone?

Even Ben? Joe? Ruby Sue? Lying dead with their attackers? Is that what happened?

Nancy needed badly to cry, to scream, to do anything but lay there, trembling like some frightened animal. The sense of loss—Sam and now possibly Ben—was huge and overwhelming, a feeling of violation. As if all the rules of normalcy had been set on their heads by some lunatic, giggling god. She couldn't take it, couldn't take anymore.

She pulled herself up gradually.

Slow, shuffling footsteps.

She froze, fear clinging to her like a sheet of ice. She lay under its weight, shivering, her brain desperately seeking the peace of blackness, of oblivion.

But she wouldn't allow it.

She bit down on her lower lip, bringing pain bright and real.

The silence was heavy, filled with ominous potential or the lack of it. Someone was near. She knew that much. She could hear them breathing. Drawing in low, rattling breaths. Louder now.

And then a smell...Christ, like rotting meat.

Although her brain demanded she hide, that she be still and silent, she could not be. She raised herself up careful inches, brought her face up over the lip of the counter to look, to see what form her death would take—

And something struck her square in the face.

She fell back, black dots before her eyes.

She never passed out, but it was close. Blood ran from her nose. She could taste it on her lips. Reality swam back in completely.

Whatever had struck her brought pain, but she was unaware of it, her mind locked now in battle mode, ready to fight to the death. She still had the rolling pin. Her fist was wrapped stiffly around it. As she moved, something rolled off her lap.

A softball.

Softball?

Yes, of course. That's what had hit her. That's what—

There was a little boy standing before her dressed in a muddy, rumpled blue suit. Looked like maybe he'd just come from choir practice. Seven, eight years old. No more. Nancy made to smile at him, but she saw his eyes, leering and yellow like full moons, filled with a total, unflinching hatred. A blind hate that was not human, not animal, but something feral and rabid.

Yes, he looked like a little boy, but he was not a little boy.

Some atavistic nightmare from the dawn of the race when people were predatory things that lived only to hunt and kill.

He smiled down at her, drool running from his lips.

His hair was wild, leaves stuck in it, his face was the color of fresh cream, but mottled and streaked with grime.

Not a boy, just a thing from a grave.

Nancy drew herself slowly to her feet. "Please," she said, close to tears, very aware of the weight of the rolling pin in her hand. "I know you're sick...you can't help what you are, but I don't want to hurt you. Don't make me."

He kept smiling, but came no closer. *"Please,"* he mocked in a choking voice thick with phlegm. *"I don't wanna hurt you, don't make me."* Then he started to laugh, cold, baying laughter like the shrieking of a maniac.

Nancy took a step back, the flesh crawling on her bones, and he leapt.

She swung the rolling pin at him, but missed as he rammed into her, spilling the both of them to the floor. He was wild in her arms, fingers clawing, legs kicking, head thrashing, teeth snapping. Alive and deadly like a sack of copperheads, contorting and twisting in every direction as Nancy tried to keep his teeth from her. The feel of him...hideous, like living, breathing meat. She managed to hook a foot under him and launch him backwards.

He slammed into the counter with a sickly, fleshy thud.

He came again, a macabre grin slitting open his pallid face.

Nancy brought the rolling pin down and it crashed into the crown of his head. She heard a soft cracking sound. He pulled himself up and she kept bringing the rolling pin down until blood spattered her face and his head was caved-in like a rotting pumpkin. Until his skull was opened like a can, the contents running to the floor. And even then, she had to peel his cold fingers from her ankles where they were seized in a death grip. The back of his hands were gray and flaking.

Nancy staggered off, felt the wind being sucked from her lungs.

She went down to her knees, whimpering and shuddering, finally vomiting.

She only wanted to die then.

She'd killed a little boy.

That's what this fucking town had done to her. Maybe it hadn't acted like a boy or even looked too much like a boy, but once, yes, once it had been. An innocent child corrupted by this place, polluted. Cut River had done that to him and she'd supplied the final unspeakable denouement to his lamentable existence.

Again, totally numb, the part of her that had been human and hopeful just a windblown memory, Nancy got to her feet.

She started towards the back of the store to find the stairs, knowing it was where she had to go. Dragging her feet, she continued on.

She saw the stairs now, the door that hid them nearly ripped from its hinges. There was a tumble of bodies on the steps, great sections of their anatomies blown away. A scene from some medieval hell. Bodies heaped like jackstraw.

She would have to climb over them.

No other way.

Then she heard motion behind her.

She turned and brought up the rolling pin limply, no longer noticing that it was caked with blood and brains and tangles of hair.

Sam was standing there.

Something like October moonlight filled his eyes. They were a brilliant yellow, yes, the yellow of a pumpkin skull lit by a candle, but they seemed almost silvery, reflective like the surface of mirrors. She could see herself quite plainly in them. His flesh was colorless and he stank like death.

Nancy felt something wet tickle her lips and realized it was her tongue.

She took it all in and something in her shut down completely, refused to accept this. She could see the grisly wound on his neck, swollen purple, blackening at the edges, dried blood everywhere like rust.

He was dead.

He had to be dead.

No one could live with their throat laid open like that.

Sam grinned at her, a broad toothy smile of shining white teeth that was as evil and vicious as anything she'd ever seen. A baboon's grin. He was no more human than that. There was nothing but desolation in those shining eyes, a ravening insanity.

"Nancy," he said and it sounded like water dumped on a hot stove lid. "It doesn't hurt at all, it just feels good."

"Sam..."

But he was already too close, pulling her in with those terrible lies, a beast spinning half-truths, luring children into a dark wood. And Nancy went because she simply couldn't help herself and she was tired of fighting and she just wanted to sleep now.

Sam had her hands in his own, his fingers like icicles.

The rolling pin clattered uselessly to the floor.

Before she could do so much as protest, he yanked her left arm up and sank his teeth into her wrist. And he lied, for it hurt. It hurt bad. His teeth were sharp, his tongue so cold, the foaming slime from his mouth thick and burning. She felt it snake its way into her bloodstream, a malignancy taking her cell by cell.

Then the world exploded and exploded.

Sam jerked and jerked, stumbled away from her. He let out a high, piercing scream of utter rage and utter suffering and then his face blew apart. He pitched over, striking the floor face first, his bullet-ridden body twitching.

"Nancy?" she heard a voice say. "Nancy?"

Then blackness, sweet and welcoming as the confines of the womb.

16

Lou Frawley drove mindlessly through the streets of the dead city.

He had half a tank of gas, deciding morosely that he would continue driving until he either passed-out or the needle hit empty. Regardless, he was surely not going to stop.

They would not have him.

In the thirty-odd minutes he'd been driving, he'd come to the same realization that Ben and Nancy Eklind and company had come to: there was no way out. He'd run into the same barricades they had, seen the same horrors, knew that Cut River was a cage, a maze, and that the psychos out there were just waiting for him to fuck up so they could have him.

So he drove and thought about the life he'd once had and wished to God Steve had survived so he could at least have some human company. Because being alone was the very worst thing. Nothing in creation compared to the phobia of solitude.

Though Lou had never been a religious man—he thought most churches were the theological version of pawnshops—he sincerely believed now that men and women had souls. After seeing the things that had once been the people of Cut River he was convinced of this.

Because they had no souls.

They were animals, monsters, walking deadwood, but not human beings.

Not like him.

And he realized after seeing the lack of souls in Cut River how precious a commodity the soul was. And his was decaying. From terror. From solitude.

As he drove, he saw the good citizens of the town going about their wicked business. He saw white faces leering from behind parked cars, trees, and shrubs. Saw them lurking in shadowy doorways and cul-de-sacs. Saw them peering from darkened windows and storefronts. They watched him pass, but did not attack. Not yet.

He saw an old lady wearing nothing but a scarf and a blanket standing guard at a stop sign with a double-edged axe.

He saw a throng of vile children dragging the butchered body of an obese woman into a side yard.

He saw a young yuppie couple standing on the curb, hand in hand, their naked bodies painted up with what almost looked to be runic symbols.

He saw a naked teenage girl digging a hole in a lawn and pushing a body down into it, burying it for later...and then urinating on the spot as if marking it with her scent.

And he saw others crawling over sloping roofs like cats, leering down from the high branches of trees. Many of them were doing this, as if seeking some high perch like human raptors.

Yeah, the town was gone.

There was no point in fighting.

The battle—if there had been one at all, which Lou doubted—was waged and lost. The enemy had won. They seemed to be somewhat intelligent, many of them. At least, he thought, intelligent enough to erect barricades of automobiles at all the roads leading out. And if they were smart enough to remember how to drive, to position those cars and trucks, then they were smart enough to use advanced weapons and technologies. It stood to reason. Sure, maybe they'd just pushed the cars in place, but that meant they knew enough to manipulate the keys and put transmissions in neutral so the vehicles *could* be moved.

But for some reason, he thought they'd probably driven them in place.

And that was a scary thought. But if that was true, then why weren't they hunting him down in cars and trucks?

Why weren't they using guns?

There were plenty of guns in this part of the state. Prime hunting country, guns were everywhere. But these people didn't use them. They carried knives and clubs and hatchets and cleavers and had even fashioned spears (he had seen this). Maybe they didn't use these objects because at some base level they shunned civilization. Maybe this is why they ripped phones from walls, shattered TVs and computers, crushed cell phones underfoot. And as far as guns went, they were too impersonal; you couldn't feel your victims writhing flesh, their warm blood, taste their fear. Guns were for civilized peoples; barbarians preferred something more personal.

But was he giving them too much credit?

He didn't think so.

Because, if you studied them (and God knew he had had plenty of opportunity for that) you saw that they were organized. Loosely, perhaps, tribal units maybe, hunting clans and no more. Not yet. But they didn't wage war on one another, they seemed to coexist peacefully, cooperatively. Only the normal ones were their prey.

Yes, right now they were formed into small bands perhaps, but what if this raged on unchecked for months or years? Would they group together under a central leader?

Lou had his doubts because such a thing smacked of culture, of enlightenment, and these creatures had degenerated to a primitive, feral level and seemed to like it there just fine.

He was wondering why they only watched him and didn't attack.

He was thinking this very thing when two of them ran out into the street ahead, madly waving their arms. He slowed down to draw them in. Maybe he couldn't kill them all, but he could tag a few. It was better than nothing.

He slowed to a crawl.

C'mon, you crazy bastards, come to daddy.

They jogged up closer and as they got within range of the headlights he saw that one of them carried a shotgun. His worst fear realized, he was about to jam down the accelerator when he noticed that their eyes did not shine. Everywhere he went in Cut River, the headlights picked out their eyes shining in the dark.

These two did not have eyes like that.

And the way they moved...Jesus Christ in Heaven, they were human!

Lou threw open his door as they came up closer. A woman and a man. The woman was small, thin, dressed in a rain poncho and carried a guitar case of all things. The guy was outfitted like the cover of *Soldier of Fortune*.

"You're human," was all Lou could say.

"Yes, yes," the woman said, sounding close to tears.

The man pushed her towards the rear door of the cruiser. "We better get the fuck out of here," he said. "The natives are getting restless."

Lou looked and saw them slinking in the shadows like cats ready to pounce.

He got behind the wheel, thinking it was funny how your priorities changed. A week ago, nothing less than winning the lotto would have satisfied him...now he was simply happy that he wouldn't have to die alone.

Life...and death...were funny.

17

Schoolcraft County Sheriff's Department—Transcription

September 26—11:20-11:59 P.M.

11:20

Dispatcher: Twelve, what's your twenty?

Unit Twelve: Ten miles outside Blaney Park on seventy-seven. Returning.

Dispatcher: Negative. Request you go to Cut River vicinity.

Unit Twelve: Come again?

Dispatcher: Cut River. No radio activity from Cut River P.D. in fourteen hours.

Unit Twelve: Power's still out in that area...or most of it.

Dispatcher: Should be...some activity. Received a call for assistance earlier.

Unit Twelve: P.D.?

Dispatcher: Negative. Civilian, possibly. Might be a crank.

Unit Twelve: Probably. Ten-forty-nine. En route to Cut River. E.T.A. fifteen minutes.

Dispatcher: Ten-four.

11:39

Unit Twelve: Outside Cut River location on Junction Twenty-Three. Will advise.

Dispatcher: Ten-four.

Unit Twelve: We've got an abandoned vehicle here. Possible accident. Two miles outside location on twenty-three. Vehicle is a late-model Plymouth van...license ADAM-DAVID-FRANK two-oh-seven. Repeat.

Dispatcher: ADF two-oh-seven.

Unit Twelve: Standby.

Dispatcher: Vehicle registered to a Benjamin Thomas Eklind.

Unit Twelve: Ten-four. We're going to need crime scene assistance here...front end of vehicle bashed in. Possible hit-and-run.

Dispatcher: Message relayed.

Unit Twelve: Leaving scene. Occupants missing. Seems to be...can see a fire burning in Cut River direction. Investigating.

Dispatcher: Exercise caution, Twelve.

Unit Twelve: Will do. Ten-four.

11:53

Unit Twelve: Dispatch? Requesting back-up...possible civil disturbance. We've got a situation here.

Dispatcher: What's the Twenty?

Unit Twelve: Cut River...we've got vehicles piled up here, wreckage. Road is blocked. Fires burning...scarecrows. Something strange here...I...

Dispatcher: Repeat last, Twelve.

Unit Twelve: Code Twenty here, dispatch. Need immediate assistance.

Dispatcher: On the way, Twelve.

Unit Twelve: It's a mess...Jesus. Looks like vehicles were driven into each other to block exit or entrance. Fires burning...a group of individuals spotted. Standby.

Dispatcher: Proceed with caution, Twelve.

Unit Twelve: CODE THIRTY! CODE THIRTY! OFFICER NEEDS ASSISTANCE! EMERGENCY! ALL UNITS! PLEASE...OH MY GOD...

Dispatcher: Twelve? Twelve? Repeat, Twelve!

Dispatcher: All available units respond Cut River location! Officer needs assistance!

Unit Seventeen: En route location, dispatch. E.T.A. five minutes. Jesus, looks like fires burning down there...

18

When Nancy woke, she was in pain.

It felt like she'd been pumping iron. Her muscles were sore, her fingers numb. A headache throbbed just behind her eyes.

And she was not alone.

In fact, she was in a room full of people and she decided right then and there, as her eyelids fluttered open and closed and then open again, that she was dreaming. Had to be. Unless this had all been some seriously nasty nightmare, the last thing she could remember was the A & P. Those things attacking them. Her alone. The little boy from hell.

And then...oh Jesus, *Sam*.

Sam biting her.

She was on a sofa in what looked like somebody's living room, a blanket thrown over her. She brought her hand up, brought it up slowly. Yes, her wrist was bandaged. Sam had bitten her. Yes. Not attacked her, not really. All he wanted to do was bite her.

It doesn't hurt at all, it just feels good...

Oh, Jesus, did that mean, did that mean—

"How you doing, baby?" It was Ben, leaning over her. He looked very tired, very...used-up. But his eyes were bright. "I was worried. Christ, I was worried."

She managed a smile. "I'm okay. I...what happened? I don't remember."

He sat on the sofa near her and told her how he'd been separated from her in the grocery store, thought she'd been killed. Then the crazies started their attack. Joe and Ruby Sue were armed to the teeth. He didn't know why, but was simply glad. They spent maybe fifty rounds on the *crazies,* as he called them.

"It was like nothing you ever seen before," he told her. "You can shoot 'em five, six times, and it only slows them down. You gotta get 'em in the head.

"Ruby Sue was right," she said in a dry voice.

He nodded.

He himself owed his life to Joe. The crazies had swarmed over him and Joe ran right into their midst, shooting and fighting. Ruby Sue—a crack shot, believe it or not—had backed him up, popping those bastards right in the heads. They'd knocked Ben senseless and Joe had dragged him up the stairs, took care of him. It was also Joe who—

"He shot Sam," Nancy said.

Ben stroked her hair. "It wasn't Sam, baby. Not anymore."

She licked her lips. "He looked like he was dead."

Ben didn't say anything to that. "Joe bandaged your arm. You cut yourself or what?"

Nancy went into a bullshit story about how one of them had stuck a roasting fork in her arm, how she'd beat him off with a rolling pin. It was important to her that Ben didn't know, that any of them didn't know, about the bite. Laying there, Ben's voice droning on and on about how they'd come here to this church because they'd seen a police cruiser parked out front that hadn't been there before.

That's how they ended up with this bunch.

Ben introduced them all.

Beyond Joe and Ruby Sue, there was a stocky, balding man with a friendly smile named Lou Frawley. Lou was a salesman. The muscular, capable guy in the corner with the bald head and black mustache was named Johnny Davis. He was a citizen of Cut River and, Nancy decided, possibly a mercenary by the way he was dressed and armed. Near to him was a thin, slight brunette with huge dark eyes and jutting cheekbones. She was Lisa Tabano. She looked haunted, trembled badly, and was some sort of rock performer. Even had a guitar with her.

Joe had positioned himself at the window, was studying the night between a part in the curtains.

"Any activity?" Johnny asked him.

"Nada."

"Not yet, anyway."

They were in the rectory of St. Thomas' Catholic Church. In the priest's living room. It was large but cozy with a fireplace, shelves lined with old books, overstuffed furniture, and impressionist paintings on the walls. It smelled like leather and pipe tobacco.

Of course, Lisa and Lou were heavy smokers and there was a haze gathering in the air now. There was only one light on and it was turned down dim. Nancy thought that was for the best; she didn't think she could handle bright lights just yet.

"Hi," Lisa said to her. "How you feeling?"

Nancy looked at her, thought that though she was a pretty girl and everything that Nancy was not—petite, thin, fine-boned—she didn't look well. Sick? Yes, like maybe she'd come off a lengthy illness. Not good at all. Dark hollows under her eyes, her bones lying tight just under her skin. Rock star? Yes, looked like one of those stick figures with all the hair, on the verge of death.

She thought: *Looks like I feel.*

She sipped from a glass of water Ben brought her. It tasted good. On her lips, on her throat, but when it hit her stomach she felt nauseous. "What band are you with?" she asked the girl.

"Electric Witch," Lisa said, as if she didn't believe it somehow. "It seems so far away now."

"You guys are good."

Lisa seemed surprised. "You know us?"

"Yeah. My son has your CD. Loves it."

"Sweet."

"What brought you here of all things?"

"My mom and dad. I'm from here. I don't know where they are."

Lisa explained to her that they'd come to the church because it's where Johnny had decided to ride out the storm, watch the city go to shit.

"You could've done something," Nancy found herself saying, her head pounding so badly now she thought she might pass out.

He shook his head, had a look on his stern face like he wanted to hurt somebody. "Nobody could stop this. It was inevitable." Everyone was looking at him, but he paid them no mind. "This town's fucked. Maybe the country."

"I think it's localized," Lou said.

"You sure about that?"

"Could be spreading," Ruby Sue said. "You know? I mean, shit, maybe town by town like some kind of plague. Think I saw a movie like that once. Anybody see that?"

Ben chimed in, "Listen, everything was fine before we got here. I'm sure it still is."

Johnny shrugged. "Could be."

"C'mon, Johnny," Lou said. "When we were in the cruiser you could hear traffic on the radio. Cops calling in plate numbers, responding to calls. It sounded perfectly normal out there."

"Did you call for help?" Nancy asked.

"Yeah. I tried. I hope I got through. I told 'em to get their fucking dead asses to this shithole on the double."

Nancy thought that was good. If he got through help would arrive. Sooner or later, the cops would investigate. She was certain of that.

Ben was sitting by her on the couch, his face cradled in his hands. "Johnny? You live...or lived here, didn't you?"

"Yeah. Just outside town."

"Well, what the hell happened?"

"About five days ago—I was out of town—we got this rain. It went on all day and night. No big deal, right? Except that in the afternoon, guy told me, it looked like ink." He had their attention now if he hadn't before. "After that, well, everyone started getting sick. Started staying inside, calling into school and work. People were saying we had a flu outbreak. No big deal. Half of the country was going through it, too. Nobody gave it a second thought. By Saturday, there wasn't anyone around. Like a fucking ghost town. But Saturday night—"

"They started coming out of their holes?" Ben said.

"Yeah, you got it. Not a lot, but some. Sunday night, it was half the town...and tonight, well, you know what it's like now."

"I can't believe somebody didn't notice something," Nancy said.

Johnny looked at her. "What's to notice? The flu? Shit, it's everywhere. Schools closing, businesses not opening. Think anybody's gonna freak out about just another town coming down with it? You know how it is in the fall, winter, and spring...there's always a lot of it around. They even talk about it on TV. No biggie. By the time somebody might have noticed, the phone lines were down and we were cut off. Who knows, maybe nobody wanted help. Maybe they didn't want to admit that there was a problem in the first place. So they crawled under the covers, went to sleep. Except when they woke up that night...they didn't see things the same way anymore."

It was a chilling hypothesis, but it made a certain amount of sense.

It could've worked that way. People thought they had the flu. Even if they went to a doctor or the emergency room of a hospital with flu symptoms, they would've been sent home, told to drink lots of fluids and get some sleep.

Nancy closed her eyes for a moment.

The darkness felt good.

Her limbs were aching now, a tight ball of nausea jumping in her belly. She kept her hands hidden beneath the blanket though she was too warm, her scalp tight and itchy, sweat at her temples.

Flu? She wanted to laugh at that. But her body hurt too much.

Lou sat there, nodding. "All right. Say there was something in that rain. It couldn't have gotten everyone. Am I right?"

"Maybe it spread person to person after that."

"Could be," Johnny said. "By the time I realized something was really fucked-up, it was too late."

But they'd all gotten a taste of his nihilism by that point and they didn't exactly believe him. They pretty much figured he liked all this.

Lou lit another cigarette. "Your husband tell you we're not alone? There's some people in the basement. Got themselves locked in. Johnny found 'em before. They won't come out."

"They think we're...what do you call 'em, Johnny?"

"Rabids."

"Yeah, rabids."

Lou shook his head. "Bunch of Jesus freaks by the sound of 'em," he said, like the idea disgusted him. "They got it into their heads that it's the fucking Rapture or some crap. Rapture, my white ass."

"They're singing hymns, man," Ruby Sue said. "And they sound like shit. Why don't you go give 'em some pointers, Lisa?"

"I'll pass." She got up and left the room, taking her purse with her.

"Say the word, people, and I go clean 'em out," Johnny suggested to them.

Joe laughed at that. "Few less pests knocking at people's doors."

"They're scared," Lou said. "You can't blame 'em."

No, Nancy thought, *you can't blame them.*

There was a strange tingling where Sam had bitten her. It throbbed dully. She felt very...restless. Sore, tired. But she'd been through a lot and that had to be normal...right? Because she couldn't quite put a finger on it, but something felt wrong. And it wasn't just the pain or nausea or numbness in her hands. There was no one word she could put to it, just a sense that something in her wasn't exactly right.

Lisa came back in about five minutes later.

Nancy thought she looked much better.

"What time is it?" Nancy asked Ben.

"Almost midnight."

Midnight. Christ in Heaven. Is that all? Another six, seven hours to dawn? That much time...might as well have been a week. What time had Sam bitten her? Ten? Ten-thirty? Yes, no more than that. And already she could feel it creeping through her, that malignancy.

She jerked stiffly under the blankets as a convulsion ripped through her.

"You okay?" Ben asked.

"Cramp," she lied. "Ow."

"All we gotta do here, people, is wait for dawn," Johnny told them in a low voice. "When the sun comes up, they'll crawl back in their holes. At least until the sun goes down again."

Lou sat there staring at him, cigarette hanging from his lips. "What are you saying? We got vampires here?"

"No, not exactly."

Joe turned away from the window. "If you know something, buddy, maybe you should spill it."

Lou stood up now. It was pretty plain he'd had his fill. "Yeah, c'mon. If you know what this is about, for chrissake tell us."

They were all watching him.

Johnny looked at them each in turn. A dark species of dread crossed his face. "Okay," he said. "I'll tell you a story. I'll tell you something I've never told anyone. You see, I've seen this before. But it was a long time ago and a world away..."

-THE WALKING PESTILENCE-

18

I spent two tours in Vietnam with the SEAL teams. You know who they are, what they do. I won't go into that. Why did I join a unit like that? Late '69 and '70 they were beefing up the Teams because a lot of the conventional Army and Marine units were pulling out. Not just the SEALs, but other groups like Marine Force Recon and Army Special Forces. End of '68 I was a swabby doing basic at Great Lakes in Chicago. I was eighteen. I joined the Navy because I didn't want to fight, didn't want to die in some foreign shithole. I thought I could avoid the draft and spend my time on a battleship, getting drunk and catching the clap in port. Towards the end of boot, the chief gave us a little chat, said they needed volunteers for the riverboat Navy, the River Rats. You've probably seen those guys on the Discovery Channel or something—they cruised the rivers in patrol boats, exchanging fire with the NVA and VC. Had a high casualty rate. Grunts in the bush had nothing on these guys.

Anyway, I'd heard enough about the River Rats to know that I didn't want no part of it. The chief inferred that those that didn't volunteer might end up with the Rats anyway. Then he gave us the pitch about the SEAL Teams. As usual, I didn't pay too much attention. All I heard him say was "frogman." *Frogman?* I thought. I got this dicked in a hard way. What could a frogman possibly do in a jungle war? I'd get out of it that way. Shows you what a naïve dipfuck I was. SEAL training lasted about a year, which was exactly what I wanted. You see, they were saying on TV and on the radio that the war would be over in a year. I had her made.

So, I volunteered.

And when I did, the chief looked at me like I had a hammer hanging out of my ass.

"You sure, Davis?"

"Sir, yes, sir!" I called out like some gung ho dumbass.

"You stupid prick, you deserve it," was all he would say.

So, after a series of tests and what not, I made the cut. And for the next year they beat my ass bloody. Only ten percent of our class made it through. Frogman? Sure, that was part of it. The basis of everything we were, but only the basis—I was jumping out of airplanes, learning to live off the land, sniping, demolitions, counterinsurgency, reconnaissance, guerrilla warfare. Shit, I learned how to handle all kinds of weapons, how to kill people with knives and crossbows, with poisons, booby traps, even my bare hands. I learned how to speak some French and Vietnamese. They brainwashed the hell out of you, too. By the end of that year you were a gung ho, life-taking motherfucker who just wanted to kill for his country and got physically sick at the thought of communism. Kick ass and take names.

Beginning of '70, they mobilized us and sent us to Southeast Asia. No point in going into my first tour. I did what you think guys like us do—I killed the enemy in number. I personally greased seventy that I knew about within the first four months. After that, I gave up counting. I re-upped for a second tour and this time I was attached to a team of second-and third tour vets who were handling special operations and intelligence missions for the spooks, part of the Phoenix program.

In July '72, Naval Intelligence sent us on a search and destroy mission in the Mekong Delta. The Delta was our main area of operations, our AO. At least that's what the buzz was. Truth being, we went everywhere and anywhere—North Vietnam, Laos, Cambodia, even China itself. This time, though, it was the Delta, just like our orders read. We were heading northeast, deep into the Rung Sat. The area had been heavily infiltrated by Uncle Ho's pukes and was serious Indian Country. The Rung Sat, or "Forest of Assassins" as it was also known, was a traditional hideout for Asian bandits and smugglers and it was also home to communist insurgents. Some four-hundred square miles of mangrove swamp and thick rain forest.

Lieutenant-commander Barber was our C.O. He was an okay guy as long as you did what he told you, which you always did because after three tours, he knew exactly how to keep you alive in the boonies.

I liked Barber. He was professional and honest and had no problems tipping beers with us swabbies in Saigon or Da Nang. Our former C.O., an Annapolis squirt name of Wentz, got greased up north after we parachuted in one night to abduct an NVA colonel. We got our subject, but we left that uppity fuck behind. Wasn't much left to him after he tripped that Russian mine, anyway.

We were to be inserted by riverboat. As we sped down river to the insertion point, everyone was quiet. Even the riverboat swabbies, the River Rats, were silent. And that was strange: they were always talking about being fucked—by each other, by the slopes, by their whores, the climate, the Navy, you name it. It made me feel uneasy. This whole thing did and I wasn't sure why.

I was checking over my gear and the other SEALs were doing the same. I looked over at Roshland, the only guy I outranked. He was carrying his ruck, Starlight scope, and the usual shit like the rest of us. But he also had the M-60 machine gun, the kind we used with the barrels sawed-off real short. He was a big black mother, his body crisscrossed with bandoleers of ammo. Roshland was okay. He was a drummer back in the world. Claimed his band had opened for Jimi once. He was probably the only guy on the team I would have associated with outside the SEALs. The rest of 'em—maybe myself included— were all fucked-up and not in a good way. They were scary. Maybe it was just that I knew how good they were at killing people. Maybe I'd seen them peel the skin off one too many Viets with their diving knives and grin while they did it, keeping the screaming little pricks alive for hours.

So, there I was on the riverboat, the PBR, smoking and worrying, propped up against several stacked cases of C-rats, the mechanical cacophony of the twin diesels thrumming through my bones. Within an hour or so, the boat slowed to a stop before a small clearing. We slipped into the water, silent as hunting crocs, and made our way to the bank, running through waist-deep elephant grass towards the jungle.

The PBR didn't hang around long: soon as we deployed, it swung around back up river.

And we were alone.

After we'd entered the fringe of the jungle and secured perimeter, Barber called us together.

"Okay, listen up," he whispered. "About five clicks east there's a suspected supply route for Charlie. We'll just check it out, maintain surveillance and ambush any small groups we come across. Anything larger, forget it. Intel just wants numbers, weapons, organization, the usual."

It wasn't unusual for us to get our briefing in the jungle. Lot of the shit we did was so highly-classified we were rarely told in advance...unless it was a special op like an abduction or an assassination or something tricky like that. Then they told you beforehand and put you in quarantine until you deployed. Security.

"That's just our first stop," Barber said. "After that comes the vil. In the morning."

The village.

As far as intel knew it wasn't much more than a little hamlet. So tiny and remote it didn't even have a name, just a couple map coordinates. It was our ultimate destination, the reason for this little trip. We were to hit it with *extreme prejudice*, meaning we were to kill every living thing we came across—men, women, and, yes, children, too.

Idea of that leaves you cold?

It shouldn't. We exterminated plenty of villages in 'Nam. That's what the Phoenix program was. Fucking government will never admit to it, of course, but then they still won't tell the truth about Roswell and who greased JFK. Anyway, Phoenix was in full force and lots of villages were being erased because of communist ties. You probably heard of My Lai, but that was only one instance. You see all that shit on TV about the Nazis exterminating villages in Poland and Russia and that, but we did the same thing. See, Mao Tse Tung said that the guerrilla is the fish that swims in the sea of the population. Something like that. So how do you catch that fish? You net the whole lot, that's how. If the population shields those cowardly bastards, then they go, too. Don't get pissed off at me, it wasn't my idea to do these things. It was your *government's*, good old Uncle Sham. But having troops go in and waste some shit-nothing hamlet was messy. Too many guys traumatized, too many witnesses who might spill the beans. So the strategists in Washington got some better ideas. And you're gonna hear all about that in a minute.

Anyway, there we were in the bush.

"What's the situation?" Thurman asked.

Barber coughed quietly into his hand. "They were a little vague on that. Just that no one comes out of there."

Thurman shrugged. "Just gooks. Grease 'em and get on out. Fuck 'em."

I didn't like it, didn't like any of it, but I was in too deep and had too much blood on my hands by then to pull out.

I remember Barber looking at me and I swear something passed between us. He didn't like any of this either and I could see that. There was something weird going on. He had a camouflage bandana pulled tight over his head, his face painted black and green. It was hard to say where cloth ended and flesh began.

Thurman was chuckling; he was always chuckling. "Find 'em, fix 'em, and fuck 'em," he said, fingering the blade of his K-Bar knife.

He was this tall, blonde psychopath with a shrapnel-pitted face and a scarf of napalm burns at his neck, arms sleeved with tattoos of serpents and scorpions. Six foot four, two-hundred fifty pounds of death. I think maybe that ghoulish little laugh of his reinforced this...*and* the necklace of sun-dried ears. Thurman was scary. No one really liked him, but he was a badass boonierat and he was good to have around. A natural born killer.

I noticed Roshland was looking about nervously.

"What's up, Tommy?" I asked.

He shook his head side to side very slowly, spitting a ribbon of mucus at a leaf spider. "I don't know. I just feel strange. Something wrong about this place."

"Charlie?"

"No, not that, man. I don't know. Imagination. Beaucoup bad vibes." He didn't seem to be sure of his diagnosis. "Maybe it's just this daylight shit."

I had to agree with him on that.

I didn't care for daylight insertions. We usually went out at night. But for some reason, intelligence wanted us to hit the vil in broad daylight. In fact, when Barber was briefed by the Admiral and his spooks in Saigon, they said if it was getting dark, to scrub the operation. Under no circumstances were we to approach the village in the darkness. Go figure. Those spooks were funny sometimes. Or maybe not funny at all.

In about five minutes, Barber finished with his funny papers—maps—and we moved out. I took point. The jungle was thick and swampy. Mosquitoes and biting gnats were landing on my face and neck despite all the bug juice I'd smeared on with my cammo paint. I didn't even bother swatting at them—for each one you killed, six more would take its place. You patrolled enough jungle like I had, you didn't waste time with the local wildlife. You just acclimated yourself. Things like insects and jungle rot became as much a part of you as your skin.

I was starting to sweat a lot, so I took a salt tab. It was very quiet. Just the way I liked it, jungle birds screeching and monkeys chattering. The day had become oppressively hotter as we approached the river, a finger of the Mekong Delta system. I kept thinking about beers in frosted mugs. The farther we went, the more an uneasy feeling began to grip me. I couldn't put a finger on it, but it left me cold.

We reached our first target before long.

Map coordinate Q-14. Supposedly, there was a supply route running through here for the slopes. We found a few footpaths beaten through the brush, but they were mostly overgrown. We canvassed the entire sector in every direction, but found nothing worth noting. Thurman, however, picked up an old French bayonet. It was rusted to shit and had probably been there for fifteen, twenty years since the Frenchies got their asses kicked out of that neck of the woods by the Viet Minh.

Finally, we called it quits.

Back into the bush, humping through swamp and hacking through jungle. I was on point again. The Rung Sat was a large area, true, but I was still somewhat unnerved that we hadn't come across anyone at all. Not even a band of drug smugglers. Strange.

Then, just after sunset, we came upon a small village.

Not *the* village, but a little clearing with a couple thatched huts and a bonfire blazing away. I moved in cautiously to take a look. Thurman and the others hung back and checked out the huts. There were seven men and one old woman around the fire. The men had AKs and black pajamas on. VC, all right. Hardcore pricks spoon fed off Uncle Ho's bullshit wagon. They were giving the regular Army and Marine units nothing but trouble, but they were no match for us. We'd proved that again and again.

Thurman came back and told us the huts were empty. He'd found one VC sleeping and slit his throat. Barber decided we were going to waste them. Thurman and I made a sweep around camp to see if there were anymore dinks around. Fifteen minutes later we came back. Nothing. It was cool.

Barber signaled us to form a killzone.

Roshland took his sixty to a small copse directly across from them. Barber, Thurman, and I spread out. Thurman carried an AK like me, Barber had a Stoner LMG. Dinks didn't know it yet, but they were meat. Night, night.

Barber open up first.

He took out two of them before Thurman and I even fired. Together we cut down three more before they knew what the fuck was happening. The other two gooks rolled away and tried to scramble into the jungle, but Roshland cut 'em in half with his sixty.

We slipped from the jungle and went to the fire.

I didn't like it: standing there in the flickering light it would have been easier than shit for someone to draw a bead on us. The old woman had gotten hit in the leg and shoulder by stray rounds. She was bleeding pretty good.

She looked up at us, spoke in English. Her face was a maze of wrinkles, her eyes shiny and wet. "You go into land of dead, Joe...you don't come back...you numba ten, you numba ten thousand..."

We all chose to ignore her meaning.

"Bitch speaks pretty good," Thurman said. "Want me to see what I can get out of her?"

Barber shook his head. "Negative. No time."

"Won't take me long."

"Intel doesn't want that. No interrogation of unfriendlies in this area."

And that was weird. Interrogation was pretty much SOP with a unit like ours. We'd been extensively trained in procedures of that type...nice ways and not so nice ways. We all spoke Viet and French, some better than others. Barber could speak Russian and Chinese, too.

But orders were orders.

"Well, we can't leave the cunt," Thurman said. He was pissed—Barber had cheated the sadist out of a good hour of cruelty.

Before Barber could answer, the old bag pulled a skinning knife out of her pants and made a lunge for him. We were all caught momentarily off-guard...except Thurman. A split-second after she pulled the knife, his boot connected swiftly with her temple, sending her sprawling senseless in the dirt.

"Crazy fucking mamma-san," he said.

"Get moving," Barber whispered. "Thurman, take point. Haul those bodies into the jungle and strip 'em."

We stripped the bodies of everything they had—weapons, ammo, food, personal items—and dumped them in the bush. That way it would look like bandits got 'em and not American guerrillas. We scattered the ammo and sabotaged the AKs so they wouldn't work. Thurman took a couple ears for his collection and some greasy photos of the soldiers' girlfriends. He had quite an assortment of both. There was a well back near the huts and I dropped a vial of poison into it so any VC getting a drink would die a painful death. It was SOP to leave little presents like that behind. Deny the enemy the essentials of life.

Before we moved out, I looked back once and saw Barber break the old woman over his knee and stick his K-Bar into the side of her throat. I'm glad he did it. I hated doing women, particularly old ones.

Guerrilla warfare. It ain't just a job, it's a guilt trip.

We were all pretty deadass-tired from walking for twelve hours, so Barber decided we could bed down for a few hours.

Said it would work out perfect. By the time we hit the vil next afternoon, we'd be fresh. We crawled up on a little flattened ridge that was nearly covered by a small, low thicket of bamboo and shut our eyes. Thurman took his Starlight scope and stood watch.

By the time I closed my eyes, Roshland and Barber were breathing even and regular. I always wished I could knock off that easy, but I needed to unwind a bit. Didn't take me long, as it turned out. Last thing I saw was Thurman creeping about, setting up perimeter.

I was dreaming about an old Chevy I used to own when I felt someone shaking me. I opened my eyes and saw the dim figure of Barber hunched over me.

"Time?" I said.

"Thurman's gone," he said. "Get your gear together."

I rubbed the sleep from my eyes and shouldered my ruck and rifle. The night had gone dead quiet while I slept. A gentle breeze skirted the trees, but it didn't do shit towards stopping the sweat that ran down my brow. I popped a salt tab and took a pull off my canteen.

"What time is it?" I asked Barber.

"Just after three," he whispered.

After three? Christ, we'd been asleep for hours. We crashed out just after 2300 hours, eleven 'o clock. Thurman should've roused us at one.

"What happened?" I heard Roshland say.

Barber didn't reply. He scanned the darkness with his Starlight scope.

"VC?"

"No." Pause. "I don't think so."

I kept watching him. His fuzzy, black outline told me nothing. But, then, I didn't have to be told: If it had been Cong, they would have greased us all. There's no easier kill than a sleeping man.

I looked through the thick jungle canopy overhead. The starry sky looked down between the branches, noncommittal. Whatever it had seen, it wasn't for us to know.

We spent the next thirty minutes or so crawling through the foliage. There were no signs of Thurman...he was just gone. Almost like he had simply walked off or just disappeared into thin air. Or gotten himself zapped by Charlie. It didn't seem possible, though. Thurman was good, the best I'd ever seen in the jungle. I couldn't imagine anyone expert enough to take him without a sound.

Besides, why take him and leave us?

Barber called us together. It was 0400 by then.

"We gotta get moving. Thurman will have to take care of his own ass," he said.

Barber took point and we fell in behind him.

The further we pushed on, the worse the terrain became. The jungle grew dense with long twisting vines that coiled down like tentacles and snatched at my boonie hat and gear, snagging and tangling. It was a real pain in the ass moving through it. We had to crouch down most of the way. The ground became muddy and then turned into swamp as we passed through low-lying areas, the muck coming up to our hips sometimes. The sky was streaked with indigo blue. There were birds cawing overhead and ten-foot pythons hanging in the trees, testing the air with forked tongues. You could see them in the bluish, pre-dawn light and that was enough. Every time I got close to one, I gripped the handle of my K-Bar, ready to slash at it if it made a move towards me.

But none did.

They just hung lazily by their tails, paying us no attention as if they saw crazy, mud-encrusted humans every day. And I guess they probably did.

I never liked snakes too much, but I'd gotten used to them like everything else in that goddamn country. For some reason, harmless as they were, they were getting to me that day.

Everything was.

But it was only the beginning.

Just after first light we regrouped at the perimeter of another little village. It wasn't the one we were looking for. There was no mention of it on the maps. We sat out there in bush, reconning it, while Barber made up his mind about whether we should bypass it or not. In general, where you're on a specific mission—that vil we had to hit, for example—you'll go out of your way to avoid contact with not only the enemy, but the civilian population as well. Unless you find something so sweet and easy you can't pass it up, you know, like that other little hamlet with the gooks by the fire. They were begging for it, so we gave it to them.

"It looks deserted," Barber finally announced.

And it did.

Like a cemetery.

It was bigger than the last one, a good eight or ten huts crowded against the encroaching jungle. A place that size, there should've been some kids running around, an old lady or two at a cooking fire. But there was nothing. The silence was eerie. It was a heavy, almost physical thing. My military turn of my mind told me that what we had here was one sweet ambush, all primed and ready. Slopes were hiding in the huts, the woods, just waiting for our asses.

But I didn't believe it for a minute.

I could smell death twisting in the air—warm, pungent, but not recent. There had been killing here or mass dying maybe yesterday, maybe the day before. I knew that much because I knew death: knew its smell, its taste. And this place was full of it like a drawer in a morgue.

We walked right into it. Not exactly SOP; usually you would skirt the perimeter, check the jungle for signs of unfriendlies. But, somehow, the three of us knew this place was empty.

And it *was* empty, all right.

No pigs or chickens. No people. Barber and I started checking the huts while Roshland patrolled back and forth with his sixty, looking for trouble. I prodded open the door of the first hut we came to and there was nothing living inside. My guts pulled up sickly at the smell. There was a little boy in there, maybe eight or ten. His decayed body had been nailed to a post. He'd been eviscerated, his head nearly cut off. His eyes were missing. His jaws were sprung open in a scream. He wore a beard of flies.

Outside, Barber said, "Pretty sadistic even for the Cong."

"Yes," I said, but could say no more.

The kid smelled bad, but he didn't account for that smell of death we encountered upon entering camp. This was localized, small. The other was huge, omnipotent. It was draped over the village.

We checked two, three other huts and didn't find a thing.

In the last hut we found another body. An older guy, maybe fifty, crouched in the corner. He had one arm up over his eyes like he was protecting his face or didn't want to see something. In his other hand was a small homemade knife. He'd slit his wrist. He was stained dark with old blood. Ants and beetles were all over him.

It looked like he'd cut himself open before something got at him. As if death was better than what he was facing.

I'd seen some bad shit over there. Things that could warp a sane man. Shit so ugly, so horrible, so hideous it could've scared a maggot off a gut wagon. But by that point, nothing bothered me much. I'd long before shut down my humanity; it was the only way to survive, to hang onto what remained of your mind. So, yeah, I was steel, I was hard, I hadn't had a decent human emotion in months and months.

But I was scared.

Scared like a kid in a spook house.

Everything was hot and dry and you could hear the brush crisping in the morning sunlight. Hot, yes, but my skin had gone cold and something inside me had curled up in a tight ball. It was more than the kid's body, bad as that was. And it was more than the man's body. It was just a raw, grim feeling I had. Just a deserted village? Sure, but there was something terribly wrong about it.

Roshland broke protocol and called out to us.

We ran over and found him in a little clearing between the hootches. He was a big, black bull of a man, but at that moment he was small and weak, a stick man smothering under all that killing hardware.

We saw what he saw.

Somebody had dug a pit, scooped a hollow out of the earth. They'd dumped the bodies of fifteen or twenty villagers into it and *burned* them. What we were looking at was like some blackened mass grave of jutting limbs and screaming faces, bodies cremated nearly down to skeletons. And the smell...Jesus. Roasted flesh, charred bone. And something else, kerosene maybe.

Roshland looked at me, at Barber. "What the fuck, man?" he said, his voice breaking. "What the fuck is this all about?"

"Must've soaked 'em and lit 'em up. But why?" I said.

We turned away, each separately filing this away for future nightmares. The village was the sight of an atrocity we could only guess at. I was thinking about what that old lady said, about us going into the land of the dead and not coming back. She knew what we'd find. Maybe those VC with her had been the ones who'd done this, probably yesterday. But, for some reason, I didn't think they had anything to do with the kid or the man. That was something else. The VC were more like....what? *Damage control?* Burning those bodies like plague victims, so some pestilence wouldn't spread.

But that was crazy, right?

I started thinking about our target, the other village, wondering why the brass insisted we hit it in broad daylight. They'd even told Barber that under no circumstances were we to make contact at night. What the fuck was going on here?

"Let's go," Barber said, regaining his composure. "Whatever happened here, it's not for us."

Back into the jungle. Swamp. Hills. Insects. Brush so thick you had to crawl through it on your belly in spots. After a few hours of that, we spotted the river. The village couldn't be too far. My back was aching from being stooped over for so long. It hadn't been that sore since my first week of BUDS, frogman school.

We paused on the riverbank and looked around.

Everything was quiet and serene. For a second there, I almost forgot where I was and what I was doing. All I could hear was the rushing of the water. It could have been a river back home in Michigan, save for the oppressive heat.

And it got hotter, too.

We crossed the river quickly, the cool water feeling great as it sluiced around my waist. I wished we could've submerged ourselves in there for awhile and cooled off. But that was out of the question: We had to cross it as fast as possible, just as we had been taught.

On the other side, we slipped into the jungle and paused while Barber checked out his funny papers.

"I wonder where Thurman is right now," Roshland said. "Probably dead...all cut to shit by Charlie. We found a Lurp like that once, Davis, when you was still with Two. We were across the border on a recon patrol. Poor bastard was cut to pieces. Got himself caught in a booby trap—then they got him."

"Laos?" I asked.

"Yeah, damn straight. Pathet Lao mothers can be wicked."

"Quit it all ready," I snapped. "Slopes didn't get Thurman. He could've wasted a platoon of them with his fucking knife."

"What then?"

"I don't know. A jungle cat or something."

"Sheeeit."

"Well, it wasn't Charlie."

In about five minutes, we continued on.

"How far?" I asked Barber.

"Be there soon."

I'd heard that one before.

The terrain wasn't bad at any rate. It was high ground, dry, without an overabundance of brush. Just enough so there was plenty of cover, but you didn't have to hack your way through.

It was weird, though.

The closer we got, the deader things became: no animal sounds, no insects...nothing. I didn't like it. Something was telling me we were in the shit and it was getting deeper every minute.

We pushed on.

I can't honestly tell you what that fear was like. It was just this cold dread that made my blood feel like ice water. It was in every cell of my body, shivering. I'd known fear before, I'd lived with it day in and day out over there, but never anything remotely similar to what was in me that day.

I was ahead of Barber and Roshland by then, walking the point. Every step was worse than the last. I wasn't worried about VC or NVA, but something else entirely. I just didn't know what.

Ten minutes later, I stopped dead.

I motioned Barber and Roshland forward.

I wanted them to see what I saw, because I was beginning to doubt my own eyes.

They came up behind me and I just pointed.

"Shit," Barber said.

It was hanging all over the trees and bushes—long, gooey strands of transparent slime that looked like snot. The air was pungent with its scent: sharp, acrid, like ammonia. A dirty yellow mist was steaming from the stuff, collecting along the jungle floor in patches of ground fog.

"What the fuck?" Roshland said, prodding a dripping mass with the barrel of his 60. The stuff sizzled as it contacted the metal.

"What is it?" I asked Barber. It was obvious from the drawn look on his face that he'd seen it before or at least knew what it was.

"Laughing Man," was all he would say.

"What's that?" Roshland said. "What the hell is that?"

"Bad shit," I said under my breath.

Laughing Man was a defoliant.

The Air Force had high hopes for it at first, but something happened and they canceled the project. That was the official version...and the rumors took off from there. This Laughing Man shit didn't kill the foliage like it was supposed to, at least not right away. It took a few weeks to work.

In the interim is when the nasty things happened.

The inhabitants that came into contact with it sort of went insane and killed each other off. There were all sorts of rumors concerning cannibalism and self-mutilation. What I knew was mostly hearsay and some crazy shit a Marine Recon told me at a bar in Saigon. He and about eighteen or twenty other Recons had to lead a team of Agency spooks up north to a village the Air Force had *accidentally* sprayed with the stuff. He told me that *Laughing Man* was no defoliant, but a biological contaminant. He'd heard the spooks whispering about it. A biotoxin.

When they got to the village, no one was left: the entire population was dead, about twenty-five men, women, and children. The place stunk to high heaven; all those bodies had been lying around in the summer humidity for nearly a week. Most of 'em were bloated and decomposed and some had been eaten. The spooks opened up a few cadavers and found the stomachs full of half-digested bits of human anatomy. A few had been stripped to the bone by their fellow villagers. Some of the bones had been snapped open, the marrow sucked out.

Others were just gnawed to hell.

It was like a fucking slaughterhouse, he said.

Later that night, as they headed back to the LZ, loaded down with body-bagged villagers for further testing, an NVA patrol came at them. Obviously, they had been dusted by Laughing man, too. They were wired. They didn't have any weapons...and their eyes shined *yellow* in the dark. Just like Christmas bulbs, the Recon said. They were foaming at the mouths like rabid dogs. The Marines blew 'em to hell with everything they had: light machineguns, automatic rifles, SMGs, shot guns, grenades—and still the bastards came. He said he emptied a full clip into one gook and still the little fucker crawled at him like a piece of Swiss cheese. The Marines managed to hold them back long enough to get to high ground and call in an artillery strike on those crazy slopes. The gunners back at the fire station pounded the shit out of 'em with their 105s.

It turned out later they weren't North Viets at all, but an ARVN Ranger patrol. Laughing Man turned them into killers and they didn't give two shits what uniform you wore. Everyone was the enemy.

That's all I knew and it was enough.

Obviously, the Air Force was still spraying the shit. I had a good idea why we were supposed to waste that village.

"Maybe we should turn back," I said to Barber.

He shook his head as I knew he would. "I'll take point," he said. "Don't touch any of that crap."

"Goddammit, Davis, what is that shit?" Roshland demanded.

"Bad-ass defoliant," I told him and moved out.

The jungle thinned out as we went, dry and dead. Laughing Man was sticking to the canvas of our boots like mucus. The ochre fog was everywhere. We were breathing it in. I could feel it burning my throat and nasal passages. It was too late to turn back by then; we were all contaminated.

Land of the dead? Goddamn right.

About that time, Barber and Roshland started getting to me.

I knew I was tired and possibly even messed-up on Laughing Man, but they were starting to look funny. Like they'd changed or something. They seemed thinner, their eyes never blinking. Their skin had a strange ashen hue to it. I hoped it was my imagination. I really did.

Roshland and I were following Barber single file, a good distance behind.

We could see him moving through the dead brush very cautiously. Suddenly, he stopped. He gave us a hand signal and crouched down behind a bush. Something was directly ahead and I had a pretty good idea it wasn't the village. Roshland kept flashing me these odd grins every time I turned around. His eyes were glazed over. They were like the eyes of a dead fish on a beach. He looked like he was fucked-up on some of that nasty Cambodian shit...except worse.

Barber gave us another signal and we crept forward.

It was just some freaking zipperhead with a rice-picker hat on. He was walking towards us, stumbling drunkenly. He didn't have any weapons that I could see. But there was something wrong with him—we all sensed that. I think maybe it was the way he walked, kind of shuffling as if he were blind, his hands clawing the air in front of him.

Barber told us to spread out, which we did, each of us crouching behind a dead bush.

The guy shambled forward and Barber stood up, waiting for him. His fingers were on the trigger of his Stoner. When the guy got within a few feet of him, we all saw what his problem was. He was blind. In fact, he didn't have any eyes whatsoever, just two bloody sockets.

"Shiiiit," I heard Roshland say.

Barber let go of his Stoner and snaked a hand behind him, clasping the grip of the machete he had slung on his rucksack.

The slope staggered right at him, his hands hooked into claws and waving wildly. Barber side-stepped him and the guy's dough-white features were hooked in a manic sneer, lips pulling back from gnashing yellow teeth. It was then I noticed that his fingers were blood-stained, like maybe he'd torn out his *own* eyes. Maybe Laughing Man had shown him things he didn't want to see.

Barber held the machete out in front of him.

My finger was sweating on the trigger of my AK. I had a bead drawn on the gook's chest and I wanted to waste him, but Barber had his own ideas. He stepped into my field of fire like he knew what I was doing.

The gook made another unsuccessful lunge at him and Barber swung the machete at him. It went through the rice-picker hat with a crunch and split the crown of the head beneath like a melon. The gook went down, flopping and snapping his teeth like a mad dog. By all that I'd seen of men dying—and it was considerable—he should've been dead. But he wasn't. He was on the ground, screaming and howling. Barber moved in for the kill, chopping and hacking at the guy's head until there was nothing left above his shoulders but a few pounds of bloody meat.

When Roshland and I got there, Barber was just standing there studying the gored blade of his machete.

"Commander," I said, "let's go."

Barber nodded, wiping his machete in the grass and sliding it back into its sheath. "Village should be over that next ridge," he muttered.

Roshland was giggling.

We moved out together.

They were both fucked-up and I didn't trust either of them, so I didn't want them on point. And I didn't want them behind me, so I didn't walk point either. Barber didn't object: he and command had parted company. I didn't think there was any harm in us moving as a group; everything was dead.

As it turned out, Barber was right.

The village *was* just over the ridge. It wasn't much. Just eight or ten hooches set up on stilts, a small stream, and a few feeble-looking paddies flanking the treeline. There didn't seem to be anyone around. The air was still, soundless, not even the cry of a jungle bird disturbed it.

It was eerie.

And hot. Sweat was rolling off my brow and stinging my eyes. I prayed for a breeze, but none came. It wouldn't have helped any; the heat wasn't what was making me sweat—it was the hush, dead feeling of the place. I prayed then for normal worries. Even an ambush would've been welcome. After the other vil and what we'd seen since...I expected only the worst.

We emerged from a small stand of trees and set about checking out the hooches. I always hated crawling up those ladders and peering inside. Usually there was little more than a couple of children or an old woman huddled in the corner, but sometimes you found yourself staring down the barrel of a Russian rifle. That happened to me once. Whether it was fate or God or the tooth fairy, I don't know, but the gook's rifle jammed. I pulled him out of there and snapped his neck. I was lucky that day. Very lucky.

This time, however, they were empty.

A couple of wooden bowls and a straw mat or two were all that we found. And it was strange even finding those things. Usually, if the slopes abandoned a village for one reason or another, they'd take anything that wasn't tied down and some things that were.

No, this was all wrong. They were around somewhere.

The knowledge of that really made me start to sweat.

After we re-grouped, Barber said, "I don't understand this. I just don't...know...I don't know..."

"Bandits got 'em," Roshland suggested.

"Bullshit," I said. "Where are the bodies?"

He shrugged. "Out in the jungle. Who cares?"

"Let's take another sweep around," Barber said. "Then...then we'll see...I guess..."

I just looked at him "Fuck that. I'm going to check the perimeter," I told them. "Then I'm heading for the LZ with or without your sorry asses."

Roshland shook his head. "Take it easy, bro. Everything's cool here. Just mellow."

"Damn yer black ass," I said and moved off into the jungle.

There was a possibility I was freaking out, but I didn't think so. Roshland and Barber were contaminated with Laughing Man and I was positive of that. I didn't know how long I had until it got to me, too. I hadn't opted to check the perimeter merely to satisfy myself that the area was safe...I had to get away from them. I couldn't stand looking at them any longer.

They were starting to look like living dead men.

I was creeping around, moving from bush to bush, when I saw the hut. I wasn't sure why it was set off in the jungle away from the others. Possibly, it was a weapons stash for the VC or just a food stash. I had to know either way. I approached it cautiously, my finger stroking the trigger of the AK. I checked around the door for any trip wires and went in. It was pitch black in there. Or had been. Now a shaft of sunlight sliced a path through the murk.

Thurman was in there.

He was bound around the ankles with a length of hemp rope and suspended two feet off the ground from a bamboo tripod, his hands tied behind his back. His skin looked like old cheese and his eyes were sunken in. He was dead, but I had to make sure. I prodded him a couple of times with the barrel of my rifle...and he moved. His lids snapped open and he leered at me with yellow, venomous eyes.

"Davis," he croaked. "Cut me down, man, cut me down..."

It was then I noticed his throat was slit.

It was open beneath his chin, like a grinning, lipless mouth. I could see the tissues in there, dead and bloodless. As I aimed my rifle at him, I imagined what it must have been like for him.

The slopes tied him like that, cut his throat, and fed on him like a bunch of fucking vampires. But he wasn't allowed to die, to rest, Laughing Man had seen to that.

Clenching my teeth, I put the barrel of my AK against his forehead and emptied the clip.

I staggered back outside and threw up.

I thought about going to get Roshland and Barber, but I knew it was pointless. If my gunfire hadn't brought them charging through the jungle, nothing would. Pulling off my boonie hat, I wiped the sweat from my face. After a good pull from my canteen and a couple of salt tabs, I felt a little better. Functional, at any rate. I dug in my breast pocket and got out my pack of Lark's. I slipped one between my lips and sat there smoking, not thinking about a thing. When I was done, I butted it against a stone and buried it.

Then I went back into the hut.

I cut Thurman's mangled body down and rolled him into the corner. There was a straw mat on the opposite side of the floor and I tossed it aside. I was looking down the throat of a tunnel. I dropped my pack and rifle and shotgun, took out my .45 and went down.

The walls were sticky and damp. It wasn't made for a larger body, so I barely fit. I slithered through there until my back was sore and I was slicked with clay. All I had for a flashlight was a small penlight. Down there, it seemed pretty bright. It was hard moving, crawling through there. My head kept bumping into the low ceiling and my shoulders brushed the walls. After what seemed about an hour, I came to a room.

It wasn't very big. Only about four feet from floor to ceiling and twice that in area.

I could smell the bodies before I saw them.

Their reek was awful. There were about three or four of them sprawled on the floor, chewed to shit. Their faces were gone, nothing but skull left. They had been VC once. I saw what was left of their black pajamas and a few AK-47s half-buried in the mud.

Then I saw the girl.

She was crouched among them, hugging herself. Her blue-black hair was tangled over her face. She looked at me. A crusty blob of snot hung from one nostril and her eyes had no pupils. She was drooling.

"You boom-boom me, numba one?" she asked.

I put two slugs between her eyes and left the dead alone to do whatever they do in the darkness.

Out in the sunlight, I headed back toward the village.

I went back to where I left Roshland and Barber, but they were gone. I was close to panicking now; it had all been just too much. I ran from hootch to hootch shouting their names. But they were gone. I found Barber's Stoner machine gun lying at the edge of the forest, but nothing else. They'd gone through the jungle, I could see that much. Either gone or been taken. Maybe if I'd been sane, I would've gotten out of there right then. But all that training was too ingrained in my mind; I couldn't leave my comrades. SEALs didn't leave other SEALs behind. I'd dragged the bodies of fallen team members through miles of jungle more than once.

I spent the next hour looking for Barber and Roshland.

I patrolled through the jungle in an ever-widening search grid, but I didn't find jack shit. Just more and more jungle, all dead and silent as a mortuary. I went back to the vil and made my plans. I should've evaded to the LZ, but Barber and Roshland, they were my friends. I couldn't leave them. I found a ridge outside the vil that was heavy with undergrowth. I hid in there, set up a nice little OP, observation post. I told myself I'd give them until dark to show, then I was outta there.

Just after sunset, I was still there. I was watching the village with my Starlight scope, expecting something. Before too long, the villagers started showing up—singly at first, then in twos and threes, and finally in roving gangs. I could hear them down there howling and hissing and shrieking. Like animals. I saw Barber and Roshland in their company. Even in the murky green field of the Starlight it wasn't hard to pick out a tall Caucasian and a heavy Negro amongst those small Asians. After a time, they wandered off into the jungle.

But I didn't sleep.

I kept watch, waiting for dawn. It was the longest night of my life, just waiting and waiting for sunup so I could get out of there. The night belonged to them; there was no question of that. They were hunters. Even with all my training, all my experience, I knew I was no match for them. Off and on I could hear screams, gunfire, shouting. I wasn't sure what to make of it. Maybe some gook patrol had run into the villagers. Whatever it was, I didn't want to know.

Just before dawn, it started to rain. Before long it was pouring, turning the landscape muddy and sloppy. At first light, I went down into the village. It was dead and empty. Thurman's body was gone. I started patrolling through the jungle again, ankle-deep in mud, soaked to the skin, and finally I found a path beaten through the knife-grass. You had to be really paying attention to see it. I followed it for about three clicks to the top of a forested rise. In the distance, I could see other villages spread out. But I didn't bother with them. If there were still people in them, then it was best I stay away. One heavily-armed man is still one man.

But I knew they were empty.

I figured that's what all the commotion had been in the night, those things attacking the villages.

I followed the trail up and down through the hills until I finally found what I was looking for: a cave. It was set into the wall of a craggy, overhanging bluff. Creepers grew over the rock like ivy, they hung in knotted ropes over the entrance. I almost missed it. But when I saw it...yeah, I knew where the things, those rabids, were hiding.

I brushed aside the dangling jungle and peered inside. It was very dark, so I checked it out with my light. The slopes were real good with caves, tunnels, that sort of thing. You've heard about that. You give 'em a nice deep hole and pretty soon they've got themselves a dandy ammo dump or ordinance drop. Sneaky little fucks even ran hospitals and weapons factories, command posts and intelligence networks right out of the ground.

I was armed to the teeth, but I wondered if it was enough.

I had my pump shotgun in a sling at my side, my AK slung over my back, and Barber's Stoner LMG. I could do a lot of killing, but I knew that eventually they'd overrun me by sheer numbers and ferocity.

It was good to be out of the rain, but it stank in there—age, mildew, a wet rotting smell. I didn't like any of it; I knew I was wading into the shit. But I had to see, had to find out, before I killed them and maybe myself, too.

The entrance was barely five feet in height. The first hundred feet or so you had to crawl on your hands and knees, but then it opened up. It was huge. A shadowy, gigantic mausoleum. Stank like death, like blood, like things much worse. I kept my mind on the task at hand; once you got the spooks, you were done.

There were pooled columns of volcanic rock, stalagmites and stalactites, shattered slabs of stone that had fallen from above. But what you really had to watch for were the sudden chasms in the floor that dropped down farther than my light would reach. But the cave itself wasn't really too dark: there were crevices and cracks in the rock above and fingers of sunlight filtered in, sickly beams clotted with dust. I found a natural archway at the far end and slipped through.

The smell of death was stronger now.

I was in another passage, maybe six, seven feet in height, twice that in width. It was dank and smelling. Water was dripping somewhere. I could hear things from time to time—skitterings in the darkness, clawing sounds, squeakings. Rats and bats, I figured. Such a place was perfect for them. I came upon a colony of greasy black mushrooms growing from a rent in the rock. A pool of gray slime was leaking from them. They were huge things, like footballs. I'd never seen anything like them before. I stepped over them and one brushed the back of my leg. It was oddly warm like a newborn, pulsing with life. It made my fucking skin crawl. I started wondering what else Laughing Man was mutating.

The walls were narrowing, the ceiling drooping. The air was so thick with damp it was hard to breath. There was moss growing everywhere. Although I saw no bats, there were puddles of guano I sloshed through, alive with roaches, black beetles. In places the stuff was four, five inches deep, a livid, crawling carpet of insects. But there were bones in there, too: human, animal, covered in fungi where they poked from the filth.

I came into another chamber that was huge and vaulted. The floor began to slope downward, black stinking water coming up to my knees. The surface was scummy with clots of graying mold and bat shit. Above, bats were roosting in the darkness. I could hear rats go splashing away at my approach. I played my light around and saw more bones bobbing in the water. Jawless skulls, shattered ribcages, femurs punctured with teeth marks.

I could hear a continual buzzing sound and soon saw why. *Flies.* Hundreds and hundreds of them lighting about the twisted forms in the water. I saw limbs, heads, gutted torsos. The remains of last night's raid, no doubt. But bodies didn't bother me; I'd been wading through them for nearly two years by that point.

What bothered me was that I was in a hive.

I panned my light around and I saw, yes, I saw *them.* I saw dozens of yellow eyes shining in the darkness, all glaring out at me with hatred. They were everywhere, the villagers. Two of them came splashing and hopping in my direction, screeching like birds of prey, their rabid jaws snapping open and close. I sprayed them down with the Stoner and they dropped into the water. But the thunder of gunfire had wakened the others. The sweating walls were honeycombed with passages, worm-holes. The rabids dragged themselves out, filthy and wild, black with dirt and dried blood. I started shooting and screaming, emptying the magazine of the Stoner quickly. There was no finesse in what I did; I popped off rounds like some cherry in his first firefight.

The water all around me (up to my hips by that point) began rippling and churning.

There were wet squealing sounds and growling noises erupting everywhere. Yes, they'd heard me coming and had been waiting for me in the water. They rose up all around me, those white faces swimming at me, fingers hooked and deadly, eyes livid with hunger. I started shooting with the AK and the shotgun, firing in a crazy arc. They would drop away, but not die. Nearly cut in half, they would not know death. I fought my way through their ranks and fell stumbling into that stinking water. I felt their white, clutching hands pulling at me.

I fought free and dragged myself out into the passage.

I saw Roshland and Barber now. Their pallid, bloodless faces were split by jagged grins. They called my name and pushed forward with the others. My skin went hot, then cold, then hot again at the sight of them. My head was thundering with noise. I pulled a pair of white phosphorus grenades from my belt, popped the pins, and threw them behind me, into the chamber. I ran maybe ten, twelve feet and then there was a heaving explosion, followed by another and the acrid stink of phosphorus. The cave was brighter than midday, fire belching in every direction, engulfing the rabids in blankets of flame. I heard them howling and mewling and it drove me nearly insane. But I only heard it for a second or two and then there was a huge, rending explosion and a wave of heat lifted me up and tossed me ten feet through the air. I crashed into the cave wall and went out cold.

I came to sometime later and all was quiet.

My head was bleeding and I was singed, much of my hair burned off...still hasn't come back as you can plainly see.

The air was pungent with the sickening stench of cremated flesh. I figured the chamber must have been full of gases from the putrefying flesh and guano. Enough to trigger one hell of an explosion when the white phosphorus ignited. The chamber had caved-in, burying those things which men and women should never lay eyes upon. I got out of the cave, finally falling drunkenly into the morning air. The rain was still coming down and it felt so good.

I don't remember much after that.

Just running and running, night and day, sure they were behind me, whispering my name. Somehow, they told me later, I bumped into a Lurp patrol and they got me out. The next four months I spent in a naval hospital in Hawaii.

Specifically, in the psych ward.

Nobody believed me.

Or so they said...but somehow that didn't jibe with all the visits I got from the brass, the debriefings. And it sure as hell didn't jibe with the visits I got from a team of doctors who I knew for a fact worked for the Agency or all the comprehensive medical exams they gave me. If I was in a psych ward being treated for battle fatigue, why all the goddamn tests? Did they really think I was fool enough to believe you treated such a problem with constant blood, skin, and bone marrow samples? What about all the antipsychotics—lithium, thorazine, phenobarbitol, other names I couldn't even pronounce—why those specific drugs? And how about that team of Agency doctors (who, by the way, went by the sterile names of Smith, Jones, and Johnson) who pumped me full of drugs at one in the morning and dragged me away to some place that looked like Dr. Frankenstein's wet dream and gave me brain scans for three days?

No, I've since talked with other vets who suffered battle fatigue and they never got the attention I got. They considered themselves lucky if a doctor stopped by every few days. Me? I had my own team of *specialists*.

There was this one grunt in the ward. Ramirez was his name. He knew what Laughing Man was. He said he'd heard through the grapevine that they'd quit spraying it because a handful of slopes that had been exposed went psycho and wiped out an Air Cav platoon up along the DMZ. A correspondent for the New York *Times* had been along on the patrol. They never did find his head.

I received an honorable discharge, the Navy Cross for reasons never made clear, and was sent home. Thirty years ago now. And that's it, people, all I can tell you about what I saw, what haunts me to this day. Crazy? Maybe. But that don't mean I'm wrong. Just look around you. Thirty years and half a world away.

Now it's come home.

God bless America.

-TOXIC SHADOWS-

19

It was quite a tale.

Such a tale that for sometime nobody said a thing. They didn't even look at each other. Had it been yesterday or even this afternoon, all concerned would have immediately dismissed it as pure nonsense. But after what they'd all seen, all witnessed...well, they took it in, mulled it over.

It was Lou Frawley who finally broke the silence. "That was in Vietnam, though. How...how could something like that happen here? I mean, shit, I'll be the first one to admit I don't know a thing about biological warfare or any of that crap, but why the hell would that stuff get sprayed here?"

Johnny stroked his mustache. "I've thought about that a lot."

"And what did you decide?" Ben said.

"Let's just look at the facts. Since the war I've done some research into this. Not much—there isn't much you can find out—but some. What I know comes from other vets. A guy at the VA in Iron Mountain told me that the planes doing the spraying were from an Air Force unit called the 57th Tactical Bombadier Group." He looked around at the worn faces surrounding him. "That probably doesn't mean jack to any of you. But if I were to say that that particular unit still exists and is based out of Pierce Noolan AFB, it might start making sense."

Lou shrugged. "Sorry. Still not getting it."

Ben's eyes widened, though. "Pierce Noolan Air Force Base is about twenty minutes from here."

"That's right," Lisa said.

Johnny nodded. "What do you folks know about that place?"

"Nothing to know," Ben said. "It's high security, I know that much. It's not open to the public. Cousin of mine's a plumbing contractor. His firm won a bid to modernize the boilers there. He said you had to go through three gates to get in.

There were guys with machine guns at each checkpoint. My cousin and his crew were escorted in and out of the place, were never allowed to wander off by themselves. Said you had to show your ID card just to take a piss."

Johnny was starting to look satisfied. "It's right on the fence there, some shit about it being a U.S. Government facility and *use of deadly force authorized* etc. All that bull. It'd be easier to get into Miss America's pants than that place."

"All right, sure," Lou said. "But that's the military. They get like that. Hell, you were a SEAL and all. I bet you guys had top level clearances."

"I could've walked right into the Pentagon."

Lou slapped his hands on his knees. "Well, there you go. That's how they do shit. But that don't mean we got some sort of conspiracy here."

Ruby Sue laughed. "You people just astound me." She pulled a joint out of her coat, fired it up. Everyone, of course, just stared. "Hey, you smoke yours, I'll smoke mine."

"Why not?" Lou said, firing up another cigarette.

"What astounds you about us?" Ben wanted to know.

She coughed, blowing out smoke. "Oh shit, man. This country ain't nothing but one big conspiracy. Haven't you heard of Area 51? The JFK thing? Roswell? Shit, man, it's everywhere. This whole country ain't nothing but a nest of lies. Right, Nanc?"

Nancy was staring off into space through glazed, fixed eyes. Her lips trembled. She shifted from one position to the next. She hugged herself. She trembled.

"She's been through a lot," Ben said, stroking her cheek. It was damp and cool like the underside of a mushroom. But he told no one that.

Nancy squinted her eyes shut, then opened them.

She managed a thin smile which quickly became a frown.

There was something not right with her, but everyone pretended ignorance. Ben was right, they figured: she had been through a lot.

Ruby Sue looked away. "I say Johnny's one-hundred percent correct. CIA, NSA, DIA...all those secret black budget ops groups, man, they have no respect for human life." She sucked off her joint, coughed again. "Good shit. Anyone...*no?* More for me. But like I was saying, those groups, man, they'd spray a town down in an instant."

Lou sighed. "Whatever. But let's not digress, people."

"What I'm saying," Johnny pointed out, "is that from what I found out, the research on that stuff, on Laughing Man, was carried out many places. But the group that dispersed it is right next door to Cut River. Let me speculate here a minute. Yeah, I think there is a conspiracy here. A conspiracy of silence. Uncle Sam won't admit he has stuff like this. But he does. And he stores it at certain facilities. My guess is that Pierce Noonan is one of them."

"But you're guessing," Lou pointed out.

Johnny shrugged. "Sure, I am. Facts aren't exactly plentiful, pal. I'm offering you people an explanation for this fucking nightmare. You think some goddamn virus or something just *happened* to mutate and cause this? Bullshit. Maybe I'm wrong here, but I don't think so. I'm not saying for a moment that the Air Force did this on purpose. I'm thinking more like a mistake here. Colossal fuck-up comes to mind. How? I don't know."

Lou stared at him through a cloud of cigarette smoke. He decided he was getting pretty good at this Devil's Advocate thing, so he kept at it. "All right. It's feasible, I'll say. And it explains things. I'll give you that. But don't you think stuff like this Laughing Man would be stored in a really secure place?"

"Who knows?" Lisa chimed in. "Maybe a container of it broke open, maybe some kind of animal infected with it got out. Maybe it vaporized and came down in that rain. I don't see the point in arguing here. It happened...or something damn close to it."

She was right.

They all knew that. The *hows* and *whys* really didn't matter at present...or not too much.

"Yeah, maybe you're right," Lou said, stabbing out his cigarette. "We can sort it out later."

Ruby Sue laughed. "Sort *what* out? You guys hear what you're saying? Christ, I thought I was the one who was baked here! Sort it out? They're not going to let you do that. On purpose or by accident, people, they'll never admit to it. They'll blame this shit on the Libyans or Osama Bin Laden or something. But be sure of one thing, we won't get answers. Shit, if they find out we saw this and survived, they'll probably kill us anyway."

"Christ, you watch too much TV," Lou said.

"Maybe I do. But they'll come for us. Black ops troops. Assassins. I saw a movie like that once." She roached her joint, put the unsmoked end in her pocket. "This plane or train or something full of some chemical warfare crap crashes and infects this whole town. People there go nuts or something. Then the government comes in. *Bang!* Martial law. Even if you're not infected, man, you ain't getting out."

Lou looked to Joe who just shrugged. "Well, let's not worry about that. What we gotta think about here, friends and neighbors, is how this stuff spreads. Granted it's infectious, contagious, whatever you want to call it. But how does that happen?"

"Could be just about any way," Ben said. "Water, personal contact, animals."

"Even through the air," Lisa said. "We might be full of it and not know it. Not yet."

Lou smiled grimly at that. "Any thoughts, Johnny?"

He shrugged. "I don't know. All I can say is that I was exposed in 'Nam and never got it."

"If this is that Laughing Man junk, then wouldn't the military want a germ that was controllable? Something they could stop easy enough but the enemy couldn't?" Lou asked them.

Johnny shrugged. "Maybe. Maybe not. One thing I don't want to do is to get into the minds of the crazy, sadistic pricks who could dream up something like this."

"And use it," Lisa said.

"We might all be infected," Ben said, looking down with desperation at Nancy. Feverish heat was rolling off her clammy skin in waves. As if to show the others that she was just fatigued, he leaned over and kissed her forehead. In a whisper, he said: "If you got it, baby, then I want it, too."

Joe looked out the window, closed the drapes. "How long, you figure, before those creatures out there, them crazy shits, sniff us out and make an assault?"

Johnny looked grim. "I'd say it could happen anytime. Anytime at all."

20

Just after midnight, everyone seemed to break up into little groups. Johnny and Lisa hung together, lounging in wing-backed chairs over by the fireplace. The mysterious bikers, Joe and Ruby Sue, stayed together by the window. Lou joined Ben in a little ell off the study. No lights burned that weren't absolutely necessary.

Nancy was sleeping, but not peacefully.

She tossed and turned and sweated. She didn't look good at all.

"How you holding up?" Lou asked him.

"Peachy," Ben said dismally. He was sitting on a little window seat, studying the dark, empty courtyard beyond the glass. "How about you?"

"Nervous. Agitated. So scared, I think I might have kittens pretty soon. Other than that, hey, I'm just fine." He sat down, pulled a cigarette out, thought better of it and put it away. "I better save what's left of my throat."

Ben stroked his closely-trimmed beard apprehensively. "My wife...Nancy...she's not doing so good. I think she's on the point of a nervous breakdown. I think she might be in shock or something."

Lou licked his lips. They felt very dry. "Like you said, she's been through the mill."

"So have you. So have I. So have the others."

"People handle it different ways, Ben. It's human nature." Lou thought that sounded pretty good, even if he wasn't sure he believed it himself. "I knew this guy in Newark, right? Back in the old days when I used to drive truck. This guy—his name was Al DeAmato—owned a string of dry cleaning outfits. Big, tough

Italian guy. Honest, hard-working, doing pretty good for himself. But you know what it's like in Jersey, right? Well, maybe you don't. Let's just say that it's corrupt in spots, lot of mob action there. Had my truck hijacked two, three times in Bayonne by those fucking wops, excuse my French.

"Anyway, my friend had one of his stores in the Down Neck area of Newark. Tough area. Mob-controlled or mostly. One day these hoods show up and tell Al real sweet-like that they want a piece of his operation, that it would be in his best interest to go along with them. Al tells them to go fuck their dogs or mothers or something. Of course, these guys, they turn the heat up. But Al? He won't bend to them. They turn the heat way up finally. They firebomb his car. The union guys who fixed his machines, they'd never show. One night a couple hardass toughs jumped him and beat him to a pulp with lead pipes. Al? He still won't give in. Fuck you and the donkey you rode in on. He's in the hospital almost a month. He gets out, they burn down one of his stores. But Al keeps on plugging. Finally, they let him alone, moved on to easier pickings. He still had trouble with the union guys. And every now and then a gang of street toughs would break some windows, but eventually, even that stopped.

"So, you see what I'm saying, right? Al was tough, determined. Stood up to those guys. Nine out of ten people would've crumbled. Hell, *ten* out of ten people. But not Al. Finally, when things chilled out, Al had a breakdown. He came out of it okay. His nerves one day just said, *Hey, enough is enough, man,* and right to the rest home he goes. I tell you this story because Al rode the storm when things were tough and gave as good as he got. It wasn't until the dust settled that he fell to pieces, when he had time to think about how ugly it all was, how close he'd been to getting killed. And I think, Ben, that your wife is like that. She's a tough broad, right? Tough, capable, knows what she wants and how to get it. But now that the action's over for the time, now that there's time to sort it all out, it's tearing her up. Just like Al. That's what I'm telling you."

Ben smiled, looked him in the eye. "Thanks. I guess that makes me feel better." But the words were barely out of his lips, when a shadow crossed his face again. "I hope that's all it is. I really do. God knows I do. But if—"

"Don't even think that. Not yet."

Ben looked close to tears. "I can't help myself. She's in a bad way, Lou. We both know that. If she's a danger to the others, then, shit, I'll have to get her away somehow so she won't infect them. I'm not being pessimistic here, just realistic."

Lou admired his strength. He nodded, listened to the muted voices singing on in the basement. "Christ, how long can those nuts keep that up? They're giving me the creeps."

"Wouldn't be so bad if they'd just come out and introduce themselves already."

"Maybe," Lou said darkly, "they will when they're ready."

"I guess that's what I'm afraid of."

*

Lisa sat in her chair by the fireplace, cloaked in shadow. Johnny sat across from her. They'd been staring at each other for nearly ten minutes. Not speaking, not moving, just staring. She had this unsettling feeling that something important, something pertinent, something revelatory was about to be said.

The air between them was hush, yet electric like the atmosphere before an important presidential press conference.

"Well?" she finally said. "Say it."

"Say what?"

"You know. Whatever you're thinking."

She could see his face break into a smile. "Pretty perceptive, aren't ya?"

"That's me. They voted me Most Likely to be Perceptive in high school. Cut River High, by the way. Same place you probably went...back in the stone age."

He was still smiling. "Were you voted Miss Piss-and-Vinegar, too?"

"I was voted so many things, I can't remember them all. Problem was, I was out in the parking lot getting stoned all the time and I never did show up for those damn awards ceremonies."

"You got a nice ass," he said.

"Pardon me?"

"I said you've got a nice ass."

"Yeah, I heard you. I just couldn't believe you."

"I speak my mind."

"Remind me to be impressed."

"I'll make a note of it."

Playful exchange finished, the silence fell again. As completely and thoroughly as if an invisible sheet had dropped over them. But it was still there, Lisa knew, that something that needed to be said.

What was it?

A question? A confession?

She lit a cigarette. In the glow of the flame Johnny's face was all lines and bony pockets and shifting shadow, his eyes shining and metallic. It was a tough face, a dangerous face, but an intriguing face. Desirable, even, in some way.

Here's a guy, she found herself thinking, *that's lived the sort of life I'll only see on TV or read about in books. She wondered what all that fierce, dehumanizing training did to a man. What happened to someone's soul when they killed people for a living, when they waded through blood and guts and cloak and dagger bureaucratic bullshit for too long? What happened when they saw something they weren't supposed to see, when they were cut loose from the machine and dropped back into a society that had no practical use for them?*

But she knew what happened to them: they became Johnny Davis.

They became disillusioned and hateful and paranoid and angry. The same way she was going to be after this little waltz when the government began denying and she began to look like a fool. How long could you could stare right through the walls of society and see the crawly things that spun the wheels before you rotted inside?

"Must be quite a life," Johnny said, scratching the side of his bald, fleshy skull. "Living the way you do."

"Rock and roll, you mean?"

"Sure. Electric Witch, you say? Catchy. I like it." He looked down at the floor. "Before the war we listened to the Who, the Animals, Hendrix, Beatles, Stones—all the big groups. Some of the crazy, loud shit—Blue Cheer, MC5, Sir Lord Baltimore. Over in 'Nam, you heard a lot of CCR and Motown. A lot of Country Joe and the Fish, Janis Joplin, the Doors. When I got back, it was a lot of heavy shit. But different. They called it acid rock then. Black Sabbath, Led Zepplin, Uriah Heep, Lucifer's Friend, all that stuff."

Lisa was pleasantly surprised. "I never pictured you as a music fan."

"I was once."

She exhaled a cloud of smoke. "You are a riddle. When I spoke about being in a band, about having hit records, big tours...you didn't seem to be impressed. In fact, you didn't seem to care."

"I'm not easily impressed. Things people say they are or have done or want to do, don't mean shit to me."

"I wasn't bragging," she said, feeling her cheeks redden.

"No, you weren't. That's why I knew you were all right."

"Oh...".

He was smiling again. "What's it like playing in front of thousands of people?"

"Nerve-wracking as all hell, if you want the truth. When you start, you play in front of the mirror. Then to your friends. Then to other wanna-bees. Soon enough, if you're worth a damn, you're in a band learning. Then you play to a dozen people. First time, you want to piss your pants."

"But it gets easier?"

She pushed back her thick dark hair from her eyes. "Yes. After awhile, two, three dozen is nothing. Then you play to a hundred and it gets bad again. Then a thousand."

"How many you up to now?"

"Quarter of a million last June. We headlined a gothfest in Ohio. So many people...it's scary. You see them out there and know they paid good money to see you, that they expect their money's worth and your knees get weak. Our drummer, Sandy, she kept puking backstage. We had to dope her up the first night."

Johnny was nodding. "Sex, drugs, and rock and roll, eh? Must be lots of partying. Must be like one big high."

Lisa was having trouble looking at him now. The conversation was being steered in a direction she wanted no part of. "Sure, but it's not all fun and games. It's grueling, believe it or not, that life. On the road all the time, motel after motel, night after night. Goes on for months. Sometimes you're not even sure where you are. You can't remember."

"If it wasn't for the booze and drugs, it would be hard to get through it," Johnny said. "Am I right?"

"If you say so."

He stuck a plug of Red Man chew into his cheek, started working it. "Before I went in the Navy, late sixties we're talking here, you could get pot, pills, some hash or acid now and then. But none of the real hard stuff. Not in Cut River. In the war, Southeast Asia and all, drugs were everywhere. I saw them destroy a lot of good people. When I got back, it was different. You could get coke if you knew the right people. Even some junk."

Lisa felt her face pulling tight. She was beginning to feel nauseous, her nose was running. It was time for another fix. "Drugs are everywhere now." She started to rise, grabbing for her purse. "I gotta use the can—"

But Johnny forced her back down. He had his big hands locked on her knees, his face swam in uncomfortably close. "How long you been using?"

"What?" Lisa said, without much conviction.

"You heard me. You want me to say it loud enough for everyone to hear?" he asked her. "You're using H and we both know it. How long?"

"A year, maybe." She couldn't believe this. The sonofabitch knew and had probably known all along. She really needed a taste now. Goddammit.

He kept nodding his head, mulling it over. "You snorting or spiking?"

"Snorting," she sighed.

He released her, sat back. "I've been around, Lisa. I've seen it all. I've seen too many friends fucked by that needle. I'm not judging you, understand, I'm just saying I know it when I see it. You ever think of quitting?"

163

"It's not that easy."

"No, it's not. It's hell on earth. I've seen guys kick it before. I stayed by their side while they did it. It's ugly, it's horrible what that garbage does to you. I know, I know." He folded his hands in his lap. "When this is over, if this ever ends, you wanna get off, I know all the tricks. I can help you."

She was starting to shiver. "Why would you want to?"

He smiled thinly. "I am a friend to the friendless. You better go take care of business."

Lisa did, more and more astounded by Johnny Davis all the time.

*

Over by the window, Ruby Sue and Joe talked in hush voices. They were crowded together on a love seat, their duffel of guns and odds and ends at their feet.

Joe was said, "Half up front, half up front, babe. We're locked in and you know it. We can't back out now. These people...you know these people...they won't understand us backing out. They aren't gonna give a fuck what our reasons are. They ain't gonna give a fuck if somebody dropped the bomb."

"It won't be easy now," Ruby Sue said. "We're lucky we found her at all in this goddamn mess, man, but it won't be easy. That guy she's with, that dude's gonna be real trouble. He looks bad."

"He *is* bad. But we'll do him, too, if we have to."

"Just bide our time."

"That's it," Joe said. "The time'll come. Sooner or later. Now why don't we go cozy up to them a bit?"

*

When Lisa got back she looked revitalized.

It truly was a miracle what a little snort of heroin could do for a junkie. She left looking haggard, eyes red as beets, face drawn, nose running, trembling like a sick pup...and came back looking young and pretty and ready to take on the world. Her eyes were bright, she was relaxed, in control, all together easy and smooth.

Johnny saw the change. Had seen such transformations before and was not moved to words. Only in his heart, maybe, was he saddened.

"Better?" he said.

"Yes," Lisa told him and would say no more on the subject. Instead, she said, "My band, Johnny…Electric Witch…we're riding high now, but we're all screwed-up. Everything's a mess."

"Drugs?"

"Yeah, and then some. We're at a stage where we can't afford to screw up. But all four of us, Christ, we're hanging on by a thread. Sandy, our drummer, she's shooting all the time. Our singer's coked up and drunk ninety percent of the time. Our bass player is so strung-out, we can barely get her on stage. And I'm no better. I'll admit that."

Johnny sighed, spat tobacco juice into a paper cup he was holding. "You guys, *girls*, need to dry out. You need intervention. You need somebody to come in and clean house, get you guys into dry-out before it's too late."

"It's not that easy."

"Nothing is," he said. "Was it easy getting to where you are now?"

She thought about it. "No."

"There you go. You worked hard to make it and now you've got to work hard to stay there. But you won't do it this way. Like I said, I've seen this plenty of times. First off, you have to confront them, admit to your problem, make them admit to theirs."

She laughed mirthlessly. "Yeah, right. I tried that. They don't think they have problems and they don't think I do either." She lowered her voice. "They're afraid, Johnny. We were drugged up getting to where we are now. It's insulation against reality. Everyone's afraid we wouldn't be worth a shit without the stuff, you know?"

"You didn't get your talent out of a baggie," he reminded her.

"Maybe not."

He folded his arms across his chest. "I might be the worst person in the world to be giving advice, Lisa. My life is a total waste and I admit that. I've done my share of snorting and shooting. The best thing for your band and you is intervention. A third party. Someone who not only cares about the four of you but has a business interest in this. Someone with something to lose if you guys fuck this up. I don't know, like a manager or an agent or something. Your mouthpiece."

"Then we *are* in trouble," she said. "Because he's the one who gets us our drugs."

Johnny pulled a face. "Shit."

"Yeah, he's very much part of it. His name's Richard Chazz. He's one of the best in the business, but he's in way over his head."

"Money-wise or drug-wise?"

Ah, now there was the question. "Both. In fact, he's dropped out of sight. Nobody's heard from him in nearly two weeks."

"What gives?"

It took some time to tell.

Chazz hadn't gotten to where he was on his good looks or business acumen, though he was pretty loaded on the latter. Half of the ride to the top had been accomplished through connections and loans. Both were accomplished by the same group of people. The same people that kept upping the interest and kept wanting a bigger chunk of his management company and, ultimately, his bands.

"What? Like the Mafia or something?"

Lisa shrugged. "I don't know exactly. But they're heavy people. They're into the entertainment industry at every conceivable level. He never put a name to them. He always mentioned shit about his *silent partners* and things like that. When we asked questions, he got nervous. I'm pretty sure he gets our drugs from these people."

Johnny shook his head. "What the hell was he thinking getting involved with those hoods?"

Lisa sighed. "Richard is good, Johnny. But he's also hungry all the time. He isn't above shady deals to promote himself or his product, in this case, us. Electric Witch."

"And now he's disappeared?" Johnny asked hesitantly. "You think maybe—"

"No, at least I hope not. All I know is that last month before he took his little powder, he was a nervous wreck. Thought he was being followed. Jumped every time his cell rang. He hired bodyguards. He was coked-up and paranoid." She let that lay a moment while she sorted it out in her head. "Bottom line is we have trouble right now. We got lawyers and record execs and road managers climbing up our ass. We've been so wasted, we don't know shit about the business side."

"Get another manager."

"We have contracts."

"How about the cops? The feds? Can't you go to them?"

She shook her head. "You fuck with these people, you're done. That's what I've been told. I don't mean they kill you or anything like that. They don't have to: they just kill your career. Pretty soon the deals aren't happening. Record execs don't want you. You have a hell of a time getting studio time. And touring? Forget it, dates are cancelled. Your road crew, which are all union by the way, boycott you. It's happened before. And if all that isn't bad enough, we're so trashed all the time, we can't make sense of it. And maybe we don't want to."

"Shit," Johnny said.

"All I know is it was getting crazy in LA, so I bailed. Came home. Came home to see my parents...and look what I walked into? I think they might be dead."

Johnny squeezed her long-fingered hand in his own callused mitt, said in his deep, resonant voice, "Let's get out of this first, rock star. Then we'll worry about the next step."

Lisa attempted a smile. "You need a job, Johnny?" she said to him. "You ever thought about managing a heavy metal band?"

*

"Put that out for chrissake," Joe said. "Keep your head clean."

Ruby Sue roached her joint. "Not like we're gonna get busted, babe. I think all the cops in this town are running around naked, foaming at the mouth and pissing on hydrants."

"That's not what I mean and you know it."

"I hear you, I hear you."

Joe sat there, thinking, plotting it out in his mind. There was no going back so it simply had to happen. He couldn't go back to Detroit unless the deed was done. And if that meant that everyone in the room had to—

"How you two holding up?"

Joe looked up, saw that Lou-guy standing there, the salesman. He wasn't a bad sort, but he was just another problem in Joe's mind. Who would ever have dreamed it would get this fucked up? A simple job like this?

"We're holding," Ruby Sue said.

Joe nodded.

Lou looked a little uncomfortable. "Hey, I think my lighter puked out on me. Could I borrow yours?"

"Sure, man," Ruby Sue handed one to him. "Keep it."

"Thanks."

Joe was suddenly aware that Lou was staring at his bare arms.

"I hope you don't mind me asking...but is that an Outlaws tattoo there?" Lou said.

Joe wished then he'd kept his coat on. He covered it with his hand. "Yeah, I rode with them in the old days. I got out, though. Those boys were getting a little wild for me."

Lou nodded, seemed satisfied.

Over on the sofa, Nancy was thrashing in her sleep, moaning and bathed with sweat. Ben was at her side, mopping her down with a cool washcloth.

"Poor kid," Lou said. "It's been rough on her."

"Yeah," Ruby Sue said, "and I don't think it's going to get any better."

Lou thanked her and left the two of them.

"Hate to say it," he said, seated over near the fireplace now with Lisa and Johnny, "but that Joe fellow, he ain't the friendliest."

"I think he'll be good to have around if the shit starts," Johnny said.

Lisa nodded. "Christ, he's a frigging giant."

Lou said, "You check out his tattoos? He was with the Outlaws. You guys know who they are, don't you?"

"Outlaw bikers," Johnny said. "I knew some in Milwaukee."

"Those guys are bad news. Criminals, I guess. Hooked up pretty tight in the underworld like the Angels and the Pagans and the rest." Lou saw they weren't really interested, but pressed on undeterred. "What do you suppose these two came to Cut River for?"

Johnny shrugged. "Maybe nothing. Gypsies, man. They like to move around."

But Lou didn't believe that; Ben had told him that Ruby Sue said they'd come to do some work, that they had a lot of guns. But he supposed it didn't really matter. Right now, they needed every gun freak they could dig up. And then some. Dawn was a long way off yet.

That conversational track was a dead end, so Lou tried to lighten things up. "Hey?" he said. "You ever hear about the guy who walks into the bar with the crocodile?"

Johnny grinned. "No, but I want to. I could handle a joke."

"Yeah," Lisa said, warming up, too.

Lou cleared his throat. "Okay. Guy walks into this bar with a crocodile at his side. Right away, of course, people gather. So the guy says: 'I can put my dick in his mouth, let him close it, and when he opens it, my dick'll still be there. Untouched.' The croc's got its jaws wide now and everyone's checking out those teeth. Look like they could shred tin cans. 'Do it then,' someone says. 'Fifty bucks up front,' says the guy. The money appears and the guy unzips his pants and sticks his horn right in the croc's mouth. He smacks it on the head with a beer bottle and it closes its jaws. People cringe, but the guys still smiling. He smacks the croc with the bottle again and he opens his mouth. The guy's prick is still there, not so much as a scratch on it. Okay. So he says, 'Anyone else wanna try?' This woman walks up and says, 'Okay,' getting down on her knees, 'just don't hit me in the head with that bottle.'"

Everyone was laughing and it felt really good to laugh.

It almost seemed like a perfectly ordinary function that had somehow been lost in this awful place where nothing was funny at all.

"Hey, man," Ruby Sue said, waltzing over, "don't leave me out, I wanna hear it, too."

Lou started into it again, glad as always to have an audience. Johnny and Lisa sat raptly for the second telling (entertainment being scarce in Cut River). Even Joe came over this time. Lou had just gotten his stride down when he heard it.

"Listen," he said, not smiling now. "You hear that?"

"What?" Lisa said.

"Listen. The churchies downstairs..."

"They've stopped singing," Johnny said.

"Don't the natives stop drumming right before they attack in those jungle movies?" Ruby Sue offered, but everyone ignored her.

"You hear that?" Lou said.

They all did. A muted, distant popping.

"Gunfire," Johnny announced. "Maybe the cavalry's rolling in. Maybe."

"Do you think so?" Lisa said hopefully.

But then it was gone. After five minutes of silence, it still had not returned.

The vacuum created by the lack of muted hymns and distant gunfire only lasted a moment or two. Then another sound rose up to take its place. It came from outside.

"Jesus," Lou said, "what the hell is that?"

And that was the question that played at all their minds.

Because they could hear it rising up, getting louder and louder: a mournful baying sound as though dozens of wolves were howling in the night. It was an eerie, discordant melody.

Lou heard and it made the skin at the back of his neck tighten. The flesh at his spine began to crawl.

Someone said, "Dogs, it's dogs."

"No," Ruby Sue said. "It's not dogs. Listen. It's *them*. The rabids. They're howling..."

They went to the window to look.

Lou crowded there with the others.

Yes, the nocturnal hordes.

The moon was high and full over the town and the rabids had climbed to the peaks of roofs, the tops of cars, shimmied up telephone poles and snaked up trees. He could see them, man and woman and child, staring up at the moon with horrid fascination, baying like mad dogs, held in rapt lunatic fascination by that glowing orb. Like the tides or the weather, the rabids were moved by unseen forces.

"Jesus Christ, that sound," Lisa said helplessly, "it's driving me nuts. I...I can't think..."

It seemed to work some nerve, aggravate some atavistic memory and everyone suddenly got very restless. In fact, it seemed like those baying voices were unlocking some primitive drive of aggression and hatred. Everyone in that room refused to look at one another. Afraid, maybe, that they'd see the faces of beasts.

Lou felt it as strong as any other.

He couldn't seem to think straight. He wanted to run, to attack, to ravage. His muscles were tensed, his teeth gnashing, his dick hard in his pants.

And they were suddenly all like that.

Circling each other like beasts of prey, refusing to accept what that they were hearing, what it was doing to them. Trying without luck to block out that song, the song of the hunt, the song of some primeval festival of bloodlust and hunger.

And it was about that time that Nancy woke up.

*

She emerged from her frightful sleep like a swimmer breaking the surface of an icy lake. Her throat felt tight, her body felt cold. She sat up and the blanket fell from her. Her hands were hooked and arthritic in her lap. She could see the others. They were walking in circles, breathing heavily. She could smell them, smell something rank and musky coming off them. It made her nipples go hard, made waves of warmth tremble in her groin.

Her mouth was sticky, her lips swollen and parched.

She'd never known such thirst.

She opened her mouth to speak, but her throat was so dry that all that came out was a strangled barking sound.

There was a glass of water on the table before her. Her fingers shaking, she reached out for it, even though the sight of it made her somehow nauseous. She shook her head, trying to free herself of the strange impulses and shattered thoughts that tumbled through her brain. She brought the glass to her lips and drank deeply.

The water was like acid in her belly.

Convulsions ripped through her and she vomited it back up in a warm stew of bile that ran down her chin. She wiped it off with the back of her hand and was not surprised to see a smear of blood.

She tried to stand and fell over, crashing into the table.

She couldn't seem to draw a breath; it was like trying to breathe through canvas. The air she sucked in felt heavy and wet. The room spun and her head reeled. Black dots swam before her eyes.

Then it seemed to pass.

Drool ran from her lips and her teeth chattered. She pulled herself up, more spasms trembling through her like labor pains. She saw faces staring at her and what remained of her thinking, rational brain tried to put names to the faces, tried to fit together all the images in her mind, and tried desperately to make some lucid connection.

But it was impossible.

Her thoughts were disjointed, confused, and feral.

The people...they were saying things to her.

Moving in closer now. Especially the tall, bearded man.

Threatened.

Yes, she felt threatened.

They were trying to draw her into a trap, tightening their little circle around her. They would get her down...bite, claw, rend, and *kill*. She snarled at them, trying to frighten them off. Her skin was tight and pebbled with gooseflesh. Hairs on her arms, the back of her neck were standing taut. She remembered speech and tried to use it. Her jaws snapped wildly, her lips pulled back.

Hissing now, she slipped away from them, saw the window and knew it was a way out. But when she got close to escape, they all started to cry out and in the glass she saw a distorted, drooling face capped by a wild pelt of hair and jumped back.

It was *her* reflection.

Spasms jerked through her, convulsions hit her with the shuddering impact of machine gun fire. The world spun, steadied itself. A low hoarse growling erupted from her throat.

They were closing in on her.

She sighted on their throats, knowing it was where she must sink her teeth.

Her brain raging with hallucination and nightmare imagery, she stood her ground, ready to disembowel the first that came within reach.

*

Ben was the first to try to get within reach of her.

When he was within a few feet, she snarled and spit at him. Using her fingers like claws she tore at his face. Ben stepped back, realizing with terror that she'd been going for his eyes.

Like an animal, an animal, she's not even human now...

Lou approached cautiously from one side, Johnny and Lisa from the other.

"Don't get too close," Lou said to Ben. "Talk to her. Try to soothe her."

Ben was trying. Speaking in low, hushed tones like the sort you'd use to calm a child who'd awoken terrified from a bad dream, he tried to reason with her. He told her who he was. He told her who *she* was. He spoke about things only she would remember, hoping to trigger some memory. He spoke of their children. How much she loved them. How they loved her. He kept speaking, tears running down his cheeks now, knowing that Nancy was dead and this thing was not her.

Lou knew it was bad, the worst-case scenario.

But if nothing else it had snapped them out of whatever had possessed them. A problem had presented itself. A problem that took human minds to solve, one that required sensitivity, care, and logic—human traits.

Nancy's eyes were wide and unblinking.

They looked oddly hollow and empty, but they glistened wetly.

Canine eyes.

Lou didn't dare get too close. She was no more human now than a rabid pit bull. Her eyes were stark and mad, completely insane. She was...*obscene*. No other word seemed to fit as she snarled and snapped and clawed at them. Snotty tangles of blood and mucus swung from her lips.

Johnny worked his way silently behind her.

Lisa and Lou slowly closed from either side to distract her. Nancy looked directly at Lou and he felt his guts go to sauce. He'd never seen such vile, mindless hatred before. A high, moaning sound came from deep in her throat.

Then Johnny had her, locking her arms behind her.

Ben darted in, "Don't hurt her! Don't hurt her!" he was crying, but that didn't seem to be a worry, because she writhed and undulated in Johnny's arms like she was made of jelly. Her face was pulled into a bestial grimace of rage.

Lou tried to get in close and her left foot kicked out and caught him in the chest. It was like being struck by a sledgehammer. He stumbled back and fell over a chair.

Joe was there now, too. As he tried to take hold of her clawing hands, her fingers scraped over his face, opening bleeding ruts.

Lisa was back-handed and dropped violently to the floor.

Ben caught her around the waist, her hands pounding at his head with meaty thuds. Strips of skin and clots of hair were torn from his scalp. But he held on and so did Johnny, trying to pull back on her with everything he had so she wouldn't be able to bite her husband. She squirmed in their arms like a sack of vipers, contorting and slithering, moving with greased, repulsive gyrations.

Finally, she broke free from Johnny and went straight for Ben.

Johnny quickly brought the ball of his right hand down on the nape of her neck with a thud. Her eyes rolled back and she folded up limply like a lawn chair.

They all stood around staring at each other, panting, sweating.

"Un-fucking-real," Ruby Sue said.

Ben cradled his unconscious wife in his arms. His face was wet with tears. Rioting with emotions, he stared at her, seeing blood running from the corners of her mouth. "What did you do?" he said to Johnny. *"What in fuck's name did you do to her?"*

"I just put her out," he explained, his face white. "She was going to bite you."

Ben sat there on his knees, rocking her slack form. One of her arms fell from her lap and struck the floor, knuckles rapping.

Joe crouched down. Felt for a pulse at her wrist, her throat. He checked her eyes, put an ear to her chest. He stood up, his face striped with red welts. He shook his head. "She's dead, man," he muttered. "She's gone."

Ben covered her with his weeping form, crying out insults at Johnny. Lisa managed to insert herself, telling him it was only the disease, the germ, whatever the hell it was. That it was nobody's fault.

But Ben shoved her out of the way.

He picked up his wife and carried her over to the dining room table in the next room. He whispered things to her and placed a blanket over her after he kissed her.

The others just stood around stupidly, wordlessly.

That's when the door was thrown in.

21

First thing they saw was an overweight man, cradling a shotgun in his arms, step through the door. "Evening," he said. "Name's Earl Rawley. Pleased to meet you."

Lou stared at him incredulously. "You don't say?"

Rawley nodded, brought the shotgun up. "And if you make one wrong move, as they say in the cowboy flicks, I'll spray you all over the room. Promise."

He wasn't alone.

A thin, sparse man with a shock of silver hair and even white teeth trailed him as did two other men, one woman, and a young girl. All dressed to kill in their Sunday finest, they carried clubs made from table legs, kitchen knives. They looked crazy.

"What the fuck is this about?" Joe said, stepping forward.

Rawley moved back a bit, intimidated by Joe's sheer bulk. "This is about living and dying, about right and wrong," he said, grinning with bad teeth. "It's about doing what I say or dying."

He was round like a barrel and not much taller, barely over five feet. He wore a straw cowboy hat with a green plastic band around it. His beady eyes were framed by black Coke bottle glasses and he looked crazier than a rat in a blender.

Johnny, of course, was carefully considering his options. As was Joe.

Ruby Sue and Lisa stood there next to Ben.

"Let's just relax here," Lou said. "Way I see it, the real enemy are those outside. If we join forces—"

"We *will* join forces." Rawley nodded. "Yes sir, we surely will. See I came into this town with a truck full of frozen meat bound for the A&P. All the way from Texas. Just another stop. What I strolled into was this bullshit. Those crazies attacked my truck, ripped the goddamn doors off. If it wasn't for my shotgun here, I'd be like them now. Preacher here heard me shooting, came to my rescue."

The preacher nodded, knowing it was all too true. "Yes. The righteous are few in number now. Had we—" he swept his hand to include his little flock "—not been away the past few days, we would be among the evil ones."

"They're not evil," Lou pointed out. "Not really. Just...infected."

"Like you soon will be, friend," Rawley said.

"What're you, fucking nuts?" Lou heard himself ask.

"Maybe. All I know is that I intend to live."

Johnny moved forward. "I don't know about you folks, but I've had my fill of this redneck cocksucker."

"Not one step closer, son," Rawley said. "I swear to God I kill you plain dead."

Johnny and Joe looked at each other and something passed between them. They both seemed to know that all that was saving Rawley's pitiful ass was the shotgun.

"What you all dressed-up for, soldier boy?" Rawley asked him.

"The end. Armageddon. Don't you recognize me, you peckerwood sonofabitch?" Johnny said. "How about you preacher? I'm Death riding a pale horse, motherfucker. I got the keys of hell and death and I'm gonna ram 'em up your worthless ass."

"You blaspheme," the preacher said.

"No, you do. Look at this guy here—you're aligning yourself with him? The guy's a psycho," Johnny said.

"Easy," Rawley said.

The preacher looked at him, looked away. Like what remained of his congregation, he desperately needed to be led. By anyone or anything. Without leadership, divine or earthly, he was without substance.

Rawley stroked the trigger of the shotgun. "Don't listen to him, preacher. That sonofabitch'll slit your throat quicker than a teenager fucks. And that's the Gospel according to Earl Rawley."

Ben said, "My wife's dead. Now I'm dead, too," he said and meant it, moving forward past Lou. "When he shoots me, take him down."

Lou grabbed a shoulder, stopped him. "No, if you do that your death means nothing. Stay back."

Rawley nodded happily. "That's right, friend. You see, maybe I am crazy. Crazy enough that I've had my fill of Yankees for one lifetime. I'll kill as many as I got to. To protect myself...and the congregation, of course."

Lisa came forward now. "Yankees? *Yankees?*" she said, lit up like a flare now. "In case you haven't noticed, you hayseed fucking yahoo, the Civil War's been over 130 years and counting. Yankees? For the love of God, you ignorant moron. What barnyard did your mama conceive your sorry ass in?"

Rawley was flushed red now. "You just settle down, snatch. You're real close right now. Real close."

"Don't you be calling her that," Ruby Sue said. "Way I hear it, man, only thing big in Texas is your mother's hole."

Rawley stared. He looked for a moment like he might snap, then his face seemed to relax. "Might be some truth to that, sweet thing, so I won't attempt a debate. You do know how to push a man's buttons, I'll give you that." He made a show of tipping his hat to her. But his finger never left the trigger of his shotgun. He looked at the preacher. "While I keep these folks honest, preacher, have your boys see what they can find."

Rawley had managed to corral them together now. Even Johnny had allowed himself to be worked. Mainly because he feared for Lisa's life.

The preacher's boys were both in their twenties. They found Johnny's guns right away and then Joe's duffel. They also found Lisa's purse, her guitar, assorted personals.

The congregation were getting antsy. They wanted to do whatever it was they'd come to do.

Rawley had stopped smiling long ago. "Listen up. This is how it works. We need a diversion to get out of this place. Those goddamn Yankee crazies are lining up outside in case you didn't notice. And—"

"And we're it?" Ben said incredulously. "You feed us to them and you walk right out?"

"You catch on quick for a Northerner, son."

"And if we don't care for that plan?" Lou said.

Rawley aimed the shotgun at Lisa. "Then I kill the snatch."

Johnny looked at Joe who looked to Lou who, in turn, looked to Ben. Then they all looked at Ruby Sue and Lisa. This was it, then. This was the big one. No more fucking around here, death had arrived. They'd spent most of the evening fighting to stay alive, to stay uninfected...and now this crazy bastard Rawley was throwing them to the wolves. The irony, if that's what it was, was numbing.

Johnny accepted it, as did Joe. Both were fighters, yes, but both were experienced enough to know that you didn't attack an armed man until all possible hope was vanquished. Besides, it wasn't just Rawley now; they all had guns.

"Bring her to me," Rawley said, staring at Lisa with unabashed hunger.

One of the preacher's minions made to do just that, but Lisa pulled back.

"You either come over here, snatch," he said, "or I drop you right now."

Lisa allowed herself to be pulled forward.

Rawley was happy now. "This little girl, you see, is our insurance policy. Any of you fucks try to play hero, she gets it first. Understand?"

They did.

Rawley formed them up into ranks. Ben was in front, Rawley decided, because he didn't give two shits for his own skin. Next was Joe and Johnny. Ruby Sue and Lou were in the back. Directly behind them were the preacher's boys. They marched their little group up the aisle between the pews towards the front of the church. Outside, there was the night and all it contained.

"It isn't too late to become a human being," Lou said.

Well behind them, the shotgun pressed into the small of Lisa's back, Rawley said, "But I am a human being. And I plan on staying that way. Wish I could say the same for you, friend."

The preacher unlocked the front door.

And the shit hit the fan.

It was as if some predestined moment of attack had arrived. Without bugles blaring or so much as a rebel yell, the stained glass windows began to shatter and the siege began. Dozens of rabids began pouring into the church. Their pallid faces were cut and bleeding but it did nothing to erase their zeal. Like an insane hive, they thronged over the pews. Countless others came from beyond the altar. And, of course, before anyone could possibly register their horror or shock, the front door exploded in.

And pandemonium began.

Ben and the others seemed to literally disappear in sea of clutching, clawing white hands. The preacher's boys started shooting. And that's the way it was—screams and shrieking, gunfire and shouting, all punctuated by the inhuman gibberings of the rabids as they sought out the last few healthy cells of Cut River, attempting to absorb them into the cancerous body of the new order.

Rawley said, "I'll be dipped in shit." He shoved Lisa to the floor and started popping off rounds from his shotgun.

Lisa had barely even hit the carpet when three of the rabids ringed in Rawley. She realized that the crazy redneck hadn't been trying to save her, but had been trying to shove her at them to buy himself time. Thanks to her own natural clumsiness, she tripped over her own feet and went down. And maybe that's what saved her. The trio of rabids had no interest in her—they went right at Rawley.

She brought her face up in time to see the head of a bald man get blasted to shrapnel. He staggered backward drunkenly, fountaining blood and collapsed in a heap.

A hugely overweight woman took two blasts to the abdomen before she, too, went down.

The third, a naked teenage boy launched himself at Rawley, spraying foam and slime. Rawley swung the empty shotgun like a bat and cracked his head open. The boy went down to his knees a few feet from Lisa, head split like a cantaloupe, blood oozing down his white face in crimson rivers. He didn't seem to comprehend that he was mortally wounded. Beyond the mask of blood, his yellow eyes blazed like headlights in a dark tunnel.

He pulled himself to his feet and staggered on after Rawley who was running back the way they'd come, swinging the shotgun in wild arcs.

The preacher dropped his empty weapon—Johnny's little .38 snubby—and simply began to pray. The sound of his voice droning monotonously seemed to drive the rabids into a white-hot rage. As the 23rd Psalm tumbled from his lips, he was struck by a wave of them. A few of which were children which hung on like ticks, biting and tearing at his face, throat, belly and legs as the adults hammered him to his knees. Beneath their lunatic attentions, he came apart like a ragdoll.

Lisa crawled away on all fours.

The church was a huge echoing drum of noise. There were bodies everywhere—tumbled, heaped, crawling, screeching.

She couldn't see any of her new friends, but she *did* see what was left of the preacher's congregation. One of the young men with him was being ritually dismembered by a group of children. She saw two rabids fighting over the head of the other man.

The young girl that had been with them (who couldn't have been more than ten or eleven) was encircled by four or five teenagers, girls and boys. All naked and streaked with grime. They were visibly excited at the sight of their helpless prey. As she tried to stand, they shoved her down. As she tried to crab-crawl to safety, they rained kicks down upon her. Bleeding and bruised and whimpering, they tossed her back and forth like a ball. They were like cats sharing the torments of a mouse. The girl kept screaming and screaming.

The rabids were all grinning, foaming at the mouth, their eyes glassy and reptilian. They closed in tighter, mocking the child's screams, howling in her face.

Lisa searched frantically around for a weapon.

She found her feet and a hand locked onto her shoulder, spun her around.

She cocked back her fist...and saw it was Johnny. He was banged-up and bleeding, but his battle-scarred face was the best thing she could imagine.

"Oh...Jesus, Johnny," she heard herself weep. "Lookit them...oh Christ....this place—"

"Fuck it!" Johnny shouted over the din. "Let's save our own asses here!"

By luck or pluck, he had some of his weapons back—the Winchester and his .357. Pried from dead fingers, no doubt.

He stuck the .357 in her hand, shoved her towards the back of the church. There were more rabids now gathering outside the front door. Oddly enough, they weren't attacking; they were just standing on the steps looking in with almost puzzled expressions.

Nothing about them, Lisa decided, fit any conceivable pattern.

The young girl was being pulled apart now. A teenage girl was lapping at blood from her neck like a kitty with a bowl of warm milk. One of the boys was pushing his penis into her mouth.

Lisa turned away, unable to look anymore.

She could not sup on any more horrors. She was full now like a barrel, overflowing.

The woman who'd been with the congregation had her own troubles.

Two rabids—an elderly woman in a windsuit and a bearded man wearing only a flannel shirt were pulling at her from either side, teeth bared. They were growling and snapping and drooling. Like lover's playfully sharing a joint of beef, they began taking turns with her, each biting chunks of meat from the woman's face and neck. There was such primitive, barbaric pleasure to their actions it was literally unspeakable.

Lisa and Johnny ran up the aisle.

Behind them, the deranged throng from outside began to rush in. There was no more time to witness the fall of civilization as such.

"They're not people!" Johnny shouted, as if to convince himself of the same. "Not people..."

From the altar, more rabids came.

The initial offensive consisted of three adults, all men. An unlikely threesome they were—a business man in a soiled three-piece suit, barefoot, wielding a broom handle; a gangly farmer-brown type in bib overalls and a greasy Case cap, Junior Samples from Hell; and lastly, a huge, lolling fat man wearing the uniform pants of a cop with a badge pinned to his rolling fish-white belly.

If they hadn't been so positively sinister in intent, it might have been laughable.

Johnny shouldered the .30-06, sighted, and blew the cop's head to fragments. He did the same with the farmer. They fell into one another, dead, but their limbs continued to jump and twitch. The businessman with the broom handle vaulted over them and came on, his club held above his head for a deathblow.

He got within four feet of Johnny and Lisa.

Before Johnny could pull the trigger, Lisa brought up the .357 and shot him in the face. The back of his head exploded with a spray of meat and bone. The impact threw him up against a pew and over it.

Johnny took her by the hand, led her forward.

They weren't far from the doorway that led to the rectory. It was just beyond the altar. Twenty feet at most. But in their situation, it might have been miles.

Behind them, the rabids were swarming like hornets. The church was filled with their screechings and howlings.

The door to the rectory suddenly slammed open and two more showed themselves.

Two twin girls, naked and scrawny, their ashen flesh black with streaks and blotches of oil and dirt like they'd been crawling around in a mechanic's bay. Their blonde hair was matted with leaves and sticks, stringy strands of it hung limply over their faces. They could've been a set of porcelain dolls, so white, so perfect...except for their eyes—liquid yellow and fixed with a wolfish hunger.

They came on, arms extended, fingers clutching and clawing.

"God forgive me," Johnny said.

And killed them both.

After that, both Lisa and he were finished.

They shambled forward, through the rectory and out into the night. They met no resistance and that was a good thing because, by that point, there wouldn't have been much they could've done about it.

They made it out into the courtyard, out into the misting, damp night.

Holding each other, they fell behind a wall of cedars and trembled. Lisa sobbed and Johnny did, too, realizing it was the first time he had cried in thirty years. It went against the grain of who and what he was, but the tears felt good.

They proved he was still human.

22

Lou was armed and dangerous and pretty much out of his head.

Like Johnny, he'd survived the initial onslaught when the rabids poured through the front door of the church by simply being overwhelmed. The rabids bowled down first Ben then Joe and Johnny. The latter slammed into Lou and pitched him on his ass. The rabids went right over the top of them, trampling them to the floor.

Maybe it was sheer momentum.

Maybe they saw the men behind them with the guns and knew they were the ones who had to go first.

Regardless, Lou, bruised and banged-up from being used as a welcome mat, managed to crawl out the front door.

Scrambling away on all fours, something struck him in the back—a shotgun. It must've been tossed aside by one of the rabids as they fell on its owner. And now he had it. It was sawed-off right in front of the pump and he knew without a doubt it was Johnny's.

And now, here he was, back on the streets of Cut River once again.

Alone.

A voice in his head kept telling him he had to hang on until dawn...but that was hours and hours away. He pretty much accepted the fact that the others had to be dead. Maybe by sunrise he'd run into one or more of them again...and have to kill them. He wasn't sure he was ready for that. His tank was empty and everything seemed gray and hopeless.

But something in him told him to fight on.

If they were going to get him—and by virtue of their sheer numbers it seemed very likely—then he was going to make them pay for it.

A block from the main drag, Chestnut, he collapsed behind a parked Tony's Pizza truck and weighed his options. He thought of getting in a car again and driving all night. If the tank was full and it was an economical job, he could cruise around until first light.

But he dismissed that idea; it would only draw attention.

He considered walking out of town again.

It seemed the only rational choice.

It didn't seem conceivable to him that they could have every avenue of escape covered. Maybe the roads...but, Christ, Cut River wasn't that big. It was bordered by woods and fields to all sides and where it wasn't, there was the river. There had to be an opening somewhere. The only alternative to that was finding yet another (supposedly) defensible position and waiting out the night.

Fuck that noise, he thought. *You don't know how many rounds you have. Do the sensible thing and get the hell out.*

Okay, then. Which way?

Chestnut slit right through the center of town. Main arteries fed off of it in either direction. Those were out. To the east, the town was flanked by the river. To the west, the cemetery, the trainyards, some warehouses, and what had looked to be a trailer court. Beyond that was open country.

He'd already tried the cemetery and that was no good. Those ghouls were thick in there.

The river?

Why the hell not? Maybe if he got in the water, cold as it would be, he could quietly follow the riverbank out of town. Regardless, it was better than dying on the streets.

Staying in the shadows, he crept up to Chestnut, pressing himself to the brick façade of a jewelry store. He was stunned to see that he was only a block or so away from where he'd parked his Pontiac. It was still there, he saw, across from the Town Tap. He felt a hollow yearning in his belly. The car had brought him to this graveyard. It was his only true connection with the real world.

He wiped a hand across his mouth. Chewed his fingernails.

He felt like he was on the edge of a nervous breakdown.

Sighing, he shook his head. He couldn't let himself weaken like that.

As he squinted his eyes, he could see shadowy forms moving not far from his Grand Am.

He thought: *Cocksuckers, dirty, vile inhuman cocksuckers! Reducing me to this! I should go down there and kill 'em all! Waste those godless pricks!*

He wiped dampness from his brow, part mist, part sweat. He had to keep it together. He couldn't afford to lose it now. This was his last chance. No doubt about that.

Steeling himself, he held the 12-gauge out before him and, crouching down low, jogged soundlessly across Chestnut. On the other side, he ducked into a dark alley and waited. Five minutes. Ten. *Safe.* They would've shown themselves by now if they were going to.

It took him maybe twenty minutes to maneuver the darkened streets.

The moon was still riding high, bloated and wide like a dead man's eyeball. It created threatening shadows and illuminated the terrain. Bad and good. He saw no one, heard no one.

The only thing that stopped him was the sound of gunfire far in the distance.

Then it was gone—just a muted series of poppings, then nothing.

He wasn't even sure he'd heard it. It was so vague that there was no way he could judge its direction. Maybe some of the normal ones were still alive and battling it out.

No matter, because he wasn't going back.

If he got out, he'd bring the Marines back with him.

The houses began to be separated by vacant, weedy lots, industrial sites. Black windows reflected the moon, reflected the lone hunted man, but nothing more.

In the distance, he saw the river.

It wound like a black, glistening snake through the countryside. There was mostly open country bordering it on either side. Lou saw what he thought might be a pumping station off to the far left and a schoolhouse to the right. In-between there was a public access road and a boat dock.

But he saw no boats.

He saw only the moon riding the dark waters.

Okay, tough guy, he told himself, *this is it. You wanted to go for a swim? Now's your chance.*

There was a fringe of trees near the dock. It would be the best point of entry.

He darted across the grass to the trees. Once in their shadows, he allowed himself to breathe again. He could smell the river now—wet and fishy. A cold mist blew off it. Its current was slow, but steady. The waters were dark and looked very deep.

He slid off the grassy bank.

The water was like ice, sluicing around his legs. He had to bite down on his lower lip to suppress the yelp of shock that twisted in his throat. Good Christ. If he stayed in too long, he'd be looking at serious hypothermia. Following the riverbank was out of the question now—he'd have to make a quick crossing.

It was an easy hundred feet of open, deep water.

He wasn't much of a swimmer. There was no way he would be able to make it across with the shotgun. Far in the distance he could see the black hulk of the bridge. See dying fires smoldering away over there. Dark, still shapes waiting. He could smell the stink of wood smoke and worse odors.

You can't go over there, dip shit, so get going.

Night birds called out in the sky.

He moved in further, feet slipping and sliding on the loose rocks and muddy bottom. The entire surface was like a mirror reflecting the bright moonlight. He looked up. The moon was fringed by a shaggy beard of gray clouds. The light would be gone soon. And was that better or worse?

His legs were getting numb.

The water was up to his waist now.

He wasn't even a dozen feet into it yet. His breath was coming in short, sharp gulps, his body trembling violently from the chill wetness.

There was a splashing somewhere. The sound of something heavy being dropped or thrown in.

A fish?

A goddamn big one by the sound.

Shivering, the shotgun tight in his grip, Lou listened.

He heard the sound of water slowing rushing past, lapping at the banks and the dock. There was another splash off to his right.

He swallowed.

The river was getting deeper. Pretty soon, he'd have to dive in, swim for the opposite bank. The water was heavy in his nostrils with a dank, dark odor.

He didn't like it at all.

Something brushed against him.

He almost screamed, stumbling back, nearly going under. He held the shotgun out. Yes, he could see it now. A large, long shape just beneath the surface. He got closer. He reached out, brushed it with his fingertips and felt flesh, cold and stiff like rubber. A body. A corpse. In the liquid darkness, there was no way to tell if it was male or female. The current carried it away sluggishly.

Lou let out a breath.

Nothing to be afraid of.

The body count in this town was going to be through the roof.

Nothing to worry about.

Of course, his brain began to wonder if that poor bastard had been trying to cross, too, and—

Another splash. Just off to his right now.

Ahead of him, there was something else.

Something floating.

Something round.

It had black filaments streaming around it like weeds. A head. Yes, the top of a head, hair swimming around it like deep-sea snakes. It rose up, breaking the surface.

Lou let out a muffled cry.

It was a woman, her face white as bleached flour. Her eyes were yellow dying stars, her grin was like needles in the moonlight.

Lou felt a scream building in his throat and he swallowed it down.

"Get away," he heard his voice say. "Get away or I swear to God I'll kill you."

She didn't move.

She just waited there with her face just above the sluicing water. He could hear her breathing with a rattling, diseased sound. She licked her lips. When her voice came it was clotted and thick as though she were speaking through a mouthful of seaweed: "Hide and seek," she said.

And then her face disappeared slowly back down into the water like a sinking ship.

Lou waited.

A moment, then two.

Like a shark, she's like a shark, showing her dorsal before going under for the attack...

With that in mind, he wheeled around wildly, trying to see movement, anything.

The water before him exploded with motion. Hands took his ankles, pulled his feet out from under him. He went down into the foul blackness, fought back to the surface.

She came at him from behind.

This time, as he fell, he brought the butt of the 12-gauge down with everything he had. He felt it strike something, something that gave. The hands were gone. When he pulled himself up this time he was farther out in the river. The water was up to his chest now.

And that had been her plan...to get him out in the deep water.

He started rushing to shore and she vaulted out of the water, her head catching him in the belly and tossing him back further. Swinging the shotgun underwater to keep her off him, but with little force, he broke the surface again, gulping for air. The water was nearly to the top of his shoulders now.

She was succeeding, his raging mind told him, pushing him out further and further.

He had to make it to the shore.

The water went calm and she was nowhere to be seen.

Lou made his break for it and then she came up again right in front of him.

She clawed wildly at his face. He felt her nails dig furrows in his cheek. She smelled like rotting fish. Her bloodless face was plastered with stringy hair, lit by a vicious grin.

He saw something catch the pale moonlight in her right hand.

He lurched back, felt a blade slice open his nose, then rip through his shirt into his shoulder. He brought the shotgun around and knocked her arm away as it made for a killing blow. He stumbled back and went underwater again.

Drop-off.

He plunged down into the deep blackness, felt his shoes brush tangled weeds. He was out of breath and needed air badly, but he would not submit. He'd play her game. Instead of making for the surface, he pushed himself along underwater with powerful kicking strokes and kept going until he sensed the river bottom beneath him. He came up again, the water just beneath his chest now. His heart was hammering, hitching painfully as it skipped beats.

The moon slid behind a wall of dark, boiling clouds.

She came up again, the knife flaying at his face. He knocked it away, ducked under it, and cracked her alongside the head with the butt of the 12-gauge. She made an almost canine yelping-sound and fell backward with a resounding splash.

He went right over the top of her, feeling his shoes come down on her soft belly, then on the ball of her head. He pitched forward and was half-dog paddling, half-crawling through the violently thrashing water.

He fell back on his ass and he was only in a few feet of water now, the shadows of the willows on the riverbank falling over him with a dark chill. He could feel the sticky, warm oozing of his own blood running down his face and chest.

The woman came out of the water about seven, eight feet away.

She was small and frail, pathetically thin. She'd lost her knife, but was coming on anyway. Making a low growling sound, she fought through the water, her jaws snapping open and closed.

"Come and get it, bitch," Lou gasped.

He brought the shotgun up, aimed generally for her chest, and pulled the trigger. The chamber explosion was like thunder. Buckshot vaporized her neck, her sternum, meat spraying out over the surface of the water.

She was thrown back into the deep.

She fought free one more time, the hole in her upper chest big enough to toss a softball into. She screamed and writhed and sank beneath the water.

Lou made it to shore.

Panting, he watched and waited.

Nothing. He figured with that hole in her, she had filled up with water like an empty can and sank to the bottom, down into that loathsome blackness. In his fatigued, frazzled mind, he could see the currents dragging her along the muddy bottom, easing her past the drop-off where she would submerge into the depths, her clown-white face caressed by river weeds.

He pulled himself wearily to his feet.

Jesus, he was running on batteries here; he couldn't take much more. Dawn was still hours away. The river had turned into a nightmare. What next?

He looked and saw the schoolhouse.

And then he knew.

23

Joe was a large man and he was not designed for running.

Powerful and menacing, you didn't want to go one on one with him. He'd crush you, pull your arms off, and use your skull for an ashtray. In his checkered career, he'd ridden with both the Outlaws and Satan's Choice up in Canada.

He'd fought with them.

Killed with them.

Done time with them.

He was a tough man and a good guy to have at your side.

But he was not a runner.

Two blocks of steady pounding after they'd evacuated the church and his legs felt like they'd been pumped with gelatin. He grabbed Ruby Sue by the shoulder, pulled her to a stop.

"Can't, babe," he panted. "Can't run...no more."

She looked around desperately.

She was winded, too, but, then again, she weighed 115 pounds and not 350 like Joe. That was one hell of a wagon of meat to be pulling around.

"Over there," she said, indicating a narrow passage between two Quonset huts.

Joe nodded, dragging his ass over there, squeezing in and collapsing. "Damn," he said.

"Easy, baby, easy," Ruby Sue said, stroking his huge forearm. She peered around the corner of the hut. Wet streets reflected moonlight. Leaves were heaped in gutters. Storefronts were silent and staring.

"It's cool, babe. It's cool. They must've found easier pickings."

Joe suddenly looked up. "You hear that?"

Ruby Sue cocked her head. "What?"

"*That,*" Joe said, narrowing his eyes. "Gunfire. You hear it?"

She nodded. "Oh yeah. Somebody's bustin' some caps."

"Big time."

Joe was jealous, if anything.

They'd rolled into this shithole with enough artillery to start World War III and look where they were now—unarmed, desperate, in a world of serious hurt. About all they had were their wits and that wasn't gonna slay the beast.

Joe figured he could probably take one of the rabids out with his bare hands. Had they been people, he could've done three or four of them without working up a sweat. He'd done it before.

But these things, damn, they were wild. Vicious. And strong, too. They fought like animals.

Ruby Sue and he had barely made it out of the church alive.

As it was, he had two of those pricks hanging off him like remoras on a shark's belly. He'd tossed them—one into the bushes, the other right through the windshield of a parked car—but it had been close. Real close.

They'd scratched him, but he hadn't been bitten and that was the important thing. He figured the others got killed.

And if Lisa was among them, all the better.

Rested now, he crawled out and checked the scene. Looked cool. He had some ideas here. One of them was to get some kind of earthmover, maybe a front-end loader, a big nasty piece of iron, and plow right through the car barricade. That was a possibility.

Then he looked up the street. "You check that?" he said to Ruby Sue.

"What's that, babe?"

"Right there."

She saw it, nodded, started to smile. "We on the same page?"

"Sure as shit," he said.

There was a sporting goods store just up the block. It looked like maybe it had been ransacked—the plate glass windows were shattered, the door was hanging off its hinges...but if they were *really* lucky, they might find some guns there. And ammo. Then they could get a car, find themselves a big piece of iron and they'd be good to go.

Silently, cautiously, they moved up the sidewalk.

"We gonna leave without her?" Ruby Sue asked.

"We gotta, babe," he said. "No choice in the matter. I think she's done anyway."

"Yeah, sure."

He put his arm around her, held her tight. She felt good. "But I ain't taking any chances. We can't go back to Detroit empty-handed. That's why we're going to Utah."

She stopped. "Utah?"

"Sure. Remember Brooker? Glen Brook? Rode with the Angels? He's retired now. Got hisself a big place out in Utah— horses, cattle, bikes. Big old ranch. That's where we're going. Nobody'll find us there. We get out of here, we quick clean out our place, and head west. Fuck the rest."

The inside of the sporting good's store looked very much like a cyclone had done its thing there. Shelves were emptied, display cases broken. Everything from rubber waders to fishing poles, hunting vests to basketballs was heaped and piled on the floor.

They had to wade through the mess.

The gun cases were shattered, too, but the guns themselves, for the most part, had not been disturbed. Joe got a nice piece for himself: a Colt Python .357 Mag and some speedloaders. He found Ruby Sue a Browning .380 semi-auto. He took a 12-gauge Remington pump off the rack and filled a duffel with boxes of ammo. The guns all had trigger locks, but the keys were in a drawer beneath the cash register.

"Now we're ready," he said.

Ruby Sue went to use the head and he kept an eye out. A thief most of his life, the desire to back a truck up and empty the place was overwhelming. Overwhelming, just not exactly practical. Or smart.

He turned around, smiling at the idea, and there was an elderly man standing a few feet away.

Joe started, took two or three uneasy steps back.

There wasn't a man in the world that truly frightened Joe.

Even in prison where there'd been some truly malicious, degenerate sadists who'd slit your throat for a cigarette, he'd never known fear. But at this moment, staring down at this little old man with his yellow, crocodilian eyes, Joe was frightened.

The guy was just standing there, scrawny pencil arms extended, palms up, fingers wiggling crazily like maybe they were full of electricity. Great dripping gouts of foam and mucus ran from his mouth.

"How about it?" he said with a voice like a gurgling drainpipe.

Joe had the .357 on him. "How about what, asshole?"

"How about it?" he said again and then said something else, but a rancid clot of mucus slopped from his lips and it became unintelligible.

Joe kept watching him, figuring what an amusing, harmless creature this guy must have been before the germ did him— probably sat on the porch telling war stories, bounced babies on his lap, fished trout in the creeks (knew the best spots, too, like all the old timers). Someone's grandpa for sure.

But now...now the damage was done and this old man was dangerous.

He took a step forward and it wasn't the step of an elderly man; there was a smooth cat-like grace to it.

"Take a walk," Joe told him.

He came on.

Joe pulled the trigger and the muzzle flash turned the shadowy shop to daylight.

The old man caught a round square in the chest.

It flung him back four feet, right into an unmolested rack of baseball bats. He and the bats went clattering to the floor. He moaned and writhed and then went still.

Joe figured he'd blown his heart right across the fucking street.

"Nothing personal, old man," he said.

Ruby Sue came rushing out, Browning in hand.

"Get your ass wet?" Joe said.

"Fucking right," she said and saw the dead man. "Let's go. Place is giving me the creeps."

Outside, they moved up Chestnut, armed to the teeth and ready to do some damage. There was a sudden loud whooshing sound overhead and both of them went down low automatically.

"What the fuck was that?" Ruby Sue said.

"I think it was a helicopter."

And a fast one at that.

It got him to thinking.

A helicopter with no lights on it. Was that legal? He'd be the first to admit that he knew as much about choppers as he knew about tampons, but there had to be laws, right? For civilians, anyway. And this chopper was no civilian model. It had been jet-black and sleek-looking, definitely a military model.

Which made him start to wonder just what sort of people were about to crash this little party.

24

Lisa found it almost funny in some pathetic way how, during the action back at the church, she'd had no interest in shoveling any powder up her nose. But now that things had cooled off relatively...the need was back. It had been maybe two hours or so since her last fix and she was burning down like a pile of dry kindling. Her nose was running, her head was aching, and her guts wanted to crawl up the back of her throat.

She needed a taste and she wasn't going to get one.

That was not only depressing, it was downright criminal.

And if all that wasn't bad enough, Johnny was acting strange. The twins back at the church...it had been bad. Lisa decided she was lucky, maybe, that she had the junk habit. Go without it long enough and pretty soon, the monkey started jumping on your back, clawing at your brain, pretty much blotting out everything else. It got so she didn't even care about the guitar she'd left at the church.

Addiction, true addiction, fucked you that perfectly.

But Johnny didn't have even that.

They were walking again. She didn't ask where. She was simply overloaded by it all; functioning completely on autopilot. She saw the faces of her mother and father. She saw the faces of those she'd come to know in these past few hours. And she saw the faces of the residents of Cut River. The only thing they all had in common was that they were all dead.

All dead.

Yes, all of them.

Just like me.

Johnny was walking ahead of her. He paused, stuffed a plug of tobacco into his jaw. He chewed it, spat. "I'm going to get you out of here. I told you I would and I will or die trying. That's that."

"How?"

"We're not taking the roads. We're just going to walk out, through the woods, the fields. It's the only way."

"But Lou said he tried that. He said—"

"I don't care what he said. He's dead. They're all dead."

Lisa didn't have the strength to argue. The weight of the .357 in her fist was like a brick. Her own body weighed only slightly more. Her eyes were blank and her belly was sick and she had the shakes. If she didn't a get a taste pretty soon, she was afraid of what might happen.

Afraid that she'd run off and make for the church and her stash.

Use your head. There's too many of them—they'll get you, make you like them. You don't want that, do you?

She started wondering if it would really be all that bad.

Then she started thinking about Nancy, what it had done to her before she died. Horrible. Far worse than withdrawal...wasn't it? At least Nancy was dead now, though, and didn't feel the pain.

Or was she?

Lisa kept wondering that, too.

She'd *looked* dead...but maybe she wasn't, maybe she'd be waking up soon.

Thinking these things only made the shivering worse.

"Listen," Johnny said to her in a whisper.

She sighed, thinking maybe he was hearing gunfire and helicopters again. She'd heard the first, but not the second. He, however, swore he'd heard it. It seemed to worry him much more than the rabids or what they could do. Maybe he was ready to have a breakdown. Maybe the war was coming back—

No, not gunfire or helicopters.

This sound sent chills up her spine, yanked her mind out of the fog. It was a baby crying. Wailing pitifully. It woke some maternal instinct in her she hadn't known existed...and it also, for reasons she couldn't explain, filled her with a gnawing, relentless terror.

Johnny shrugged, spat. "Some kid," he said.

"Who needs help," Lisa said angrily, tired of apathy.

He laughed. "You think kids haven't been affected by this, rock star? Is that what you think?" he said, eyes bulging. "What is it you think I shot back there at the church? What do you think that was?"

Lisa stared at him. "I'm going to find that kid. Help her or him. You can go fuck yourself for all I care."

She stalked off into the darkness, zeroing in on the crying. The closer she got to it, the more her habit withdrew its clutches. She was pumped with adrenalin now, on a mission from God here, and nothing was going to stand in her way.

She found herself on a block of houses.

A few were lit up, but most were dark. Odd as it seemed, the darkness was gradually holding less and less threat for her. Maybe it was the gun. Maybe it was that she knew those bastards could die now. And maybe it was just experience. After awhile, they said, you could get used to anything.

She stopped before a simple two-story frame house.

A working streetlight on the boulevard washed it down in pale illumination. It had bad windows, old cedar siding. The lawn was overgrown and there was a Ford pickup in the driveway with a flat tire. The body of a woman was twisted-up in the grass, a swath of darkness where her face had been. The sight of her didn't even faze Lisa.

There was another body in the street.

Another swung from the limb of a tree next door.

So what?

The child was still crying. Very loud, very insistent. It could thank its lucky stars that its cries had brought Lisa and not someone or some*thing* else. The porch was screened-in and she let herself in. There was a recliner, an old card table in there. A few boxes of toys, a bag of empties. She saw a pack of cigarettes on the arm of the recliner. Winston. Not her brand, but, hey, they were free.

She lit up, wondering if the flickering flame would draw any unfriendlies in.

But it didn't.

It didn't even draw Johnny in. And the fact that he'd actually allowed her to run off like that...well, it both pissed her off and scared her. She dragged off her cigarette, exhaled.

The child had stopped crying now.

She couldn't be entirely certain she was in the right house.

Sighing, she tried the door.

It whispered in without even a hint of a creak. A mild rain began to fall, tapping on the windows. Wind rattled a loose rain gutter against the siding. She was in a living room—TV, couch, sofa piled with dirty clothes. All terribly ordinary, really, except for the smell in the air of death and pain.

And an empty house.

There was something terrifying about a dark, deserted house, wasn't there? Empty, echoing, a parade of clutching shadows where only stillness and silence walked.

And this was especially true of Cut River, she knew. The town the devil built.

There was a nightlight on the stairs.

Lisa started up, still smoking, clutching the .357 with renewed vigor now. Near the top, she heard movement. A quick, faint pattering like the fall of tiny footsteps. She could feel fear settle into her again, thick as molasses. If you would have asked her at that particular moment if she had a drug habit, she couldn't have told you. All that seemed worlds away now. There was only her, three or four steps from the top, and whatever waited in the gloom above.

She tried to swallow, but her throat was full of sand.

Do what you gotta do, then get out. Just do what you gotta do.

She exhaled, her pulse drumming at her temples.

She stepped up into the hallway.

It went a short way, then turned off to the left like an L. She stopped there, listening. She could hear her own breathing, the rush of blood in her head. Outside, the wind played along the eaves, rain dropping on the roof. Her senses were electric, her muscles taut and flexed.

She navigated the bend in the hallway.

A pale radiance bathed the walls from the streetlight outside. There were doors standing open. Bedrooms, she figured. But she was only interested in the one at the end. It was halfway open and beyond was the summation of mankind's oldest fear: the unknown.

Maybe a terrified child waited. Maybe something far worse.

But she had the gun. Yes, she did have that.

You sonofabitch, Johnny...how could you make me face this alone?

Through the doorway, she could just make out a suggestion of a form. A gray half-shape, a partial outline that looked oddly human. But small.

A child?

She moved further, her own steps like feathers brushing silk.

She dropped her cigarette and pushed the door open.

This one creaked.

The streetlight fed in through a threadbare curtain. The bed was unmade. The body of a woman was stretched out on it, naked from the waist up. Her breasts were mutilated, ravaged by dark gashes and scratching. But were nothing compared to the ruin of her throat.

A child stood on the other side of the bed, its face black with blood.

Lisa, an odd buzzing in ears, found the light switch and flicked it on.

The room exploded with brilliance.

The child...a toddler...screamed at the intrusion of light. Just a little girl, caked with blood, her eyes blazing with that malign pestilence. She cowered from the light. She tottered uneasily back and forth, a child who'd just learned the fine art of walking.

Lisa knew she should shoot her, but she didn't have the stomach for it.

The child was no real threat. Very small. Insane as all the others, but trapped in a far worse darkness somehow. A darkness the child could never hope to understand. The woman must have been her mother. The woman's breasts were riddled with teeth marks. The girl must have been breastfeeding in life...and in this living hell, she still was.

Lisa turned off the light and backed carefully from the room, shut the door behind her.

She heard the girl claw madly at the door, wrestling with the knob in futility. Then she began wailing again. Lisa knew she'd never forget that awful, pathetic sound. It rattled through her skull. She heard the little girl pad across the floor, heard the squeaking of bed springs...and then a congested sucking sound as she sought comfort at her dead mother's breast.

It wasn't until she was outside that Lisa began to cry.

And then Johnny was coming through the yard.

25

Lou approached the schoolyard carefully.

He still had the shotgun, but he didn't really know if it had any shot left. The idea of pausing and finding out was unthinkable.

As he moved around the chain-link fence and into the schoolyard itself, he kept an eye cast towards the river, watching for the woman, almost expecting she'd drag her blasted, dripping body after him. In his mind he could see her cadaverous face, the stagnant river water running from her wounds.

Enough.

He pressed himself up against the brick façade of the building.

It was damp and cool.

The school was single-story, spread out over the dark grounds like a spider, wings extending in every direction like limbs. He was in the back, facing the river the town was named for.

He could hear the flagpole rope out front dinging against the pole.

The entire rear of the school was enclosed by a high storm fence. Kept the kids away from the river, he supposed, and off the ice in the wintertime. He thought the school was probably newer—built in the last twenty, thirty years or so—and had probably replaced some ancient, stone monstrosity of the sort he'd attended back in the bronze age.

That made him think of his teachers and, soon enough, he thought about his third wife, Mara. Mara had been a schoolteacher. She was real good with oral exams...unfortunately, she wasn't real picky about who she gave them to.

But Lou didn't blame her. Not really.

He thought about all the women that had passed through his life. Not a single relationship had stuck for more than a few years. He was on the road all the time, but that wasn't the real problem: he was. He was the only constant in all those relationships, the only thing that could possibly be at blame.

It was funny how it took a situation like this, one of constant danger and stress, to make you finally see your life and the numerous holes you'd dug in it. What was murky and metaphysical before, now was crystal clear.

And didn't that just beat all?

He started moving again, considering his latest plan of action.

Johnny had said to wait for the sunrise and those things would slink back into their holes. That sounded like a plan.

Lou decided he needed to get up on the roof somehow.

He could wait it out up there. Maybe it was stupid and crazy and suicidal, but if he didn't rest soon...well, he was no kid anymore.

He kept going.

The dark windows looked at him like sullen, blind eyes. He saw no movement in them and didn't wait to see any. He made it to the end of the building, sucked in a breath and rounded the corner. He was in the playground now.

Feeling relieved, he walked right out into it.

And right into a nest of *them*.

And, of course, it made sense, didn't it?

Where else would they go but the playground? Not human, not anymore, but still the most basal of imperatives held: the need to play. Even beasts of the forests had that.

And so did the children of Cut River.

Lou felt hope and energy run out of him like water through a colander.

They were everywhere.

Their dark, waiting shapes were snipped from black paper. They were perched like vultures atop the jungle gym. Crowded on the merry-go-round and sitting on the swings—not swinging, just sitting there almost as if they'd been waiting for him.

And maybe they were.

Maybe they heard him coming, smelled him perhaps. Animals could do that and these children were animals now, weren't they?

As if satisfied by his presence, they began to play.

They started swinging, the chains holding the swing seats rattling against their crossbars. The merry-go-round began to turn. The teeter-totter began to move up and down, groaning and creaking in the night. It was surreal, like falling into a dream...or a nightmare.

He sensed motion behind him.

A small hand grasped his wrist. Its grip was surprisingly powerful. The flesh was cold, damp, feeling much like the pebbly skin of a freshly-plucked chicken.

With a cry, Lou turned, pulling his hand free.

There was a little girl standing there.

She was no more than seven, wearing a cute little party dress that was bunched up and stained with dirt. Her face was pallid, eyes like living yellow marbles. She leered at him, lips pulling away from teeth in a depraved grin. She pulled up her skirt. She wore nothing beneath. "Hey, mister," she seethed with that hissing voice, "you wanna fuck?"

And Lou, maybe terrified and maybe struck by the sheer profanity of it all, brought his hand back and slapped her across the face. She yelped like a kicked dog and fell over.

And that was the signal.

The others were coming now, sliding off their perches like crocodiles from the muddy banks of a jungle river.

And Lou was running.

He moved with a speed he thought had abandoned him in his twenties.

He sprinted around the front of the school and the first thing he saw were three yellow school buses parked at the curb. He turned and saw a boy making good time on him. He was older boy, maybe a sixth grader.

Without remorse, Lou went down on one knee and pulled the trigger of his shotgun. The buckshot nearly tore the kid in half.

As Lou got back to his feet, he saw that it had done just that. The kid was mewling like a sick cat. Divorced of his legs and pelvis, he was dragging his upper body across the grass, teeth still snapping.

Lou tried the door of the first bus.

Locked.

Their footfalls were pounding through the grass now.

The second bus.

Locked.

He turned and saw their ashen faces coming through the darkness.

A dead man now, he went to try the third bus and the door was standing wide open. He fell through it onto the small, mat-covered steps. He hauled himself in and threw himself towards the chrome lever by the driver's seat. He pulled it with everything he had and the folding door snapped shut.

And then they were all around the bus, howling and shrieking, the bus rocking as they threw themselves at it.

Lou was crouched on the floor, trembling.

It was about that time that he saw the guy in the driver's seat.

26

Ben was still alive, contrary to popular opinion.

He was still alive and he was still at the church. Yes, he was in bad shape—the rabids hadn't gone easy on him. He was bitten, clawed, scratched, his body a map of bruises and contusions and swollen cuts.

But he was very much alive.

Soon after the final members of Rawley's gang had been murdered, the rabids, leaving Ben for dead, had slipped back out into the night like shadows, back to the hunting grounds of Cut River.

Ben accepted certain things now.

They had bitten him and the germ, or whatever it was, was inside him now, too. He could feel it beginning to work. It didn't waste any time.

Maybe there was a certain clarity that came with knowing your end was imminent, but he believed everything Johnny had said. He hadn't been certain before—not one-hundred percent, even though, crazy as it sounded, it made perfect sense—but now, yes, he believed.

And conversion of faith had come at an expensive price.

This disease or what not was simply too insidious to be of natural origin or freakish mutation, it had been designed to do what it was doing...by assholes in white lab coats with no more compassion or respect for human life than terrorists planting a bomb in a hospital.

Maybe he was being too hard on them, but he didn't think so.

Like Johnny, he had lost all respect for the power brokers of this country.

But that was over now. Soon, it wouldn't be his problem.

He was in the dining room of the rectory of St. Thomas' Catholic Church. On the dining table, shrouded by a white sheet, was the form of his dead wife.

It was the result of a short cut. A quicker way home from the casino. It had cost the life of his brother-in-law Sam and now his wife, too. And before long, Ben himself.

He was alone.

The rabids had abandoned the church, dragging off the dead with them.

The church was silent.

Ben sat in a chair in the corner, the chandelier burning at a low setting. It had to be that way—Ben had an aversion now to bright light. A voice of optimism kept telling him he was just tired, but he knew better. There was a numbness in his fingertips. His limbs were trembling. Spastic convulsions ripped through him now and again. He was nauseous, feverish, his head aching. His throat was dry and constricted...but the idea of water made him violently ill.

He had the germ.

He was infected with Laughing Man.

It was inside him, working its malignant magic. Soon, soon...

He went to the table, drew the sheet from Nancy's still body.

Dear sweet Jesus my wife my wife oh God oh God oh—

He tightened his jaw, pressed his lips together. There was no time for emotional outbursts now. He would keep watch over her body until dawn, then he would kill himself. He had a big carving knife from the kitchen drawer.

Nancy's face looked compressed, eyes sunk deep into their sockets. She had a gray, mottled pallor, lips bloodless and flaccid. He lifted her again, checking for lividity. If she was truly dead, then her blood should have settled—but it hadn't. Rigor had not set in, either. Her limbs were supple and limp. But he could find no pulse, no heartbeat, no evidence of respiration.

And her flesh was cold.

Terribly cold like a body pulled from a frozen lake.

What did it all mean?

Is this how it happened? Some near-death coma, some bastard form of suspended animation or metabolic suspension occurred and then...and then...

He covered her.

She was dead. She had to be dead.

He sat back down, maintaining his deathwatch. There was a painting of the Last Supper on the wall. Nearby, a simple wooden crucifix. It made him think of horror movies he'd seen. Cadavers rising from the mist of death, being held at bay with religious symbols. But that was fiction, dark fantasy channeled with religious myth.

He sat in his chair, slumped forward.

Fatigue swept over him.

He kept drifting off, his limbs aching, his eyes heavy. The only thing that kept him from passing out were the convulsions that ripped through him at irregular intervals. Sweat poured in rivers from him...icy, sweet-smelling perspiration.

He drifted off again...then his eyes snapped open.

Something had changed.

He wasn't sure what, but something. Was it cooler in the room? And what was that smell, that whisper of raw decay? Maybe it was all in his imagination, maybe it was only in his dreaming brain.

He looked at the cross on the wall, mumbled some half-remembered prayer from childhood.

The hairs on the back of his neck were standing erect as if the air were crackling with some strange electrical discharge. Gooseflesh covered his arms, crept up his spine. He could smell something sharp, inexplicable, almost like ozone.

The sheet covering Nancy was trembling slightly. It was barely evident, but there...almost as if something was surging through her body.

Ben was shaking now.

Alone in this church, this huge empty silence, breathing and brooding. Alone with his wife.

He sat there, black horror dawning in him.

He stood up. He had to see, had to see...

The body under the sheet began to thrum with evil force. It writhed and thumped against the table as if were being electrocuted. Then it went still.

The air was heavy.

Nancy's arms slid out from under the sheet to either side, suddenly snapping stiffly erect. They rose up, the fingers splayed and shuddering as if with exertion. A ragged, hollow breathing came from beneath the sheet. She sat up slowly, wearing the sheet like cerements of the grave.

Her fingers twisted and played in the air.

Ben was shaking his head slowly side to side, telling himself there was an explanation for this, that it didn't mean she had come back from the dead. All around him he could feel dark shadows crawling like worms.

The sheet slid from Nancy's gray face.

A low, grating sound like an airless, wolfish growl came from the depths of her lungs and became a hissing, inhuman voice. "Ben...oh Ben...I'm better now, I'm better now..."

Her eyes, which had been closed, snapped open.

They were yellow hunting moons rising in that shadowy, pallid face. Slowly they swept the room, found Ben, fixed on him with a flat hunger. Her lips peeled back from even white teeth. She grinned like a rabid dog, tangles of ooze running from the corners of her lips.

Ben backed away, realizing with a bleak, godless terror that, yes, Nancy was indeed dead.

This thing was not his wife.

It only looked vaguely like her.

He kept moving back and fell over the chair.

Nancy flowed off the table with a smooth fluidic motion, one that a human being would have been incapable of. She found her feet, swayed uneasily for a moment like a heaving ship, then steadied herself.

Ben picked up the carving knife from the floor.

She saw it and snarled, lips pulling away from gnashing teeth. "Ben, Ben, Ben," she managed and it was slithering, wet sound; awful like the noise from a viper pit. Her face seemed to slide and undulate on the bones beneath, creeping with shadow. Her hands were held out to him, fingers wriggling like earthworms caught in sunlight.

He was on his feet then, ready to use the knife. "Nancy," he said, his voice more of a dry croaking than anything. "Please...just sit down."

Her eyes were polished glass, reflective like those of an animal as if some shining and invisible membrane had grown over them. Ben could see twin images of the haunted, broken man he now was in her gleaming saffron eyes.

"*Hold me, Ben,*" she said with a whisper of lonely places. "*Come to me, my lover.*"

But he would not.

Knife firm in his grip, he kept backing away.

She did not know him. She might have used his name, retained some instinctive memory that he was a friend, but it was only means to an end. She said his name in a mocking voice like a parrot.

"I don't want to hurt you," he warned her, "so please, just stay away."

Nancy abandoned the idea of humanity then.

She made a ghastly hissing sound like water thrown on a hot stove and went down low, stalking now like an animal. Rancid loops of drool hung from her chin, frothed from her lips, swung side to side with her creeping motion. Sounds came from her throat, insane barking noises.

"Nancy!" Ben shouted. "For the love of God, listen to me! I was your husband! Do you understand that? Do you know who I am? Who *you* are?"

But it was obvious she didn't and did not care.

Reasoning with her was like reasoning with some loathsome queen wasp, stinger bared. And she was much like that—cold and insectile and predatory, human in form only. Unblinking, her glaring eyes were fixed on him, shimmering with a glacial appetite. They were mirrors reflecting some dark and barren void.

She let out a chilling screech and launched herself at him with a frenzied, spidery motion.

Ben brought the knife down and sank an easy three inches of it into her left shoulder. He might as well have jabbed her with a toothpick. She was on him immediately, throwing him down with an easy flick of one white hand. She pinned him down effortlessly. Her face swam in with a wolfish grin, her breath like moldering canvas.

Ben screamed.

Her tongue was blackened and glistening. It played across his trembling lips, feeling cold and fleshy like wet leather. Clots of sour-smelling mucus rained into his mouth. He felt her slimy, frigid lips at his throat. And then her teeth, biting in deep, penetrating like needles.

And then all he was vanished in a cloistral fog.

All that he had been was no more, lost in a haze of thankful madness.

But from some distant room, he could hear the sound of her cackling.

And feeding.

27

"Pass me another one, baby," Ruby Sue said, reaching down into the GTO and getting another gas bomb from Joe. It was a simple creation—Blatz bottle filled with gasoline, tampon stuffed in its neck. She upended it, getting the tampon wet. She brought it up close to her nose, sniffed it.

Nothing like a little headrush.

What was it about gas that made you want to sniff it?

She flicked her Bic lighter, got the rag burning. "I see a target coming up."

They passed by a little video store and she threw it with everything she had at the window. The window shattered and so did the Molotov cocktail. The front of Northern Video went up in flames.

"Fucking yeah!" Ruby Sue screamed. "Fuck the world!"

Behind them, three or four other establishments were burning, flames licking from broken windows, plumes of black smoke rising over the streets.

It was all part of Joe's new plan.

Originally, what he had in mind was something like a front-end loader to smash their way through the barricade of cars and get the fuck out of Dodge. But they couldn't be wandering around Cut River on foot seeking it out, no more than a blind man was wise to wander around in a cellar filled with rattlesnakes.

When Joe saw the GTO, he knew he had to have it.

Ruby Sue was against the idea, thinking that driving around in a car would attract too much attention in a town where no one was driving. But after Joe hot-wired it and she heard the purr of that big block 400, she was a believer. Problem was, they couldn't find any front-end loaders. They found some bulldozers and backhoes at an excavating yard, but no front-end loader.

That's when Joe got the idea.

What they needed to do was to attract attention.

If they couldn't get out, then bring the people in. There were four or five gas stations in Cut River. Two of them were wide open and waiting. The others could be opened by the right guy. And if the town was burning...somebody would show up.

Besides, Joe figured they already had, what with those helicopters flying over—twice now—and that shooting coming from the north end.

Something was coming down.

Nothing like a little fire to bring rescue.

The GTO had a sunroof.

Not original equipment, but some crazy sonofabitch had decided to cut a hole in the roof of a classic. Joe showed his respect by tearing it off. It made a good bombing port for Ruby Sue.

"Hey, there's a credit union," Ruby Sue said, manning her lookout. "Those bastards turned me down for a loan. Let's do it."

Joe popped the curb, drove right across the lawn and Ruby Sue lit up two bombs and let them fly. The shadows retreated as huge balls of orange and red fire engulfed the side of the building.

"HOO YEAH!" she called out.

A trio of rabids were standing at the entrance of an alley, just watching.

She lit up another and heaved it in their direction.

A canvas of flame erupted mere feet from them and they ducked back into the shadows. She slid back into the car.

They'd hit an Amoco convenience store—wide open and empty—and helped themselves to four cases of Blatz and a few boxes of tampons. They dumped the warm beer out and filled the bottles at the pump. They were on their third case already. She looked out the rear window and saw the flickering glow of flames as the town went up.

"What we need is something quicker," Joe said, bringing the GTO around in a complete circle, sacrificing rubber.

This time they found a Citgo station.

Like most stations these days they sold everything from beer to broasted chicken. The electricity for the pumps was on, all four tiers of them, some sixteen pumps. Giggling, he turned on the hoses one after another, setting the latches so they would not shut off after he let them go. Before long, gasoline was flooding through the parking lot, into the streets. Oceans of it flowed through the grass flanking the lot, pooled around parked cars, and washed up to the station itself.

But the best thing was the tanker truck parked in back.

With any luck it was full.

Joe ran back to the GTO, splashing through the sea of gas.

Behind the wheel, he said, "Ready for some pyrotechnics, babe? Tonight be the night."

He brought the GTO out into the street and got within three, four feet of the nearest stream of gasoline.

"Man your position," he told Ruby Sue.

She did just that. She upended a firebomb and got the wick nice and wet. She lit it with her Bic and let it go. It crashed in the street, flames splashing in all directions. Joe saw the fire moving in a blazing yellow-orange wave towards the station.

"ROCK AND ROLL!" he shouted, stomping down on the accelerator and squealing out of there, the back of the GTO fishtailing wildly until he got it under control.

They were maybe a block away when night turned into day.

A vivid cloud of fire easily forty feet high rose above the rooftops. The explosion was so intense it actually jarred the GTO nearly off the road. The plate glass windows of storefronts shattered and a great surge of heat passed through the car making the chill September night feel like a July afternoon.

But it didn't end there.

More explosions followed as parked cars went one after the other.

Ruby Sue was hollering like a cheerleader.

But the really big one came next.

The tanker truck went maybe three, four minutes later. Thousands of gallons of gas went up with a deafening peel of thunder. Fireballs and black, rolling clouds of sooty smoke were sent skyward.

"Let's see 'em ignore this," Joe said.

He figured it was only a matter of time before the underground tanks tasted a flame or spark and went up in a blazing, explosive inferno—no doubt, taking a city block or two with them.

With that in mind, it made good sense to get the hell away from there.

"What now, babe?" Ruby Sue said. "We still got more bombs left."

Now that they were a good distance from the spreading inferno, Joe slowed down, navigating the dark streets. "No need. Not just yet. Let's just wait around now and see what develops. Something's gotta happen pretty soon. Half the county's gotta be wondering what in fuck just happened."

And when the underground tanks went up it would sound like Hiroshima all over again.

Ruby Sue was sucking on a cigarette, wishing she had some weed. Sitting sideways on the passenger side of the GTO, she watched the glow of the fire behind them. It painted the treetops red.

"You ever see that movie where those people are trapped in that burning skyscraper, Joe? It was awesome. Fire kept getting closer and closer. Shit, I hope we don't roast-up, man. That would suck."

Joe coasted slowly up a blacked-out street. "We're okay, we're...*what the fuck was that?*"

Something had thudded against the car.

"Something hit us," Ruby Sue said.

Thud.

"What—"

Then another thud right on top of the roof.

And then there was no time to discuss as a white arm snaked in through the sunroof and took hold of Ruby Sue by the hair, pulling her up towards the opening. She started screaming and thrashing, kicking out wildly and accidentally catching Joe in the ribs.

The GTO swerved crazily, thumped over a curb, barely missed a tree, and came back down in the street only to sideswipe a parked pickup truck in an eruption of sparks.

Ruby Sue was still shrieking, shoulders nearly drawn through the sunroof now, legs bicycling madly and striking the dashboard, popping open the glove compartment, and spinning the wheel from Joe's hands more than once.

"Joe, help me for god's sake! *Help me they got me oh shit oh shit—*"

Joe had hold of one leg and pulled with everything he had, yanking Ruby Sue maybe a foot or so back into the car so that he could just see her chin, but then, as if attached to a bungi cord, she sprang back up again.

"Cocksucker!" Joe spat, trying to reach behind him for the guns they'd lifted from the sporting goods joint. No dice. He got his hand on the butt of the Remington pump and then it fell behind his seat.

They were at the verge of a lighted neighborhood now.

He made it into the light and stamped on the brakes.

The GTO squealed to a halt, going sideways in the middle of the street, coughed and died.

Ruby Sue let go with a bellowing cry and dropped back into the car.

Her assailant—a thin man with a face white as putty, wearing a pair of jeans and nothing else, his bleached torso dark with what looked like ritual symbols panted in dried blood—slid down onto the hood, clinging there like some huge, bloodless beetle and started slamming his fists into the windshield. A few hairline cracks appeared almost instantly.

Joe tried in vain to get the engine to catch and smelled gas.

Jesus, I flooded her, I flooded her.

The rabid pressed his face to the cracked windshield, staring in at them with vapid eyes, the pupils dilated obscenely and glittering with a demonic yellow shine. He made a hissing, angry sound...or maybe it wasn't angry, because he knew he had them.

"Sonofabitch," Ruby Sue said as he leaped off the hood and landed in the street.

Joe threw his door open and the rabid was on him.

His fingers hooked into claws, he slashed at Joe's face. Joe sidestepped him and smashed him in the mouth with one meaty, broad fist. The rabid stumbled back in a daze, but did not go down.

Ruby Sue was out by then, on the other side of the GTO. "Hey, shit-fer-brains," she called out. "Over here."

The rabid turned towards her, a black grin on his dead white features.

She brought up the Browning .380 and pumped two rounds into him.

The first struck him squarely in the chest and spun him around in a complete circle. The second opened up a third eye in his forehead. Dark blood bubbled over his snarling face.

He screamed at her, bleeding profusely, but still on his feet.

He took one stumbling, drunken step forward, his hungry eyes scanning her like a cut of beef.

She shot him in the mouth and he went over stiffly, slamming flatly against the pavement. He twitched and flopped, making horrible gurgling sounds and going still.

Ruby Sue said, "Well, ain't that just the shits?"

Joe started laughing, amazed as always by her choice of words and her incredible durability in the worst possible situations. "We better let the car rest a minute," he managed. He turned and opened the back door to get his guns.

"Yeah, I'm for that," Ruby Sue said, studying the orange horizon as the fire spread. She sat on the curb, gun in her lap.

Joe turned his head slightly, hearing a roar, thinking maybe it was the fire.

But then knowing with a dread certainty it was not.

A car raced out of the darkness at them.

Lights off, it was on him before he could do much more than move a foot or two. Ruby Sue was on her feet, up against the GTO, mouth open, attempting to say something, but it was too damn late.

Joe saw a radiator grill winking at him like a silver eye.

And beyond it, a few white, grinning faces pressed to the windshield.

The impact was sudden and irresistible, the black Lincoln traveling at well over seventy miles an hour. Joe was sandwiched momentarily between the front end of the Lincoln and the open door of the GTO.

But only momentarily.

The hinges snapped free and Joe and the driver's side door were dragged fifty feet in a shower of sparks and smoking flesh before they went tumbling across the pavement.

The Lincoln continued along, swerving frantically from side to side, seeming to pick up speed. It crossed an intersection and leaped a curb, slamming into a stout oak with a screech of twisted metal and shattering glass.

It came to rest there, nearly ripped in half, the front end crushed back into the driver's compartment. The hood was detached and driven through the windshield. There was a stink of gas and it went up in flames. Not a dramatic movie explosion this, but a gentle, almost casual engulfment by flame.

The impact of the Lincoln striking the GTO had sent Ruby Sue careening to the street. Her head smacked the curb and her left wrist was twisted sickly beneath her body. Moments later—her face smeared with red from a gash in her head and her left arm clutched limply at her side—she was on her feet, stumbling up the road.

Joe was lying in a tangled heap, blood pooling out from him.

The air was ripe with the stench of scorched metal and flesh.

He was moaning.

Alive, but just.

28

They were throwing themselves against the bus.

The progeny of Cut River, the children of the night.

But with the bi-fold door safely locked down and the emergency hatch in the back only accessible from the inside, Lou wasn't worrying about them. Not yet. When the evil bastards started busting through the windows, *yes*, but not right now.

He was staring at the guy in the driver's seat.

He felt a wave of gooseflesh go up his back. If he'd have been a cat, he would've raised his hackles. He'd made a good run of it, found safety here...and now this.

Shit.

He kneeled there on the floor of the rocking bus, breathing, trembling, waiting for the moonish face of the driver to turn towards him, look at him with hollow eyes.

But it did not happen.

Because the guy was dead.

Lou prodded him with the barrel of the shotgun and he slid down further in the seat.

Dead, all right.

Lou muttered something about it not being personal and pulled him unceremoniously from behind the wheel. He slumped over and fell onto the steps, his face mashing against the door window. This drove the children outside into a veritable feeding frenzy. They began fighting for space at the door, licking and biting at the glass, trying to dig through it with their fingers.

The keys were in the ignition.

The seat and wheel were sticky with what Lou figured was old blood. The driver must have slit his wrists or throat.

Sweating profusely, barely able to keep his fingers steady, Lou turned the key.

The bus roared into life.

The gauges lit up and told him he had half a tank. He pushed down on the clutch and threw the shift lever into gear, pressing down gently on the accelerator and easing off the clutch. Last thing he needed was for the bus to stall.

It began to move.

He gave it some gas and most of the rabids fell away from it.

Others clung like leeches and still others (he could hear) were clinging to the roof.

No matter now.

He kept shifting gears until he was doing an easy forty-five miles an hour, speeding through what passed for an industrial sector in Cut River. He veered wildly from side to side, throwing off the little monsters. But there were still more on the roof, banging and screeching.

A white hand snaked down from over the driver's cabin and took hold of a wiper blade, snapping it off like a twig.

In five minutes, Lou made Chestnut, the main drag.

He took the corner barely bothering to slow down until he was into the turn, then riding the brake for all it was worth. He popped a curb, smashed a little Ford Escort out of the way, knocked a STOP sign over, and thudded back into the street, the bus careening unpleasantly to one side like maybe it was going to roll over. But it didn't.

In the rearview, he could see that he'd shed the remaining children.

He could see them crab-crawling off into the darkness.

Breathing a sigh of relief, he slowed down.

Shotgun at his side, he felt kind of like Dirty Harry in that one movie, plowing through the streets in his bus. Rabids popped out from behind parked cars from time to time, but scattered when he veered towards him. After awhile, he saw none, so he turned onto a side street looking for victims like a teenager trying to run down dogs or squirrels.

It was about that time that he heard a series of explosions and saw the eastern side of town light up with fireballs rolling above the treeline. Whether it was to his benefit or not, he let out a battle cry as the glow of flames not only didn't die down, but raged with new life.

He'd heard gunfire off and on for some time now.

But what was this?

Had the Marines landed and called in an airstrike? The image of canisters of napalm incinerating Cut River made him grin ferociously.

That'll put those rabids on the run.

His hi-beams illuminating the blackened streets, he saw rabids everywhere, hiding and skulking and sticking to the shadows. Only a few dared cross his path. Maybe it was the bus they were afraid of and maybe it was just the headlights.

He heard more explosions as he tooled around an avenue of brooding, dark houses and that's when he saw two figures coming right up the middle of the street, waving their arms wildly.

Jesus, it couldn't be.

Not again.

He slowed down and yes it was!

He skidded to a halt.

Johnny Davis and Lisa Tabano.

They came up to the folding door, weapons drawn. He took a good look at them before he pulled the lever and opened the door. He wanted to be sure their eyes were normal.

They were.

He opened the door.

Johnny leapt in, sticking a .30-06 in his face, then withdrawing it. "You?" he said, dumbfounded. "What in the hell are *you* doing alive?"

Lou shook his head. "I'm too pretty to die."

Lisa dragged herself in and Lou shut the door behind her.

"We gotta stop meeting like this," he told her.

She laughed or tried to...but hell, she looked like ten miles of bad road. She smiled grimly and tossed him a pack of cigarettes, then collapsed into a rear seat.

Lou took them, lighting one up, wondering, though, if she'd been infected.

Johnny and he looked at each other and Johnny shook his head. "No," he said, reading his mind, "it's not that."

Lou saw figures creeping from the shadows and got the bus going again. And while he did that, Johnny told him yet another story. Except this one was about a certain rock star with a particularly bad habit.

Lou exhaled a column of smoke, keeping the bus under twenty-five to save fuel. "You mean...you mean like a...a..."

"*Junkie*," Lisa said in a croaking, broken voice. "That's me."

He supposed it didn't matter.

It wasn't any of his damn business...except, Christ, she looked rough. A bag of bones topped by tangled mess of long, dark hair. Even her breathing seemed ragged. She hugged herself back there, rocking back and forth. He had to wonder if infection by the Laughing Man germ could really be any worse than heroin withdrawal.

He searched for words, finally found them. "If we can get our asses out of here, Lisa, we can get you to a hospital. They have things, I bet, that would make it easier."

She said nothing. Her chin was resting on the seat before her, her eyes shining dimly in the dark.

Johnny said, "First we have to get out."

Lou nodded. "Exactly what I've been thinking about. You know that barricade of cars? What do you say the chances are of us ramming through it with this rig?"

Johnny considered it. The green dash lights winked off his bald head. "I'd say maybe it'll work." He shrugged. "And if not, beats the living shit out of sitting here doing nothing."

"How about you, Lisa?" Lou asked. "You concur?"

She mumbled in assent.

That was that then.

Lou pulled a U-turn, plowing through a few yards and taking out some rose bushes and a few withering flowerbeds. Off in the darkness, he could see the ever-present eyes of their silent witnesses. A few minutes later, he was moving up Chestnut.

"I suggest everyone hang on now," he told them.

Lisa crouched down between the seats.

Johnny stayed next to Lou, putting down his rifle and clutching the chrome handbar with everything he had.

"There's gonna be a jailbreak," Lisa said in a low, tortured voice, an old Thin Lizzy song echoing in her brain.

"Lot of steel in this bitch. But she's light, rolls easy," Johnny said, more to himself than the others.

Lou navigated his way up Chestnut, leaving the way he'd originally come in. The bus was doing fifty by the time he passed his little Grand Am parked at the curb, doors wide open. At sixty the bus started to rattle a bit. The steel floor plating began to vibrate and it went right through their feet and up into their bones.

"Keep it there," Johnny said over the noise of the engine. "She ain't made for too much speed. Fifty, sixty's plenty. If there's no heavy metal in that barricade—big trucks, heavy equipment and the like—we'll smash right through. Those sonsofbitches'll never stop us."

Half a block from the barricade, they could see lights.

But these were not the flickering, burning lights of bodies being roasted. These were electric lights—from vehicles, from searchlights. Closer they got, they could see now that the barricade had been pushed aside.

"What the hell is this?" Lou said. "The army?"

"Slow down," Johnny said with an air of urgency.

"What—"

"Slow the fuck down!" Johnny snapped. "*Now!*"

He was up at the dash, face to the windshield, checking out what they were driving into and not liking it one bit. Beams from searchlights played over the bus, blinding him.

Lou downshifted and brought the bus to a crawl.

"Turn around," Johnny said. "Right now."

Lou was going to ask him why in the hell he should do that when he heard the popping of automatic weapons. The front of the bus was grazed by bullets. Two or three holes appeared in the windshield.

"Sonofbitch!" he said, wheeling the bus around in a huge, rocking circle and coming back onto the street again.

The bus was filled with light now.

A vehicle was coming up fast behind them. It looked to be some sort of assault vehicle. More bullets slammed into the back of the bus. There was a gun mounted on the approaching vehicle.

Lou saw fire belching from it.

The rounds that struck the bus didn't ricochet off this time, they ripped right through the metal. Suddenly, the bus was full of flying lead and shattering glass, bits of metal spraying around like shrapnel. They were firing a machine gun at them. There was no doubt of that. Slugs were ripping through the seats, tearing into the dashboard. The windshield took a volley and collapsed into itself, a sheet of safety glass fell into Lou's lap.

He got the bus going—forty, fifty.

The bullets still rained down on them. One of them burst through his shoulder, another grazed his leg.

He cried out and pushed down on the accelerator.

The pursuing vehicle fell behind.

"We're losing 'em!" Johnny called out.

The vehicle—Lou was pretty sure it was a Hummer, like the troops had used in Iraq—was falling behind now. He figured it was on purpose, as if the troops weren't allowed to chase them beyond a certain point.

He was driving with one hand now, his left arm numb from shoulder to wrist.

He was bleeding profusely.

More searchlights played over them now. These from above.

"Helicopter!" Johnny said.

Lou could heard the rapid thunk-thunk of its rotors as if it were right on top of them. There was a sudden flash of light and the street ahead of them exploded, air-to-surface rockets blowing great chunks of road into fragments.

He knew what came next.

He saw the plate glass front of a department store and spun the wheel.

The bus rocked over the curb, took out two parking meters in a spray of pennies, and went right through the front of the store. Shards of glass and wood exploded in the air. Mannequins were dismembered. Lawn furniture was turned to kindling. A display of gas grills was sent airborne. The bus rammed through a counter, coughed, jerked, and died.

Lou was hurting.

Not only his shoulder and leg now, but his face and arms which were a mass of tiny, innumerable cuts from flying bits of glass. He'd managed to shield his eyes, though. And they were about the only thing that didn't hurt.

Johnny pulled himself from the floor, scraps of glass and wood rained off him. "Everyone okay?" he said.

"Yeah, I'll live," Lisa sighed.

Lou dragged himself from behind the wheel, a mannequin arm wearing a cheap, flashy bracelet slid from his lap. "I'm hit," he said to them.

Johnny said, "How bad?"

Lou told him.

"You'll survive."

"Gas," Lisa said. "I smell gas."

They all did. It was getting stronger by the moment.

Johnny helped Lisa to her feet. "They must've got the tank. Everybody out. Right fucking now!" He found his rifle and Lou's shotgun, took them with.

Bruised and battered and bleeding, they helped each other from the bus, wading through the wreckage of the department store. Carefully, quiet as they could be with glass crunching under foot, they stepped out into the street. The chill night air stank not only of gasoline, but of cordite and smoke.

They could see the glow of the expanding fire in the east.

They hobbled up the block

They ducked into an alley and collapsed there, waiting.

The helicopter did not return. The pilot must've figured (wrongly) that he'd hit the bus, sent it careening into the storefront. They could still hear gunfire, occasional booming explosions.

"What the fuck's wrong with those bastards?" Lou wanted to know. He slipped a cigarette between his lips and Lisa lit it with badly trembling hands.

She shook violently, pulled in a ragged breath. "Maybe...they think we're rabids."

Johnny was watching the streets. "I don't think it matters to them by this point," he said grimly. "I don't think those boys are from a conventional unit. Some sort of emergency response group, a containment unit, NBC. Sort of troopers that are trained to crush and quarantine an area in the wake of a biological or chemical attack."

"So we're fucked?" Lou said.

"Maybe. As far as they're concerned, we're all infected. Whether this whole clusterfuck was on purpose or by accident doesn't matter now. Nobody's coming out of here. They can't have that."

Lou shook his head. "They can't get away with that."

"Sure they can. They've been planning and preparing for an emergency like this for years."

"The media, though," Lisa said. "If they get a hold of this..."

Johnny smiled. "And they will, but they'll only learn what the feds want them to know. Cut River? Attacked by terrorists, maybe. Militias. Some bullshit like that. We can only be sure of one thing—they'll have every eventuality covered."

"They can't. It's too big."

Johnny shook his head. "They do it every day, Lisa. Every time you hear about a a political scandal or an act of terrorism...you can be sure that what you are told and what *really* happened are not the same thing. Perception management. That's why nine out of ten people surveyed prefer bullshit. It makes it easier to sleep at night."

Lou grunted. "Johnny is like our own Jesse Ventura."

"It must be spooky in your head," Lisa said.

"You have no idea," Johnny said. "I've seen things that would turn your hair white. If we had the time, I'd tell you what *really* was behind Watergate."

Lou found it easy enough by this point to accept everything Johnny said. He didn't argue. "We have to contact the outside world," he said. "That's what we have to do."

Johnny shook his head. "No phones. Even if some were working, they'd cut the lines. They've isolated us, people. They won't let us out. Even CBs and Ham radios will be jammed, I bet."

Then Lou thought of it. "The municipal building. The police cruisers there. They have radios."

Johnny was going to object, but didn't. "Damn straight," he said. "Even if we don't make it out, we can broadcast, tell the world what's going on here." He seemed very happy suddenly. After all these years, he'd finally found a way to fuck the government that had fucked him.

They made their way out into the streets.

The municipal building was about a half mile from them, they could see its cyclopean girth squatting on the hill, overseeing the entire town. It was a long way in a warzone, but it was the only way.

"Let's do it," Johnny said.

29

"Oh my God...oh Christ..."

Ruby Sue was kneeling next to Joe.

A bloody smear marked his progress to this unremarkable spot on the street, his deathbed. His face had been scraped clean of meat from the friction. He had died only a few moments before, living long enough to tell her he was sorry about it all, bringing her here.

And now, he was dead. Crushed and broken.

She trembled in the night. First with terror and loss and violation, then with rage. "I'll get 'em, baby," she told Joe's raw face. "I'll make those sonsofbitches pay for this."

His corpse was unconcerned.

Warmth bled from it into the cool September air. He had finally found a way out of the asylum that was Cut River. He was at peace.

Ruby Sue kissed his dead face, her own washed by tears.

Something in her had died with Joe.

What was left was hard and mean and pissed-off. Her left wrist was sprained, she figured, but her right was just fine. She was scraped and bleeding, but very much alive. Back at the car, she got her Browning .380 and stuck it in her coat pocket. She took Joe's Colt Python and left the shotgun behind.

Then she went to kick some ass.

She walked towards Chestnut. A pair of rabids—teenage boys, hideous imitations of the same—came at her slithering and snapping their jaws. She killed both of them and continued on.

The town was burning, gunfire everywhere.

Much of it was very close now.

She hid behind a row of bushes as a group passed.

But they weren't rabids.

Soldiers dressed out in white hooded suits. The sort guys wore on TV when there was a nuclear accident or something. They looked like invaders from Mars. They were all carrying M-16s except for the guy in the back who had tanks strapped to him, a short pipe in his grip.

She was just willing to bet it was a flamethrower or something.

She let them pass and continued on.

The air was thick and acrid with rolling black smoke now as the fires she and Joe had set ate up the town.

Gunshots.

Just ahead.

She cut between two houses and saw a group of rabids (ten or more) assault a squad of soldiers. Lead was flying in every direction, but still the rabids came on, smothering the soldiers with their superior numbers. She saw white suits being shredded, heard screaming and enjoyed it all maybe too much.

A lone solider, weaponless now, was encircled by rabids, mostly women. He was pressed against a brick wall, a solid line of them approaching him. He tried to climb the wall, ran to the left, the right.

Slowly, inexorably, they pressed in, making awful hissing sounds, hands held out before them.

Ruby Sue watched until his screams subsided and then slipped away into the night.

A pack of rabids found her on Chestnut.

She faced them fearlessly.

They tried to ring her in and she squeezed off shots with the Browning semi-auto until they were all down. Then she used the .357 on them. Most were dead, but a few were only gutshot, crawling at her through tangles of their own viscera.

She left them like that. Let them suffer.

In the distance, she saw the municipal building.

She remembered Lou telling her that was where the police were headquartered. She had one speedloader left for the Colt, about eight rounds for the Browning. She would need more ammo before she was done.

Eyes fixed and determined, she made her way towards the towering building.

The night was still young.

Plenty of darkness to kill by.

-GENOCIDE-

30

They made it maybe thirty feet into the rambling confines of the municipal building when one of the crazy bastards came stumbling out of the shadows to meet them.

Lou and Lisa hung back while Johnny faced the psycho dead-on.

Something he didn't mind too much, considering he'd gotten his shotgun back now.

The rabid was a big, ugly man that could've passed for Joe's twin brother, save that he was balding and beardless. He was shirtless, wearing stained jeans and rubber boots. There was something almost profane about that jiggling mountain of ashen flesh before them. Drool hung from his chin like stalactites. He had something in his filthy right fist that at first looked like a club but upon closer inspection could be nothing but a human femur, dyed dark with old blood. A cord of gristle hung from the hip ball.

"I've been waiting all night, friend," the flabby, leering monstrosity said. "What took you so long?"

Johnny shook his head.

He hated the idea of shooting this creature, repellent though he was; he started busting caps all over and everyone and everything would know right where to find them. He had high hopes they could do what he had in mind covertly.

But the rabid came on, swinging the thigh bone.

Johnny stood his ground and gave him a burst to the belly.

The rabid stumbled back three, four feet, but did not go down. There was a huge, smoking crater where his belly had been. Intestines—what was left of them—trailed out like burnt sausages. He reached in there with one shaking hand, rooted around in his abdomen, brought his hand back out. It was dark with blood and cinders of flesh.

His raging yellow eyes never left Johnny.

A good deal of his anatomy had been sprayed against the marble wall behind him. With a crazy, agonized smile, he shambled forward, bone raised high to strike.

Johnny stepped back now, a cold terror in his belly.

He racked the pump and aimed for the guy's head.

He pulled the trigger.

It blew away the left side of the guy's face, leaving a ruin of blistered meat, tendrils of smoke puffing from the bleeding cavity. He made it two, three steps and pitched over face-first, limbs still attempting locomotion.

"C'mon," Johnny told the others in an airless voice.

They passed a bank of elevators and then paused before a set of steps climbing into the darkness. There was a body sprawled near the bottom. A naked woman.

Johnny approached her carefully, nudged her with his combat boot.

A surge of panic rode through him as she began to move, but it was only gravity, he saw, her body tumbling down the last few steps onto the floor. Her chest was riddled with bullet wounds, the trail of blood—still wet—glistened on the steps. Somebody must've shot her (and with an automatic weapon, judging by the pattern of wounds) and she dragged herself down the steps and died near the bottom.

Nothing spooky about that.

Johnny started up.

"Shouldn't we try the police station?" Lou suggested, clutching the wound in his shoulder Johnny had bandaged with strips of rags. "It might be worth a shot."

Lisa licked her lips, shook violently. "I thought...I thought you said the place was trashed?"

"Maybe I overlooked something."

Johnny shook his head. "You didn't. It won't do us any good. Even if we found a working radio, we couldn't transmit. It would be just like the radios in the cruisers. That army out there, they're jamming everything. They don't want any messages getting out."

Lisa and Lou didn't argue with that.

They both remembered how Johnny had tried in vain to raise the outside world with one of the radios in a parked police car and had gotten nothing but static.

Isolated. Contained. That's what they were.

They submitted. They both knew what Johnny's alternate plan was and it was as good as any. Make for the roof. It was defensible. Lock themselves up there and wait for dawn.

At least that's what he told them.

His real plan was only slightly different in that it had something to do with a glorious death.

He led them up through the darkness, his bald head gleaming with sweat.

Go slow, he told himself. *There's probably rabids everywhere. And there might be soldiers, too. You run into a group of them and you're all dead.*

So he moved slowly, quietly up the steps, knowing he had only two rounds left in his shotgun and they were valuable. More priceless than gold now.

They made it to the second floor, or Johnny did.

Lou and Lisa waited on the stairs. The second floor was much like the first, dimly lit, corridors snaking this way and that, studded with doors.

Johnny waved them forward.

He kept the 12-gauge before him, the stock greasy beneath his sweating fingers. He rounded a corner, coming down low. There were a few bodies sprawled on the floor. Dead rabids, a man and a woman. They were both naked. Looked like they'd been fucking when the soldiers found them. Their bodies were riddled with bullet holes. Brass shell casings littered the floors.

The rabids were tough.

They could take shit that would have killed normal people five times over. But, still, this many rounds spent on these two was a real waste. Johnny could see those soldiers in his mind, spraying down the copulating rabids on full auto. He'd seen plenty of that in Vietnam—cherries, newbies, spending magazine after magazine when two, three well-directed bursts would have done the job quite nicely.

It told him something about these troops.

Either they were scared shitless or inexperienced.

He figured it was probably both.

Okay, keep going.

He led the other two past the bodies. A few offices were lit up, light spilling into the hallway. He didn't like that—either the lights had been left on or somebody had turned them on.

The latter was a possibility he didn't care for.

Why he didn't see the guy squatting in the doorway of the dark office was beyond him. In the old days, the guy would have been dead. But tonight Johnny had walked practically right up on him. He didn't even notice him until he'd seen the gleam of metal from the rifle barrel.

Johnny went down low, bringing the shotgun to bear.

"Don't even think about it, motherfucker," the guy said. "You touch that trigger, I cut you all down."

And that was what stopped Johnny.

His finger touched the trigger, then retreated.

He knew he could grease the guy...but he didn't want Lou and Lisa paying the price for it. So he let the shotgun down, knew that they were at the mercy of this sonofabitch. Good thing was, his eyes were normal. They didn't shine at all. If rabids started using guns, the jig was up.

"Come in here," the guy said. "It's cool."

They filed into the office, sat next to each other on the floor in front of a big desk. It was just a typical office—desks, filing cabinets, computers, water cooler in the corner.

The guy stayed in the doorway.

With the moonlight flooding in through the big windows in the rear, they could see him well enough. He was one of the soldiers. He had a white protective suit on, sans hood. Some young white guy, early twenties maybe, narrow face, crewcut.

"I ain't gonna shoot you," he said. "You're the first normals I've seen in an hour. Creepers are everywhere, man. Them bastards'll eat your ass for breakfast soon as look at you. If they don't fuck you first."

"What's your name?" Johnny asked.

"Johnson...*nah*, fuck that, name's Tony Terra. You?"

They introduced themselves.

"Why'd you say Johnson?" Lou wanted to know.

He laughed at that, plugged a little cigar in the corner of his mouth, lit it. "Smoke 'em if you got 'em," he said. "Not supposed to, you know. Smoke, that is. Creepers can see in the dark like fucking cats. They can smell body heat. That's what they told us. A cigar? A cigarette? Like a bonfire to those animals. But, fuck it, right?" He dragged off his cigar, blew smoke into the shadows. "Reason I said *Johnson*, man, was because we all got code names, you see? Smiths and Johnsons and Browns and Blacks—you get the idea. Must be a hundred Johnsons. I was Johnson-12, see? We never knew each other's names. That's the way this shit works."

Lou said, "You're in the army?"

"Yes and no. I was part of the force, man. ERG. That's Emergency Response Group. My battalion is one of dozens, so they say. Some shit comes down, we're trained to contain it. We don't take our orders from the army, though." He laughed. "Nobody knows *who* we take our orders from. Ain't that a rush?"

Lisa was moaning, her body shuddering with spasms.

Terra was keeping an eye on her. "She infected?"

Johnny assured him she wasn't. "She's coming down from her drug habit."

"Junk?" Terra said. "Yeah, my brother was on that shit. Bad news."

"What the hell happened here?" Lou asked, lighting a cigarette.

Terra shrugged. "I ain't supposed to say. We're not even supposed to talk to civilians. We're supposed to consider 'em all infected and shoot 'em dead. Jesus H. Christ. I trained for this— nuclear, biological, chemical, NBC—for the past three years. But, oh shit, none of us ever thought—fuck, man." He cradled his head between his knees, sobbed. Sighing, he looked at them. "They told us there was an outbreak. We thought it was another goddamn drill, a war game. But it was real. They told us an unfriendly foreign power had dumped some germs on this little town. I don't even know what fucking state I'm in!"

"You're in Michigan," Johnny said. "It's okay now, pal. Just tell us."

Terra sat there silently for a moment, rolling the cherry of his cigar across the sole of his boot. "So, we were sent here to contain this mess, see that it didn't spread. But, holy shit, those creepers...like zombies or vampires or something straight out of them horror movies, right? They don't die easy." He licked his lips, looking close to a breakdown. "We came in three, four hours back, surrounded the town. We came in by helicopter—all of us. Even the hummers and equipment came in by air. They started sending in recon teams right away, but none of 'em came back. Once we were deployed, they broke us into platoons and told us to kill everyone. Even the kids, the *babies*." He started crying for real now. "All the little kids are monsters...oh, oh, oh, Jesus...we were shooting down toddlers. Oh Christ in Heaven, I'm gonna burn in Hell, I'm gonna burn in Hell..."

Johnny went to him, put an arm around him. "No, you're not. People who created this stuff, let it loose on this town, yeah, they're going to burn."

It took Terra about five minutes to compose himself. "Okay, I'm all right. I'm cool. They told us to kill everyone. No exceptions. It's what we were trained to do, so we did it. When we were done, we were to burn this town to the ground. Nothing could be left." He motioned towards the window, the orange glow reflected on the glass. "Somebody already started that, though."

Johnny thought it all through and still had questions. "Did they tell you what it was? What these people are contaminated with?"

He shrugged. "A virus of some kind. Spread by bites, body fluids. Supposed to be some shit they engineered from the rabies virus. Agent-X. That's what they said. But there were rumors..."

"Yeah?"

Terra started talking in a whisper now. "Fucking-A. Guys have been saying that it ain't fucking terrorists or any of that shit, they're saying it's *us*. Saying we created it. That we used it—"

"In Vietnam?"

Terra looked like he'd been slapped. "How the hell you know that?" He looked concerned.

"I was in Vietnam," Johnny told him. "I saw what it did there. We called it *Laughing Man* because it drove people stark crazy. They told us it was a defoliant. But nobody bought it. We saw what that garbage did. My team got infected."

Terra nodded, patting Johnny's knee. "Yeah. My platoon, man, creepers wiped 'em all out...downstairs. Motherfucker. I got away, hid out." His face looked like it had been sculpted from sallow wax. "Rumor says they developed it back then, but they shelved it for further study. Then, I don't know, while back they pulled it out of the freezer and started refining it or something."

The ash on Lou's cigarette was an inch long. It fell onto his lap. "Why did they spray it here? What the hell were they thinking?"

"Guys were saying it wasn't on purpose. An accident or something," Terra told him.

Johnny felt suddenly vindicated.

After all these years of bullshit and denial, it had all come full circle now. There was no getting around the truth any longer. Oh, sure, they'd kill everyone and burn the town down, but the truth would come out...eventually.

In one form or another.

There would be too many questions.

"Why don't you come with us?" Johnny asked Terra. "We're making for the roof. We're gonna hide out until dawn."

"Yeah, fucking vampires, they don't like the sunlight. They told us that much." Terra looked half out of his mind. "I can hear the boys out there, can't you? Boom, bang, boom. Mopping up this here burg. Fucking right. Flamethrowers and everything. Shit yeah. They go crazy when you crisp 'em, creepers do. Start jumping around and trying to fight the flames. Sometimes, they don't even give a shit that they're burning—they come right at you. Then you gotta pop 'em. Pop 'em and drop 'em. Blood and bodies and brains. I'm covered in it. Fuck if I ain't."

Johnny led the others back out into the corridor.

Terra took up the rear, with Johnny in front, the others in the middle.

"Let's be careful out there," Terra said and started giggling. He pulled something out of the ammo pouch slung around his shoulder. He hung it over his neck.

A necklace of human ears.

31

"Stone-two?"

"Johnson-four?"

"Smith-Seventeen?"

Silence. Maybe a minute, maybe two.

"Where the fuck are you guys?"

From where she hid, Ruby Sue was hearing it all.

Unlike the others, she'd come into the municipal building from the back. She'd slipped through the rear courtyard and waded through dozens of dismembered corpses dressed in red protective suits that had once been sparkling white. She'd didn't spend too much time studying the fallen soldiers, just long enough to know they were dead, to see that they'd been mutilated, partially devoured.

Now she was in the garage.

But she wasn't alone.

On the other side, hidden by the looming hulk of a fire truck were the soldiers. They sounded panicked and with good reason: most of their comrades had been wiped out, apparently by a large force of rabids.

Ruby Sue was crouched behind a pump truck.

The garage was huge and shadowy, lit dimly by emergency lights and moonlight seeping through tall windows set along the far wall. There were two fire trucks in there, a half dozen other city vehicles...not to mention the bodies of other soldiers, sprawled and twisted in heaps along the concrete floor. There was one a few feet away from her. He was missing his left arm and his protective hood had been ripped off, his face meticulously stripped down to the skull beneath. The grinning death mask watched her, but offered no suggestions.

What to do?

She waited there and contemplated it.

Her original mission had been to kill as many rabids as she could. Payback for Joe. Now she was starting to wonder who the real enemy was here.

She could hear the soldiers whispering amongst themselves.

She had to wait until they moved; the state they were in, they'd shoot anything they saw.

Not good.

About ten minutes later, she saw them crawl up towards the front of the garage, moving beneath vehicles on their bellies like lizards. They were uncomfortably close when they re-grouped.

"There's only four of us," a voice said. "That's all."

"We had thirty guys here," another said, his voice breaking with stress. "They...they can't all be dead."

"Why the hell not?"

"Shit."

"Don't be such a pussy. This is what you trained for."

"Oh, for fuck's sake."

"Lock and load. Let's do this. We don't have a choice."

"The radio—"

"Piss on that," the first voice said. "We're transmitting, but they're not receiving. Stupid pricks are jamming the secure channel, too."

"I knew this would happen."

Ruby Sue was grinning at the exchange.

It was somehow satisfying to see the military hamstrung by the situation, too. If Johnny was right, they had created it, so let them suffer along with the rest. It was only fair, wasn't it?

She crept towards the front of the truck, bare inches now from the dead soldier. She looked down at the raw meat of his face glistening in the moonlight. It didn't bother her; nothing seemed to bother her anymore. There was something lying by his side. Something dark and shiny. She touched it. Metal.

Jesus, it was his rifle. His M-16.

Carefully, she picked it up.

She'd never fired one before. It was remarkably light, fitted with a bayonet. The barrel was short and ribbed, the magazine jutting from beneath banana-shaped. She stuck her Colt in the other pocket of her jean jacket. The soldiers were standing up now, approaching a door which read EXIT in glowing red letters.

Breathing hard now, more out of fear and apprehension than any exertion, she moved soundlessly to the front of the pump truck. She aimed at the silhouettes, no easy task with her sprained left wrist. They were still arguing as to whether they should go into the building proper or escape out the back way.

"I got a better idea," she said under her breath.

She pulled the trigger.

The M-16 came alive in her hands, the bullets going everywhere but where she'd aimed them. The rocking motion of the rifle sent knives of pain into her damaged wrist. But then, in a split second, beyond pain, she had the rifle under control, pressing the stock into her shoulder where it rode easily. Shell casings rained in the air.

The soldiers instinctively went down low, but not fast enough.

They were clumsy in their spaceman suits.

She hit two of them and then a third as he opened fire in her direction, taking out his aggression and terror on the windshield of the pump truck. He screamed as bullets ripped through his face shield. The last soldier tried to scramble away, but she shot his legs out from under him. He screamed and started shooting in every direction.

By then, she was on the other side of the vehicle.

She drew a bead on the solder's head and let go with another burst. He went down face-first.

She waited then.

She could hear one or two of them moaning, whimpering, begging for help.

Here comes your fucking help.

She walked over to them, nearly slipping on all the brass scattered over the floor. She couldn't see their faces in the hoods, but she could see that there was no way they could get to their rifles. And that was the most important thing.

One of the soldiers held bloody, gloved hands out to her.

She swatted them away with the barrel of her 16. "Welcome to the jungle," she told him and rammed the bayonet into his chest continually until he quit writhing and screeching and her arms were sore and his blood was spattered over her in a fine, coppery mist.

She took the man's rifle and slung it over her shoulder.

He had some sort of ammo pouch with him. In it were three smooth-bodied grenades and two others shaped like blunt cylinders. She shouldered the sack, stuffed her pistols in there and some more magazines for the M-16s. It was heavy by then and bulging, but she was ready for war.

She stepped into the corridor on the other side of the fire door.

It was empty.

Too bad. She liked using her new rifle. Liked the way it put out the rounds. She wished Joe were here, though. For many reasons, of course, but mainly because he'd been in the service and he knew how to load these things.

She supposed she'd figure it out, though.

The walls were cement block painted an ugly piss yellow. She went through the first doorway she found and into a bank of offices. Fluorescents were on overhead. A few of them, anyway.

The rabids had been through here.

There was no doubt of that. Desks were overturned, computers shattered into plastic shards, phones ripped from walls. The floor was littered with papers and file folders.

She found a cell phone, but all she got was static on it.

She moved to the end and around a corner. More of the same. A framed sepia photo of the municipal building, probably taken back in the 1920s or '30s was shattered on the floor. It looked like somebody had vomited on it. The only constant was the smell of urine, as if the rabids had gone through here and then marked their territory like dogs.

Nothing else except the woman.

She was sitting in a swivel chair up against a bank of file cabinets. She was naked save for a pair of orange knee-high socks. There was a bullet hole in her forehead, a few of them in fact. Congealed brains and blood trailed down her face onto her chest. There was a rose tattoo on her left breast. Her legs were spread wide, her cold sex on grisly display.

Ruby Sue looked at her for a long time. "There's no dignity in death in this fucking town, sister," she told the corpse.

What she was most perplexed by was the woman's position in the chair. It wasn't the position in which someone would sit in a chair—her ass was down low, almost hanging off the seat, her back had slid nearly to the bottom of the backrest, head slumped forward. Maybe she had been killed and slid down like that, but it didn't fit: Why were there no bullet holes in the chair? In the file cabinets behind her?

No, she'd been killed somewhere else and put there.

But why? And by *who*?

And then Ruby Sue saw the dried patches of clear material around the woman's vagina and thighs. She'd been laid out in the chair like that so her body could be screwed. That's what it was.

And although Ruby Sue had gone deep cold inside now, she still found it sickening.

And that's when she heard them coming up behind her.

She wheeled around with the 16, but never even squeezed off a shot.

The rifle was snatched from her grip and sent spinning across the office. Two naked men—rabids—stood before her. They were giggling, drool running down their chins. Their yellow glaring eyes were swimming with a ghastly hunger.

They tried to speak and succeeded only in making morbid gurgling sounds like bad plumbing.

She did not panic.

This was no place for someone who couldn't keep their head. The two of them held her by the arms now and with their huge, erect penises pressing against her like missiles, there was no doubt what they had in mind. They'd rape her. Then kill her. Then keep raping her until there was nothing left.

The M-16 she had around her shoulder was stripped free now.

But not the ammo pouch. There was still hope.

Use your head, outsmart them.

They threw her roughly atop a desk.

So much for foreplay.

One rabid held her head down by the hair, brushing his frigid, damp penis against her face. The other began ripping her pants off. He didn't bother with niceties like zippers and buttons. He yanked them down with savage force, the button popping and sailing away. He tore everything away.

And Ruby Sue, despite the almost phobic horror that trembled in her, did not fight. If she fought, she knew, they'd hold her arms down and she couldn't have that.

Her pouch was still at her side, the strap wedged around her shoulder. They didn't seem to be concerned about that.

They were pawing her with their contaminated fingers.

That shouldn't have mattered, but it didn't.

The man holding her down leaned in close, a slimy grin stitched across his bloodless lips. A thread of germ-rich drool broke across her face like a spider web. It was cold and gelatinous like old snot, but its touch made her skin feel hot. Waves of nausea rolled through her. She needed badly to vomit, to scream, but since she wasn't about to lose control like that, she did nothing.

She steeled herself, internalized it all.

The rabid leered at her with a lewd, degenerate mockery of carnal need.

She laid there motionless, her right hand inching slowly to the pouch.

He pushed her legs apart with the hands of a man who'd just handled frozen meat.

Her fingers brushed the pouch.

His breath was rancid, his penis hard against her thigh.

Her fingers slipped into the pouch.

She felt his cock press against her sex.

He started to giggle. A wet, horrible sound. The laughter of the criminally insane.

Her hand closed around the butt of the Browning .380.

The head of his penis found where it had to go.

It slid roughly into her and she gasped.

With a quick, economical motion, she brought out the Browning and shot him in the face. His nose exploded in a spray of blood and he fell back, screaming and clawing at the air in front of him.

The other rabid went into instant action.

He literally pulled Ruby Sue off the desk by her hair and tossed her through the air. She tumbled across another desk, taking the blotter and lamp with her. Her knees cracked the desk and her head cracked the floor. The Browning slid away.

The rabid came right at her.

He kicked her in the belly with enough force to knock the wind out of her. He aimed another for her face, but she darted back quick enough so it only caught her shoulder, flipping her over on her back.

But she still had the pouch.

The rabids came on.

The one with the hole in his face knocked the other out of the way, lurching forward, baying like a hound, spraying blood from his mouth.

She brought out the Colt Python.

It was heavy in her hand. She pulled the trigger and it went off like a cannon, the recoil almost throwing the weapon from her hand. It blew another hole in the rabid, this one right in the center of his chest. He flew back, dead before he hit the floor.

The other one came on and she shot him in the throat, the side of his neck pulverized. He went down, dying, but refusing to go quietly. His fingers wriggled in the air.

Ruby Sue pulled herself up, pressing her wrist against her side. Her right hand, the one that had held the Colt, was numb from the recoil. She slid the weapon back in her pack and retrieved the Browning.

The rabid with the gored throat was up on his knees, head hanging to one side, blood gushing from the ruptured tissues. She put another round in his head and he went down and stayed down.

She went to her knees, vomiting, then began to cry.

But not for long. She found her pants, hitched them up the best she could and found her M-16. The spare one she couldn't seem to find and didn't want to take the time. She could hear gunfire again, the poppings of automatics. Sounded like it was both outside and inside the building. She could smell smoke and not just the acrid stink of her own cordite.

Was the fire that close?

She ducked back into the hallway and someone came running at her.

At her and past her.

It was hard to tell whether it was a woman or a man.

Just a figure completely engulfed in flames, stumbling up the corridor, bounding off the walls, making some high-pitched whining sound. The smell of cremated flesh was sickening. The figure made it to the fire door and actually tried to work the handle futilely before dropping into a smoking, roasted heap.

The fire didn't do that.

The soldiers had flamethrowers.

32

They were moving up the stairs to the third floor.

Johnny was leading the way in a low crouch. The stairwell was like being inside a black box. They could see the lights from below and some illumination from the bend in the stairs above, but that was it.

"We should've taken the elevator," Lou said.

"Sure," Johnny said, "and get trapped between floors? That would be great. Might take maintenance awhile to reach us."

He kept going.

He was figuring that if they were extremely lucky, they might make the roof. He knew where the doorway was. It would be locked, but that wouldn't be a problem. When he was sixteen he'd worked here mopping floors and cleaning the shitters. He was pretty certain everything would still be pretty much the same.

That was, if they could make it there.

The building, he knew, was crawling with rabids and soldiers now. It was like some sort of war and they were trapped in-between. If the rabids didn't get them, the soldiers would.

He could hear gunfire. It was closer all the time.

Just because Terra and his boys had gotten wiped out, that didn't mean shit, he knew. The troops would keep coming and coming. They wouldn't stop until they'd mopped up the entire town.

Nobody had commented on the necklace of trophies Terra was sporting.

That was probably a good thing, Johnny figured. He'd seen guys mutilate cadavers in the war. It was a very solemn thing to them, symbolic of their ferocity perhaps.

Truth was, it was also the act of a damaged mind.

And Terra? He was damaged, all right.

At the top of the steps, Johnny paused.

It was quiet, but he knew there were people up here. Maybe human, maybe not.

His fatigue shirt plastered to his back with sweat, he slipped out into the corridor. It was dimly lit like those below. In either direction were doorways. Some open. Some closed.

The others followed him up.

Their footfalls were very loud, echoing in the stillness.

"Well, what took you, partner?"

That voice...

They turned and Rawley was standing in the doorway of an office. He had an M-16 rifle pointed in their direction, a big shit-eating grin on his piggish features. Somewhere along the line, he'd lost his hat and had his shirt nearly torn off. His face was bruised, crusted with fingers of old blood.

Lou saw him, his jaw dropped. "Oh, for fuck's sake."

"Back at you, buddy."

Terra had his weapon on him. "Who's this greaseball?" he wanted to know.

"Just call him Greaseball, everyone does," Lou informed him with a very straight face.

Rawley was pretty much as they remembered him—save that he looked like some pissed-off mongrel had chewed him up and shit him back out again. He still had the same crooked smile, the same unreadable eyes.

"Hate to break up the fun and games," he said, "but you may have noticed that I have a rifle here in my hands and if you don't drop your artillery, well, shit, in about five seconds you'll be deader than Jesus."

"If we stand around bullshitting much longer, we'll all be dead," Johnny said.

Terra laughed that high giggle again. "I ain't about to drop my weapon. You're either with us or I kill your redneck ass right here."

Rawley nodded. "Could be. But first, how do I know you aren't infected?"

"How do we know you aren't?" Lisa managed.

"Morning, cutie-pie," Rawley said, bowing slightly. "Hate to be the one to say it, but you look like three-day old dog shit."

"Go...fuck yourself."

Rawley laughed. "That's my girl."

"We're going to the roof, Texas. We're gonna make a stand," Lou explained to him very calmly. "You're either in or you're out. Make your choice. We're not fucking around here, okay? You can pretend you're Jim-fucking-Bowie or some shit. That ought to make you happy. Now move or fucking die."

Rawley did not move. He kept his gun leveled on them.

Lisa let out a grating moan and collapsed.

Lou pulled her to her feet with his good arm, pretty much using up what remained of his strength. "She's okay," he said to them, to Johnny in particular. "She needs a rest. We all need a rest."

"All right, Rawley," Johnny said with a look in his eye like maybe he had the urge to play a little fast-pitch with the man's testicles. He had his rifle on Rawley now. "What's it gonna be?"

Rawley shrugged. "You Yankees certainly are a violent bunch. Must be the climate." He lowered his sixteen. "Of course, I'll join you. I was only playing a bit, relieving the tension."

Terra glared at him. "I came real close to relieving your brains all over the wall, motherfucker."

"Don't say?" Rawley acted like this was very interesting. "Where's your Buck Roger's helmet, soldier boy?"

"I shoved it up my ass to keep it warm."

Rawley was still grinning.

"Let's go," Johnny said and started down the hall.

Terra turned his back on Rawley for just a second. Then he came around real quick with the barrel of his rifle, slashing the bayonet across Rawley's face. Rawley screamed and dropped his weapon.

His face was splashed with blood.

He had barely hit the ground when Terra started jabbing him viciously with the bayonet—in the belly, the ribs, the throat, the balls, the ass. Anywhere that was soft and unguarded, the bayonet got him. Pretty soon Rawley was curled into a frayed red ball, the floor wet with his fluids.

Neither Lou nor Johnny intervened.

They just looked at each other and made a mutual decision to let the man die. The world—Cut River, at least—had been thrown back into the Stone Age. Atrocity was nothing new. Barbarism was the norm. Why fight it? Besides they were too damn tired to save the ass of some Texican peckerwood who would have fed them to the dogs the first chance he got.

Terra stooped down next to Rawley's cooling body.

"What're you doing?" Johnny asked him, though he well knew.

Terra laughed, thinking it was all pretty funny. He slid a K-Bar knife from its sheath and slit off Rawley's left ear. Then, in no hurry whatsoever, he carefully threaded it onto his necklace. He had an even ten now. He seemed happy.

"Just a hobby," he said when he saw Lou staring at him.

Lou nodded dumbly, nervously. "Yeah, you should see my football cards. Mint."

And then there was the sound of feet coming up the stairs. Many of them.

33

"Boy, am I glad to see you guys," Terra told the half-dozen soldiers watching him through the goggle visors of their protective hoods.

"Are you?"

The soldiers wore no insignia, so Terra didn't know if he was talking to a private or a major. Didn't matter, he figured.

"Johnson-12," he said, saluting. "Bravo Company, 1st Platoon." He swept his hand towards his trio of new-found friends. "These ones are okay. Norms."

The soldiers stood there with weapons raised. They muttered amongst themselves.

"Where's your hood, Johnson?" another said. "You know the rules."

And he did: anyone without full protective gear was to be considered infected, as was anyone found within the city limits of Cut River.

He knew that.

He hadn't forgotten.

He couldn't help it if his hand casually (or not so casually) drifted up to his face and then slid down again. "Creepers tore it off me," he explained. "But I drilled 'em all. I'm okay."

"*Are you?*" the first one said again.

"Course I am."

Lou felt like he was stuck in a maze.

A maze full of crazies—some that way by accident, others by training.

He said, "We're just survivors. That's all. We're not foaming at the mouth. Our eyes aren't lit up like Jack-o-'lanterns. So cut the shit for chrissake. We're taxpayers. Now do your duty and get our asses out of here."

Johnny watched them. He expected the worst and kept his mouth shut.

Lou lowered Lisa to the floor because she was getting too goddamned heavy to lug around with his busted-up shoulder and aching leg. She started to tremble and gag, writhing around like she was about to swallow her tongue.

They were all watching her then.

How thin she was.

The sweat beaded on her face.

The bubble of snot in her left nostril.

They were watching her and although nobody could see their eyes behind the visors, it was obvious what was going through their little minds.

"What about *her?*" one of them said stepping forward. He carried a H & K submachine gun.

The others inched forward. Including the guy with the flamethrower strapped to his back.

"She's just sick," Lou said.

"She looks it."

Terra shook his head. "No, she ain't got it, man. She's an addict. She's strung out."

Another of the soldiers said, "The town's burning. It'll get here soon enough. We should be gone by then."

"So let's go," Lou said.

"We will. Soon enough."

He whispered something to the other soldiers.

They drew their weapons and formed a defensive perimeter.

"Here's how it works," the soldier said. "You and these other two drop your weapons and step away from the girl. She's infected. She's gotta go."

Johnny's hands tensed on his rifle. "I don't think so."

"Then you all burn."

A tongue of flame licked out of the end of the flamethrower two or three inches. Just enough so all present could see it was primed and ready to do some damage. The guy carrying it stepped forward.

"She's not infected," Terra maintained.

"Don't tell me my business, soldier. I know infected when I see it."

Terra turned away and then came back with his M-16, sprayed a volley of rounds into the soldiers chest. He stumbled back, pissing red, and went down.

The other soldiers didn't move.

Nobody moved.

Except the rabids.

A howling, screeching pack of them came flooding down the corridor, bringing the stink of death with them. There had to be nearly twenty of them. Some running, some hopping like insects, others barrel-crawling on hands and feet.

The soldiers didn't care about Lisa or the others then.

Terra opened up on them.

Johnny and Lou hit the floor, both trying to cover Lisa. A spout of flame whistled over their heads, singeing Lou's hair.

The rabids ran right into it.

It barely slowed them down.

A few were thrown into a deranged mania as flames swallowed them up. They ran right into the ranks of the soldiers, throwing themselves madly into the walls, the floors, dancing and jumping and shrieking, looking like flaming puppets with clipped strings.

The soldiers were overwhelmed instantly.

They kept shooting, but it did little good.

Some of the rabids dropped and died, but the main force—many of them lit up like Guy Fawkes effigies—fell on them.

The air was putrid with the stench of scorched flesh and hair, gunpowder and blood. There was smoke and tumbling bodies everywhere. The floor was littered with spent brass.

Terra felt teeth bite into the nape of his neck as he smashed his empty rifle down on the head of a rabid. He wheeled around, got hold of his assailant and flipped him through the air. He slipped through the grasp of the others, shoved a whimpering soldier into their midst, and threw himself down the stairs.

Johnny and Lou dragged Lisa away through an open doorway and into a conference room.

A naked woman decided to come with them.

Her hair was smoking, blasted away from the side of her head.

Lou tried to knock her back with his fist, but she absorbed the punch and took hold of him. Her anemic face darted to bite at his throat and he blocked it, trying to elbow her in the mouth. She bit down on his forearm, her yellow sepulchral eyes blazing with delight. He cried out and managed to throw her back out into the hallway, back into the haze and smoke.

He slammed the door shut after her and instantly fists began to hammer on it.

It began to buckle in its frame.

He locked it almost casually, studying the blood welling from the wound in his forearm. It hurt much worse than his shoulder or leg. He stood there looking at the bite marks, the torn tissues, the blood dripping from them. The snotty mucus all over his skin.

It didn't matter now. Any of it.

Because he wasn't getting out alive.

34

Tony Terra stumbled blindly down the stairs, lost in an unreasoning panic.

He was infected.

He could feel the burning wound at the back of his neck. God, yes. The virus, Agent-X, Laughing-fucking-Man, was in him now, too.

He tripped down the last three steps and landed on the body of a dead rabid.

Her head was blown open by gunfire. She was a big fat woman. He pulled himself off her. Fat...no, *not* fat. Her belly was a huge, hard mound.

She'd been pregnant.

Terra started to weep.

He ran a hand across the hill of her abdomen. Wasn't there any end to what this shit could do? Even expectant women. My God, my God, my God—

The flesh under his palm undulated with a slow, sudden movement. The baby. The baby was still alive in her.

Terra thought of things he could do, might do in a sane world. But not here, not in this awful, hellish place.

The woman was dead. Her flesh was cold.

But her belly...it was hot, waves of heat emanating from it.

The baby couldn't possibly be alive.

Her belly began to shudder and palpitate with obscene life; the flesh literally began to squirm with a fluidic motion.

He watched, transfixed with terror.

Her body was rocking back and forth as her progeny raged within, a caged animal.

Terra screamed and jumped to his feet.

He didn't want to see what might chew and claw its way out.

He ran down the corridor, vaulting the bodies of dead rabids and soldiers alike. He saw a restroom door and piled through it. The door swung closed behind him and he was lost in limitless blackness. His fingers pawed the wall, found the switch. Overhead lights buzzed into life.

There was another body on the floor.

Another dead woman.

Maybe a rabid, maybe just some poor civilian caught by them. Didn't matter one way or another because she was stone cold dead. Dead as a squashed woodchuck on the interstate. Her skirt was hiked up to her flat belly, nothing on beneath. He refused to speculate what that might mean.

He paid her no mind.

Frantically, he went to the row of sinks. He splashed water on his face, all over his neck. He kept dousing the bite until the skin there began to cool slightly. Then he took a handful of pink disinfectant soap from the dispenser and scrubbed it liberally into the wound. The pain it caused brought tears to his eyes, but he kept it up until the bite was numb. Then he doused it again with water. He repeated the entire process three times.

He let the water continue to run.

He put his face in it. God, it felt so good.

As he splashed water onto his face again and again, he told himself that what he needed here was a plan. Any plan. Somehow, he had to get a hood for his suit and link up with one of the units. If he had a hood, he might be able to pull it off. If not, they wouldn't even show him the courtesy the soldiers upstairs had—they'd shoot him on sight.

Okay.

Maybe, just maybe he'd be okay.

He stood up, rivulets of water running down his shoulders, his back, making their way into the suit. He was going to survive this. He'd show them all. Then maybe when this was all over with (if it ever was), months from now, he'd tell them he'd been bitten. Maybe. Maybe not.

He looked at his haggard reflection in the mirror.

There was someone standing behind him.

A soldier in a protective suit.

The suit was filthy, soiled with patches of dried blood, soot, and dirt. There was a huge tear in the sleeve.

Terra's heart hitched in his chest.

What bothered him the most was that this soldier had no weapon.

Terra turned and faced him. "I'm glad to see you," he said. "My unit got wiped out upstairs."

The figure waited there, face veiled behind the visor.

Terra licked his lips. He remembered the knife on his web belt, the 9mm Smith & Wesson. His hand drifted slowly toward it.

The soldier moved now.

Terra brought out the knife because it was quicker and jammed it into the rip in the suit, felt it find flesh and bisect it. The soldier came on regardless, took Terra in his arms, slammed him up against the sink.

Terra tore the hood away. Easy enough: it wasn't attached.

What he saw came out of a nightmare.

The sunless face was the embodiment of black, barren hatred. Nothing with a soul could look like that. The face was ashen, the mouth hooked in a drooling, noxious grin.

With the sweep of one arm, Terra was thrown to the floor.

His attacker came on like some relentless wind-up toy. His luminous graveyard eyes were merciless and unforgiving.

Terra tried to speak, but all that came out was a dry croaking.

No matter. This thing was not human. The only thing that propelled it was cold, flat hunger and the lust for blood and killing.

The soldier fell on Terra, fingers like icicles digging into his throat. His breath stank of morgues, teeth drawn back, toxic tangles of drool swaying from his cracked lips like braids.

Terra found the 9mm Smith.

As the rabid made to bite him, he put the barrel alongside the maniac's head and splashed his brains all over the stalls.

He had to pull the fingers from his throat.

Then, gun in hand, he stumbled back into the corridor. He started running to the left, then the right, finally sliding down the wall and whimpering. He put the barrel of the 9mm into his mouth...but he just couldn't bring himself to do it. Tears rolled down his face. He stayed that way for some time, listening to distant screams and gunfire, explosions and howling sounds.

Finally, he got to his feet.

He dragged himself down the corridor, towards the stairs. He felt empty, deflated, and hopeless. He wanted out. He wanted it to end. He wanted—

He went down into a crouch as he heard a strange, sloppy sound.

He inched forward, his heart thudding.

He heard a loathsome, wet mewling noise that reminded him of the squeal of a newborn kitten, but blasphemous somehow, degenerate. It set his flesh to crawling like there were worms knitting his skin.

He saw the corpse of the pregnant woman...saw the blood everywhere, the grisly smeared path of something black and oily.

It went up the wall.

Right up the wall and he followed it with his eyes...

Oh, Jesus, I forgot, I forgot.

There was something up there clinging to the ceiling like a pink and gray fleshy spider, an eyeless and pulsing mass that dropped down onto him, fell over him in a squirming, writhing horror.

It was flabby and warm, like being caressed by a placenta.

It forced itself into his eyes and down his throat, up his nostrils and through his pores. Wherever he was open, it surged and flowed and consumed. It was the first true citizen of the new Cut River.

And for Terra, it was an unspeakable death.

35

It was time to make a run for it.

Out in the corridor, they could hear battle being waged— soldiers screaming and dying, rabids falling on them like animals. There was the constant report of rifles and submachine guns, the acrid stink of flamethrowers. The occupying force was intent on cleaning out the municipal building which had become something of a hive.

It was here that the end would be played out.

That much was obvious.

The door was under constant barrage as the rabids tried to get in.

Lou, Johnny, and Lisa were in a conference room. Its primary features were the long, polished oak table and the windows that looked down on the burning city. Other than that it was unremarkable. There was a pegboard on the wall with various civil announcements and the minutes of previous city council meetings.

There was another door at the far end of the room.

The one they came in was buckling in its frame. It was a big heavy job or it wouldn't have even lasted this long. The one at the far end seemed unmolested...so far.

"It's death to go out there," Johnny said, "but we can't stay here."

Lou said, "Then let's do it. I don't have shit to lose now."

Lisa, who swam in and out of her fugue, made a few grunting sounds which they took as assent.

Lou stood before the door. He had Lisa's .357 now. The shotgun was empty.

Johnny, holding Lisa at his side, said simply, "Ready?"

Lou nodded.

The other door burst in and two or three rabids fell in with it, along with a lot of billowing black smoke and the nauseating stench of burning flesh and blasted wood. No sense in discussing it any longer.

Lou led the way out into the hall.

The corridor was hazy with smoke.

As Johnny and Lisa slipped by, Lou watched the far end. There was no more shooting. Just a lot of moaning. Cries for help. The slithering, hissing sound of the rabids as they mutilated and possibly devoured the soldiers. Lou could hear violent thuds, wet ripping sounds, sucking and tearing noises. The smoke, thankfully, blocked his view. Tongues of flame licked up the walls. The smoke made his eyes burn.

"Come on," Johnny said as he led Lisa away.

And Lou had every intention of doing so, except that out of the smoke three forms came walking. Rabids. Three men. One of them had several bullet holes in him, but he came on regardless. Demented eyes swam in bleached faces, a moldering stink of sick wards drifted off the trio.

Lou shot two of them in the head and they fell back into the wall of smoke, spraying blood. The third simply snarled, went down low and disappeared the way he'd come.

"You okay?" Johnny asked him when he caught up.

"Fine," Lou said. "Let's go."

The soldiers, it occurred to him, were losing this battle.

The dire army of rabids were overwhelming them by numbers and sheer ferocity. How could you hope to fight savages like that by conventional means? And that got him to thinking that if this went on any length of time, Terra's Emergency Response Group would start using more lethal means to control and crush the good citizens of Cut River.

No matter.

He wouldn't live to see it.

They moved up the smoky corridor, coughing, eyes watering. The fog of smoke was good and bad—it helped to hide them, but it also concealed the forms of their enemies. Lou kept seeing the faces of his ex-wives and lovers and wished to God he would have had the chance to say good-bye to them. But such a thing was far beyond the realm of possibility now.

They moved around a bend in the corridor and right away found more bodies. There were holes punched into the walls— literally hundreds of them—from gunfire. Great areas were scorched from the flamethrowers.

And bodies.

Dozens.

Rabids and soldiers.

Many locked in death embraces. The hallway looked like a litter pile from an extermination camp. The smell of smoke was overpowered here by the corrupt and polluted stink of mass death.

Johnny lowered Lisa to the floor and stripped a flamethrower and a 9mm sidearm from a soldier.

Lou, following his lead, took a gun off a corpse, too. They'd need everything they could get.

"There's a doorway up ahead," Johnny explained. "It leads into a maintenance corridor. The stairs to the roof are in there."

"If we make it."

"Sure, if we make it."

Johnny led the way again.

Lisa was still lost in her narcotic dreams (or the lack of them), but she was able to shuffle along if she had an arm to hang onto. Lou figured she was the lucky one. She'd been out of it for hours now. With any luck, he figured, maybe she'd die without truly coming to her senses and, really, what else was there to hope for?

And that's when the woman stepped out of the murk.

Lou saw her and cringed.

She reminded him vaguely of the rabid police woman he'd fought earlier that evening downstairs. She was equally as lovely—tall, elegant, completely naked, a sweep of blonde hair falling down one shoulder. She had a knife in one hand and something in the other. A head. The head of man which had been decapitated crudely, dripping meat hanging from the stump like confetti. She offered Lou a sardonic, hungry grin, a skullish rictus really, and a single rope of glistening drool ran from her mouth, oozing down the cone of one perfect breast, pooling at the nipple.

He remembered his gun and brought it up.

Something struck him in the chest and he went on his ass.

The head.

With one fluid sweep of musculature, she'd flung the head at him and with such force it was like being hit by a medicine ball. The wind was literally knocked out of him. He'd lost his gun and she was advancing like a starved wolf that had separated a weak stag from the pack.

She dove on him.

He fought with everything he had left which wasn't much. She overpowered him effortlessly, pinning him to the floor and slavering his screaming face with kisses, with licks from her long discolored tongue which was so cold, so very cold...like a snake from a meat locker. Drool washed over his face and he fought hopelessly as she licked a spot at his neck and playfully nipped it with her teeth, sucking up the blood that ran out like an infant at its mother's teat.

He was locked down by her glaring vulpine eyes...and suddenly, was liking it.

And then there was a gunshot.

Followed by a second and a third.

The woman went taut, began to shudder, her mouth split open into a bestial cry of defeat. She howled and screeched and then slumped forward, vomiting a sea of black blood and toxic waste all over him.

Lou kicked free.

Johnny was a few feet away, but his weapon was lowered. He was looking past Lou at the rabid woman clawing her way up the wall with snake-like gyrations of her trunk.

Ruby Sue was standing there, gun in hand.

She was bloody and beaten and looked like she'd just escaped from a tiger cage. But her eyes were normal, if not glazed and empty. They mirrored recognition of those she saw in the corridor.

The woman pulled herself up the wall, three gaping bloody holes in her back. She turned and leered at her attacker with poisoned eyes. She growled and snapped her jaws and spit out clots of blood and phlegm. Her eyes found Lou and fixed on him with that vicious, boiling hatred.

And then Ruby Sue shot her in the head.

She slid down the wall slowly like a raindrop down a window, leaving a smear of gore behind her. But not for one moment did her manic eyes leave Lou's own. Even in death, cheated of prey, like some morbid human lioness, that flat and cold appetite remained.

Ruby Sue looked down at her, stepped over the armless body of a soldier. "Well," she said very nonchalantly, "let's get moving."

Lou sat there on his ass, bitten, clawed, bruised and bleeding. Through a mask of blood and bile he began to laugh. In fact, he began to cackle madly as if it was all the funniest thing he'd ever heard of.

Ruby Sue took him by the arm and helped him to his feet.

"So you finally went crazy, eh?" she said. "Well, goddamn, it's about time, man."

Nobody bothered to ask her what she was doing there or if she'd been infected. It was pretty much a given thing by this point: outside of Lisa, there were no more virgins among them.

They all had it.

They all had tasted the teeth of the rabids and carried the dark secret of Cut River within them.

Johnny was in the lead again.

Lou was the rear guard man.

Ruby Sue helped Lisa along.

No group of soldiers had seen worse action than they, had waded through more blood and viscera and insanity. And even if by some crazy, impossible set of circumstances one or more managed to survive, they would never be the same again, would never be whole, would never be human as such.

They were moving lower now, almost at a staggering crouch.

The corridor was so thick with smoke it was like to trying to suck breath from the tailpipe of a Buick.

"Door should be just ahead," Johnny said to them, leading on.

He stopped suddenly, hearing a shrill cackling sound.

It reminded him of fingers drawn over a blackboard. Not even remotely human. An elderly woman wearing the bedraggled, bloody remains of a bathrobe squatted in a doorway. She dropped what she'd been nibbling on—a human hand.

Her voice was wet and congested like the lungs of an ammonia victim: "How's about a kiss, handsome?" Then the voice dissolved into a hissing like acid dissolving flesh.

She stood upright and came at him, drool spraying from her lips.

Her hands were almost at his throat when he pressed the trigger of the automatic he'd taken from the dead soldier. Her body jerked as a volley of three rounds punched through it. Her eyes glazed-over, went wet and vitreous, translucent like high-gloss enamel. She stepped back, fingering her wounds.

Johnny shot her in the face and she pitched stiffly over, trembling on the floor, arms slapping at her sides. Ichor and filth bubbled from her lips and she went still.

Another woman came to take her place.

She wore a short business skirt slit at the thigh and high heels, but nothing more. A river of foamy drool flooded from her mouth and painted her large, jiggling breasts like a slime of oil. She opened her mouth and let out a peal of wailing torment at them. Her tongue flicked across her lips and she spat a wad of mucus into Johnny's face.

He brought his 9mm up.

Hands on her knees, she rocked from side to side like some child daring to be hit with a ball. A stream of sour-smelling urine ran from beneath her skirt and rained to the floor. Her flesh was glistening with plague excretions, issuing a sharp, caustic mist.

But she did not attempt an attack.

Johnny pumped four rounds into her.

The first went between her legs, missing entirely. The next went into her thigh, the others into her belly. She spun around bleeding and screaming like a woman in a padded cell.

He shot her in the chest, pulverizing one breast into a drooping sac of meat.

She turned and clawed at the air, barked at the ceiling, eyes rolling madly like marbles on a roulette table. A steady stream of something black and oozing poured from her wounds. The raw bile of human evil. The stuff that flowed in the veins of child molesters and rapists and mass murderers. She shook all over like a wet, stinking dog, then went down in a heap, spasms running through her.

Then the survivors were moving again and they could hear more gunfire and much closer. Not only small arms, but heavy machine guns now. What sounded like helicopters buzzing the building as if they were hunting wasps on a mission.

Then the door.

It was locked. Johnny put a few bullets in it and threw it open.

He led the way in followed by Ruby Sue and Lisa. Lou came last.

Only he never actually made it in.

Because he heard them coming: the pounding feet and hissing voices and knew there was too many this time, just too many. He turned and decided it was as good a place as any to make his last stand. He thought of matinees as a kid, old movies on TV. Heroism. It had never been in him. Not until now. And he decided that heroism, though once a very unthinkable, abstract concept, made perfect sense now that he didn't give a flaming shit about his own life and had absolutely nothing to lose.

"COME ON GODDAMMIT!" Ruby Sue called out to him and Johnny said something familiar.

"Go!" he ordered them. "It's Alamo-time, people! I'll hold 'em off!"

His eyes connected with theirs one last time and some sliver of hope, of selfish survival lodged momentarily in his mind: *Just what in fuck's name are you doing, Lou? What do you hope to accomplish here?* But there was no real answer to that, only a warm pervading sense that for the first time in his life he was doing something completely unselfish and damn if it didn't feel good.

He shut the door behind him, pressed his back to it.

They were coming, maybe drawn by the shooting or the rich smell of fresh blood, regardless, they were coming.

He saw them moving out of the smoke, swimming out of the murk like piranhas. Jesus, so many.

Hundreds?

Could there really be that many?

Was it even remotely possible?

He chewed down on his lip until it bled, his guts gone to jelly, as utterly terrified as he'd ever been in his entire life. So many of them. God, how he wanted to run, to make it easier on himself and fuck the rest.

But he wouldn't.

Not this time. And not ever again.

And maybe the true measure of a man, of a human being, was how he faced death. Not biting and clawing like an animal, like them, but as a human being.

As a man.

As the rabids poured forth he suddenly saw them as they were: a hive. A mass army under a single set of imperatives and drives. A single cold, relentless intellect. Like ants or wasps they lived only to serve the hive, to crush intruders, to gather food and defend their lair.

And that's how they came at him, scampering forward like rats, all teeth and eyes and clutching fingers. He was what Terra had called a *norm* and, yes, he was the enemy and they could smell it on him.

Mostly, the ones that came for him were children.

He wondered if he'd encountered any of them back at the playground.

He brought up his guns, one in each hand, feeling oddly like a gunslinger in a surreal, nightmarish western and started shooting. They absorbed his bullets and, although some fell, the mass crawled and hopped and lurched forward.

And then he was out of shells.

Staring into their cruel, sadistic faces, he said, he shouted, "I AM NOT THE ENEMY! DON'T YOU SEE THAT? THE SOLDIERS! THEY'RE THE ENEMY! THEY'RE PART OF WHAT MADE YOU LIKE THIS!"

But those baneful white faces did not care.

They came on, a noisome throng, rustling and slithering and growling and hissing. He could see their sharp teeth and the pawing nails at the end of their pallid hands, the matted hair and yellow eyes like harvest moons rising above blighted October fields.

Yes, they came on in a swarm, totally detached of humanity, human insects ritually purging the hive of dangerous elements much as our ancestors might once have done under a boiling black sky of slaughter. Theirs was a fixed society and there was no room for those who did not fit seamlessly into the mass.

Lou heard his voice scream as they got closer, as he smelled their dark stink.

They circled around him and pressed in slowly, in no hurry whatsoever.

As he felt their cold fingers open furrows in his face and their teeth divorce him of flesh, all he could think of were their eyes. Those phobic, predatory pits.

He kept watching them until his own eyes were torn free from their housings.

36

"We're all going to die," Lisa heard someone say. "All of us. It all ends here. This is where it all ends for us."

It took her a moment or two to realize that *she* was saying it.

She wasn't entirely sure whether she was dreaming or awake and in this goddamn town, did it really matter? Because that was one thing she *was* sure of—she was still in Cut River. She could feel fresh air brush her face. Fresh, damp, yet carrying the smell of smoke.

So they'd made it to the roof, had they?

No matter, it was all coming down now and there was little she or any of the others could do but accept it and pray it happened quick.

She knew she personally couldn't take much more.

Her nerves were frayed and her body ached and, God, this is what the junk had done to her. The one night of her life when she couldn't afford to be anything but sharp, she'd fallen apart.

She was awake now.

The world was ending and she could smell the smoke and feel the fear of those around her. Although it was night, she could see plumes of smoke drifting against the retreating face of the moon and smell the burning stink of the town as it died. Beyond the rooftop, the horizon was blazing orange and red and yellow like the perimeter of hell itself.

She suddenly realized that her head was cradled in Ruby Sue's lap and that Ruby Sue was droning on and on.

"...it was never nothing personal, girl, you have to understand that. That manager of yours...well...he played with the wrong people. The day you came here, I guess that would be today or was it yesterday? Fuck it. They found him, dragged him out of hiding and, well, you get the idea. They whacked him out, you know? Joe was hooked up with...well, I guess it doesn't matter...but he got the contract on you and that brought us here. It was never anything personal. You believe that, don't you?"

Lisa didn't really care.

In the back of her mind, sure, it explained things, but it seemed so trivial now. What did any of it matter?

She blinked her eyes and saw Johnny.

Saw the way he was looking at her.

His eyes radiated a certain fuzzy warmth and she was pretty certain that in these few short hours he'd fallen in love with her. She smiled at him and it felt good to do so. She imagined she looked a real fright, like an extra from an Italian zombie movie.

But he didn't seem to care.

"We made it?" she said.

He nodded. "Yeah, finally."

Ruby Sue stroked her face. There were tears in her eyes. "Joe didn't...he didn't make it here. Not this time."

"Lou?" she said.

Johnny shook his head, looked away.

So it was only the three of them now. She guessed it really didn't matter. She could hear gunfire and explosions and figured the army, or whoever those people were, were closing in, cleansing the town of its infected elements. Which, she knew, would include them eventually.

"I think the shit's about to get deep," Johnny said.

And he was right.

"I don't mind dying," Lisa said to him, "as long as I'm with you."

37

Johnny smiled at her in the glow of the burning town, beneath the baleful eye of the full moon which was slipping away now into the western sky. He wanted to tell her many things, but there was no time. War had broken out below and there was gunfire and explosions and screaming and dying. A main force group had probably made it up to the third floor and encountered the mob that had gotten Lou.

Hell was breaking loose now.

The rooftop was pretty much the same as Johnny remembered from when he was a teenager. There were two maintenance sheds up there as well as some sort of radio shack with an antenna climbing into the hazy sky. Probably for the police and fire radios.

The three survivors were hidden around the side of one of the sheds, backs up against the projecting outer ledge of the southern exposure. They were on the only flat expanse of roof. The rest was all sheer and pitched, jutting domes and towers and you name it. Behind them, if you were to look up above the four-foot ledge, you could see the town burning.

Johnny had looked for some time and then forced himself to look away. The destruction of his hometown wasn't as pleasant a thing as he'd once envisioned.

They were waiting for the killers.

Crouched in a tight little formation, they were waiting to die.

Ruby Sue said, "Maybe we should just get the fuck out of—"

"Quiet," Johnny whispered.

They were coming.

The only true advantage the three of them had was that their assailants did not know precisely where they were. Maybe they had a general idea there would be something up here, but not who or what. The door on the far side swung open and out came a soldier, moving low and defensively, M-16 cradled in his arms. His vision was obscured by his hood, so he had to stop and scan his surroundings from time to time.

"He's mine," Ruby Sue said, picking up her rifle.

The soldier was followed by three others, part of a recon team.

They would check the roof and if there was trouble, they'd call in a main force body. They fanned out, paying particular attention to the radio shack. The first guy crept over near the maintenance sheds.

Ruby Sue got a bead on him with her M-16, aiming the barrel in the general direction of his upper body. It was unlikely she'd miss—the bastard was close enough to spit at now.

In his hood, he hadn't seen her yet.

Then he did.

As he made eye contact (or what passed for it under the hood), Ruby Sue pulled the trigger. He took two three-shot bursts directly in the chest. His rifle went one way and he went the other, his arms flaying, his suit painted red. He hit the ground kicking and wailing and gurgling, trying in vain to strip his hood off. In a moment or two, he was still. Only the stink of cordite in the air remained.

The other three charged out, shooting in every conceivable direction.

Using the .30-06, Johnny dropped both of them with head-shots, their visors exploding with blood and meat.

The last man carried a flamethrower and he squirted a barrage of fire in their general direction. It struck one of the sheds and lit it up. As the guy tried to make it back through the doorway, Johnny shot him in the tanks and there was eruption of fire as burning fuel engulfed the man and everything around him. Like a villager caught in a napalm burst, the guy danced around wildly before collapsing in a blackened, sizzling heap.

There was more gunfire then, coming from the stairwell.

Lisa screamed.

Near where the body of the first soldier lay, a white and skeletal hand swung up and over the ledge, a rabid pulling itself up onto the roof. It was hard to say whether it was a man or a woman.

Lisa looked over the ledge and saw chaos.

The parking lot and courtyard below were a hive of activity.

There were assault vehicles with searchlights scanning the night, scanning the building. Hordes of rabids were attacking groups of soldiers and there were the continual reports of machine guns and small-arms fire. Grenades were bursting and flamethrowers spitting out streams of flame. A lot of dying and screaming and madness. The stink wafting up from down there was the smell of crematory ovens—thick, pungent, and nauseating.

But it was hardly the worse thing.

For the façade of the municipal building was actually alive with creeping, slinking motion as rabids scaled the walls. They were crawling upwards like spiders. Literally hundreds of them fighting for space. The building was infested with them. Some fell, only to be replaced by three or four others.

Many were very near the top.

As evidence of this, two or three more of them made it over the ledge, hissing and angry.

"Jesus Christ," Johnny muttered.

Thirty or forty others were creeping over the peaked roofs, dragging the bodies of dead soldiers with them. The only thing all of this had in common was that they were all making for the same place: the section of roof Johnny and the others had once considered a safe haven.

More soldiers came through the doorway.

Ruby Sue's body jerked as slugs swept across her chest.

Johnny watched, squeezing off shots as did Lisa now.

But who to shoot at?

Rabids?

Soldiers?

They were all congregating here for the final, apocalyptic battle as the building burned and the town raged and death hung in the air like a shroud.

Ruby Sue got to her feet and dropped two soldiers, despite the fact that she was badly wounded. There were fifteen or twenty soldiers on the roof now and more coming from the mouth of the stairwell all the time.

A cloud of flame inundated both Ruby Sue and a pair of rabids closing in on her. They stumbled into each other, human candles, greasy black smoke coming off them in churning plumes.

Johnny and Lisa shot alternately at rabids and soldiers until they were just out of ammunition.

Rabids swarmed over the ledge.

Many were gunned down or lit on fire before they stepped onto the roof, but they kept coming, a human wave attack of the damned.

The air was black with smoke and the stink of cremated meat and fresh blood.

The rabids that had come over the rooftops dove on the soldiers.

Others formed themselves into ranks atop the maintenance sheds. In a grisly, almost cartoonish display, they pelted the soldiers with the only things they had at their disposal: body parts. They dismembered the bodies of their kills and heaved heads and legs and arms at the white-suited troops. Entire trunks spun through the air and flattened troopers.

The confused soldiers were firing in all directions, dropping rabids and their fellow soldiers as well.

Lisa and Johnny stayed down low and fought on.

Johnny picked an M-16 up off a dead soldier and cut down an advancing wave of rabids, catching two, three white suits in the process. He felt a stray round rip through his shoulder and then another pulverize his right kneecap.

Lisa had the sidearm of a fallen trooper—a 9mm auto—and she was shooting pretty much at anything that moved.

The rooftop was a perpetual motion machine of fire and bodies and shooting and blinding smoke and howling rabids.

She dropped a rabid that beat a soldier to the ground with a severed limb.

Then she heard a high, whining sibilance like the buzz of a pissed-off hornet.

She spun around and a rabid whose face had been blasted right down to the bone clawed out at her. She kicked out, catching him in the thigh and knocking him momentarily off balance. She blocked another lunge, felt a spray of drool splatter against her face, and put two rounds in his chest. He fell back and was replaced by two, three others and she just kept shooting until there was nothing left to shoot.

The rooftop was a gray, spiraling haze of smoke and flames and she couldn't tell any longer where the rabids and the soldiers were.

It was a free-fire zone.

The flames were eating away at the building and occasional muffled explosions rocked everyone to the ground. The fire was advancing through the city and Lisa could hear something in the distance like an air raid siren. But it was nearly blotted out by the confused shrieks of the dying and the screeching of killers and the sounds of blaring loudspeaker horns and gunfire.

A rabid was on top of Johnny—a naked, barking woman with a cleaver in her hand.

She was bringing it down in lethal arcs.

He was blocking its edge with his rifle, but stroke after stroke, she was whittling through it.

Lisa ran over there and pounded the woman's head with the butt of the empty automatic. She kept at until the maniac dropped her cleaver and her head was pulped and bleeding.

But it didn't stop her.

She wrapped her fingers around Johnny's throat despite the blows he rained into her face. Lisa dug her fingers into the woman's cold neck and screamed as the flesh peeled away in strips like flaking dough.

Johnny cracked the woman in the face with the butt of his Remington and both she and Lisa went over in a fighting heap.

Lisa fought free and pulled Johnny to his feet.

His body jerked as bullets shredded through it.

His hand brushed Lisa's face and then more slugs ripped into him and he fell back over the ledge and into the night.

The soldiers were losing.

Most of them were dead and the rabids were still coming on, driven into a manic feeding frenzy like sharks in a bloody sea. They mutilated soldiers and bit the flesh from their faces, stripped away containment suits and skin in the process. A woman was sucking at the bleeding throat of a fallen soldier as a man raped her from behind. And that seemed to be all they wanted to do or were interested in doing in this stinking envelope of scorched bodies: feeding, killing, and fornicating.

Beneath the sinking moon, they celebrated this night of festival with feasting and fucking.

Lisa took up a gun and killed a few, but it was all really quite pointless.

A bloody leg slammed into her face and she fell back against the ledge, nearly going right over and not really making much of an attempt to stop herself, knowing it would be better that way.

And then they were on her, too, three of them.

They fell on her and teeth sank into her throat and fingers gouged valleys into her flesh. She propped her foot against the side of the maintenance shed and, drawing upon every remaining bit of energy that pulsed in her veins, she kicked off with everything she had.

She and her host of rabids flipped over the edge, careening down.

Still they held her, though, biting and pulling at her.

They were in free fall, the four of them, flipping over and over through the air, and then Lisa was riding atop them and they began to smash through the upper limbs of a tree. Their bodies took the impacts, breaking and crushing beneath her. And then the final resounding, jarring impact as they slammed into the grass below.

Lisa was knocked numb and senseless, but unbroken.

After a time, she crawled away from the human wreckage, away from the burning building and the attacking rabids and the peals of machine gun fire. Uninjured except for bites and scratches and numerous lumps and bumps, she crawled like a baby through the grass over mutilated bodies and into the darkness.

Soon, there would be nowhere to escape the flames.

She pulled herself over a curb and into the road.

The pavement was cold beneath her, wet leaves sticking to her pants and shirt. She found a manhole cover. Pressing her fingers into the lip, she began tugging at it until it loosened, came up a few inches. She managed to get it standing upright in its cavity...but then it slipped from her fingers and fell into the murk below with a splash.

She crept down the ladder after it.

It was cool down there.

Cool, dank, and quiet.

She splashed on through the maze of tunnels until she finally felt safe. She found a shelf of frigid concrete sticking out above the waterline and lowered herself onto it. Stretching out like a corpse on a slab, she folded her hands across her bosom and closed her sore eyes.

Sleep came almost instantly.

In the darkness, rats splashed through the water and moved across the brickwork industriously. A few rabids took shelter down there, too.

But Lisa knew nothing of this. She slept on as a coma settled over her and would for hours and hours until the mop-up and extermination above was completed.

But she wouldn't sleep forever.

Maybe tonight or the next she would waken.

Waken and claim the night as only her kind could.

-The End-

www.ingramcontent.com/pod-product-compliance
Lightning Source LLC
Chambersburg PA
CBHW050721180626
46814CB00002B/550